BREATHING WATER

BREATHING WATER

TIMOTHY HALLINAN

WILLIAM MORROW

An Imprint of HarperCollinsPublishers

This book is a work of fiction. References to real people, events, estab-
lishments, organizations, or locales are intended only to provide a sense
of authenticity, and are used fictitiously. All other characters, and all
incidents and dialogue, are drawn from the author's imagination and are
not to be construed as real.

HarperCollins books may be purchased for educational, business, or
sales promotional use. For information please write: Special Markets
Department, HarperCollins Publishers, 10 East 53rd Street, New York,
NY 10022.

FIRST EDITION

Library of Congress Cataloging-in-Publication Data has been applied for.

ISBN 978-0-06-167223-1

09 10 11 12 13   OV/RRD   10 9 8 7 6 5 4 3 2 1

This book is dedicated to the memory of Raleigh Philp,
who left behind an ever-widening wake of inspiration,
and to Alicia Aguayo from her *hijito*

PART I

THE GULF

Pinch It

The man behind the desk is a dim shape framed in blinding light, a god emerging from the brilliance of infinity. The god says, "Why not the bars? You're pretty enough."

The girl has worked a finger into the ragged hole in the left knee of her jeans. The knee got scraped when the two men grabbed her, and she avoids the raw flesh. She raises a hand to shade her eyes so she can look at him, but the light is too bright. "I can't. I tried for two nights. I can't do it."

"You'll get used to it." The god puts a foot on the desk. The foot is shielded from the light by the bulk of his body, and she can see that it is shod in a very thin, very pale loafer. The sole is so shiny that the shoe might never have been worn before. The shoe probably cost more than the girl's house.

The girl says, "I don't want to get used to it." She shifts a few inches right on the couch, trying to avoid the light.

"It's a lot more money. Money you could send home."

"Home is gone," the girl says.

That's a trifle, and he waves it away. "Even better. You could buy clothes, jewelry, a nice phone. I could put you into a bar tonight."

The girl just looks down and works her finger around inside the hole. The skin around the scraped knee is farm-dark, as dark as the skin on her hand.

"Okay," the man says. "Up to you." He lights a cigarette, the flame briefly revealing a hard face with small, thick-lidded eyes, broad nostrils, pitted skin, oiled hair. Not a god, then, unless very well disguised. He waves the smoke away, toward her. The smoke catches the glare to form a pale nimbus like the little clouds at which farmers aim prayers in the thin-dirt northeast, where the girl comes from. "But this isn't easy either," the man says.

She pulls her head back slightly from the smoke. "I don't care."

The man drags on the cigarette again and puts it out, only two puffs down. Then he leans back in his chair, perilously close to the floor-to-ceiling window behind him. "Don't like the light, do you? Don't like to be looked at. Must be a problem with a face like yours. You're worth looking at."

The girl says, "Why do you sit there? It's not polite to make your visitors go blind."

"I'm not a polite guy," says the man behind the desk. "But it's not my fault. I put my desk here before they silvered those windows." The building across Sathorn Road, a sea-green spire, has reflective coating on all its windows, creating eighteen stories of mirrors that catch the falling sun early every evening. "It's fine in the morning," he says. "It's just now that it gets a little bright."

"It's rude."

The man behind the desk says, "So fucking what?" He pulls his foot off the desk and lets the back of the chair snap upright. "You don't like it, go somewhere else."

The girl lowers her head. After a moment she says, "If I try to beg, I'll just get dragged back here."

The man sits motionless. The light in the room dims slightly as the sun begins to drop behind the rooftops. Then he says, "That's right." He takes out a new cigarette and puts it in his mouth. "We get forty percent. Pratunam."

She tries to meet his eyes, but the reflections are still too bright. "I'm sorry?"

"Pra . . . tu . . . nam," he says slowly, enunciating each syllable as though she is stupid. "Don't you even know where Pratunam is?"

She starts to shake her head and stops. "I can find it."

"You won't have to find it. You'll be taken there. You can't sit just anywhere. You'll work the pavement we give you. Move around and you'll probably get beat up, or even brought back here." He takes the cigarette out of his mouth, looks at it, and breaks it in half. He drops the pieces irritably into the ashtray.

"Is it a good place?"

"Lot of tourists," he says. "I wouldn't give it to you if you weren't pretty." He picks up the half of the cigarette with the filter on it, puts it in his mouth, and lights it. Then he reaches under the desk and does something, and the girl hears the lock on the door snap closed. "You want to do something nice for me?"

"No," the girl says. "If I wanted to do that, I'd work in the bar."

"I could make you."

The girl says, "You could get a fingernail in your eye, too."

The man regards her for a moment and then grunts. The hand goes back under the desk, and the lock clicks again. "Ahh, you'd probably be a dead fish anyway." He takes a deep drag and scrubs the tip of the cigarette against the bottom of the ashtray, scribbles something on a pad, rips off the page, and holds it out. His eyes follow her as she gets up to take it. "It's an address," he says. "Go there tonight, you can sleep there. We'll pick you up at six-thirty in the morning. You'll work from seven to four, when the night girl takes over." He glances at a gold watch, as thin as a dime, on his right wrist. In English he says, "How's your English?"

"Can talk some."

"Can you say 'Please, sir'? 'Please, ma'am'? 'Hungry'?"

"Please, sir," the girl says. "Please, ma'am." A flush of color mounts her dark cheeks. "Hungry."

"Good," the man says. "Go away."

She turns to go, and his phone buzzes. He picks up the receiver.

"What?" he says. Then he says to the girl, "Wait." Into the receiver he says, "Good. Bring it in." A moment later an immaculately groomed young woman in a silk business suit comes in, carrying a bundle of rags. She holds it away from her, her mouth pulled tight, as though there are insects crawling on it.

"Give it to her," the man says. "And you," he says, "don't lose it and *don't drop it*. These things don't grow on trees."

The young woman glances without interest at the girl with the torn jeans and hands the bundle to her. The bundle is surprisingly heavy, and wet.

The girl opens one end, and a tiny face peers up at her.

"But . . ." she says. "Wait. This . . . this isn't—"

"Just be careful with it," the man says. "Anything happens to it, you'll be working on your back for years."

"But I can't—"

"What's the matter with you? Don't you have brothers and sisters? Didn't you spend half your life wiping noses? Just carry it around on your hip or something. Be a village girl again." To the woman in the suit, he says, "Give her some money and put it on the books. What's your name?" he asks the girl holding the baby.

"Da."

"Buy some milk and some throwaway diapers. A towel. Wet wipes. Get a small bottle of whiskey and put a little in the milk at night to knock the baby out, or you won't get any sleep. Dip the corner of the towel in the milk and let it suck. Get a blanket to sit on. Got it?"

"I can't keep this."

"Don't be silly." The man gets up, crosses the office, and opens the door, waving her out with his free hand. "No foreigner can walk past a girl with a baby," the man says. "When there are foreign women around, pinch it behind the knee. The crying is good for an extra ten, twenty baht."

Dazed, holding the wet bundle away from her T-shirt, Da goes to the door.

"We'll be watching you," the man says. "Sixty for you, forty for us. Try to pocket anything and we'll know. And then you won't be happy at all."

"I don't steal," Da says.

"Of course not." The man returns to his desk in the darkening office. "And remember," he says. "Pinch it."

FOUR MINUTES LATER Da is on the sidewalk, with 250 baht in her pocket and a wet baby in her arms. She walks through the lengthening shadows at the aimless pace of someone with nowhere to go, someone listening to private voices. Well-dressed men and women, just freed from the offices and cubicles of Sathorn Road, push impatiently past her.

Da has carried a baby as long as she can remember. The infant is a familiar weight in her arms. She protects it instinctively by crossing her wrists beneath it, bringing her elbows close to her sides, and keeping her eyes directly in front of her so she won't bump into anything. In her village she would have been looking for a snake, a stone in the road, a hole opened up by the rain. Here she doesn't know what she's looking for.

But she's so occupied in looking for it that she doesn't see the dirty, ragged, long-haired boy who pushes past her with the sweating *farang* man in tow, doesn't see the boy turn to follow her with his eyes fixed on the damp bundle pressed to her chest, watching her as though nothing in the world were more interesting.

2

Mud Between Her Toes

The boy sees her go, assessing her without even thinking about it: Just got here. Still got mud between her toes. Doesn't know anything. Looks stunned, like someone hit her in the face with a pole.

The baby's not hers. Too pale.

He thinks, *Another one.*

The nervous man behind him slows again. The boy hesitates grudgingly, feeling like he's trying to lead a cat. For a moment weariness washes over him like warm water. He longs to disappear into the crowd and leave the foreigner to fend for himself, but the others are waiting, and they're hungry.

"Come on," he says in English. "Nothing to worry."

"I don't know," the man says.

The boy stops. He draws a deep breath before he speaks; it will not do to show his frustration. "What problem now?"

"It's not dark enough."

"When it dark," the boy says, "they all gone."

"Just ten minutes," the man says. He is in his forties, with hair brushed forward over a plump baby's face that seems to be mostly lower lip. Despite his eagerness not to be noticed, he wears a bright yellow shirt and green knee-length shorts across wide hips. A fanny pack dangling below his belly thoughtfully announces the location of his valuables. To the boy he looks as conspicuous as a neon sign.

"Ten minute too long." The boy's eyes, tight-cornered and furious, skitter across the man's face as though committing the features to some permanent archive, and then he turns away with a shrug.

The man says, "Please. Wait."

The boy stops. Plays the final card. "Come now. Come now or go away."

"Okay, okay. But don't walk so fast."

The sun is gone now, leaving the sky between the buildings a pale violet through which the evening star has punched a silver hole. The boy sometimes thinks the sky is a hard dome lit inside by the sun and the moon, and peppered with tiny openings. From the outside the dome is bathed in unimaginable brilliance, and that light forces its way through the pinpricks in the sky to create the stars. If the sky dissolved, he thinks, the light from outside would turn the earth all white and pure, and then it would catch fire like paper. But in the dazzling moment before the flames, it would be clean.

"We go slow," he says. There may not be another man tonight. The crowds on the sidewalk are thinning. The kids are hungry. He drags his feet to prevent the man from falling behind.

The man says, "You're handsome."

"No," the boy says without even turning his head. "Have better than me."

They turn a corner, into an east-west street. They are walking west, so the sky pales in the sun's wake until it slams up against a jagged black line of buildings. Before he returned to Bangkok, this city he hates, the boy had grown used to the soft, leaf-dappled skyline of the countryside. The horizon here is as sharp as a razor cut.

"There," the boy says, indicating with his chin. "The window."

Across the street, nine impassive children loiter against the plate glass of a store window. They wear the filthy clothing of the street, mismatched and off-size. Three of the five boys are eye-catchingly dirty. The four girls, who look cleaner, range in age from roughly eleven to fourteen. The boys look a year or two younger, but it might just be that girls in their early teens grow faster than boys.

They pay no attention to the man and the boy across the street.

"Keep walking," the boy says. "Don't slow down too much, but look at the window, like you're shopping. When we get around the corner, tell me the sex and the color of the shirt of the one you want. Or take two or three. They don't cost much."

The man looks toward the shop windows. "Then what?" he asks.

"Then they come to the hotel," the boy says.

3

The Big Guy

The Big Guy's eyes keep landing on Rafferty.

He's developed a visual circuit that he follows every time a card is dealt: look at the dealer's hands, look at the new faceup card in the center of the table, look at Rafferty. Then he lifts the corners of the two facedown cards in front of him, as though he hopes they've improved while he wasn't paying attention to them. He puffs the cigar clenched dead center in his mouth and looks at Rafferty through the smoke.

This has been going on for several hands.

Rafferty's stomach was fluttering when he first sat down at the table. The flutter intensified when the Big Guy, whom no one had expected, came through the door. Like the others in the room, Rafferty had recognized the Big Guy the moment he came in. He is no one to screw with.

But Rafferty may have to.

He has grown more anxious with each hand, fearing the moment when he'll have to test the system. And now he can feel the Big Guy's gaze like a warm, damp breeze.

With a flourish, the dealer flips the next-to-last of the faceup cards onto the green felt. It's a six, and it has no impact on Rafferty's hand, although one of the other men at the table straightens a quarter inch, and everyone pretends not to have noticed. The Big Guy takes it in and looks at Rafferty. His shoulders beneath the dark suit coat are rounded and powerful, the left a couple of inches lower than the right. The man's personal legend has it that it's from twenty years of carrying a heavy sack of rice seed, and he is said to have punched a tailor who proposed extra padding in the left shoulder of his suit coat to even them out.

A massive gold ring sporting a star ruby the size of a quail's egg bangs against the wooden rim of the table as he clasps fat, short-fingered hands in front of him. Rafferty finds it almost impossible not to look at the man's hands. They are not so much scarred as melted, as though the skin were wax that had been stirred slowly as it cooled. The surface is ridged and swirled. The little finger on the left hand doesn't bend at all. It looks like he had his hands forced into a brazier full of burning charcoal and held there. The mutilated left hand lifts the corners of the facedown cards with the careful precision of the inebriated, the immobile little finger pointing off into space. The Big Guy was drunk when he arrived, and he is well on his way to being legless.

"What are you doing here, *farang*?" the Big Guy asks very quietly in Thai. The soft tone does not diminish the rudeness of the question. His mouth is a wet, pursed, unsettling pink that suggests lipstick, and in fact he swipes his lips from time to time with a tube of something that briefly makes them even shinier.

"I'm only part *farang*," Rafferty says, also in Thai. "My mother's Filipina." He smiles but gets nothing in return.

"You should be in Patpong," the Big Guy says, his voice still low, his tone still neutral. "Looking for whores, like the others." He picks up his glass, rigid pinkie extended like a parody of gentility.

"And you should watch your mouth," Rafferty says. The glass stops. One of the bodyguards begins to step forward, but the Big Guy shakes his head, and the bodyguard freezes. The table turns into a still life, and then the Big Guy removes the cigar from the wet, pink mouth and sips his drink. Minus the cigar, the mouth looks like something that ought not to be seen, as unsettling as the underside of a starfish.

The others at the table—except for Rafferty's friend Arthit, who is wearing his police uniform—are doing their best to ignore the exchange. In an effort to forget the cards he's holding, which are terrifyingly good, Rafferty takes a look around the table.

Of the seven men in the game, three—the Big Guy and the two dark-suited businessmen—are rich. The Big Guy is by far the richest, and he would be the richest in almost any room in Bangkok. The three millionaires don't look alike, but they share the glaze that money brings, a sheen as thin and golden as the melted sugar on a doughnut.

The other four men are ringers. Rafferty is playing under his own name but false pretenses. Arthit and one other are cops. Both cops are armed. The fourth ringer is a career criminal.

One of the businessmen and the Big Guy think they're playing a regular high-stakes game of Texas Hold'em. The others know better.

It's Rafferty's bet, and he throws in a couple of chips to keep his hands busy.

"Pussy bet," says the Big Guy.

"Just trying to make you feel at home," Rafferty says. In spite of himself, he can feel his nervousness being muscled aside by anger.

The Big Guy glances away, blinking as though he's been hit. He is an interesting mix of power and insecurity. On the one hand, everyone at the table is aware that he's among the richest men in Thailand. On the other hand, he has an unexpectedly tentative voice, pitched surprisingly high, and he talks like the poorly educated farmer he was before he began to build his fortune and spend it with the manic disregard for taste that has brought him the media's devoted attention. Every time he talks, his eyes make a lightning circuit of the room: *Is anyone judging me?* He doesn't laugh at anyone's jokes but his own. Despite his rudeness and the impression of physical power he conveys, there's something of the whipped puppy about him. He seems at times almost to expect a slap.

The two architecturally large bodyguards behind him guarantee that the slap won't be forthcoming. They wear identical black three-button suits and black silk shirts, open at the neck. Their shoulder holsters disrupt the expensive line of their suits.

The Big Guy's eyes are on him again, even though the dealer's hands are in motion, laying down the final card of the hand. And naturally it's when Rafferty is being watched that it happens.

The final card lands faceup, and it's an eight.

Rafferty would prefer that someone had come into the room and shot him.

4

They Could Be Anywhere

Just an alley.

Bangkok has thousands of them. To a newcomer—like the girl with the baby, the boy thinks—they're just places to get lost in: filthy concrete underfoot, the chipped and peeling rear walls of buildings that turn their painted faces to the streets, hot exhaust and dripping water from air-conditioning units, loops and webs of black-rubber-coated wiring. Piles of trash and the rats they attract. The barbed, high-throat reek of urine.

But to the boy this alley is as good as a compass. He knows precisely how many steps it is to the busy brightness of the boulevard. He can feel on the surface of his skin the open space of the smaller alleys that branch off to the left and right. He could tell you without looking how many stories make up the building at his back.

It's just one of the thousands of alleys in the boy's mental navigation system, as safe or as dangerous as the person he shares it with. The person he shares it with now is definitely dangerous, but probably not under these circumstances.

He wears a polo shirt and a pair of cheap slacks, robbed of their crease by Bangkok's damp heat. Barely taller than the boy, the man is as

wide and unyielding as a closed door. The square face is so flat it seems
to have been slammed repeatedly against a wall. The man's eyes scan
the boy's face as though they're trying to scour the skin away.

The boy says, "You're lying. I saw his wallet when he paid me."

Behind the door-shaped man is another man, taller and more slender, but equally hard-faced. The taller man has both hands wrapped
firmly around the elbow of a third man, who studies the concrete beneath his feet as though he's looking for the faint lines that will betray
a secret door.

The third man is handcuffed, his arms behind him.

"It's full, but it's mostly ones," the door-shaped man says. "Here.
Look for yourself,"

The wallet he extends has been taken from the handcuffed man. It is
sticky, damp with the sweat of heat and fear. The boy doesn't touch it.
"Ones now," he says. "But tens and twenties before."

The man in handcuffs hears the argument without understanding a
word. He speaks German and English, but no Thai. His face is blank
with the sheer effort of running mentally through all the things he
might have done, all the choices he might have made, dozens of them,
large and small—anything that would not have led him to this minute.
This minute when his life, his life as he has come to know it, ends.

"Look at it, damn you," says the door-shaped man.

The boy says, "One hundred dollars."

"You little shit," the door-shaped man says. A scuff of shoe on concrete draws his attention, and two children enter the alley from the
even narrower passage that runs off to the left. He turns back to the
boy and gives the wallet a shake. "Are you saying I'm lying?"

The boy looks past the wallet, at the man's eyes. "One hundred," he
says.

The man stares at him, then nods abruptly, as though agreeing with
himself about something. He shoves the wallet into his hip pocket. "In
that case," he says, "fuck off." He starts to turn to go, but the boy's
hand lands on his arm, and the man yanks his arm away as though the
boy carried disease.

He brings the arm back, as if to hit the boy, but then his eyes go past
the boy's face and settle on something behind him. Four children have
come into the alley from the boulevard. Behind them are three more.

The taller man, the one holding the prisoner's arm, feels a presence at his back. He glances over his shoulder. Three children stand there, although he could not have said where they came from. He's almost certain the alley dead-ends behind him. He licks his lips and says, "Uhhh, Chit . . ."

"One hundred," the boy says. "Now. In one minute, two hundred."

Half a dozen children come out of the alley to the right.

The children are ragged and dirty, their hair matted, their upper lips caked with sweat and snot. Many of them are barefoot, their feet so filthy it looks like they are wearing boots. Some of them are only eight or nine, and some are in their early teens. They say nothing, just stand there looking wide-eyed at Chit, the door-shaped man.

There are fifteen or twenty in all. Over the hum of traffic from the boulevard, Chit can hear them breathe. Three more appear at the alley's mouth.

The boy says, "Thirty seconds."

Chit draws his lips back, baring his teeth as though he is about to take a bite out of the boy's throat. His hand goes to his pocket and emerges with a wad of twenties. With his eyes fixed on the boy's, he counts off five of them, holds them out, and drops them to the ground.

The boy bends down and picks them up. "Thank you," he says, as politely as if they'd been neatly folded and handed to him in an envelope. He puts them into his pocket and turns to go.

"Wait," Chit says. The boy pauses, but the other children are already melting away. "Tomorrow night."

The boy says, "No. There are other police, not as greedy as you."

"Try it," Chit says. "See how long you live."

The boy turns back to him. "I could say the same to you." He looks up and down the alley, taking in the remaining children. "They could be anywhere," he says. "Any time. Waiting for you."

Chit surveys the upraised faces, smells the dirt and sweat. He raises both hands, palms out. "All right, all right. No more bargaining. Fifteen percent off the top." The boy is impassive. "Twenty," Chit says.

"Tomorrow," the boy says. He saunters to the end of the alley and goes left, onto the sidewalk of the boulevard. The children drift away.

Chit's eyes burn holes into the boy's back. He turns to the handcuffed man and slaps him hard, then slaps him again. Then he catches the taller man's eye and jerks his chin upward, a command. The taller man reaches behind the prisoner, and a moment later the man's hands are free.

This is not what the prisoner had expected. The thought ricochets through his mind: *Shot running away?*

He flinches when Chit's hand comes up, but it holds nothing except the prisoner's wallet. Chit removes the cash, then pulls out a slender deck of credit cards. "Gerhardt," he says, reading the name off the top card. "Gerhardt, around the corner is an ATM. You withdraw everything you can get on all your cards and give it to me. Tomorrow morning you leave Thailand. Understand?"

Gerhardt says, "I . . . I leave? You mean, no jail?"

Chit says, "And you never come back."

Gerhardt starts to thank him and then bursts into tears.

5

All In

It's an eight.

The other six men at the table barely give it a glance, but Rafferty suddenly has a buzzing in his ears that sounds like a low-voltage power line. He squeezes his eyes closed and opens them again.

It's still an eight.

The Big Guy leans forward, watching him. He passes the tube over his lips and says, in that high, buttery voice, "The *farang* is interested."

Rafferty barely hears him. If he were forced at gunpoint to make an estimate—and it's looking increasingly likely that someone *will* be at gunpoint soon—Rafferty would put the value of the chips in the pot somewhere in the neighborhood of 750,000 baht—about $24,000 U.S. Not exactly the national debt, but certainly the largest amount he's ever risked on the turn of a card.

Of course, he's only been playing for ten days.

Feeling the Big Guy's eyes on him, he grabs eight chips off his stack and clicks them together four times. He does his best to make the gesture seem natural, but it feels like the staged business it is, transparently phony, bad blocking in an amateur play. He closes his hand around the chips and finds them wet with sweat.

The Big Guy leans back in his chair, his pink mouth puckering around his cigar. The bodyguards watch everyone else.

The man three seats to Rafferty's right had dealt the hand. He's a sallow-faced man in a shiny suit that's either brown or green depending on the light, but not a good shade of either. He waits indifferently for the man to his left to make his move. The man, one of the businessmen, makes a tight little mouth like a reluctant kiss and throws in a couple thousand. The uniformed man on the businessman's other side, Rafferty's friend Arthit, has the bet in hand and tosses it into the pot with the air of someone making a donation at the temple of an unreliable god. The moment Rafferty has been dreading has arrived. He tries to look thoughtful as he waits to be told what to do.

The one whose job it is to tell him, seated directly opposite him at the round green felt table, is as lean as a matador and as dark as a used teabag, with a hatchet-narrow face, and hair that has been dyed so black it has blue highlights. With his eyes resting lazily on the pile of chips in the center of the table, he turns the signet ring on his right hand so the stone is beneath his finger and then brings it back up again.

The hum in Rafferty's ears rises in pitch, as though the power line has been stretched tighter. The room seems to brighten.

It takes all of Rafferty's willpower to keep his hands steady as he pushes his entire pile of chips toward the center of the green felt. He says, "I'm all in."

There is a general shifting around the table as people adjust themselves in their chairs and survey the new landscape of risk. Rafferty has about 290,000 baht in chips—he's been having a selectively good night, just barely not good enough to be suspicious. This is a bet that could remove at least two of the players from the game.

One of them is the Big Guy.

Four days ago, when this game was being planned, there had been only three people in the room: Rafferty, Arthit, and the hatchet-faced man. They had been sitting in a dingy meeting room in a police station, a room to which the hatchet-faced man had been brought directly from his jail cell. He'd been promised six months off his sentence if he succeeded in fooling the pigeons—the businessmen—at the table, thereby guaranteeing that he'd do his best with the four dodges he was to perform during the game. Arthit and the other policeman, whose name is Kosit, had been promised a "consideration" of 50,000 baht apiece by the casino owners who were looking for ways to spot the dodges, and for whose enlightenment the game is secretly being videotaped.

But no one had expected the Big Guy.

And now, seated to Rafferty's left, he blows out a quart of cigar smoke and leans back in his chair. His eyes flick to Rafferty again and then away. Late forties, strong as a horse beneath fifteen pounds of soft, wet fat, he holds the cigar dead center in a tightly pursed mouth.

He says in English, "Bluff."

"Easy to find out," Rafferty says. His heart is beating so hard he can actually feel the cloth of his shirt brush his chest.

A cloud of smoke, waved away so the Big Guy can peer down at Rafferty's chips. "How much is that, *farang*?"

"Two hundred ninety-two thousand," Rafferty says.

"I've only got two-eighty-five."

"In or out?" asks the dealer.

"In," says the Big Guy. He pushes his chips into the center of the felt and then drops the last few thousand-baht chips on top of the pile, one at a time. Then he switches to Thai. "Look at your money," he says, "because you're never going to see it again."

The hatchet-faced man throws in his cards. The dealer and the man next to him also fold. Arthit takes a last look at the faceup cards and then mucks his own, making it unanimous. The man to Rafferty's right, who has already folded, shifts in his chair to watch the showdown.

"After you," Rafferty says to the Big Guy. The Big Guy moves the cigar to the corner of that pink mouth and flips his cards. He's got a straight: four, five, six, seven, eight.

"Gee," Rafferty says. He looks at the Big Guy's hand and shakes his head in admiration. Then he turns over one of his hole cards: an eight. "Let's see," he says, squinting at the table. "I haven't played for very long, but this is an eight, and there are two more of them over there, so that makes three, right?" He flips the other card. "And here's another one. So that means I've got four eights." He looks around the table. "Who wins?"

The Big Guy's chair hits the floor with a bang, and the bodyguards step forward to flank him. "Who *wins*?" He takes three steps back, one of the bodyguards whisking the fallen chair out of his way. "You're a cheat, you and that blue-haired freak over there. And you picked the wrong game." He pushes back his suit coat, and suddenly Arthit is standing with his police automatic in his hand.

"Don't *move*," Arthit says, and Kosit, the man who dealt the hand, also pulls a gun and waves it around as though to say, *Look what I have,* although he doesn't point it at anyone. "Khun Pan," Arthit says to the Big Guy, "if you're thinking about getting that little gun out of your shoulder holster, I have to advise against it." The dealer's gun comes to rest pointed at the nearest bodyguard.

"This . . . this game is fixed." Pan is so furious he's spluttering.

"Of course it is," Arthit says. His eyes flick to the bodyguard at Pan's right, who's looking jumpy. "By the way, just to put all the information on the table, there's no reason not to shoot you, so don't get silly."

"You should be ashamed," Pan says. "Siding with this *farang* against a table full of honest Thais. He's a cheat."

"Yes, he is," Arthit says. "But as you pointed out, he's not the only one." Neither the dealer nor the hatchet-faced man reacts, but two of the businessmen draw sharp breaths. "Tip here," Arthit says, indicating the hatchet-faced man, "joined us this evening straight from the monkey house, where he'll be staying for—how long is it, Tip?"

"Four years," Tip says.

"With a little time off for tonight," Arthit says. "Because Tip is way, way too lucky."

"I saw the signal," Pan says. "But if he's so fucking good, how come he hasn't won anything tonight?"

"He's not supposed to. He's been feeding Mr. Rafferty."

"Feeding?"

"He's been watching you," Rafferty says in English, with Arthit providing more or less simultaneous translation and, to all appearances, enjoying it. "You're watching him to see whether he's cheating, but what he's doing is lighthousing me, based on what he sees you do and what I have in my hand. Before I bet this last hand, I picked up eight chips and rattled them four times to tell I was holding four eights. He gave me a sign that said bet the house, and I did."

"You shit *farang*," Pan says. Rafferty starts to get up, but Arthit waves him back to his seat.

"You should be grateful," Arthit says. "Tip pulled this trick in a game a few months ago that cost a friend of yours almost four million baht. So you got a free lesson. And before you get any more disagreeable, this is a sanctioned police operation, and you're all going to get your money back."

"And you're going to lose your job," Pan says. "I don't want my fucking money back. I came here to play cards."

"Tough," Arthit says. To the dealer he says, "Give him the two hundred seventy-five thousand he came in with. Mr. Vinai," he says to the man on Rafferty's right, "you came in with a hundred and eighty-seven thousand. Officer Kosit here will count it out for you. You had two-ten," he says to the other businessman.

"He's a cop also?" Pan says, glaring at the dealer. He grabs the glass of brandy in front of him but doesn't drink. "Is he? A cop?"

"Why?" Arthit says. "Are you going to get him fired, too?"

"I might," Pan says. "What was the point of all this?"

"We, by which I mean the Bangkok police, arranged this game at the request of some people you know, actually—two of the guys who run the casinos on the Cambodian border. They face this stuff all the time." He pauses, glances at Rafferty, and adds, "Also, in the interest of full disclosure, there's Mr. Rafferty's book."

"A book?" This is one of the businessmen. "He's writing a book?"

"He is," Arthit answers. He is answering the businessman, but he's watching with thinly veiled pleasure as Pan's face turns an even deeper red. "What's it called, Poke?"

"*Living Wrong*," Rafferty says. "I apprenticed myself to seven different kinds of crooks and then went along on an operation. Tip here is the last of my mentors."

Pan seems to be having trouble breathing. "I'll have you sweeping streets for this," he says to Arthit. Kosit, the other cop, has been counting out chips and has slid several stacks toward Pan. Pan backhands them, scattering them across the table, then turns to Rafferty. "And you," he says, "I'll have you run out of the country." He takes the cigar from his mouth, drops it on the carpet, and steps on it.

"That's going to cost you," Rafferty says in Thai. "Somebody's got to pay for the rug."

"One more word out of you," Pan says, "and I'll put my foot on your head." This is a violent insult for a Thai.

"Sorry," Rafferty says. He is so angry he feels like his throat has been sewn half shut. "I forgot that you're used to dirt floors."

Arthit says, *"Poke!"* and Pan brings back his hand and slings the cognac, glass and all, at Rafferty. The glass strikes Rafferty in the center of his chest. Cognac splashes down his jacket and onto his trousers, and before he knows it, he's up and leaping at Pan even as the bodyguards push in front of him, and then there's an earsplitting bang and all eyes turn to Arthit, who's just put a hole in the ceiling.

"That's enough of everything," he says. "The evening is over. Each of you just take your money and go somewhere else to play. Is that clear?"

Rafferty is chest to chest with the nearer bodyguard. Everyone is now standing.

"I said, *'Is that clear?'*" Arthit demands.

The two businessmen are already backing away from the table, but Pan takes a step forward. "Colonel," he says to Arthit, "do you doubt I can have you fired? Do you doubt I can have this cheat's visa canceled?"

"I think money usually gets its way," Arthit says, his eyes as hard as marbles. "But not without consequences."

Pan's flush deepens. "You're threatening me?"

"Oh," Arthit says, "I think we're past threats." To Kosit he says, "Shoot the bodyguards if they so much as move."

Even the businessmen who were backing away from the table stop. Someone's cell phone begins to ring, but no one makes a move to answer.

Most Thais have an exquisitely accurate ability to read the emotional temperature of a confrontation and to veer away, even if it's at the absolute last moment, from the point at which no one can back down without a serious loss of face. In the part of Rafferty's mind that is functioning clearly, he knows that the line has just been crossed. And he knows that—since he's not a Thai—he's the only one with no significant face at stake, the only one who can step back, the only one who can retreat to the safe side of the line.

Slowly he eases himself away from the bodyguard and toward the table. He raises his hands, palms out, and sits. Then he looks down at his sport coat and brushes beads of cognac off it. The movement draws the attention of everyone in the room. "Since I offended you," Rafferty says to Pan, "what could I do to calm you down?"

Pan licks the pink lips. The look of uncertainty is back. "What . . . what could you . . ."

"What would it take?" Rafferty says. "To wrap this up, to send you home happy."

Two heavy blinks. "There's . . . there's nothing. . . ."

"Sure there is," Rafferty says. "You're too busy and too important to waste time making trouble for us, and Arthit doesn't want to have to deal in consequences. And neither do I. So what would it take? An apology? A promise to leave your name out of the book? What?"

"Ah," Pan says. His eyes dart around the room, and then he says again, "Ah." He moves to the table and picks up some chips, then lets them trickle through his fingers, apparently giving them all his attention. "An *apology*," he says, as though the concept is new to him. He brings his eyes to Arthit's and says, "You. Would you apologize?"

"Sure," Arthit says, although the word seems to hurt.

"And you, *farang*? Would you apologize?"

"I'll apologize for playing unfairly," Rafferty says. "And for being rude. Would that do it?"

For a moment he thinks it will work, but then Pan shakes his head.

"No," he says. "I want a fair game."

"I'm out," says one of the businessmen, and the other nods agreement.

"No problem," Pan says. He lifts his chin to Rafferty. "*He's* the one I want to play against."

"He doesn't have any money," Arthit says.

"I didn't say anything about money," Pan says.

Rafferty says, "Then what?"

"You like it here, don't you?" Pan asks, and Rafferty feels a sudden dip in the center of his stomach.

Studying Pan's face, Arthit says, "I don't know about this."

Pan looks at Arthit and then at Rafferty. "Aren't we looking for a way to walk out of this room?"

Rafferty says, "We are."

"Then these are the stakes," Pan says. "If you lose, you will voluntarily leave Thailand."

"Poke," Arthit says.

"I can't do that," Rafferty says. "I have a wife and daughter to take care of."

Pan shrugs the higher shoulder. "That should make the game more interesting."

"Forget it."

The flush on Pan's face deepens. "Consider the alternative," he says. "I destroy your friend here, and then I have you thrown out of the country, and then your friend undertakes some act of vengeance that probably gets him killed."

A vista of emptiness opens up in front of Rafferty. It feels like part of the walls and floor have fallen away and there is nothing above or below but gray, empty space with drizzle falling through it. Life without Thailand: life somewhere else, uprooting Miaow, explaining it all to Rose.

Possibly losing both Rose and Miaow.

Rafferty says, "And if I win?"

Pan shrugs. "Name your bet."

Suddenly Rafferty thinks of something he might actually like to have. More important, it's something Pan will never give him. If Pan won't bet, they might all be able to walk away from the table. "I'm a writer," he says. "I want your permission to write your life story, without interference."

"You're joking," Pan says. His biography is a kind of holy grail among Thai publishers, as unattainable as it is desirable. Several well-known writers have announced plans to write the man's life, only to abandon the project later for unspecified reasons. The only book that actually made it to press was lost when the printing plant burned down.

"That's what I want," Rafferty says. "Gives you something worth playing for."

Without taking his eyes from Rafferty's, Pan raises his right hand and massages the lower left shoulder as though it is still sore from the seed sack's strap. He seems completely unconscious that he is doing it. Then he laughs, but without much conviction. "Write my life story? And I don't try to stop you?"

Rafferty says, "You not only don't try to stop me. You cooperate."

"I'm leaving," says one of the businessmen. "Send the money to my office." The other joins him to leave, but Pan says, "You're staying here. Keep an eye on the *farang*. I'm not going to get cheated again."

His eyes drop to the green surface of the table and then come up to Rafferty's. The room is silent and as motionless as a window display. He purses his lips and drums his fingertips on the table for a second. His eyes make their quick circuit of the room. Then he says, "I can beat you."

"Poke," Arthit says. "Don't do it."

"Got an alternative?" Rafferty still can't believe that Pan will accept the stakes. He reaches over and grabs the deck of cards, squares it, cuts and shuffles it once, puts it in front of the spot where Pan had been sitting, and waits to see what the man will do. With an abrupt jerk, almost a muscle spasm, Pan lifts the low shoulder and lets it fall again. Then he adjusts his jacket and points to his fallen chair. One of the bodyguards picks it up and puts it back in position, and Pan sits. He puts out a hand, and a bodyguard gives him a cigar, which he centers in the pink mouth. He waits a moment, until the lighter has come and gone, and then shuffles the deck twice and passes it to Rafferty to cut again.

"So tell me," he says, picking up the deck. "Why are you so interested in writing about my life?"

"Something Balzac said," Rafferty answers. "I just want to know whether it's true."

The first two facedown cards hit the table, one for Rafferty, one for Pan. "Who is Balzac?"

"A French writer who died a long time ago."

Rafferty's second facedown card lands.

"And what did he say?"

"Something to the effect that behind every great fortune lies a great crime."

Pan's second card lands eighteen inches from his first.

6

Mound of Venus

The owner has taken advantage of the cool air towed in by a late-night drizzle to kill the expensive air-con and prop open the door to the street. It's one of Arthit's regular haunts; he had stopped at the bar to grab a full bottle of Johnnie Walker Black before heading for a corner booth. Rafferty followed along.

The place is funereally quiet, the drinkers solitary islands of silence, except for Arthit and Rafferty, who whisper, heads together, in the corner. Now and then the gloom lifts as a car passes in the *soi*, the small street outside, with a sizzle of tires on wet pavement, its headlights throwing the drinkers near the door into sharp silhouette.

"Call him in the morning," Arthit says, putting down the bottle for the fourth time. He's knocked back about a third of the contents, and the ice over which he poured the first few drinks is now a memory. "Tell him you've changed your mind." He hoists his glass.

"He gets his way too often," Rafferty says. "He needs his goddamn face slapped."

Arthit takes two long swallows, the way Rafferty drinks water. "Far be it from me," he says over the rim of the glass, "to remind you of one of the foremost precepts of your adopted culture: Keep a cool heart."

"Like you did," Rafferty says, and immediately regrets it.

Arthit lifts his drink and sights the bar through it, turning his head slowly with the glass in front of one eye. He doesn't speak.

Rafferty says, "Sorry."

"You're right," Arthit says. He takes yet another numbingly large slug of Black. "I behaved like a child. And Pan should never have been in that game. I put Vinai in charge of choosing our pigeons, and I am-most—" He shakes his head. "*Almost* called the whole thing off when he brought Pan in. But Vinai said Pan would enjoy it, said he'd think it was a terrific joke."

"He might have, if he hadn't been so drunk."

"Well," Arthit says, and drinks, a sip this time. "He was." He looks idly around the bar, just a cop survey, obviously not expecting anything interesting. "You don't want to write the book." His eyes wander to the glass in his hand, and he sets it on the table again and picks up the bottle.

Rafferty has seen his friend knock it back before, but never quite like this. "What's that thing with his lips?"

"He got burned, don't know how. You saw his hands. The file on him said the lip balm is psylochogical—psychological. He thinks they're hot, his lips, so he cools them down with menthol."

"If I'm going to quit, tell me what I'm missing. What's the story I'm not going to write?"

Arthit closes his eyes, and for a moment Rafferty thinks he might be going to slump sideways, but then he opens them again, looking at a spot in the center of the table with an intensity that suggests that he's trying to get the room to hold still. "Father was a farmer. Had some land, Isaan dirt, all rocks and scrub. Every year they'd work themselves to death, and every year they'd borrow money. They were going to lose everything. So Pan came to Bangkok." He sits there, regarding the invisible spot on the table.

"And?" Rafferty prompts.

Arthit tilts his head back as though it is too heavy for his shoulders. "And he's a tough boy. You can see that when you look at him, even now."

"He's gotten soft," Rafferty says.

"He's hard underneath it." Arthit's eyes go to the wall, and he squints slightly. "He came to Bangkok, I said that, right?"

"Right."

"Okay. Good to know I didn't imagine it. *So.*" He blinks heavily. "He chose three blocks in Pratunam, not far from where Rose and Peachy have their office now. Sidewalk market, lots of stalls. Remember, he's about seventeen years old. He goes to the stallholders and tells them they need protection." Arthit turns the glass in his fingers. "They say they've already got protection, and he says no they don't. The next day the guy who's collecting the protection money gets thrown out of a car in the middle of one of the blocks."

"Dead?"

"*Deeply* dead. Pulverized. So everybody takes a good look, and the body gets hauled away, and next day there's Pan again, telling them they need protection." Arthit picks up the bottle and squints at the label. "It's really whiskey," he says, sounding surprised. "My head should be on the table by now."

"Keep trying."

Arthit presses the bottle to his cheek, as though his face is hot. "Of course, the guy who got tossed out of the car had a boss, and Pan gets grabbed and taken to him. They're going to chop him up and prolly— probably—use him for bait, but the boss wants to take a look at him first. They're all there, Pan and the three guys who grabbed him, in the boss's office. And the boss, a management-level crook named Chai, asks Pan why he shouldn't just be killed right there. Pan says, 'Choose one of these guys.'"

As long as he has the bottle in his hand, Arthit pours and drinks. "You understand that this is hearsay, right? It's not like it's in his file or anything. Anyway, Pan says that thing about choosing a guy, and Chai figures what the hell and points at the biggest one, and in about five seconds the big guy is dead on the floor with an ice pick through his temple, and Pan has the dead man's gun and it's pressed against the back of Chai's skull. But he doesn't pull the trigger. What he does is say, 'Choose another one.'" Arthit looks toward the door as a car hisses by, narrowing his eyes against the glare through the door.

"There's buckets of this kind of stuff at the beginning, but of course if it's not in a file somewhere, it never happened. Anyway, Pan becomes one of Chai's enforcers and works his way up, and the next thing we know—say he's twenty-three, twenty-four—he's taken over a massage place, just a dump off Sukhumvit. Real junk pile. Cops called it 'the armpit,' because it was hot and dirty and wet and it smelled. A total bottom-level, ten-dollar pounding parlor. Women, the kindest way to describe them would be 'motherly.' Title to the place changes hands, and trucks pull up, and a bunch of heavyweights go in with sledgehammers, and a couple tons of dirt get dumped in front, and there are a few weeks of banging and hammering and painting and flower planting, and the dirt gets turned into a big hill leading up to the front door, which is now black glass—etched, okay?—and a huge purple sign goes up that says 'The Mound of Venus,' and Pan owns the fanciest public whorehouse in Bangkok. And then he owns two, and then three. And they've all got that little hill outside, and they're called, I don't know, Mound Two and Mound Three."

"The Mound of Venus?" Rafferty asks. "In English?"

"That touch of class," Arthit says.

"And from that he got into everything."

"You name it," Arthit says, "and he's in it. The first Mound was maybe nineteen years ago, and now he's in everything. Hotels, apartment buildings, office blocks, toy manufacturing." He wipes a palm over his forehead although the bar is cool. "In fact, manufacturing of all kinds—shoes, clothes, dishes, anything with a label on it. Factories everywhere. He's a baht billionaire. For all I know, he's a dollar billionaire, too."

Rafferty drains his beer and watches the remaining bits of foam form little bubble continents as they slide down the inside of the glass. Finally he says, "Something's missing. Where's the connective tissue? I mean, there's a gulf between baby thug–slash–sex mogul, as opposed to getting manufacturing rights to half the logos in the world. You don't just buy into the kind of businesses he runs. For that you have to get to the really big boys. That's a closed club."

"You're right," Arthit says. "There's something hidden there. And that's probably the reason he doesn't want his life story written."

"You've mentioned his file a couple of times—"

"Have I?" Arthit's eyebrows rise. "I shouldn't have." He picks up the glass and regards it with severity. "Muss—*must* be the drink talking."

"Why?"

Arthit says, " 'Why' is an extremely broad question."

"Why shouldn't you have mentioned his file?"

"If you ever looked at it, you'd know."

"I don't think I'm likely to get a look at it."

"You're certainly not. It's sensitive information. Privileged."

"Privileged how?"

"Strictly cops only. You'd have to get a cop *very* drunk for him to tell you that Pan's file is about three pages long, with wide margins and big type, and it reads like the stuff the Catholic Church gives the pope when they want somebody sainted, except shorter. Zero real information. And this is a guy everybody knows is dirty."

"But he's a Boy Scout on paper."

Arthit leans forward, pushing his face toward Rafferty's. "You're only hearing part of what I'm saying. The file's interesting, but what's more interesting is the amount of *power* it took. 'Nough power to get somebody who's way, *way* up there to pull a big, fat, dirty file, hundreds of pages thick, and replace it with a box of candy. And I mean it's been pulled everywhere. It's not on paper at the stations, it's not online, it's not in the backup systems. Least not the ones I can access."

"How unusual is that?"

The glass comes up again and gets tilted back. Rafferty watches the level drop. "Very," Arthit says when he can talk again. "Extremely. Almost unprecedented." He fans his face, which, thanks to the alcohol, is as red as the liquid that indicates the temperature in an old-time thermometer. "Poke. You don't want to get anywhere near whoever deleted those files. Which means you don't want to get near Pan."

AN HOUR LATER Rafferty steers Arthit's car along the shining street, still wet from the drizzle, to the curb in front of the house that Arthit and his wife, Noi, share. Arthit has his head thrown back and his eyes closed, but when the car stops, he sits forward and looks around at the neighborhood as though he's never seen it before.

He turns to face Rafferty. His eyebrows contract. "My car, right?"

"Right," Rafferty says, pulling the key from the ignition.

Arthit blinks lids as heavy as a lizard's. "How'd I get over here?"

"Seemed like a good idea, since you'd drunk most of the Johnnie Walker Black in Bangkok."

"Did I?" Arthit seems pleased to hear it.

Rafferty gives his friend a second to find his way into the present. "I have a question for you."

"And I," Arthit says with careful precision, "am hip-deep in answers."

"You knew all about Pan, about the amount of power behind him, earlier this evening."

Arthit says, "Oh," and turns to look out the window at his house, at the place where he had once thought he and Noi would raise their children. He breathes on the window to fog it. "That."

"Well, knowing all of it, why did you let things get so out of hand at the card table? Why didn't you defuse it earlier?"

"The right question," Arthit says thickly, "is, why didn't I give a fuck?"

Rafferty waits.

Arthit slumps sideways, his cheek pressed against the passenger window. "Between us," he says.

"Fine."

"I mean it. Not even Rose."

This stops Rafferty for a moment. There's nothing he keeps from Rose. He looks at his friend's drained, crumpled face and says, "Not even Rose."

"Noi needs . . . pills to sleep," Arthit says. The words seem to require physical effort. "The pain's worse and worse. It keeps her up. I can hear her breathing. So the doctor, the new one, he gives her sleeping pills. Strong ones. She's been getting them for more than three months."

Noi has been Arthit's wife for seventeen years. Her nervous system is being ravaged by multiple sclerosis. In the last few months, her decline has been brutally swift. She is a burning match. Arthit has been reduced to the role of helpless bystander.

"Do they work?"

"I wouldn't know," Arthit says.

"Why not?"

Arthit opens the glove compartment and snaps it shut again. "Every night she goes into the bathroom and she brushes her teeth, and then I listen as she fills a glass with water and shakes a pill out of the bottle, and then she comes to bed. Just like the doctor told her to. And I lie there and listen to her breathe, hear the catch in her breath, and I know she's awake." He opens the little compartment door again and leaves it hanging, the dim splash of light from inside it bringing his thighs and belly out of the darkness. "And this morning I went into the kitchen to make her some pancakes, as a surprise. She loves pancakes."

Rafferty feels a tremor of dread but says, "Okay."

"And in the tin of flour, a couple of inches down, I found one of those plastic bags that's got the little zipper along the top, and it was full of pills. There were eighty-one of them, Poke."

Rafferty says, "Oh?" Then he says, *"Ohhhh."*

Arthit puts both hands on his friend's arm. "Eighty-one of them," he says. "Hidden from me."

7

The Silk Room

The phone in the Silk Room rings at 11:17 P.M.

The man in the big bed is awake immediately. Late-night phone calls are so common that his wife sleeps in the Teak Room, more than thirty meters down the hallway. It is a very big house.

"Yes." He switches on the bedside lamp, and the pale silk walls of the room appear. He listens for a moment, until something he hears brings him up to a full sitting position. His forehead wrinkles and then smooths immediately, automatically erasing the display of concern even though there's no one to see it. "Seriously? A *farang*?"

He peels back the blankets and gets up, a lithe, slender, balding man in his early fifties, whose face retains the fine bone structure that had made so many well-bred hearts flutter when he was younger, the bone structure that landed him the problem daughter of one of Thailand's oldest families, now sleeping down the hall. He wears silk pajamas. "Was he drunk? He must have been drunk."

A desk, the work of some English craftsman who's been dead for three centuries, gleams between the heavily curtained front windows. On one corner is a silver tray holding a decanter of water and a heavy, deeply cut crystal glass. The man cradles the phone between ear and shoulder and uses both hands to pour, being careful not to splash any water onto the wood. He picks up the water and sips. "No," he says, "not at all. You were right to call." He puts the glass back on the tray and picks up a pen. "Spell it?" He listens and then writes, *Rafferty.* The man on the other end asks him a question.

"Let me think about that for a second." His underlings call him "Four-Step" behind his back, because of his insistence on thinking things through four and sometimes even five steps in advance. He closes his eyes briefly, his finger making tiny circles on the wooden surface of the desk.

His eyes open. "Good idea," he says. "Two in English and two in Thai. All morning papers, and one of them should be the *Sun.* You'll need to make the calls right now and use my name to make the morning editions. And I need information about Rafferty. By the time the papers come out." He listens again for a moment, and impatience twists his face. *"Everything,"* he says. "I need everything."

8

Six Separate Hells

The children who joined the boy in the alley have eaten their fill at a roadside soup stand, and the boy has given each of them a small amount of money for the needs of the following day. The little ones are already curled up on old blankets spread over the dirt floor close to the damp wooden walls, since they go to sleep earliest. The older kids take the middle of the room, with the biggest ones in front, near the door, next to lengths of two-by-four with nails driven through them at one end.

Just in case.

The boy steps outside into the misting rain, pushing the shack's wooden door closed behind him. The mud, thick beneath his flip-flops, slopes down toward the edge of the river, which is low at this season. A cloud of mosquitoes orbit him, but he waves them off and makes his way up to the boulevard, where he flags down a motorcycle taxi.

There's a one-in-three chance that he's guessed right about where the village girl with the baby will end up. She came out of Wichat's building, and Wichat maintains three holding pens, or at least three the boy knows about. There could be more.

But his luck is good. He is sheltered in a doorway when another moto-taxi bounces over the ruts and stops in front of the empty-looking building across the street. She is on the backseat, the baby at her chest and a white plastic bag dangling from her free hand. He retreats into the darkness as she climbs off and takes her first real look at her destination.

PARTWAY ACROSS THE stretch of mud, Da stops.

Six or seven steps distant, seen through the gaping doorway, the hall is ghost-dark. To Da's heightened senses, the building teems with spirits. It is roofed but unfinished, surrounded by an expanse of mud behind a rusted chain-link fence. Pitting its surface are dark, empty windows that look to Da like missing teeth. Patches of plaster have peeled from the walls, exposing sagging layers of crude, handmade mud bricks. The place smells of piss and abandonment.

Da takes two more steps, peering into the hall that yawns in front of her. There is enough city light reflecting off the low clouds to dilute the blackness of the hall into a kind of darkness in suspension, like a glass of water into which a writing brush has been dipped repeatedly. A long pool of black rainwater has collected against the left wall. Dimly visible at the hall's far end is a staircase.

The baby sleeps, heavy and loose-limbed, in her left arm, curled against her chest. The baby's blanket stinks of ammonia. A heavy plastic shopping bag cuts into the fingers of her right hand. Behind her she can hear the mechanical heartbeat of the motorcycle taxi that brought her, as the driver waits to make sure she's in the right place before he abandons her.

A thin wash of light dances on the ceiling of one of the rooms on the second floor. A candle. So someone *is* here. Da turns and lifts the bag, swinging it back and forth as a good-bye to the driver. She tries to smile. He pops the moto into gear, and Da stands there, watching the red dots of his taillights disappear in the falling mist.

Then she hoists the baby higher, takes a deep breath, climbs three steps, and passes through the doorway.

Instantly something scuttles away from her along the opposite wall, the one to her left, creating a V-shaped wake in the water: a rat. Da doesn't like rats, but she's lived with them all her life. There are worse things than rats.

The only doors in the hall are on the left, but they are closed, and nothing could make Da step into the water. That leaves the stairs.

Da has climbed stairs more frightening than this one.

On the edge of her village in the northeast was the house where the woman died. It was the largest house in the village, with two stories above the ground, this in a town where most families shared a single wooden room.

The woman had lived alone. She was not born in the village, and she was not friendly. She moved through the streets without talking to the other women. She didn't use the town shops. The shutters over her windows were kept closed.

So no one knocked on her door. And when she died, when Da was eleven, it was more than a week before the smell announced it, and two of the village men forced their way in and came out running, their hands over their noses and mouths.

In the year that followed, people gave the house a wide berth. One of the village grannies, a woman who had dreamed several winning lottery numbers, said she heard the sound of weeping coming from the house. No one else heard it, but no one else had dreamed winning lottery numbers either.

Naturally, the boys talked about going in. And talked about it and talked about it, until finally Da said *she* was going in. And quickly, before she could lose her nerve, she pried open the front shutters, hoisted herself over the sill, and let herself drop to the floor. Stood there, holding her breath, listening to the house creak in the heat. Felt the dust on the floor beneath her bare feet. Heard the rustling of mice in the walls.

Heard the weeping.

It came from upstairs. It flowed like water, without pauses for breath, a river of grief. Whoever or whatever was making that sound, it did not need to breathe. But it needed comforting. With every hair on her arms standing upright, Da went to the stairs.

There was no increase in volume as she climbed. The weeping filled the air evenly, like dust in a storm, the same everywhere.

The stairs took Da up to a short hallway. The weeping came through the open door at the end of the hall, a room that was tightly shuttered, because it was even darker than the hallway. Da slid one foot forward, then the other, moving as silently as she could. It seemed to her that it took a very long time to reach the door, and when she did, she put a hand against the jamb for balance and looked in.

The bed was terribly stained. Da's mind reeled back from considering what had caused the stains, and she forced her eyes past the stain, to the edge of the bed, to the corner of the room. And stopped.

Slowly she looked back at the bed. Nothing, nothing but the stains. She looked away again, and felt her knees weaken.

The woman was sitting on the edge of the bed, slumped forward over her lap. Long gray hair hung loosely all the way to the blanket, covering her face. But when Da looked at her, she was gone.

Da grasped the doorframe with both hands and let her eyes scan the room. While her eyes were moving, the woman was clearly visible. When she looked directly at the bed, it was empty. But the weeping continued whether the woman was visible or not.

Da forced herself to study the empty bed. This time she could see something: The pillows beyond the spot where the woman had been sitting were *wavering*, as though Da were looking at them over a steaming kettle.

"Please," Da said, and then stopped to clear her throat. "Please don't cry."

The weeping continued.

"Don't cry," Da said. "It's all over. Whatever broke your heart, it's over. You need to go."

A moment of silence, and into it Da said, "And if you can't go yet, I can come back. If you don't want to be alone, I mean. I can come see you again. I can be your friend."

Nothing.

"You don't have to be alone," Da said.

Then the bed creaked and the crack between the shutters seemed to widen, letting in more light, and Da took a lightning step back.

She could see the pillows clearly.

Da heard the house again, heard the wood groan and shift, heard the mice in the walls. Heard, as though from very far away, the boys outside calling her name. She felt the weight of her own body return to her, and she shifted from foot to foot, wondering what would be the most polite way to take her leave, just in case something remained to say good-bye to.

After a moment she backed away from the door. Halfway down the hall, she stopped and said, "Bye," and gave a *wai* of respect. Then she turned and walked, without hurrying, to the head of the stairs, and down them, then across the living room and through the window into the bright sunlight and the circle of waiting boys, all demanding to know what it was like, what she'd seen, and all unsatisfied when she said, "Nothing," and walked home alone.

And now, with the weight of the strange baby against her chest, with her left arm aching from the burden and the handle of the plastic bag cutting into the fingers of her right hand, Da looks at the stairs in the unfinished apartment house and begins to climb.

On the second story, there are no doors in the doorways and the openings are pale with light. Da peers into the first one and finds herself in one of the waiting rooms for hell.

A kerosene lantern. Its glow falls on hunched shoulders, bent backs, sharply angled necks, open wounds. Four of the people are fragments: their limbs are twisted or missing, their torsos folded over stunted appendages. The effect is of a roomful of people assembled, in the dark, from the litter of a battlefield. The fifth one, the whole one, is a child of ten or twelve. Da has to look twice to see the harelip that pulls her face up into a permanent grimace, like a painting smeared by a malicious hand before the oils were dry.

"Excuse me," Da says, backing away. One of the adults sees the baby and waves them off. "No," he says sharply, "not here." He rises, his knee dangling, crimped at the end like a sausage, and Da backs out, into the hall.

Huddled in the next room are old-looking children, all teeth and joints and fingers; one of them hisses at her. The room after that reeks with whiskey and is crowded with men, dangerously full of unhealthy heat. Da looks into six rooms, six separate hells, before a heavyset woman in her thirties smiles at her and waves her in. This woman, ten or twelve years older than Da, also has a baby.

The older woman has somehow made the unfinished room feel warmer, although all she has done is lay a faded, threadbare blanket over the cement floor and made a soft mound of clothing to put her infant on. A candle burns in a bottle in the corner. Da offers a grateful *wai*, her palms pressed together as if in prayer, and then sets down the bag containing her new T-shirt, the blanket, the cake of soap, the milk, the small bottle of whiskey. Giving the other woman as much space as possible, Da sinks to a sitting position with the baby in her lap and says, "Thank you."

The woman makes a fluid movement, precise and economical, from mouth to ears. She can neither hear nor speak. She puts her hands side by side and extends them toward the baby in Da's lap as though she wants to pour water on it. She brings her hands back to her chest and repeats the gesture, and Da realizes what it means and hands the child to the woman.

In the woman's arms, the heavy, stinking bundle becomes a baby. She gently unwraps the cloth, and a tiny hand emerges and opens and describes an arc through the air. The woman extends an index finger, and the baby's fist closes on it.

Da feels herself smile.

The woman looks up and catches Da's smile and returns it. At the sight of the smile, of the tiny fist around the finger, something breaks in the center of Da's chest, something that has been hardening there for days. Her eyes fill with tears. The woman shakes her head slowly and extends her free arm, and Da creeps beneath it. With a stranger's arm around her shoulders, Da wipes her eyes and looks down for the first time to study the face of her new child.

A Towel and a Frown

The Day of the Telephone begins at 6:20 A.M.

He rolls over blindly at the first ring, his hand slapping the surface of the bedside table and knocking the alarm clock to the floor, and Rose stirs and mutters beside him, although it takes more than a ringing phone and a falling clock to awaken her.

The side of his hand hits the phone, sending it skittering to the edge of the table, but he manages to grab it before it follows the clock down. "What?" he says, his voice a frog's croak in his ear.

"Mr. Rafferty?" A woman's voice.

"Time is it?" Rafferty says.

"Mr. Rafferty, this is Elora Weecherat with the *Bangkok—*"

"Elora what?" He is rubbing scratchy eyes with his free hand.

"Weecherat. With the *Bangkok Sun.*"

"I don't want a subscription."

"I'm wondering whether you have a comment about the story on page three."

Rafferty says, "Ummmm."

"Is the story accurate?"

He hauls himself to a sitting position. "Give me a number," he says.

She recites a phone number, and he hangs up in the middle of it. He sits there, feeling the edge of sleep recede like the shoreline of a country he's been forced to leave. The phone begins to ring again, and he pulls the jack out. This silences it in the bedroom, but he can hear it chirping away in the living room. He wraps himself in his robe as though it were a grievance and goes through the bedroom door, into the stuffy heat of the living room.

The air conditioners in the bedrooms make sleep possible in the hot season, which this year seems to be twelve months long, but it makes little sense to cool the living room when no one is in it. The door to the balcony is closed, and the air is heavy with the stink of Rose's cigarettes. For the thousandth time in his life with her, Rafferty wonders why cigarette smoke smells so much worse in the morning than it does at night. At night it has a sort of sinful razzle to it, but in the daytime it smells as toxic as asbestos. He goes to the sliding glass door and opens it. The clouds responsible for the previous evening's drizzle have thinned to a high, pale ghosting, semitransparent as a film across the sky, a brilliant chromium heat-yellow in the east, but still a sleepy, pillow-feather gray to the west. As he checks his watch—*6:25?*—the phone rings again. Or, more accurately, it chirps like the world's biggest, most aggressive cricket, the ring tone Miaow programmed into it.

He glares at it, but it doesn't explode, so he goes into the kitchen.

He has taken lately to grinding the coffee beans before he goes to bed, not so much because of the noise the grinder makes in the morning, since nothing short of a collision with an asteroid would wake Rose, but as a way of shortening the amount of time it takes him to get the first gulp of coffee into his system. All he has to do now is turn on the pot, pour bottled water into the reservoir, and then stand there in suspended animation while the coffee drips. And drips. And drips.

The phone rings four more times as he waits, his forehead pressed against the cool of the refrigerator door. As he pours his first cup, it begins again. He ignores it, sipping the hot liquid and waiting for the daily miracle, the renewal of consciousness and judgment and volition, that coffee always brings. At the twenty-fourth ring, the phone stops.

And, with the chirping silenced, he hears his cell phone ringing. The surge from the coffee gives him the energy to go into the living room and check the display, which says ARTHIT.

His throat tightens as the previous night comes back to him. Noi's stash of pills. What it might mean.

"Arthit," he says.

"One of our friends has been busy," Arthit says. He sounds thick as sludge, as befits a man who drank his weight the previous evening.

The fact that this is not about Noi sends a porous buoyancy through Rafferty and makes the day visible through the open door look less stifling. "We have friends in common?" He sucks down most of the coffee that remains in the cup.

"One of our friends in the card game. You're famous."

Rafferty says, "Well, don't worry, I'll still say hello to you. If we should happen to meet, I mean. However unlikely that may be."

After a moment Arthit says, "How much coffee have you had?"

Rafferty looks down into the mug, which is empty. "One cup."

"You have a very responsive system."

"Some people are Ferraris," Rafferty says, "and some are Land Rovers."

"And some are in the *Bangkok Sun* and the *World*," Arthit says. "And a couple of the Thai-language papers, too."

"Wait. What's in the paper?"

"You and Pan," Arthit says. "You're big news."

Rafferty puts down the cup. "Let me go get the papers," he says. "I'll call you back."

THERE HE IS: page three in the *Sun* and page seven in the *World*. The *Sun* even has a dark, fuzzy picture, cribbed from the color shot on the back of Rafferty's book *Looking for Trouble in Thailand* but oddly mutated by being cheaply converted into a black-and-white halftone.

"I look like an ax murderer," Rafferty says.

"With all due respect," Arthit says on the other end of the phone, "how you look is the least of your problems."

"No," Rafferty says. "How *you* look is the least of my problems. How *I* look is a matter of some concern. Who talked to the press?"

"None of them. They don't have this kind of clout. One of them, probably Vinai, talked to someone who *does* have this kind of clout."

"Why Vinai?"

"He's the one who brought Pan."

"And why don't you think he made the call himself?"

"As I said, clout. By the time the game ended, the papers were coming up on deadline. It took somebody with weight to get the stories into the morning editions. And then look at what's *not* in the story. The card game, any hint of resistance on Pan's part—practically everything is missing except the fact that a *farang* has been selected to write Pan's biography, with Pan's blessing."

"So what does that mean?"

Arthit says, "I don't know yet."

Rafferty's adopted daughter, Miaow, comes into the living room, her hair wet and pasted to her head from her morning shower, on her way to another challenging day of fourth grade. She has been detached and even sullen lately, but she's sufficiently surprised to see Rafferty— who's not often up at this hour—to give him a startled little wave. Then she damps down her enthusiasm and heads for the kitchen.

"My phone's been ringing all morning," Rafferty says to Arthit.

"Oh, sure. This is news. Bangkok's most profligate billionaire, the guy who gold-plated his Rolls-Royce and is known not to care for *farang,* has suddenly given one of them the right to tell his story."

As if on cue, the other phone begins to ring.

"There's my public," Rafferty says. "Do you know somebody on the *Sun,* a reporter called Eloise or Eleanor or something?"

"Elora?" Arthit asks. Miaow comes into the room with a can of Coke in one hand and an orange in the other and starts toward the ringing phone. Rafferty holds up a hand to stop her.

"That's it," he says to Arthit. "Elora."

"Elora Weecherat," Arthit says. "Business section. Looks like a fashion model, but she's as tough as nails."

Miaow tucks the orange under her chin and picks up the phone, ignoring Rafferty's attempt to wave her off. "Yeah?" she says.

"Is she pro or con on Pan?" Rafferty asks.

"She's got a kind of horrified fascination," Arthit says. "Mainly because of all the girls."

Miaow says, "He's on the other phone. This is his daughter."

Hearing Miaow refer to herself as his daughter makes Rafferty smile, although he knows she won't like his smile any more than she seems to like anything else these days. "What's she going to think when I quit?"

"*Are* you going to quit?"

"No," Miaow says, in the put-upon tone Rafferty's been hearing a lot of. "I won't write down a number. I'm eating breakfast. Call him back." She hangs up and takes the orange out from under her chin, and her eyes drift to the newspapers on the table.

"I thought we'd decided that last night," Rafferty says. "I'm going to call him today and tell him I changed my mind."

"Just checking," Arthit says. "I didn't know we'd come to a firm decision."

"All this nonsense this morning has, as the British say, stiffened my resolve. I am stiffly resolved not to do it."

Miaow nudges Rafferty's arm. He glances up to see her finger pointed at his photo in the *Sun*. He nods, and Miaow tugs down the corners of her mouth and lifts her eyebrows, looking grudgingly impressed. At least, Rafferty thinks, it's a reaction.

"Well, when you tell her you're not going to write it," Arthit says, "give her a reason, or she's going to think you've been scared off."

"But if Pan has given me permission to write it, why would he scare me off?"

"There are other people," Arthit says, "*lots* of other people, who would much prefer that a book, especially a sympathetic book, not be written."

"Who?"

"People who are worried about his personal power base. He's extremely popular among the poor, especially in the northeast."

"Why?"

"Ask someone who's poor," Arthit says. "Or used to be."

Miaow is reading the story that accompanies the photograph. She gives a low whistle, which comes as a surprise. Rafferty hadn't known she could whistle.

Watching Miaow run her finger along the lines of type, Rafferty says, "What would you do if you were in my shoes?"

"I'd take a careful look around, assess the total situation, add up the pros and cons, and then scream."

"Thanks. How's Noi?"

"We'll talk about that later," Arthit says, and hangs up.

"What *is* this?" Miaow asks. She is rubbing the surface of the photo with her index finger as though she expects it to come off the page.

"It's a picture of me."

"You look really ugly," Miaow says, and the door to the bedroom opens and Rose comes out, wrapped in a towel and a frown, just as the phone begins to ring.

"Why is it so *noisy*?" she asks.

"Poke's in the paper," Miaow says, rotating the *Sun* to face Rose. Then, without another word, she turns her back on both of them and heads for the kitchen.

"What?" Rafferty says into the phone.

"Listen to me," says a man's voice.

"I have the phone at my ear and everything," Rafferty says. "Just poised to listen."

Rose says, "This is a *terrible* picture."

"You will not write this book," the man says. "If you write it, you, your wife, and your daughter will die."

"Who is this?" Rafferty says, and the tone of his voice brings Rose's eyes up.

"Did you hear me?" the man asks.

"I asked who you were."

"All three of you will die," the man says. He hangs up.

Both Rose and Miaow, who stopped at the kitchen counter, are staring at Rafferty now. He brings up the corners of his mouth, hoping it looks like a smile, and says, "I don't think the picture's that bad."

10

Or What?

He's a great man," Rose says. She blows on her cup of Nescafé.

"Are we talking about the same guy?" Rafferty's on his third cup of coffee, waiting for Miaow to finish getting ready for school, since he's decided not to let her go alone today. She has grudgingly agreed to allow him to accompany her.

He eyes Rose's cup of instant with resignation. He's abandoned his two-year campaign to get her to give up Nescafé, the coffee she grew up on. He's spent a fortune on exotic beans, coffeemakers, gold filter cones, and bottled water to convert her, and her dream cup of coffee still involves hot water run from the tap onto a heaping clot of brown powder.

"We're talking about Pan," she says. "The gold car and the girls."

"He's a thug. And a drunk."

"So what? The way he acts, he knows what he's doing. He's like a bone in their throats."

"Whose throats?"

"The *good* people," she says, and he is taken aback at the bitterness in her voice. "The big people, the people who have everything and want more. The people who take, take, take, own, own, own. The people who go to fancy parties with blood on their hands. With their expensive cars and their big houses and their beautiful clothes and their terrible, spoiled children. The people who own the streets underneath the bars the girls work in and the rooms they sleep in when they're finished screwing tourists. And then sell them the drugs for AIDS." She slaps the cup down, loudly enough to straighten his spine. "You know. The people who have run everything forever."

They are seated opposite each other at the counter that divides the kitchen from the living room. The brilliance of the new day spills into the room behind Rose, catching flyaway locks of her hair and exploding what seems like a hundred colors out of the long fall of black that stretches to the dimples at the base of her spine. He leans across and touches her wrist.

"He drives them crazy." She turns her hand palm up and wraps her fingers around his. "He's dirt, up from some pigshit village, and he rubs their noses in it every day of the year. He shoved his way in here, with his awful skin and his burned hands and his one low shoulder, and grabbed a place at the dinner table without being invited, and then he pushed all their plates and glasses onto the floor, and spit on them. And then he bought everything they owned, two or three of everything, and covered them with gold just to make them uglier. And he takes the most beautiful women in the country, the ones they all want, and drags them behind him like a parade."

"What's the point?"

Rose shakes her head. "To prove that someone like him can have everything *they* have, everything that makes them special, and then shit on it. That someone can get rich without pretending to be one of them or trying to hide where he came from. The richer he gets, the cruder he gets. It scares them. They think he does it on purpose, just to build his personal power base."

Power: the word Arthit had used. "Does what? Act like a pig?"

She turns the cup in the saucer, just doing something while she thinks. "That's one side of it. But then he also gives money away like old newspaper. He sets up what he calls 'banks' up north. But they're not really banks. Real banks lend money at interest and take away houses and things. *His* banks make small loans, maybe three or four hundred dollars, to poor people who have an idea for a business. If the business works, they pay back a little more than they borrowed. If the business fails, they don't owe him anything. There are weaving villages now, woodcarving villages, silver-jewelry villages. There are men who own three or four trucks that they rent to farmers whenever they're needed."

"Why does that upset anyone?"

She dips her index finger into her cup and flicks coffee at him. "You're supposed to understand this country. You wrote a book about it, remember?"

"I've never claimed to understand it. That's why I married you."

She pushes the coffee aside. "It upsets people because poor people are supposed to stay poor. They're not supposed to have papers that say they own their land. They're not supposed to have money in the bank so they can stockpile their harvests until the prices go up. They're not supposed to do anything except live and die, and get fucked over in between. Grow the rice and sell it for nothing. Clear the land so some godfather can kick them off it and build ugly, expensive houses. Go where they're told and stay where they're put. Present themselves for sacrifice on a regular basis so the rich can stay fat."

"And Pan is rocking the boat?"

"Sure. Rich people steal from the poor and pretend they're giving. And here he is: He was poor, he still behaves like a peasant, and he's *really* giving. He's built two hospitals in Isaan, not big hospitals but good ones, and he pays doctors to work there, to take care of people who have never seen a doctor in their lives." She stands and goes to the sink. He looks at the day heating up through the window, hearing the clink of her spoon against the jar of instant coffee and then the flow of water as the tap goes on. "Do you remember a girl from the bar, short and a little fat, always laughing, named Jah?"

Rafferty searches his memory. "Sort of. Maybe."

"You have to remember her. There was that girl, the ugly, awful one, who was dancing when you first came into the bar. She wore glasses, and you can't tell me you've forgotten that."

Rafferty feels his face go hot.

"So you thought she was a college student or something, and you gave her—"

Rafferty tries to wave the rest of the story away. "I remember."

"—you gave her five hundred baht. Because you were a sap. And the next night when you came in, *everybody* was wearing glasses."

"Oh," Rafferty says, the light dawning in the east. *"Jah."*

"Right. She was the one whose glasses were so strong she walked off the edge of the stage and landed on that foreign woman. Anyway, Jah tested positive."

"Oh, I'm so sorry." Rose is right, Jah had always been laughing.

"She's okay." She comes back and takes her seat again. "She got into a place here in Bangkok with about a hundred and fifty women in it. I know five or six of them. They get the drugs without having to pay for them, they have a place to sleep, they get three meals. They're not out on the street, dying, or curled up in some shack up north, with the whole village pointing at them. Pan pays for it all."

Rafferty says, "Last night he was calling the women on Patpong whores."

"They are," Rose says.

"Well, yeah, I mean, sure, literally." This is not his most comfortable subject. "But he used the word—I don't know—contemptuously."

"That's who he is. He uses the worst words he can think of. And then he goes and sets up a place like the one Jah is in."

"I'm ready," Miaow says, coming into the room in her school uniform. Her hair has been meticulously reparted and slicked down, and the skin on her cheeks literally shines. She is, Rafferty thinks, the cleanest child on the face of the earth.

"Let's go, then," he says, standing up.

"Why are you taking me?" Miaow demands. "I get there by myself every day."

"Why not?" Rafferty says. "I'm awake, it's time, and you're my daughter. You said so yourself."

Miaow slips into the straps of her backpack. "He's weird today," she says to Rose.

Rose says, "He's weird every day."

FOR THE FIRST five minutes of the taxi ride, Miaow gives him the brooding silence that seems to be her new default mode.

When she finally talks, he gets the topic he wants least. "Something's wrong, isn't it?"

"Why would something be wrong?"

"I saw you when you were talking on the phone. You got all tight and squinched."

"Squinched?"

"That's English," she says. "I think."

"I suppose it's closer to English than it is to anything else."

"Anyway, you looked like that."

Rafferty gazes longingly out the window, which is too small for him to escape through. In retrospect, being alone with Miaow right now is not a tremendous idea. For some obscure reason, possibly because she knows he loves her with all his heart, she thinks she can ask him about anything. And, of course, she's right.

He opts for selective honesty. "You know that book they mentioned in the newspaper?"

She blows out, her upper teeth against her lower lip to create a very long and slightly irritated "Ffffffffffff" sound. "I remember. It was only half an hour ago."

"Well, that was someone who told me not to write it."

Miaow says, "Or what?"

He should have known better. "What do you mean, 'or what'?"

She crosses her arms high on her chest. "People don't tell you not to do something without saying 'or what.' You know that."

"You've been watching too many movies."

"No. He said 'or something,' and then you got all squinched."

The cab, at long last, makes the right into the street that leads to the street that leads to the street that Miaow's school is on. Rafferty exhales heavily and says, "Jesus, this is a long ride."

Miaow's not giving him an inch. "That's because you can't think of anything to say."

"Why have you been so grumpy lately?" Rafferty asks.

"Don't change the subject. They said 'or something.' "

"All right, you're absolutely correct. They said if I wrote the book, they'd attack me with garden tools, chop me up, and make me into sandwiches."

"I'm not *five,*" Miaow says. "Why would anyone make a sandwich with garden tools?"

"They're farmers," Rafferty improvises. "That's all they have."

"Why don't they just back the buffalo over you?"

"Then they wouldn't have the sandwiches."

The remark gets the silence it deserves, and Miaow allows it to stretch out. Then she puts a small brown hand on top of his, the first time she's touched him in days. "Are you going to get us into trouble?"

"Absolutely not."

"How can you be so sure?"

"Very simple," he says. "I'm not going to write the book."

IT TAKES ONLY a second for his life to change.

The thrust of something hard into his back. The solid grip on his upper arm.

"It's a gun," a man says in English. "Stop walking. Don't look around."

"Or what?" Rafferty says, Miaow's voice in his ears. The door to her school is a few yards behind him. She disappeared through it ten seconds ago.

"Or I'll blow your spine to bits." The English is almost completely unaccented.

"Just asking."

"Hold still," the man says, and something dark brown is pulled over Rafferty's head and he's shoved forward. "Bend down, pull the hood away from your chest, and look at your feet. There's an open car door in front of you. Get in. Leave the door open behind you and sit in the middle. Clear?"

"Crystalline."

"Then go."

The car is black, and the bit of it he can see is clean and highly polished. He climbs in. It is cool and smells of leather. He slides to the center of the seat, his feet straddling the bump for the drive shaft, and waits. The front door opens, and the car dips as someone very heavy climbs in. A second later the back door to his left opens. A man gets in, and then there is another man sitting on his right. A gun probes his ribs on each side.

"With all friendly intent," Rafferty says, "if those bullets go through me, you're going to be shooting each other."

"They won't go through you," says the man who had spoken before, who is now to Rafferty's right. "They're .22 hollow-points. They'll just turn you to hamburger inside and stay there."

Rafferty says, "Good. I'd hate to worry about you." He hears a ticking that he identifies as the turn signal, the driver preparing to enter the stream of traffic.

"On the other hand," the man says, "no exit wounds. You can have an open-casket funeral."

11

Peep

The baby's name is Peep.

The night whispered the name in Da's ear just before she dropped off to sleep. She had spent hours, extravagantly letting her candle burn down, studying the child's face. He is a beautiful baby with features of bewildering delicacy, especially the impossible miniature perfection of the nose and ears, the long, dark fringe of eyelashes, the soft curls of black hair. All of it so defenseless, all of it so *new*.

"Peep" is the first sound a chick makes, when its wings are silly, useless elbows and its feathers are yellow baby fluff. It's a small sound, breath-edged, perfect for a baby.

So: Peep.

Don't drop it, the man in the office had said.

How could she drop him?

Early the next morning, they were jostled down the stairs and across the drying mud into the back of a pair of vans. The men and the cripples were herded into one van, the women with children into the other.

The windows were covered with ragged pieces of sacking that had been glued to the glass. The covered windows frightened Da: Why shouldn't they see where they were going? She pointed to the cloth and made a palms-up, questioning gesture to the deaf and dumb woman, who smiled and shook her head: *Don't worry.* One of the other women, older than the others, with a skeletal, stunned-looking four- or five-year-old child clinging to her, said, "It's so nobody can see in. People aren't supposed to know that we get driven back and forth."

Da said, "Oh." Feeling stupid, feeling naive. Feeling lost. Wishing she were back in the drowsy cluster of wooden shacks at the bend of the river that is now dry, its water stolen. The shacks empty now, knocked off balance by the big machines until they sagged drunkenly sideways. Even the dogs are gone.

The sidewalk that has been given to her is hard and hot and dusty, another kind of dry riverbed, a river of people. The booths from which the vendors sell their wares begin half a block away, while this stretch is given to store windows, small office buildings, foot traffic, and beggars. Da sits exactly where she was put by the man who had driven the van, a thickset tree trunk of a man in a bright blue Hawaiian shirt with brown girls all over it. He had looked at her incredulously when he realized she didn't have a bowl, and then he'd tightened his mouth and stalked away, down to the booths. When he returned, he tossed a red plastic rice bowl into her lap. It had just missed Peep.

"You owe me eighty baht," he'd said.

Now she sits there, the bowl upraised, hopelessly fishing the river of people. Most of them push past her, the same way they would sidestep a hole in the pavement. Once in a while, someone—usually a woman—will slow slightly and drop a coin into the bowl, often with a glance at Peep. Every time a coin strikes the bowl, Da feels a wave of shame wash over her.

The noise of the street is deafening.

Everything is in motion, but nothing seems to change: The people flow past, the cars glint cruelly, the sun slams down, the noise hammers her ears. How can the world be this noisy? How can the air smell like this? How can the people who live here endure it? Sweat gathers under Da's arms and between her breasts and runs down her body. She feels repulsively filthy.

How will she survive this day?

One of the problems is that everything—the noise, the people, the dust, her shame—distracts her. It breaks to pieces her sense of who she is and scatters them unrecognizably at her feet. Where she grew up, silence was always available. There was always someplace she could go to reassemble herself when her grasp on who she was became frayed by distraction or anger, or even love. And now, sitting here, she feels as soulless, as valueless, as a piece of furniture abandoned on the sidewalk.

And she has been this way, she realizes, for days. Since her mother and father slung their packs over their shoulders and took her younger sisters by the hand and said good-bye to her and to their lives together. Since the bulldozer knocked the shacks crooked and made them unlivable. Since the moment she began the long, slow flight to Bangkok.

She has lost herself.

But now that she has recognized it, this is something she knows how to deal with.

She gathers her attention, reeling in the bits of her she left here and there over the days and nights that she was moving, no, *running,* as blindly and absently as the people who push past her now. She focuses all her attention on the sweat coursing down her skin. Feels the separate drops, feels their faintly cooling progress toward her belly. Feels the reassuring pressure of buttock on sidewalk: There is someone here after all. Slowly she broadens her focus to include her breath. In and out, in and out. An endless cycle with something at the center of it. Something doing the breathing, or perhaps something being breathed through, that she has come to know as Da.

The noise gradually fades.

After an undefinable period of time, she becomes aware that Peep has stopped shifting restlessly in her lap. She looks down to find him gazing at her. His tiny eyebrows are very faintly contracted, as though he is seeing something different when he looks at her. The look that passes between them is a pulse of some sort. A fine thread of connection.

Peep brings up one arm, fingers spread wide, and swings it up and down. It looks to Da as if he is waving at her. The thought breaks her concentration and makes her laugh.

And she feels eyes upon her. Someone is looking fixedly at her. She can feel this kind of thing. It is the dim, warm pressure of a gaze, fainter than the most tentative breeze, as faint as the weight of light falling through an open door. From behind her.

She turns to look, and someone stumbles into her, hard enough to knock her to an elbow and send the bowl into the air, the coins spiraling loose and ringing against the pavement. Hard enough to make her grab Peep so tightly he squeals and then begins to cry.

Someone is gabbling at her in some language—*Sorry sorry sorry*—it's English, Da realizes, and she looks up, Peep squalling against her chest, to see a thin *farang* woman with hair the color of copper, a color that doesn't even pretend to be real. The woman is waving her hands around, almost in tears, loudly saying the same thing, *Sorry sorry sorry.* She drops to her knees and begins to pick up the coins that hit the sidewalk.

"Okay," Da says, embarrassed for the woman, with the sweat dripping off the tip of her long, bony nose. "Me okay. Baby, him okay."

"I just wasn't looking," the woman says. She snatches a coin just inches in advance of a man's shoe, barely getting her raw-looking knuckles out of the way. "Are you sure he's all right?" She looks at Peep more closely and says, "Oh, my God, he's *adorable.*"

"Him . . . pretty," Da says.

"*Pretty?*" the woman says. She is dropping into the bowl the coins she picked up. "He's precious, just a real little heartbreaker. How the girls will love him—he is a boy, isn't he?"

Da says, "Boy."

"And look at those *lashes.* Why is it always boys who get those beautiful eyelashes? Although *you* didn't exactly get shortchanged in that department either. I feel like Bigfoot," the woman says, looking around for more coins. "Just hoofed over you like a heffalump. Honey," she says, putting a red-nailed hand on Da's arm, "I am *so sorry.*"

"No problem," Da says. Peep has stopped crying and is regarding the woman's hair with wide-eyed uncertainty.

"Look at that little angel," the woman says. "Just look at him. Couldn't you just eat him up?"

Da says, "Eat?"

"Oh, you poor thing," the woman says. "Here I am, gabbing on and on like this. Of *course* you need to eat. A lot more than you need a bunch of sloppy sympathy. Here." She unsnaps a big straw purse and pulls out a wad of red five-hundred-baht bills. "You just buy as much food as you can choke down, and get that little angel a new blanket. The one you've got needs a couple of hours in a good strong bleach solution." She puts two of the notes, and then a third, into Da's bowl.

"Too much," Da says.

"Nonsense. Plenty more where that comes from." The eyes on either side of the sunburned nose are a pale, faded blue that Thai people associate with ghosts, but they seem kind. "Look at you," she says. "Probably never done anything wrong in your sweet little life, and here you are. I have to tell you, honey, with all due respect to your beautiful country and everything, it stinks."

Da takes the third note out of the bowl and extends it. She says, "Please?"

"Honey, you knock that off. Put that back, or I'll give you a bunch more." The woman gets to her feet. "I'm Helen," she says. She jabs her chest with an index finger. "Helen. Me Helen." Then she points at Da. "You?"

"My name me, Da."

"Da," Helen says. "What a pretty name. And Junior there?"

"Sorry?"

Helen points at Peep. "Name?"

"Name him, Peep."

"Name him . . ." Helen says, her voice trailing off. "Oh, oh. *His* name, his name is Peep. Peep, right?"

Da says, "Peep."

"Da and Peep," Helen says. "Peep and Da."

"Happy," Da says, and then runs the sentence through her mind once and says, "Happy meet you."

"Oh, well, *honey*," Helen says, blinking fast, "I'm happy to meet you, too. And I'll be back here tomorrow. I'll be back here every day this week, and I'll be looking for you." She tugs her blouse straight, puts the strap of the big straw purse over her shoulder. She waves at Peep. "You take care of that little treasure," she says. "Bye, now."

Da says, "Bye-bye," and Helen is gone.

And immediately the space is filled by the tree-trunk man in the blue shirt, who snatches the five-hundred-baht bills out of the bowl, bends down, and says furiously, "*Never* do that. Never. Never give money back. Do you understand me?"

Da lowers her head. Peep begins to cry again. "I understand," Da says.

"You're here to get it, not give it away." And then the man is gone.

Da sits there, bouncing Peep to quiet his crying, trying to reassemble the feeling she had before Helen bumped into her. But what she feels instead is the warmth of that fixed gaze.

When she turns this time, she sees him: a spectrally slender boy of thirteen or fourteen, with a sharp-featured face and long, knotted hair. A moment later, like an animal disappearing into the brush around her village, he is gone.

12

The Chuckle Is a Perfectly Acceptable Form of Laughter

You guys do this often?" Rafferty asks.

"Often enough," says the man on his right, the one who spoke before.

"The driver must be built like a sumo wrestler. When he got in, it felt like the car was going to tip over."

"You hear that?" the man asks in Thai. "A sumo wrestler."

The man in front makes a sound that Rafferty identifies as a chuckle. Despite having read countless novels in which characters chuckle more or less continuously, this is the first time Rafferty has actually heard someone do it.

Rafferty says, "He chuckled."

"He's a merry soul," says the man to his right.

"It's important to be happy in one's work," Rafferty says.

"Do you always chatter like this when you're frightened?"

Rafferty says, "I'd be frightened if you hadn't put the hood on."

"That just means we're not going to kill you. It doesn't mean we're not going to beat the shit out of you."

"When I'm frightened, I shut up," Rafferty says.

After a moment of silence, the man to his right chuckles.

"You chuckled, too," Rafferty says. "Did somebody teach all you guys to chuckle?"

"The chuckle," the man to his right says, "is a perfectly acceptable form of laughter."

"You speak very good English."

They ride in silence for a few moments. Then the man says, "Here's the problem: It doesn't matter whether I like you. I'll do anything to you that I'm told to do. Kill you without a thought. So go ahead and entertain us, but it won't make any difference."

Rafferty says, "Why waste good material?"

DOWN A RAMP and over some speed bumps. The car stops, and a hand grasps Rafferty's arm.

"Let's go. And don't suddenly get stupid."

"I don't suddenly get stupid," Rafferty says, sliding across the leather. "I have to work up to it."

A few short steps, a wait, and then a bell rings. Rafferty hears the doors slide open, and he's guided in. The man says, "Use the key for express. No stops." Rafferty counts his pulse as the elevator rises, not because he thinks it'll be useful but because it seems to be the only information available. At the count of seventy-three, the elevator does a stomach-churning deceleration, and at seventy-seven it comes to a full stop. An amplified woman's voice with a fruity, phony-upper-class British intonation, says, "Thirty-six." Then she repeats it in Thai.

"Shit," says the man who has been doing all the talking. "I forgot about that."

Rafferty says, "I didn't hear it in either language."

"No, you didn't. And you don't mention it while you're talking to the man, understand? If you want to get through the day alive, you'll forget all about it."

"It's gone."

"Good." Hands take his elbows as the doors slide open and a wave of cold air rolls at them. "You're going straight now. I'll tell you when we've got to turn."

Four turns later he is stopped. He hears a very faint tapping sound that could be fingers on a keyboard. Several keyboards. A secretarial pool? It's easy to envision one of those big open rooms with chest-high walls. A secretarial pool, in the kind of office where a hooded man doesn't invite speculation.

So an office suite. On the thirty-sixth floor of some building, almost certainly in the Sathorn district.

A door squeaks open to his right, and hands grasp his shoulders and turn him ninety degrees to point him toward it.

"Walk four or five steps directly forward and then stop. When you hear the door close, take the hood off."

Rafferty counts off five steps, feeling thick carpet underfoot. The door closes with the same squeak. He removes the hood.

He is in a conference room. A single glance makes it clear that what is conferred about here is money, gobs and gobs of money. The table, at least sixteen feet long, is teak. It doesn't look like a veneer. It looks like twelve hundred pounds of extremely valuable, endangered hardwood. Surrounding it are eight high-backed teak chairs with sky blue woven-silk cushions, the precise color of the carpet. Dead center in front of one chair is a bright yellow legal pad and a single ballpoint pen.

Other than the pad and pen, the surface of the table gleams empty except for a squat black high-tech object at one end, an obviously expensive Whole Geek Catalog item that looks to Rafferty like it might spring a set of pincers and decide to crawl across the table toward him. The walls, covered in a cream-colored fabric, host large rectangular pale patches, announcing where pictures or posters were probably removed for his visit. Near the top of the wall to his right are two small square windows: a projection booth.

Rafferty takes a couple of steps, and a tinny voice says, "Sit." The voice comes from the techno-thing on the table, which Rafferty belatedly recognizes as a conference-call terminal. He glances up at the windows of the projection booth, but the glass is dark. Whoever is watching him is sitting well back in the gloom.

"Here, I assume." Rafferty pulls out the chair in front of the legal pad and sits. "Listen," he says. "I appreciate you sending the car and everything, but if this is about the book, you should know that I'm not going to—"

"Of course it's about the book," the man says. "I want it written immediately."

Rafferty parrots, "You want it *written*." He feels like a man who's just been shown proof that two plus two is a subtraction problem.

"Beginning today. You'll be paid a substantial advance, which will be transferred into your account at Thai Fisherman's Bank, the Silom branch, in ninety minutes. It's account 044-35-11966, is it not?"

"I'll take your word."

"Look under the legal pad."

Rafferty says, "No."

A pause, just long enough for Rafferty to swallow.

"Excuse me?"

"I'm not going to write the book."

"You're mistaken. You're not only going to write it, you're going to file regular reports on your progress. You're going to share the chapters with us as you finish them. We'll have suggestions. You will accept them."

"It's not going to get that far. I'm not going to write it. So, with that out of the way, you can go back to standing behind the screen and working the levers or whatever it is you do with your time." He starts to get up.

"If you go through that door before I excuse you, you'll have a very brief time to regret it."

Rafferty analyzes the sentence for a moment and lowers himself back into the chair.

"Mr. Rafferty. Has someone told you not to write this book?"

"No. Actually, I've decided to write a children's book. *Mr. Bunny's Bow Tie.* It's about a little rabbit who's frustrated because her husband wants to wear bow ties and she can't tie bows. You see, her paws—"

"And were there threats involved?"

"The problem is that rabbits don't have fingers—"

"Against your wife and daughter, perhaps?"

Rafferty says nothing.

"I'll take that as a yes. Two things you need to know. First, we can protect you and your family better than anyone else in Bangkok. Second, whatever you may have been threatened with, I promise you that it would be a feather bed compared to what we will do if you don't cooperate with us."

Rafferty realizes that he has crumpled the top sheet on the yellow pad. "So let's not waste time. Lift the legal tablet. Look beneath it."

He does as he's told, forcing his hands to be steady. He finds two sheets of paper, stapled together.

"Those are names," the man says. "Most of those people will talk to you willingly. The book will also require some investigative work, nothing you can't handle, judging from what you've already written. The last number, at the bottom of the second page, is the one you call to communicate with me. Is all that clear?"

What's clear to Rafferty is that he needs to get out of the room. He can't do anything until he's out of the room. "What else?"

"Now and then we'll have people watching you, just to make sure you're giving us the time and energy we expect. Occasionally an addition to that list will probably occur to us, and we might call to tell you about it. Your cell phone number is 012-610-2230, isn't it?"

Cell phones aren't listed. Rafferty says, "Don't showboat."

"This is Wednesday. You'll get the advance in your account today. You'll leave most of that in the bank. We'll know how much you withdraw, down to the last baht. We don't want you running around with so much cash it gives you stupid ideas. I'll expect the initial report on Monday, and it will be substantial if you don't want things to get uncomfortable. Your family will be under continuous surveillance, which you should find reassuring."

"Not exactly."

"Well, you're right. It's a two-edged sword. But as long as you're doing what you should, they'll be better protected than the prime minister."

"And when this is over," Rafferty says, "how do I find you?"

"You won't have to worry about that. If you're foolish enough to try, we'll find you."

Rafferty says, "I'll look forward to it."

"Don't waste energy being angry. You have work to do."

"So," Rafferty says, holding up the two pages, "I take these with me?"

"Of course not," the man says. "You copy the information onto the legal pad and take it away in your own handwriting. And you leave the pen on the table."

"I like the pen."

"Fine. One of my men will buy a box of them and then, when no one is in your apartment, he'll pick your locks and put them on your daughter's pillow. That's the bedroom to the left of the front door, I believe. Before you get to the bathroom."

Rafferty sits for a long moment, feeling the blood pound in his ears. Then he picks up the pen and begins to write.

13

They Dimple the Surface

Standing on the sidewalk, counting to fifteen as he's been told to do before removing the hood, Rafferty smells something tantalizingly familiar. He hears the surge of the car's engine. At the count of twelve, he pulls off the hood and finds himself in a small *soi*. At the end, a black Lincoln Town Car makes a left onto a broad and busy boulevard. Mud has been smeared over the license plate.

Two passing women look at him, standing there, dangling a brown pillowcase from one hand. One of them says something, and they giggle. They step into the street to avoid him.

He needs to know where he is, but before that he needs to know he still has a family. He yanks his cell phone from his pocket with so much force that he pulls the pocket inside out. Baht notes flutter to the pavement. He leaves them there, just putting a foot on one, as he dials.

Rose answers on the second ring.

"Everything okay?" he asks.

"I'm making noodles. Does that sound okay?"

"Sounds like heaven." He stoops to pick up the money.

"I'm such a housewife," Rose says. "If anyone had told me three years ago I'd be awake at this hour, making noodles with an apron on, I'd have laughed at them."

"I knew it, though," Rafferty says. "I knew the first moment I saw you, up on that stage wearing ten sequins and that crooked tinfoil halo, that there was a vacuum cleaner in your future."

"Good thing you didn't say it. I'd have had them throw you out of the bar."

"Listen," he says. "Be careful today. Don't open the door to anyone you don't know. And I think one of us ought to go get Miaow when school's out."

Rose sighs and says, "Why does life with you have to be so interesting?"

He says good-bye and works his inverted pocket back inside his pants, then takes a survey. Down at the end of the *soi*, several stands cluster, nothing more than dusty awnings tacked to the backs of buildings and propped up in front with wooden doweling. As he moves toward them, he sees that they're selling luggage, mostly knockoffs of Tumi and Louis Vuitton. And then the fragrance in the air resolves itself into curry and basmati rice, and he knows where he is: He's in the Indian district.

And the ass end of Bangkok, as far as Rafferty is concerned. He knows that it can be difficult to get either a taxi or a *tuk-tuk* here. He's sworn off motorcycle taxis since he went down on one a couple of months back. He has forbidden Miaow to ride them, too, giving her extra money every school day for taxis.

Six dollars a day, he thinks, trudging toward the boulevard. *Twenty-four, twenty-five every week.* When he first came to Bangkok, those taxis would have cost a buck, a buck twenty-five. In a week that would have been—

He stops, halted by the realization that he's taking refuge in details. The part of his mind that earns its keep by imposing order on the world is offering up bright little beads of factual material for him to string into a reality that doesn't include anything that's happened since he sat down at the card game last night: Pan's drunkenness, the threats, his abduction.

Noi's pills. The sound of Arthit's voice when he told Rafferty about them. Noi's pain.

And today's displays of naked power.

The floor plan to his apartment. His bank-account and cell-phone numbers. The kind of power most *farang* never experience.

Rafferty knows Thailand well enough to be aware that people above a certain social and political level are virtually unaccountable, shielded from the consequences of their actions by layers of subordinates and networks of reciprocal favors and graft that corrupt both the police and the courts. These are the people, the "big people," whom Rose despises, the people who attend dress balls with blood on their hands. There are not many of them, relatively speaking, but they have immense mass and they exert a kind of gravity that bends tens of thousands of lives into the orbit of their will.

Most *farang* pass through the gravitational Gordian knot of Bangkok unscathed, like long-haul comets for whom our solar system is just something else to shoulder their way past. *Farang* have no formal status here. They come and go. They dimple the surface of the city's space-time like water-striding insects, staying a few months at a stretch and then flitting elsewhere. They don't have enough mass to draw the gaze of the individuals around whom the orbits wheel.

But Rafferty is being gazed at. And he knows all the way to the pit of his stomach that it's the worst thing that can happen to him. If they decide it is in their best interest, they can blow through him and his cobbled-together family like a cannonball through a handkerchief.

If he goes in one direction, Rose and Miaow are in danger. If he goes in the other direction, Rose and Miaow are in danger. And "in danger" is a euphemism.

He is leaning against a building. His skin is slick and cold with evaporating sweat. Panic is barking useless orders at him: *Get the family to the airport.* (Rose and Miaow don't have passports.) *Hurry them out of Bangkok.* (We're being watched.) *Disappear into the city.* (Not possible.) *Kill everybody.* (Who?)

He pushes himself free of the building on legs that feel as numb as prosthetics and makes his way down the *soi* to the boulevard.

Where he stops, looking left, then right. Which way to go?

Both directions are wrong, but one must be less wrong than the other.

What he needs to do is buy time. He needs to do things that both sides will see as compliance while he figures out which chunk of Bangkok masonry he can pry loose to make a hiding place for his family. Once they're out of the line of fire, he can think about next steps. About removing himself from the equation. Finding some way to step aside at the last possible moment and let the opposing forces annihilate each other.

Just as he figures out where he needs to go next, his cell phone rings, and it's someone summoning him to the one place in Bangkok he wants to be.

14

The First Paradise

Y ou wait," the guard says, shutting the little glass door in the booth. The glass is at least an inch thick, certainly bulletproof.

The booth occupies the base of a semicircular clay-brick turret beside an enormous pair of weathered bronze gates that stretch twenty feet toward the paper-white sky. Mesopotamian lions rear up on them, claws extended and teeth bared. The Mesopotamian theme continues on the clay-brick walls, covered with bas-relief figures of standing kings, slender and stiff-kneed and tightly robed. Sprouting here and there among the kings are outcrops, planted with vegetation that spills over the edges. Green streamers dangle downward.

The Hanging Gardens of Babylon, Rafferty realizes. Not even remotely what he'd expected.

The wall is perhaps a fifth of a mile long. It occupies the entire block. Rafferty tries to remember what used to be here, but nothing comes to mind. Bangkok is like that, he thinks: One day you look up and there's a building, and the field, the house, the slum—whatever it was before, it is gone forever.

The sun's glare makes him uncomfortably aware that it is almost noon. He is glancing at his watch when the guard opens the little window again and says, "Through here." A narrow door, barely wide enough for one person to pass through, opens in the left gate. On the other side of the door stands a short, slender, dark-complected man in a pale yellow shirt and triple-pleated, salmon-colored golf slacks.

"Please," he says in English, "come in, come in."

The door in the gate clangs closed, and the slender man in the bright clothes climbs into a little white electric golf cart that has been remodeled to look like a very large and steroidal swan. One wing is improbably upraised to shade the passengers. All that Rafferty can see as the cart whirs into motion is greenery, thickly tangled and thorny, a second wall. At the wheel of the cart, the slender man says, without turning to Rafferty, "I am Dr. Ravi."

"I recognized your voice from the phone," Rafferty says. Dr. Ravi's receding hair makes his noteworthy nose seem even larger. His entire face points forward, like a 1950s hood ornament.

"I'm often told I have a distinctive voice," Dr. Ravi says. "I think it's the influence of Cambridge."

Arthit also went to school in England, but his linguistic suitcase isn't packed with such plummy vowels and half-chewed consonants.

"Sounds like you were there for years."

He gets a quick glance, but the wall of foliage is upon them. Dr. Ravi slows the cart, slides a hand into his pocket, and brings out a slim remote, which he points at the green barrier. A portion of it detaches itself and begins to swing inward.

Rafferty says, "Lot of protection."

"Human nature," Dr. Ravi announces gravely, "is to want."

"I've noticed."

The paved track they're following describes a slow turn through the tangle of scrub, and the view widens suddenly. Rafferty stifles the urge to gasp.

They are entering the Garden of Eden.

The cart passes through a flaming gate, from the top of which a gigantic hand points a single finger outward. The flames are made of gold, beaten thin and curled into phantasmagorical shapes. Large red stones glow at the base of the flames, simulating coals. On the far side of the gate are green, gentle hills, pools complete with swans, ferns, and willows, and, in the center of the garden, an artificial apple tree hung with glistening red and green fruit. A gleaming silver snake curls around the trunk of the tree. It has a red apple in its jaws.

Rafferty says, "Um."

"The first paradise," Dr. Ravi says.

From several hundred possible questions, Rafferty randomly chooses one. "How did he get the apples to glow like that?"

"That's what everyone asks," says Dr. Ravi smugly. "The red ones are covered in tiny rubies, thirteen or fourteen hundred on each. The green ones are made with emeralds."

"It's like a fundamentalist theme park," Rafferty says maliciously. "Faith World."

Dr. Ravi says, "Hardly," in a voice like a pair of tin snips.

A brace of peacocks wander by, the males wasting their time trying to dazzle each other. *Men,* Rafferty thinks. White ponies dawdle and trot here and there. A couple of them have spiral horns protruding from their foreheads.

"I didn't know there were unicorns in the Garden of Eden."

"Obviously there weren't," Dr. Ravi says. He's still offended. "Or they'd exist today, wouldn't they? One assumes that God works in first drafts and doesn't revise, or there wouldn't have been such a flap about evolution. But this is Khun Pan's Eden, and he wanted unicorns."

Rafferty watches the apple tree recede. The bed of deep green moss that surrounds it looks like it was created to be reclined upon. "Is Eve home?"

Pursed lips and a pause. "On occasion."

"I'd like to see that."

"I rather doubt that you will."

The narrow road they are navigating is so smooth and the cart so silent that Rafferty has the illusion of being towed over ice. "Why Mesopotamia? Why Eden? Why not something Thai?"

The pursed lips again. "If you had done any research this morning, you would know that Khun Pan enjoys annoying certain people. Spending this kind of money to re-create the Judeo-Christian paradise in a Buddhist society . . . well, it . . . it—"

"It pisses people off."

"And occasionally he opens the grounds for a charity event. Tonight, for example. It'll draw movie stars, television crews, newspapers, and pour more salt into the wounds of the wellborn. All of this did not come cheap," Dr. Ravi says. He allows the corners of his mouth to lift, revealing unexpected dimples. "If it doesn't upset people repeatedly, it's not cost-effective."

For the second time, Rafferty catches a whiff of something that is quite distinctly not the perfume of paradise. "What am I smelling?"

The smile, such as it is, reappears. "That's the *other* creation myth. You'll see it in a moment." The golf cart labors up a hill. "I must warn you, your reception will probably not be a warm one."

"I'm not expecting a corsage."

"He seems to regret the entire evening. And especially you."

"Oh, fuck him," Rafferty says, and Dr. Ravi's startled sideways glance makes the cart swerve. "I'll give him whatever he gives me. And something really stinks. It smells like—"

The furrows in Dr. Ravi's brow are so pronounced that he looks like a basset hound. "I'm quite serious. He's not at his best this morning. I would avoid offending him."

"Or what?" Rafferty says. "That's the question of the day. Or what?"

Dr. Ravi says, "Oh, dear."

"What do you care? I suppose you have to put up with him, but that's not my problem. And you know what? You don't actually have to put up with him. There are lots of jobs for a broad-voweled Oxford graduate like you."

"Cambridge."

"Just checking."

"You really are a disastrous choice. I don't know what he was thinking." The cart crests the hill, and Dr. Ravi says, "There it is. Your other creation myth."

At the foot of the gradual downslope before them gleams a white marble mansion, a Parthenon of twenty or twenty-five rooms, marble columns and all. In front of it is a small, rickety, blow-the-house-down northeastern farm village: four raggedy stilt houses and a rice paddy half the size of an Olympic swimming pool. A bamboo fence surrounds a churned-up sea of filth in which five mammoth pigs wallow. From the sheer volume of the stink, rich enough to thicken the air to an unwholesome syrup, it's clear that the pen has not been mucked out in some time. During Rafferty's weeks in Rose's village, he has become familiar with pigsties.

"It's not usually this bad," Dr. Ravi says, averting his face from the smell without taking his eyes off the road. The paved track, Rafferty sees, will take them past the pigsty before delivering them to the classical pretension of the front porch. "As I said, he's got an event tonight, an antimalaria fund-raiser, and lots of the big folks will come. He likes to let it all ripen when they're here."

"My wife says he rubs their noses in it, but I didn't know she meant literally."

"Your wife is Thai?"

"As Thai as tom yum kung." Tom yum kung is the national soup, eaten everywhere.

"Was she poor?"

Rafferty glances over at Dr. Ravi, but he seems to be giving all his attention to the task of steering the cart. "Very."

"Then she'll appreciate this," he says as the stench envelops them. "The pigs are named after our last five prime ministers."

AFTER THE SCRAMBLED symbolism of the grounds, the house is just another ordinary Greek Revival mansion roughly the size of the Taj Mahal. Rafferty follows Dr. Ravi across gleaming marble floors until they reach the big, closed double doors at the back of the house.

Dr. Ravi's knock, so feathery it wouldn't wrinkle linen, is answered by something that sounds like a sea lion nailed to a rock. With a final glance that combines haughtiness and supplication, Dr. Ravi opens the door and gestures Rafferty through. Rafferty has the feeling that Dr. Ravi wants to hide behind him.

The room they enter is square, with walls approximately twenty-five feet long. The focal point is a teak desk inlaid with mother-of-pearl. The far wall is glass, opening onto a sun-soaked vista of plants and flowers. Seated behind the desk, his back hunched defensively against the glare, is Pan. Without looking up, he says, "You."

"Always a good guess." Rafferty bends down to look at Pan's face. The man cradles his head in both hands as though afraid it will roll off his neck and crack open on the desk. His eyes are deep-sunk and red-rimmed, and a silvery little aura of gray bristle glints on his chin. He has not shaved this morning. The silver dusting his chin looks odd beneath the bootblack sheen of his hair.

"You didn't waste any time, did you?" Pan snaps in Thai. Dr. Ravi starts to translate, but Rafferty raises a hand.

"If you mean the newspapers," he replies, also in Thai, "I didn't have anything to do with it."

"Of course you did."

Rafferty says, "Good-bye, and good luck with your hangover."

"Wait," Dr. Ravi says, putting a placating hand on Rafferty's arm.

"Like I said in the cart, fuck him. I took all the shit last night I'm willing to take."

"I'm sure he doesn't mean to offend you," Dr. Ravi says with an imploring glance at Pan.

"Who else?" Pan squeaks. "Who else had anything to gain?"

Rafferty has a hand on the doorknob. "Any of them. Anybody who wanted a journalist in his pocket."

After an evaluative moment, Pan mops his face, lowers his head even farther, and says, "Owwwwww. I hurt."

"Tell somebody who cares."

"Okay, okay," Pan says. He closes his eyes in a long wince. "How much not to write it?"

Rafferty hasn't expected this, although he realizes he should have. He thinks for a moment and says, "I'm not sure I can have this conversation."

"Five hundred thousand baht. Cash, right now." Pan slowly opens a drawer, like someone pushing his way through a thick liquid, and pulls out a wad of thousand-baht notes.

"Even disregarding everything else," Rafferty says, "and there's a lot to disregard, that's peanuts."

Pan's face is suddenly a deep, choleric red, and he slams the drawer closed with a sound like a pistol shot. He starts to sputter something, then removes one hand from his temple and actually covers his mouth with his fingers and lets his eyes droop shut. He sits there for a moment, breathing heavily, then lowers his hand, opens his eyes, and says, "All right. You're angry. Pim told me it was my fault."

"Pim?"

"One of my bodyguards. He said I was terrible."

"You were."

"I'm not—I'm not a good drinker," Pan says.

"You were—" Rafferty turns to Dr. Ravi and says, in English, "I don't know the Thai. Tell him he was appalling."

"I think . . ." Dr. Ravi swallows. "I think he's already gotten that message."

"A bodyguard can level with him and you can't? What kind of amanuensis are you?"

"I'm not an amanuensis. I'm his media director."

"Goddamn it," Pan says in heavily accented English. "Speak Thai. Or translate."

"Sorry, sorry." Dr. Ravi switches to Thai. "The *farang* said he also sometimes behaves unwisely when he drinks."

"I did?" Rafferty asks.

"He is certain he contributed to the problem." There is a sheen of perspiration at Dr. Ravi's hairline.

Pan's eyes look like they were pounded into his head solely to hold up the bags of fluid hanging beneath them. They creak around to Rafferty's. Pan waits, the pink mouth half open, like someone watching to see whether the water will ever boil.

"I did," Rafferty says. "We all did."

A sigh escapes Dr. Ravi.

"*All* of us," Pan says. He burps and pats the center of his chest. "We all behaved badly."

"Fine."

Pan nods. "One million baht."

Rafferty says to Dr. Ravi, "Am I allowed to sit down or what?"

"Please, please," Dr. Ravi says. "Sit."

"Thanks." Rafferty pulls a chair to the edge of the desk. "I need to think for a second."

"Fine." Pan puts his forehead back into his hands. "If I start to snore, wake me up."

"How are you going to get in shape for your party tonight?"

Pan says to the desk, "Steam, sauna, herbal tea, massage, boom-boom with triplets from Laos, a few drinks."

"Triplets?"

Pan grunts. "I really only like one of them, but I'm never sure which one it is."

"I want to ask you a question."

"So?"

"Why do you care about sex workers with HIV?"

Pan separates his fingers and peers at Rafferty between them. "Who says I do?"

"The hundred and fifty of them you're taking care of."

Pan brings the scarred hands back together. All Rafferty can see is the Elvis-black hair and the silver grizzle on the chin. "Who else will?" Pan says.

"I didn't think you liked prostitutes."

"You were wrong. It's *farang* I don't like. Those women and me, we're mushrooms, sprung from the same shit. They're my sisters for life. 'Whore' is just a word for something they have to do for a while."

"Do you mean that?"

"Look at me," Pan says. He opens his desk drawer, pulls out a tube of lip balm, and applies it. "Look how handsome I am. Am I any better than they are?"

Rafferty thinks, *No,* and he's heard enough. "We need to talk." He moves his head a quarter of an inch in Dr. Ravi's direction. "Alone."

Pan's glistening mouth contracts as though he's about to whistle. Dr. Ravi sputters.

Pan says, in English, "Go."

"Khun Pan," Dr. Ravi says, "I don't advise—"

"If I have to get up and push you out the door," Pan says, "I'll probably break your back."

"Very well." Rafferty can hear Dr. Ravi's lips tighten around the words. Then the door closes.

Rafferty says, "I'm going to put my life in your hands."

Pan is watching the door as though he's trying to see through it. He seems to be listening, but not to Rafferty. After ten or fifteen seconds, he nods and says, "Why would you do that?"

"Because my wife thinks you're a great man."

"Women are bad judges of character."

"Oh, turn it off. You've already outraged me. Give it a rest."

Pan puts his fingertips to his temples and rubs circles, about the size of a quarter. "This is about why you don't want the million baht."

"Actually, the million baht confuses me."

"Why? A million is a thousand thousands, right? What's confusing?"

"I had a threatening call this morning, telling me not to write the book."

The circles stop. "You did? Who— Oh, oh, I see. No, not me. I don't do things that way."

"You used to. Back in the old days."

"Think about it," Pan says. "I have someone threaten you this morning—what? Four, five hours ago?"

"Something like that."

"And then I ask you to come here so I can offer you money. Without even waiting to see if you've been scared off. Does that make sense?"

"Then you have no idea who—"

"None. But I'll think about it. So," Pan says, leaning back in a relaxed position for the first time, "are you going to write the book or not? The million's still on the table."

"It'll have to stay there. I had two conversations this morning, not one. In the second chat, my life and the lives of my wife and daughter were threatened if I don't write the book."

He jerks forward as though Rafferty had yanked a rope tied around his chest. "If you *don't*—"

"And the book they want me to write is probably not the monument of your dreams."

Pan settles back in the chair. The wet-looking eyes go from side to side for a second, as though Rafferty were moving, and then something ignites in them. He leans forward again, almost eagerly, and says, "Who?"

"I don't know. But they're serious." He tells Pan about the snatch in front of Miaow's school and what followed.

"Do you have the list?"

"Sure." He hands it across the desk.

Pan scans it, and the color mounts in his face. "No," he says. "Not the book I'd want." His eyes come up from the page. "Do you know any of these people?"

"I recognize some of the names. Anyone would."

"Spiders, the bunch of them." Pan passes the side of a scarred hand across the page as though he could erase the names. "Bloated, greedy, venomous. They suck people dry and spit out the husks. Strip the land, poison the rivers, turn men into drunks and women into whores. Buy rice at low prices and sell it at high ones. Let people starve and count the money." He fills his cheeks with air and releases it. Rafferty can smell the sourness of the previous evening's cognac all the way across the desk.

Rafferty says, "You're saying they're pigs."

"Not on their best days," Pan says. "Give me a good pig any time."

"When these people threaten my family, how seriously should I take it?"

"How seriously do you take breathing?" Pan squirms himself a bit lower in his chair. Then one foot, clad only in a sock, hits the top of the desk. He laces his fingers across his belly and regards his foot critically. "What you said last night," he says, "about there being a great crime somewhere. That didn't sound like you were planning to write a fan letter."

"I was pissed off. I was surprised you took the bet."

Pan drops his eyes to the center of Rafferty's chest, and then, suddenly, he grins. "I'm really not a good drinker."

"No, you're not."

"So, just to be clear, you want to get out of writing the book."

"With a qualifier," Rafferty says. "I have to get out of it alive."

Pan waves a hand in the air, as though to clear smoke. "Be specific. Let's say I'm disposed to help you. How would I do that?"

"To start, I want a list of everybody who will tell me the story you'd want the book to tell. That way, I can let them know you're cooperating."

Pan nods. "And you'll look busy, if someone is watching."

"Someone will be watching."

"Yes, they will." He looks over Rafferty's shoulder and then raises his eyes to the ceiling. Then he closes them. After a moment he says, "I'm having an event here tonight. Malaria relief."

"I heard. How many of the people on that list will be here?"

"A lot of them."

Rafferty says, "Got an extra ticket?"

Pan opens his eyes, still looking at the ceiling, and says, "Your wife, the one who thinks I'm a great man. Is she from Isaan?"

"Yes."

"Is she pretty?"

"I think it's absolutely safe," Rafferty replies, "to say she's pretty."

"Good." Pan leans back and puts his other foot on the desk. His eyes close again. "You get two tickets."

15

No Witnesses

He leans against the carved Mesopotamian wall, his shoulders midway between a king's sandaled feet. After the mausoleum chill of the house, the heat actually feels good. He settles his shoulders against the warm brick, reaches into the rear pocket of his jeans, and pulls out the yellow sheets containing the list he copied on the thirty-sixth floor.

The list Dr. Ravi gave him at Pan's command is in his shirt pocket. He opens it, too, and spends three or four minutes going back and forth between them.

Not a single name appears on both lists.

He is pushing that around in his mind when the low growl of an engine brings his head up.

Idling at the curb six or seven feet from him is a carbon-black, dark-windowed SUV, expensively pimped out in customized chrome. The word *LEXUS* is inscribed on the door in silvery italics eighteen inches high. Deep blue lights blink beneath the chassis and bounce off the asphalt, in time to a throbbing bass line that makes the entire vehicle pulsate. The windows are heavily tinted. The behemoth just sits there, a sort of right-hand drive Death Star energized by techno music. It doesn't seem to be going anywhere.

A movement at the edge of his vision draws his gaze. In the turret beside the gate, the guard has picked up the phone. His eyes, like Rafferty's, are on the SUV.

There is no one on the sidewalk. Except for the guard behind his bulletproof glass and whoever is in the SUV, there are, Rafferty realizes, no witnesses.

Not a comfortable way to look at it.

He could move, but there's nowhere to go, just the wall with its frozen kings and hanging gardens, which he can neither climb nor melt into. A look at the guard's anxious face makes it clear he's not going to open any doors. Even if Rafferty turns and runs the long block to the corner, the SUV can keep up with him easily, and there's no place to run to.

The SUV's horn is tapped twice, like it's clearing its throat for attention. A back window goes down five or six inches, and something long and shiny comes through the opening and points at Rafferty. It is the barrel of a rifle.

Rafferty can feel the precise spot in the center of his chest on which the rifle is trained, as though a stream of cold air were pouring through the muzzle of the gun. He can feel his knees loosen. He rests more of his weight against the wall just to stay upright. He feels his pulse bump against the band of his wristwatch.

After what feels like an eternity, someone in the vehicle laughs, and it pulls slowly away from the curb.

The license plate is not Thai. It has only five digits. Rafferty doesn't even need to write them down.

"THIS IS ELORA." The voice is brisk and cool. Rafferty has an image of a slender vamp from the 1940s, wearing seamed stockings and a dress with shoulder pads, her hair loosely rolled up around her head. A sort of executive big-band singer.

"Ms. Weecherat. This is Poke Rafferty." This is his third cab in twenty minutes, and no one seems to be following it. His body still feels loose and nerveless, emptied by the draining of all that adrenaline.

"You were going to call me back."

"And here I am."

"This morning. While you were news." The words are in precise English, with a faint accent that could be French.

"I'm still news."

"That's what everybody thinks." Definitely French. "But it's not true unless you have something new."

"Do I ever."

A moment's evaluative pause. "If you want to talk to me, I'll need to meet you," she says.

"That could be difficult."

"Call me again when it's not."

"Wait. You want what I have."

"Because."

"Because it's sensational."

"Then I *definitely* need to meet you."

Rafferty says, "Someplace we won't be seen."

"Where are you?"

"New Petchburi Road." It's not true, but it's not far off.

"How's traffic?"

"I'm in Bangkok," Rafferty says. "How would it be?"

"Where are you headed?"

"Toward Silom. Okay, I know where. Write this down." He gives her an address on Silom and then a suite number. "That's my dentist. I know her well enough for this."

"A dentist? This had better be worth it."

"Can you make the deadline for tomorrow's paper?"

"Yes."

"Then it'll be worth it."

HE HAS BEEN in the fourth cab only a minute when his phone rings.

"What the hell are you doing?" It is the man who sat next to him in the Lincoln.

"I've been thinking about buying a cab. Thought I'd try a few out."

"Where are you?"

"Rama IV Road," Rafferty lies. "You mean your guys lost me?"

"Yes," the man says. "But we know exactly where everyone else is."

"When this is over," Rafferty says, "I'm going to pull your teeth one by one and shove them up your nose."

"No point getting mad at me. Just don't disappear again, or there will be consequences."

"What was that cute thing with the SUV?"

"I don't know what you're talking about."

"Do you want this book or not?"

"*He* wants it."

Rafferty says, "And he'll be unhappy if things go wrong."

"Things won't go wrong."

"They will if you ever pull anything like that again," Rafferty says, and disconnects. Then he sags back against the seat and works on his breathing.

16

Fair

The day is endless.

The river of people continues to flow past her, sometimes in full flood, sometimes at a trickle. Occasionally the people arrive in knots and tangles, as though they were snarled in the branches of a floating tree. People are most likely to give when the river is trickling. They can see her from farther away then; they have time to make up their minds, to fish out the money so they can drop it into the bowl without slowing. No one wants to slow. Most look no further than the upraised bowl, as though it were floating unaided above the sidewalk. A few glance at her very quickly and then look away, embarrassed.

The tree-trunk man in the blue shirt is always somewhere nearby. Every time someone drops paper money into her bowl, he is there, snatching it.

Da has begun to keep a count in her head, just as something to do. When she was small, she discovered she was good with numbers. She did the math, mostly subtraction, that spelled out her family's finances. She is surprised by the amount of money that has fallen into the bowl. Counting Helen's 1,500 baht, it comes to 3,200, plus the coins that she hasn't counted yet. So say 3,500 baht.

The man in the office said they took 40 percent. That means she keeps 60 percent. To do the math, she divides by ten—let's say that's 350 baht—and then multiplies by six.

More than 2,000 baht.

There were twenty or twenty-five beggars in that building. If all of them take in as much as she, the man in the office is making something like 28,000 baht a day. There are probably other beggars in other buildings. He is probably making . . . she works out the answers, but she has to stop and double-check the zeros in her head. He is probably making more than a million baht a month.

Da's father earned less than 13,000 baht a year.

Still, she thinks, they have people to pay. Money to the police not to chase the beggars away. There are businesses behind her, their front doors opening onto the sidewalk. The business owners probably get paid something, too.

Someone drops a coin into her bowl, and she looks up to see a little boy of nine or ten, scurrying away as though he's done something he's ashamed of. He is the first child she has seen since morning. That means school is out. It's after two-thirty, perhaps three. At four o'clock it will be over.

They have to pay the drivers, she thinks, the man in the blue shirt. Maybe rent for the half-finished building they sleep in. The vans, the gasoline. Expenses.

Still, it's a lot of money. It's the most money she's even thought about in her life. She sees again the shoes the man in the office had worn, shoes that looked as if their soles had never left a carpet.

Maybe he has a hundred beggars. Maybe two hundred.

Peep makes the rising sound that means he wants her to look at him. She drops her eyes to her lap, and sure enough he is gazing at her, the gaze that makes her feel he can see right through her. She feels the smile spread over her face, and then a thought chases it away.

Did they have to pay for *him*?

How much do you pay for a baby? Do they all cost the same? Are they priced by the pound, like meat? Do beautiful ones cost more than ugly ones? Is there an extra charge for light skin, like Peep's, or a discount for dark babies? Do children of different ages cost different amounts?

Different ages.

The oldest undamaged child she has seen is the skeletal boy of four or five. Where are the older children?

"How are you doing?"

It's a woman's voice, and there he is, the skeletal boy, and behind him is the woman from the van. The child looks at nothing, clutching the woman's sleeve in a hand that's all knuckles.

"Can we go now?" Da asks.

"Another hour. Kep has gone to eat something. He does this every day. We've got half an hour before he gets back." The woman shakes her sleeve free, but the child immediately reclaims it, without even glancing at it. His dusky skin is stretched tightly over his bones and his eyes have the unblinking luster Da associates with the simple-minded.

"Kep?"

"The one in the blue shirt." The woman puts her folded blanket on the pavement and sits on it. The boy immediately sits beside her. He puts an open hand, dark and elongated as a monkey's paw, on her leg, palm up. "How much money has Kep taken from you today?"

"More than three thousand baht."

The other woman raises her eyebrows. "Good day."

"One woman gave me fifteen hundred."

"The *farang* with the metal hair?"

"Yes."

"Lucky you. She comes every day. She works somewhere down there. One of the buildings."

"Does Kep tell the truth about how much money he takes?"

"No. He'll put a thousand in his pocket and pass the rest on to Wichat."

"Wichat? The man in the office?"

"That's Wichat."

"He doesn't make enough money without stealing from me?"

"For these people there's never enough money. They'd eat the world if they could get their jaws wide enough."

"It isn't fair."

The other woman laughs. The sound draws the skeletal child's empty gaze, but then his eyes drift downward again. "Fair," the woman says. She laughs again.

"Well, it's not."

"No," the other woman says. She fans herself halfheartedly. "You've had a good day," she says, "but it was luck. I've been watching you."

Da is looking at the boy's eyes. He seems to be gazing at a point four or five feet in front of him, about as high as the center of his chest. Da says, "Am I doing something wrong?"

"You don't move around enough. You need to get their attention. Push the bowl in their direction, get up on your knees so they can't pretend they don't see you."

"But if I get up, it wakes Peep."

"Who?" the woman asks.

"Peep," Da says. "The baby. If I get up, it—"

"You *named* it," the other woman says. She looks at Peep and then averts her eyes and shakes her head as though in distaste. "You shouldn't do that."

"Why? He needs a name."

"You shouldn't," the woman says. "But you already did, didn't you? So why talk about it? Anyway, move around more. If you don't make good money, they treat you badly. Kep especially." With a grunt she gets to one knee. "Not much longer," she says. The boy rises to his feet and extends a hand to her, but she pushes it away, not ungently, and gets up unaided.

"Wait a minute," Da says. "Why shouldn't I name him?"

The other woman says, "You'll find out soon enough." The boy grabs the back of her blouse and knots it in his hand, and she rests her hand on the nape of his neck as the two of them wade into traffic, zig-zagging through it as though the cars and motos and *tuk-tuks* are an elaborate mirage. Only when they are safely across does Da take her eyes off them, and when she does, she realizes that someone is standing beside her.

She looks up. It is the boy with the tangled hair.

He leans down, and she is startled by how clean he is. His clothes are filthy, but his skin shines.

"When you want to run away," he says, "turn your bowl upside down and put it in front of you."

"Run away? Why would I want to run away?"

"Just turn the bowl upside down," the boy says, backing away from her, his eyes scanning the sidewalk. "Don't look for me. Just turn your bowl upside down."

17

Charm Doesn't Make the Cut

Flora Weecherat is fearsomely stylish, nothing like the retro siren of Rafferty's imagination. The instant he sees her in the sparse, creatively wrapped flesh, the faint French accent becomes a heady, even cloying, whiff of Paris, the Paris of haute couture and hold the sauce, the Paris that Rafferty glimpses on the pages of Rose's fashion magazines, where "beautiful" means undernourished and overdressed. Beneath the drape of expensive clothes, Weecherat is as thin as a piece of paper and probably, he thinks, as easy to cut yourself on.

By the time he comes through the door, her tape recorder is already on, its little red eye glowing on the table. She is seated in regal state on one of the two pumpkin-colored chairs in the corner of the dentist's waiting room, and she starts talking before the door has closed behind him.

"You don't look like your photo." She redrapes her skirt and crosses her legs in a single choreographed motion. Her cheekbones are so prominent that her face is almost diamond-shaped, and her eyes have sunk deeply into her face. The eyes may be deep-set, but they are very bright eyes, and they don't look like they miss much.

"Ah, but I've brought my personality," Rafferty says.

"Charm doesn't make the cut."

"Is that English?"

"The *cut*," she says, the word itself sharp. "The twenty-five percent of my story that my editor will remove just to remind himself that he can." She turns the tape recorder a fraction of an inch toward him. "Let's get to it."

"First," Rafferty says, and he reaches over and turns the tape recorder off.

Weecherat gathers her draperies around her. "No tape, no talk."

"This is background," Rafferty says. "If the discussion goes well, I'll let you turn that thing on again and I'll give you the stuff for attribution."

She settles back and realigns her shawl, which is the color of a buttercup, until it is at a precise vertical.

"You're interested in Pan," he says.

She shrugs, and her lower lip pops out. It is a very French shrug, and suddenly Rafferty has a plausible biography: rich family, French education, interested in fashion, but not enough talent to make a living at it and too hardheaded to specialize in writing about it. Therefore, the business beat. "In the way one is interested in faulty plumbing or a grotesque tattoo," she says. "Good plumbing is a blessing. A really marvelous tattoo is an enhancement. Pan has the opportunity to be both and has chosen to be neither. He eats money and vomits it in public. Pan is a swine."

Rafferty reaches into his shirt pocket and pulls out the two lists, the one Dr. Ravi gave him and the one he copied onto the legal pad. He puts the second yellow sheet in front of her and points at a line halfway down the page.

She looks at the name that is written there, which is her own. "Yes?"

"You're one of about seventy people whose names I was given this morning. Would you say that most of these people share your opinion of Pan?"

She holds out a hand, its nails painted black. He passes her the remaining yellow pages. Her eyes go down them quickly, and then she flips through the sheets as though looking for a contradiction. The lower lip makes a reappearance. "These people would not be invited to his wedding, if that's what you mean. Or, if they were, you'd be a fool to eat the cake."

"Do you think a good book can be written from these sources?"

"Of course not. Whatever he is, Pan has done *some* good. He has a kind of prehensile charm that some people find attractive. A biography, if it's going to be worth anything, needs to get as much of the story as possible. Otherwise it'll be Mao's Little Red Book. Of interest to no one but the people who already believe it. Who gave this to you?"

"I'll tell you in a minute. Maybe."

She shakes her head impatiently. "I don't see how you could even be considering this approach, since he's authorized you to write the book. I'd think he'd want something that would position him for the Nobel Prize."

"Like the perspective you'd get from these folks?" He hands her the list Dr. Ravi gave him.

She looks at it, and then she does what Rafferty had done; she puts them side by side, her eyes going from one to the other. When she turns her gaze to him, there is a glint of amusement in her eyes. "Exactly."

"Okay," Rafferty says. "You can turn on the tape recorder." He waits until the red light glows again and she nods at him to proceed, and then he says, "This morning my life and the lives of my family were threatened. I was snatched off the street, hooded, shoved into a car, and taken someplace where I was given the names on the yellow sheets and told that we'll all be killed if I don't write this book—and I mean *this* book, the one I would get from these sources. I can't tell you who threatened me, because I don't know, but I can give you some information, off the record for now, that might help the police to identify them if my family and I are killed. Does that sound like news to you?"

"I can't print the information that would lead the police to them?"

"No. You can say you have it but that it might violate the libel laws."

"In Thailand it probably would." She glances down at the tape recorder, making sure it's running, then flicks the yellow list with an extremely long index finger tipped in black polish. "Before we go any further, you realize there's no way I can verify this story."

"No," he says, "but you can report truthfully that the *farang* who was authorized to write Pan's biography says that his family's lives have been threatened by unknown persons unless he writes a violently anti-

Pan book. And just so you know that it isn't a publicity stunt, you can also report that he's going public with this in the hope that the reduced risk will allow him to quit the project."

She studies him for a moment. "You're not going to write it?"

"I'm going to try like hell not to."

"And you think this story will reduce the threat?"

"I hope so. At least we won't be killed in a vacuum. Whoever's behind this will know that the American embassy will demand an investigation, a real one, not just going through the motions. It might scare these people off. They'll know that the investigation will focus on the information you didn't print."

"Why don't you go to your embassy directly?"

"What could they do? Get me out of Thailand? My wife and daughter are Thai. They don't have travel documents."

The buttercup scarf seems to require her attention again. She is still fiddling with it when she asks, "How old is your daughter?"

"Nine."

"My daughter is seven," Elora Weecherat says. "It's a magical age." She aligns the strands that make up the shawl's fringe until they are precisely parallel. "Let's start from the beginning," she says. "You're a travel writer. How in the world did you get into this?"

18

The Furniture Takes a Vote

Arthit says, "The thirty-sixth floor." His face is rigid, the mask of muscle he wears when he's just been with Noi. His eyes are still poached from the previous night's alcohol.

"In both English and Thai." Rafferty is trying to conceal his dismay at the way his friend looks. Arthit's composure seems thin as a coat of paint. The hands clasped on the table betray a faint tremor. A cup of coffee cools untouched in front of him, the cumulus burst of cream in the center not even stirred smooth.

"Even in the New Bangkok we keep hearing about, there aren't that many buildings with talking elevators," Arthit says. "But as much as I hate to say this, it won't mean anything even if you figure out who it is. You're not going to get anywhere near him. If I'm right about what's happening, this is a level where I can't help you. I don't even know who *could* help you."

"Then what do you suggest, Arthit? Should I just roll over and die?"

"It would save you a lot of effort." Arthit rubs his face with both hands, as though he were trying to erase his expression.

"Well, in the absence of that kind of wisdom, here's what I've done." Poke tells Arthit about the meeting with Elora Weecherat.

"Not bad," Arthit says, in a tone that suggests it's not very good either. "Still, you should get Rose and Miaow off the map somehow, just in case the reaction to the newspaper story isn't what you want it to be."

"Moving them will be hard. I think the other side is four deep on them all the time. The followers got a little chesty today when I shook them."

"And why did you shake them?"

"That thing with the gun and the SUV. I got pissed off."

Arthit takes a fistful of his own hair and tugs at it in sheer frustration. "You can't afford to do that," he says. "I don't think you understand what's going on here."

"Has that *just* occurred to you?"

"Let me give you an image," Arthit says. He picks up the coffee and drinks half of it at a gulp. "If it would clarify your situation to think about it visually, then imagine this: You're at the bottom of the Chao Phraya, wandering around on the riverbed without a map, and breathing water. You just haven't realized it yet." He erases the image with his palms. "No, actually, it's more like this: You're in the crevice of a deep canyon with very steep walls, and there are some enormous boulders directly above you. Let's say the size of an apartment house. You've built a cute little straw roof to keep you dry, something a songbird could dent. These boulders can decide, any time they want, to roll down on top of you. For any reason. You go to the wrong place. You talk to the wrong person. You ask the wrong question. You go out too much. You stay home too much. You eat meat on Friday. They don't like your socks. So they roll down on you and squash you to paste."

"Okay," Rafferty says. "What's the downside?"

"The downside is that even if you do everything they want, they still might kill you."

Rafferty nods. "That qualifies."

"You're not taking this seriously."

Suddenly Rafferty is furious. "What do you want me to do, Arthit? Run in circles, scream in soprano, wring my hands? Give me an option. You've pretty much said there's nowhere I can go for help and that it barely matters what I do. For all the difference it makes, I might as well yell at the weather. If I write it, we're dead. If I don't write it, we're dead. If I write it wrong, we're dead. According to you, if I somehow defuse the people who don't want it written and then write it exactly the way the other side wants, we're dead anyway. Would you like to tell me how taking it seriously is going to help?"

Arthit drains the cup and curls his lip at the dregs in the bottom. It makes a jittery little clatter against the saucer when he puts it down. "You have a point."

"One thing that *might* help would be for you to do what I thought you were going to do just a minute ago, which is to tell me what the hell is going on. Why is this book such an issue?"

Arthit picks the cup up again and turns it upside down on the saucer. "I thought you understood this country."

"That's what Rose said, too. And I'll tell you what I told her. I don't."

"Actually," Arthit says, "you know all of it. You just haven't put it together." He pushes his chair back slightly and eases a leg out from under the table. "Let's start with the coup."

Rafferty says, "You're kidding."

"No. It's a good starting point. And it'll suggest the kind of weight you're up against."

"Why? What does this little whirlwind of stupidity have to do with who governs the country?"

"Everything," Arthit says. "Okay. Here's the dummy's guide to the coup. Point One: Thaksin Shinawatra, a rich guy but not really a member of the traditional power elite, gets himself elected prime minister by purchasing the votes of a group of people who have never really turned out for an election before. The poor of the northeast."

"Rose's people," Rafferty says. "The ones she says are supposed to go where they're told and stay where they're put."

"The least powerful people in Thailand. And so what if Thaksin paid for some of their votes? What *mattered* was that we had the first prime minister in the history of the country who was voted in by the poor."

"Yeah, yeah."

"Well, that development didn't sit well with the people who have been in charge forever. They wanted to get rid of Shinawatra, and luck-ily for them he got caught apparently cheating the country, ducking millions in income tax, and they saw their chance. *Bang,* a military coup; the army overthrew him and set up a new government."

"And it was the Marx Brothers."

"Yes. But it represented the old guard, so the folks who are traditionally in charge were comfortable with it." Arthit clanks the inverted cup against the saucer a couple of times to get the attention of the ethereal, almost transparent youth behind the counter, who is devoting his entire being to getting his bangs to fall across his forehead at a forty-five-degree angle. The boy locates the noise, registers the police uniform, and gets up. "So you've got a government of generals, and they can barely figure out which shoe to put on first."

The boy with the bangs says, "Yes, sir?"

"Some sort of pastry with chocolate in it. And fill this." The boy takes the cup and fades. "And the generals hold an election, and guess what—the peasants vote Thaksin's friends back in."

Rafferty says, "What a surprise."

"It was to the power elite. The second prime minister in a row, voted in by poor people. The old guard is flabbergasted. They feel like they went to a party and while they were out, the furniture took a vote to change the locks. Suddenly they see themselves standing on the doorstep, trying to get their keys to work."

A chocolate eclair appears in front of Arthit, followed by a napkin, a fork and a knife, a full cup, and a discreet retreat.

"And okay, the new prime minister, the one the poor elected, breaks some obscure rule and appears on a cooking show because he likes to cook, and the powers behind the scenes are shocked, do you hear, *shocked* that he'd accept a couple thousand dollars U.S. to make an omelet on TV. So they kick him out. Only in Thailand could a prime minister be overthrown for the way he handles a spatula. But of course that's not what it's about, is it?"

"No," Rafferty says. "It's about poor people having political power."

"That's it exactly. Something fundamental has changed. *Poor people have learned that their votes count.* This is new in Thai politics, and it terrifies some very powerful people, all of them pale-skinned, most of them Thai-Chinese. Some of the old-power families have been in charge for generations, since Bangkok was built more than two hundred years ago. And they've gotten amazingly rich. Billions of dollars, Poke. Year after year, billions of dollars. They dip their scoops everywhere: the national budget, the banks, the corporations, the army, the police—you name it. All of it based on the assumption that they'll hold power forever, which always looked like a good bet. But now the foundation is suddenly shaky. The ground they built on could be turning to water."

"And this has what to do with me?"

Arthit empties the cream container into his coffee. "To bring you up-to-date, since you don't read the papers. The elected party put up yet *another* prime minister, and the elite went on a rampage. Formed a group with *Democracy* in the name, which is kind of amusing since they want a mostly appointed government. So they demonstrated, took over the airports, and finally got some people in the Assembly to change sides so they could put one of their own in."

"I actually do remember that."

"So nothing is resolved. Nobody thinks the current situation is stable. Here's the point, Poke. Shinawatra mobilized the poor, but he was never one of them. He was never Isaan. He's Thai-Chinese. But Pan *was* poor. Pan *is* Isaan. Look at the way he's lived, Poke. He never stops reminding people where he came from. He gives constantly. He's *dark-skinned*. The poor liked the former prime minister, but—what did Rose say about Pan?"

"She worships him."

"Then let me ask you a question. Given everything that's happened in the past few years, if Pan suddenly decided he wanted political power, how much do you think he could get?"

"If he lived through the election," Rafferty says, "as much as he wants."

"And how much power would be lined up against him?"

Rafferty turns to look out through the window at the darkening street. "Pretty much all of it."

ON THE SIDEWALK outside the coffeehouse, Rafferty forces himself to bring it up. "Listen, I know you don't want to discuss this—"

"It's not that I don't want to," Arthit says. His voice is remote, tone-less. "But it won't do any good. There's nothing I can do."

"What does that mean? You're her husband. You can talk to her. Get it on the table."

"It doesn't belong on the table. She'll lie to me. She'll tell me she doesn't like the pills, that they nauseate her or something. What am I going to do? Contradict her? I'd sit there nodding, hating myself for making her tell me a lie." He passes the back of his hand over his forehead, erasing a sheen of sweat. "Because when you get right down to it, it's actually none of my business, is it? What could be more personal than the decision to stop living? Is there any action that belongs more completely to the person who commits it? It's Noi's life. She shared it with me, but I'm not the one to tell her she has to continue to live it when it's just one wave of pain after another."

"I'm so sorry," Rafferty says. "It feels like I should be able to do something."

"And I'm grateful for the thought," Arthit says. "But you've already got more than you can handle."

19

Canaries

Rose starts to laugh when she smells the pigpen.

Her reaction startles Rafferty, and he's further surprised to see a grin put dimples in Dr. Ravi's face. The swan cart has carried them in grim silence across the grounds thus far, even when they drove past a dramatically lit Garden of Eden. Rose is in agony over what she's wearing, a white, flowing, two-piece outfit she bought to meet Rafferty's father in. He thinks she looks beautiful, but she behaves as though she's wrapped in a rice bag.

But the pigpen makes her laugh out loud.

"How long?" she asks, wiping her eyes. "How long since he had it cleaned out?"

"*Weeks,*" says Dr. Ravi. "Imagine their faces," and the pair of them go off again. Dr. Ravi has a falsetto laugh that flutes along half an octave above Rose's alto. Together they sound like a pair of mice on the keyboard of an organ.

"Oh," she says, half gasping for breath, her fingers splayed over her heart. "This is enough, Poke. You can take me home and my evening will be complete."

"No you can't," Dr. Ravi says. "There's something you'll want to see."

"What?"

"A surprise. You'll love it. I promise you, it's going to be worth it."

Rose says, "I doubt it." She looks down at herself and tugs at the sleeve of her blouse with an intensity of loathing that Rafferty can hardly comprehend. They are obviously deep in female territory.

"Besides," Dr. Ravi says with the secure air of someone who knows he's got a first-class closer, "Khun Pan would kill me if I allowed someone as beautiful as you to leave without at least an introduction."

Rafferty says, "What do you mean, 'at least'?"

"He's jealous?" Dr. Ravi asks.

Rose drops her sleeve like a rag that's been dipped into something disgusting and says, "He can't believe his good fortune."

"I can't either," Dr. Ravi says.

"Hey," Rafferty says.

"And here we are." Dr. Ravi pulls the swan to the bottom of the broad marble steps leading up to the front porch. The double doors have been thrown wide, and even at this distance Rafferty can feel the cool air pouring out. A small orchestra is cricketing away inside, and he hears the usual party montage of conversation, laughter, and ice cubes hitting glass. Two women wearing, as even Rafferty can tell, several thousand dollars' worth of clothing apiece float across the doorway on a cloud of privilege.

"Absolutely not," Rose says. "I can't go in there."

"Oh, come on," Rafferty says. "You look beautiful. And, Jesus, look at me."

"He's right," Dr. Ravi says. "You'll be the most beautiful woman in the house."

"What I'll be," Rose says, "is a dark-skinned, big-footed peasant girl wearing a dust rag." She puts a hand on Rafferty's arm. "Poke. I want to go home."

"Well, well," someone says from the top step. Rose turns at the sound of the voice, and her jaw very discreetly drops.

"You *are* surprising," Pan says to Rafferty. "You must have strengths you haven't shown me. Goodness," he says, turning to Rose. "What jeweled box does he keep you in?"

Rose says, "Oh, my." Her nails dig into Rafferty's arm.

"You said she was pretty," Pan says, coming down the steps, "but you didn't tell me she was stunning." Halfway down, he tosses his partially smoked cigar to smolder on the marble. He wears bright yellow silk slacks with burgundy patent-leather shoes, lavender socks, and a shirt of a vibrating grass-snake green, the precise color to set off the pink lips. He looks, in all, like a newly successful pimp who hasn't found the right haberdasher yet. Rafferty would bet everything he owns that the look is intentional, down to the last agonizing detail. "I have a show planned that will curl their hair," Pan says to Rose, "but nothing compared to you. You'll drive them completely crazy." He puts a hand on Rose's shoulder and studies her face as though he were memorizing her bone structure. "You're Isaan, of course. Where?"

Rose's face is flushed with embarrassment. "About a hundred kilometers from where you were born."

"We were neighbors," Pan says. "This *farang* is lucky that I never saw you when you were growing up. I'd have stayed in Isaan, and he'd never have laid eyes on you."

"Of course," Rose says. "You'd be loafing barefoot on some hammock while I nag you to feed the chickens."

Rafferty says, "Go ahead. Talk as though I'm not here."

"Get used to it," Pan says. "No one's even going to notice you."

"Since someone has to have some manners," Rafferty says, "this is my wife, Rose. Rose, this is—"

"I know who he is," Rose says. "It's an honor to meet you."

Pan says, "And you're the . . ." He pauses, screws up his eyes, and says in English, " . . . *whipped cream* on the evening. You're so beautiful it's almost wasteful." He glowers at Dr. Ravi. "Why didn't you think of this?"

"I hadn't seen her."

"No, of course not." Pan looks at Rose again and actually rubs his hands together. "I've made a life out of excess," he says. "Improving the lily—"

Dr. Ravi says, "*Gilding* the lily."

"Actually," Rafferty says, "it's 'painting.' Painting the—"

"Oh, fuck the lily," says Pan. He leans in toward Rose as though to whisper in her ear. "I have an idea for you, something that will ruin the evening for most of my guests. We know they think of Isaan as mud. Let's remind them that mud is where the lotus grows." He turns and says over his shoulder, "Please, please come with me."

Rose and Rafferty follow Pan's broad yellow bottom up the steps as Dr. Ravi climbs back into the swan and heads for the gates. Pan leads them at an angle, chatting with Rose all the way, partly in Lao, which Rafferty doesn't understand. They top the steps to the left of the door and follow Pan around the side of the house. Halfway back they come to a marble wall with an iron gate in it. Beside the gate is a combination pad, which Pan prods with a sausagelike index finger for a second, and then Rafferty finds himself in the garden he'd seen that morning from Pan's office.

"This will take me a minute," Pan says, shoving a glass door aside and motioning them to file into the office. He comes in behind them and closes the door. "But, believe me, it'll be worth it." A few steps take him to a corner, where he opens a closet door, revealing a safe the size of a refrigerator.

"I don't give up easily," Pan says to Rose as he twirls the dial, "but I was beginning to think I'd have to return these. You'll know what I mean at a glance. Not just anybody can wear them. They'd look ridiculous on someone who isn't tall, for one thing. How tall *are* you?"

"Almost two meters," Rose says.

"You should think about modeling, except you'd have to kill eight or nine society girls to get a job." The door swings open without a murmur, although it must weigh three hundred pounds. "And even most tall women would disappear behind these. Just vanish, like the stars when the sun is out." He pulls out a long, gray box covered in velvet and pops it open.

Rose emits something that sounds like a long hiss.

"They're canaries," Pan says, looking closely at her face. Draped over the swirl of burns on his fat little hand is a concentration of golden light: solid yellow drops of brilliance chained together somehow. "Average size is four carats," Pan says, "but the one in the center is six. Canary diamonds this size are very rare, I'm told. I don't know anything about it. I just thought they were pretty."

"Why . . . why are you showing me these?" Rose asks.

"To wear, of course," Pan says. "Oh, don't worry," he says to Rafferty. "I'm not trying to dazzle your wife with presents, although I would if you weren't here. These are a loan for the evening, just to give those snobs out there something to stub their noses on. Let's show them an exquisite Isaan girl, the most beautiful woman in the room, wearing three million dollars' worth of yellow diamonds." He holds up the necklace. "What do you say?"

Rose reaches out a hand and says, "Let's make their teeth hurt."

RAFFERTY'S FIRST IMPRESSION when Pan plunges into the thick of the gathering, dragging him and Rose in his wake, is that everyone is surface, brought to a high polish. Everyone shines, everyone glistens, everyone seems to reflect everyone else. Gold, jewels, hair, the shimmer of fabrics, the mysterious gleam of money. He practically squints in self-defense.

The men are a mixed lot, although all have the sheen of power he noticed in the poker game. Despite the occasional immaculate uniform, glittering with medals, most of the men wear suits, sober garments with the effortless drape achieved through highly paid effort. The men are mostly in their fifties and early sixties and look like they would put on a suit to pull a dandelion.

Seen from six or eight feet away, the women seem younger than the men, and some of them actually are—trophy wives or favored *mia noi*, "minor" wives who have been towed into public as a treat. Silk is everywhere, bordered at neck and wrists by the hard sparkle of precious stones. Young or old, most of the women are variations on a theme. They are grimly slim and brilliantly made up. Noses too broad in the bridge have been subtly shaded to appear narrower. Thin lips have been plumped up and thick lips minimized. White skin is the ideal, and those who do not have it wear pale, almost ghostlike powder to simulate it. Hair is architectural: sculpted, layered, lacquered against gravity. Perfume is everywhere. In the midst of the crowd, Rafferty feels like he is being attacked by flowers.

Rose, her face scrubbed and gleaming, the diamonds dazzling at her throat, towers above the women and most of the men as Pan hauls her and Rafferty along behind him, introducing them right and left as proudly as if he'd just whipped them up in the kitchen. He pretends not to see the stiffness with which they are met.

It usually takes a moment for the stiffness to set in. Rafferty can almost see the thoughts chase each other through people's heads as they first look at Rose: *She's beautiful. Maybe she's someone I should recog-*

nize. Hmmmm, very dark-skinned, low bridge of the nose—Isaan. Oh, of course, she's one of Pan's little popsies.

Pan not only ignores the stiffness, he intensifies it. He has a trick of taking between both of his hands one of the hands of the woman he is greeting and then, when he introduces Rose, putting Rose's hand into the woman's. Some of the women manage the situation; their breeding comes to the fore, and they hold on to Rose's hand and make conversation as though they had grown up neighbors, rather than on the opposite sides of one of the world's widest gulfs of power and possession. The others—mostly, Rafferty thinks—those who fought their way into rooms such as these, go rigid. They actually tilt slightly backward, as though Rose smelled bad, and they snatch their hands away the moment Pan lets go.

At first Rafferty is worried about how Rose will handle the rejection, but this is a woman who stepped onstage nightly in a crowded, testosterone-filled bar, wearing little more than an attitude. The women who try to escape her learn that she is eagerly friendly, that she will follow them, puppylike, as they back away across the marble floor. She asks them the kinds of questions they would be asked in a small village: How many children do they have, how old, were the births painful, how *do* they get their hair to do that?

The woman Rafferty likes least retrieves her hand and wipes it on her thigh. Her eyes go to Rafferty and then back to Rose, and he can almost see the word "whore" form in her mind. "I'll bet there's a *fascinating* story here," she says in English, for Rafferty's benefit. "Where in the world did you two meet?"

"The King's Castle," Rose says, the English name of the Patpong bar she danced in.

"The Royal Palace," Pan translates into Thai.

"Really," the woman says, her eyebrows elevated. "Were you on a tour?"

"Oh, no," Rose says. "I worked there. For years."

The woman hesitates for a second, weighing the probabilities, then says, "Doing what?"

"Guest relations," Rose says with her sweetest smile.

The woman says, "Ah."

Pan says to Rose, "You don't need me," and disappears.

Rafferty snags a passing waiter and grabs two flutes of pink champagne, and he and Rose wander the crowd. There is no question that Pan was right: Rose is easily the most beautiful woman present. The yellow diamonds throw hard little points of golden light on the flawless skin of her neck and the underside of her chin. Most of the men follow her with their eyes, and most of the women watch the men, although their gaze eventually floats to Rose. But Pan was wrong about one thing: Even when Rafferty is standing right beside Rose, there *are* people who pay attention to him. Men, three of them. He can feel their eyes on him and see them slide away when he turns.

They are scattered throughout the crowd as though some sort of territorial imperative were in operation, keeping them apart. Orbiting each of them is a muscular little knot of men, three or four of them, wearing dark suits of anonymous cut. These men keep their eyes in motion. Some of them wear discreet earplugs. When one of the men in the center wants a drink, one of the satellites peels off and goes to get it. When the drink bearer returns, he stands like a human tray with the drink extended until the top dog condescends to notice him.

The three men's eyes keep flicking to Rafferty.

At eight-thirty the little orchestra, which is seated on a raised platform midway down one of the room's walls, strikes up the triumphal march from *Aida*, and two long screens, painted with gold bamboo and blindingly iridescent hummingbirds, are folded back to reveal a room filled with food and white-jacketed waiters. There is a general movement toward the buffet, and Rafferty takes advantage of the shift in focus to navigate through the crowd to Pan's side.

"Three men," Rafferty says. "I'm going to describe them, but don't look for them while we're talking."

"I won't have to," Pan says. "It's good business to know your enemies."

"High-ranking policeman," Rafferty says. "Full uniform, fat, looks a little like a monkey—"

"Thanom," Pan says. "*Very* bad. He runs a little squadron of killer cops. They scare people to death. He was one of the top cops who resisted the crackdown on drug dealers because he was taking so much money off them. Millions of baht a month."

"Why is he here tonight?"

"His wife is ambitious. Got a set of claws and uses them to climb. Also, we were in business once, he and I. When we were both younger and poorer." His eyes scan the room. "But most people are here to show me I can't chase them away. They would rather this fund-raiser had been held anywhere else in the world. They'd prefer a rat-infested slum or a mountain of rubbish. But since I outbid all of them to host the event, they have to show up to prove they've got the balls."

"Dark suit, short, mostly bald. Not skinny but gaunt, got a face like a skull. Not eating or drinking anything."

"Porthip. He's the guy who owns the cranes you see all over the city. Imports steel for skyscrapers. His steel partners are Tokyo yakuza. Once or twice they've sent him help when he needed to persuade builders that they were buying their steel in the wrong place." Pan seems to be enjoying himself. "Three or four years back, one of the reluctant customers was found in Banglamphoo. And Pratunam. And Lumphini Park."

"I get it."

"Something very sharp," Pan says. "*Japanese* sharp."

"Does he live on air or something? He can't weigh more than a hundred and twenty pounds."

"He's lost maybe twenty kilos in the past year or so. Word is he's got stomach cancer." Pan looks around the room. "It's a good thing we're not raising money to cure that. Half the people here wouldn't give a penny until Porthip is dead."

"This last one's harder," Rafferty says. "Maybe the best-dressed man here, really beautiful suit. Late forties, early fifties, goes to the gym a lot—"

"In the middle of a gang of bodybuilders?"

"Right."

"Mmmmm," Pan says, the pink lips pushed out.

Rafferty says, "Mmmmmm?"

Pan pulls a cigar case from his jacket, opens it, and takes one out. He snaps the case closed without offering one to Rafferty. Then he stands there, looking down at his hands as though the cigar and the case come as a surprise to him. He opens the case, drops the cigar back in, and shoves the case back into his pocket. He smiles at Rafferty and takes his arm.

"Let's eat," he says.

20

Wrecking Ball

It takes Rafferty less than a minute in the privacy of Pan's office to confirm that Thanom and Porthip are both on the yellow list.

While everyone eats and Pan proudly leads Rose around the room, Rafferty grabs Dr. Ravi. Dr. Ravi has a plate in his hand and doesn't seem overly happy at the interruption.

"Where's the list of the people who showed up tonight?" Rafferty asks.

"Down at the guardhouse."

"Do me a favor? Call and tell them to show it to me. And can I borrow your swan?"

The swan starts with a purr. As Rafferty guides it back toward the gates, he becomes vividly aware that the stink from the pigpens has increased incrementally. Passing the ramshackle village, he sees the enormous fans that have been placed behind the pen, wafting the scent of *merde de cochon* toward the Garden of Eden.

The smell chases him up the long hill. When he crests it, he sees that the lighting in the garden has been shifted to create an island of brilliance around the apple tree. The jeweled fruit gleams green and red through the leaves, and the verdant moss that surrounds the tree has been raked or fluffed up to make it seem deeper, lusher, more sensuous. As befits, Rafferty thinks, the spot where the world's most pleasant sin had its world premiere. Half a dozen men are at work around the apple tree. Several of them are up on ladders and seem to be putting something into its branches. In the relative darkness on the far side of the garden, behind red velvet ropes policed by two uniformed guards, is a gaggle of people whom, from their cameras and casual dress, Rafferty identifies as members of the press. They have their own bar and are using it with some enthusiasm; its surface bristles with bottles, and the voices he hears have the tone-deaf loudness of the freshly drunk.

A guard gives Rafferty a few minutes with the RSVPs. About a third of the attendees are on the yellow list, the anti-Pan list, and about a fifth of them are on the list Pan gave him. He pulls out his copies of those lists and circles the names of the people who are present. He wants to get a look at as many of them as possible tonight. Pan's line comes to mind: *It's good business to know your enemies.*

He works as fast as he can. The booth is hot, even this late in the evening. His shirt is damp by the time he finishes. He refolds his lists and pockets them, thinking that by tomorrow morning it may all have proved to be a waste of time. Elora Weecherat's article will be out by then, with its hidden threat: If anything happens to Rafferty and his family, the paper has information that could lead to the person responsible.

If he weren't American, he thinks, it wouldn't have a chance of working. The potency comes from the threat of the embassy pushing the Thai investigation along. And if Arthit is right and this has something to do with the national political scene, pressure from the United States is the last thing the people who are threatening him would want.

During his time in Bangkok, he's learned not to take too much comfort from a string of hypotheticals, but it's all he's got.

HE APPROACHES THE policeman, Thanom, first. The picket fence of protectors parts as though he's expected, and Thanom offers him a wet hand to grasp and a fat-faced smile of welcome that almost makes his flat little eyes disappear. "Certainly," he says. "I'd be happy to talk to you. Anything to help a writer with such an interesting subject."

"Isn't it?" Rafferty says. "And of course I want to do it well."

"I'm sure you do," Thanom says, and one of his guys snickers. Thanom's smile remains in place, but his eyes, when he turns them to the man who laughed, look as if smoke should be coming out of them.

When Rafferty reaches the other side of the room, the living skeleton, Porthip, is more difficult. "No time," he says.

"I'm sure you're busy—"

"I have *no time*. Didn't you hear me? I'm working twenty hours a day as it is. And Pan no longer interests me." There's a tremor to his voice that could be lack of breath support. It could also be pain.

One of Porthip's guardians puts a hand on Rafferty's arm, and Rafferty shakes it off. "That's going to disappoint some people," he says. The guardian takes Rafferty's arm again.

"Who?"

"Tell you what," Rafferty says. "Rather than discuss a bunch of names in front of everyone, I'll have one of them call you tomorrow."

Porthip extends a shaky hand and touches the shoulder of the man whose hand is on Rafferty's arm. The man lets go. "Do that," Porthip says. "If they're the right people, I'll talk to you. But you arrive ready to work. No matter who calls me, I can only give you an hour. If that."

"That'll be fine," Rafferty says. He turns away.

"Wait," Porthip says. "Who is she?"

"Who?"

The tip of his tongue touches his lower lip. "You know who."

"Oh, *her*," Rafferty says. "She's a spirit of the forest. She only assumes human form when the moon is full."

Porthip looks past him, to where Rose towers over Pan, yellow fire at her throat. "The moon isn't full."

Rafferty says, "I guess I was misinformed."

The third man, the beautifully dressed man whose name Rafferty doesn't know, won't allow Rafferty anywhere near him. The bench-pressing phalanx that surrounds him simply stand, massive shoulder to massive shoulder, a human Stonehenge, several feet in front of their employer, and stare Rafferty down.

"At least let him tell me himself," Rafferty says.

One of the musclemen says, in English, "Fuck off."

"Is that message from you?" Rafferty calls over the muscleman's shoulder.

The beautifully dressed man simply turns away. Rafferty has been snubbed before, but this is a whole new level. He starts to push between two of the men in front of him, but the one to his left, a short, wide, dark-skinned man whose teeth stagger drunkenly across his mouth, leaning in all directions, reaches around the side of Rafferty's neck and digs an iron thumb into a spot behind Rafferty's jaw, just below his ear. Pain radiates outward in all directions. Rafferty lets his knees go loose, trying to drop out of the hold, but the other man grabs his necktie and holds him up. It has taken almost no movement, nothing to draw attention, but Rafferty's entire awareness is focused on pain. By the time the two men release him, the beautifully dressed man is gone.

"Next time," says the one with the drunken teeth, "you'll be limping for a week."

Then he brings up his right hand and, with his index finger, flicks Rafferty across his open left eye.

The pain is dazzling, enough to take Rafferty to his knees, both hands cupped over the assaulted eye. Tears stream down his face. After what seems like ten minutes, he becomes aware of an open hand extended down to him.

He looks up with his good eye to see a man in his early fifties with long, wavy hair, worn brushed back without a part, in a senatorial style. His hand is framed by half an inch of immaculate white French cuff fastened by a link of lapis lazuli set in gold. "Please," the man says. "Let me help you up."

"Thank you." Rafferty reaches up to give the man his hand and is more or less hauled to his feet.

"I saw that," the man says. "Filthy trick."

Rafferty mops his face with the sleeve of his jacket. The vision in his left eye is badly blurred. "And he'll have an opportunity to regret it."

The senator smiles gently. "Don't say it too loudly. There are people in Bangkok who could wipe you up like a spill, and Ton is one of them."

"Ton?"

"Oh," the senator says, dropping his eyes to adjust an immaculate cuff. "I thought you knew." When he looks back up, he is smiling. "Given the beauty of your companion, you have good reason to stay alive. If I were you, I would think of Ton as a wrecking ball and stay out of his path." He nods slightly. "Please excuse me."

The senator moves off, doing a little genteel glad-handing here and there, and Rafferty turns to find Rose standing behind him. "Nice-looking man," she says.

"He returns the compliment. In fact, everyone returns the compliment. You're all anybody here wants to talk to me about."

"That's not surprising, considering that one of your eyes is bright red. You look better when they match. What happened?"

"I ran into a finger."

"Who was it attached to?"

"Captain Teeth."

Rose says, "Is this something *else* I have to worry about?"

"Worry?" Rafferty says, blinking against the pain. "In a gathering like this one?"

21

Net Profits

The evening's final act begins about nine-thirty as Pan steps up onto the orchestra's platform. He raises both hands, gesturing for silence. The fiddlers desist.

"Ladies and gentlemen," Pan says. "On behalf of the Malaria Relief Fund, I want to thank you all for coming and invite you out into the garden for our closing presentation. I'm sure you'll find it worthwhile."

He steps down and weaves his way through the crowd, as conspicuous in his awful clothes as a peacock among pigeons. He winks at Rose as he passes. They wait a bit and then go out and down the steps, following the crowd along the narrow paved track, and the little village is to their left. "By the way," Rafferty says, "the votes have been tallied, and it's official. You obliterated every woman here."

"I already married you, Poke," Rose says. "But don't stop just because of that."

Someone jostles Rafferty's shoulder roughly and pushes past him. It is Captain Teeth, the man who flicked Rafferty's eye. He turns back to stare at Rose and makes a loud slurping noise with his tongue.

"If you learn how to swallow," Rose calls to him, "you won't have to do that."

"He knows how to swallow," Rafferty says, his eyes on the man's. "He eats shit every time the boss loosens his belt."

Captain Teeth flushes and starts to pivot, but the man next to him grabs his arm and gives it a yank. With his upper lip pulled back to bare his awful teeth, Captain Teeth makes a V with his index and middle fingers, jabs them in the direction of Rafferty's eyes, and then allows himself to be dragged away. The beautifully dressed man is not with them.

Rose says, "Would that be—"

"It would," Rafferty says.

"He doesn't like you much." She fans her hand beneath her nose. "Ohhh, those pigs."

"Half an hour ago, Pan had wind machines, like in the movies, set up behind them, just to move the smell around."

"He doesn't trust much to chance, does he? The diamonds for me, the fans for the pigs. He really piles it on."

They are cresting the hill that slopes down to the garden. "It's probably a good thing it didn't occur to him to put the diamonds on the pigs," Rafferty says.

"We should suggest that for next time." Rose passes her fingertips over the stones. "It was nice to wear them once, though." Rafferty doesn't say anything, and Rose hits him in the ribs with her elbow. "You dummy," she says. "You say *one word* about how you wish you could buy me something like this and I'll stick my finger in your other eye."

"At least they'd be the same color."

"Look at *that*," Rose says, stopping. Rafferty stands there, feeling the crowd part around them and flow past, apparently unimpressed by the sight below.

The garden is an explosion of light. Six-story palm trees, gilded by light, dazzle against the black sky. Enormous ferns are transparent green, backlit by thousands of watts. Apples glisten in the foliage of the tree, and a pinspot picks out the snake as it winds its silver spiral down the trunk. The whole thing nestles like an emir's jewels against the dark velvet wall of greenery. It is vulgar, ostentatious, biblically ridiculous, and absolutely beautiful.

Movement beyond the garden catches Rafferty's eye. The members of the press have been released from their eighty-proof cage and are streaming toward the lights like moths. Nipping at the heels of the press, herding them like a border collie, is Dr. Ravi. He and two guards shepherd them to an area on the opposite side of the tree from the crowd.

"This could be interesting," Rafferty says. "Look, he's set it up so the guests are in the picture."

Pan emerges from the greenery and steps up onto a wooden platform, about eighteen inches high, positioned beneath the tree. Flashbulbs explode, making Pan's movements as jerky as stop-motion animation.

"Welcome to the garden," Pan says. He is wearing a microphone on a headset, and his voice echoes. "And to Net Profits." He says the words in English and then reverts to Thai. "You'll see why we're calling it that in a moment. When the Malaria Relief Fund proposed this event, I decided immediately that we should end the evening here, in the Garden of Eden." He pauses as Dr. Ravi and the two guards finish jamming the press into their assigned area and then reaches into his pocket and pulls out a fan of three-by-five cards. "Most of us here tonight are Buddhists. But for Christians and Muslims, this garden was the setting of creation." He is reading now; the words—which, Rafferty thinks, he obviously didn't write—sound stiff and uncomfortable in his mouth. "It was here that the Deity shaped, from clay and divinity and a rib, the creatures who would sit on the throne of the world He made. They were perfect in form and perfect in health. And they were perfect in their innocence."

A murmur starts to run through the crowd, and Rafferty sees heads turn, sees people step back and bump into those behind them. He hears Rose start to laugh, and say, "Oh, no."

The thick ferns to Pan's left part. Adam and Eve enter their garden, holding hands. Neither of them is a minute over nineteen, and they are as naked as the day they were born except for a couple of strategic and mysteriously adhesive leaves. As the beautiful couple walks to the base of the tree, seemingly unaware that the garden is full of overdressed millionaires, every flashbulb in Thailand goes off, and it suddenly occurs to the people in the front of the crowd that they have just been captured in a front-page photo. There are more attempts to back away, and Pan has to raise his voice to speak over the protests.

"But there was something else in the garden," he reads from the cards, "a creature whose sting we continue to feel even today. And no, ladies and gentlemen, it wasn't the snake with his shining apple of temptation. It was a much smaller creature, a tiny, seemingly harmless creature, that finds us at our most vulnerable." Adam and Eve lie down together on the moss at the base of the tree. Their arms intertwine as the flashbulbs reach the intensity of antiaircraft artillery. The people at the front of the group are trying to back away while the people at the rear are pressing forward for a better look.

"The anopheles mosquito," Pan says. He starts to grin but fights it down. "It took its first drink of human blood here in the garden, and it went forth and multiplied. It multiplied by the millions and became a swarm that fills the night with the world's number-one killer. The humblest, bringing down the most mighty. But it could have been stopped right here, ladies and gentlemen—" Adam has wrapped both arms and one leg around Eve, and a fig leaf flies into the air from between them and dawdles its way down again. Now the crowd is seriously trying to get out of camera range, and Rose is laughing so hard she has to lean against Rafferty.

"It could have been stopped here, but it wasn't, because *one thing* was missing from the garden." Pan raises his hand and makes a magical pass at the tree, and a glittering gold net drops from it, covering Adam and Eve only seconds before the pictures would have become useless for news purposes. Movement continues beneath the net. Pan takes advantage of the diversion to light a cigar. "A *net*, ladies and gentlemen," he says through a haze of smoke. "A simple net. A net that still stops malaria today, that can help us to eradicate it from the face of the earth. And I'm proud to announce that my own initial contribution to Net Profits will be ten million baht. That'll buy one hundred and fifty thousand nets, but that's just a beginning. I'm hoping we'll buy a *million* nets with the money we raise tonight, and, fortunately, there are people here this evening—good friends of mine, each and every one of them—who will make me look like a tightwad." He creases the cards up the middle and tosses them over his shoulder, then glances down at the golden net, which is still in motion. "So," he says, "why don't we give these kids a little privacy and go up to the house and write some checks?"

22

Buttercup

It's almost eleven when Elora Weecherat steps onto the sidewalk. Late for her, but it's been a frustrating evening.

She'd stopped for a quick dinner after her meeting with Rafferty, just a simple coq au vin and a fresh baguette at a French bistro on Silom where she knew the cooking was actually French, not *Thai*-French, which she supposes has its charms, but not for her. A glass and a half of Côtes du Rhône had washed everything down with the dusty red taste of the Left Bank, and she was feeling carefree and mentally limber by the time she plopped into the chair in her cubicle in the newsroom, logged onto the computers, and started to slap out Rafferty's story.

It came easily, but it came wrong. The opening was too leisurely, the language didn't achieve the muted tension she was aiming for. This man has been threatened with death, and the death of those he loves. The people behind that threat are almost certainly overwhelmingly powerful, and their motive is probably to create a book that would serve as a preemptive strike against Pan, should he decide to take advantage of his political potential.

Halfway through rewriting the opening paragraphs, she stops and asks herself how she feels about that. She loathes Pan for his vulgarity and the way he treats the women who are foolish or greedy enough to rise to his bait. On the other hand, there is no doubt that Thailand should be moving toward real democracy, untidy as that may be. Weecherat has little innate sympathy for the poor, primarily because she believes that beautiful things are always created by the privileged. One may wish for the proletariat to rise above poverty without also wanting them to design one's clothes.

So she detects a little bias problem in the story's point of view. And, perhaps more important, the piece isn't sufficiently discreet. No matter how big the story is, she has no desire to feel on her own back the sights that are presumably trained on Rafferty's. She needs to get her personal opinions out of the way and make the language more suggestive and less explicit. She needs to make the reader see something she doesn't actually say. And amp up the tension at the same time.

She reaches out and straightens the small photograph of her daughter, the only personal item in the cubicle, then kisses the tip of her index finger and touches it to the child's nose.

She has worked most of her way through the story, feeling more in control of the material, when an instant message pops up on her screen. The night editor would like to see her.

She gets up, irritably redrapes her scarf, and threads a path between the empty desks to the office at the far end of the room. The night editor, a fat, balding hack who has gained thirty pounds since smoking was banned in the building, swivels in his chair to face her. He holds up a printout.

"Where's this going?"

"If you'll let me finish it," Weecherat says, "you'll see."

"Just tell me. My eyes are tired."

Weecherat sighs and talks him through the story, painstakingly telling it exactly as she intends to write it, eliminating her personal bias and skirting the occasional misdirection that will allow her to imply more than she actually says. When she finishes, he regards her long enough for her to feel uncomfortable.

He drops the printout on the desk. "So you're selling me a story that could bring the cops down on the paper if anything happens to this *farang*. We become the keepers of the keys if things go wrong."

"That's one way to look at it."

"Give me another."

"I just told it to you. The first person ever authorized to write Pan's biography is being forced under threat of death to write a character assassination. That meets my definition of news."

He nods slowly, as though considering her argument. "And what's this mystery information? The stuff you're leaving out?"

The nape of Weecherat's neck suddenly feels cold. "You don't need to know," she says. "It won't be in the story."

His index finger snaps against the edge of his desk with a *thwap.* "Don't tell me what's material. You're taking us in a direction that could put us in a courtroom."

"Oh, don't be silly. If the police do come to us, we'll tell them everything. We can't be sued for libel if the police demand the information, and you know it." She hears the pitch of her voice and takes a step back in an attempt to lower the temperature. A question occurs to her. "What are you doing reading this? You don't usually monitor stories in real time."

His gaze drifts past her, and she has to fight the urge to turn and look over her shoulder. The tips of his fingers land in the middle of the printout and scrabble it back and forth over the surface of the desk. "You're right," he says at last. "Don't tell me. It's probably better that I don't know."

"You didn't answer my question."

He stands, picks up her printout, wads it into a ball, and drops it in the trash. "Didn't I? Sorry. Go finish your story."

Back at her cubicle, she rereads what she's done, types in a few minor changes, and then finishes. She spends twenty minutes fast-forwarding through her tape of the conversation to make sure she's quoted Rafferty accurately, and then pushes "send." After she gets up and hefts her purse to her shoulder, she turns to look across the dim room at the bright window in the night editor's office and finds him looking at her.

She gives him a cool but proper fingertip wave. He nods and swivels his chair to turn his back to her.

The moment she is gone, he swivels around again and gets up. He goes to Weecherat's cubicle and picks through the things in her drawers until he finds her tape recorder. He opens it and checks that the tape is inside. Then he returns to his office.

Traffic is thinning at this hour. Weecherat steps into the street and extends an arm, palm down, and pats the air to signal a cab. One pulls out from the curb a short distance away, swings into the traffic lane, and swerves toward her. She glances down to gather her shawl so it won't catch in the taxi's door, then the glare of headlights brings her eyes up and she sees the cab bearing down on her. The two steps she manages to scramble back, toward the safety of the curb, put her directly behind a parked truck, and that's where the cab hits her, slamming her against the lower edge of the truck so hard she is almost cut in two.

The driver flicks on the wipers to clear blood from the windshield and shifts into reverse. The transmission lets out a squeal of protest. Something is caught beneath the truck. The driver throws his door open, climbs out, and slams the door on his thumb. He yelps in pain, opens the door, and lopes away into traffic, dodging between cars and holding his injured thumb close to his chest.

As traffic whisks past the scene, Weecherat's buttercup scarf flutters in the windstream.

Close Enough

The moment the apartment door opens, Miaow pushes through, saying, "It was on *television*."

"Then I guess it really happened," Rafferty says, standing in the bluish fluorescent light of the hallway. He puts a hand on Miaow's head. "Don't you have something to say to Mrs. Pongsiri?"

"Thank you," Miaow recites dutifully. "I had a very nice time."

"It was a little holiday for me," Mrs. Pongsiri says. She is wearing full evening makeup and a silk robe in all the hues of the rainbow, plus a few that were deleted for aesthetic reasons. Her apartment, the lamps mysteriously sheathed with colored scarves, gleams behind her like a Gypsy caravan. "This is the first night in months I haven't gone to the bar."

"Were they really naked?" Miaow says. Her eyes are so wide he can see white all around her irises, and the evening's excitement seems to have driven away the clouds that have been hovering over her head. "I mean, *really*?"

"Close enough," Rafferty says. "Thank you, Mrs. Pongsiri. I'll baby-sit your bar girls some evening."

He gets a flirtatious smile and a disapproving shake of the head. Rafferty doubts there's a man in the world who could mix messages like that. "You wouldn't say that if your wife could hear you."

"No, I wouldn't," he says. "And she's not going to hear it from anybody here either. Is she, Miaow?"

"Why couldn't I go with you?" The petulance returns.

"No kids allowed. Just a bunch of rich people standing around sneering at each other. Bye, Mrs. Pongsiri." He leads Miaow down the hall. "Anyway, it was all boring except for the two minutes you saw on television."

"The garden was pretty. I would have liked it."

"It didn't smell as good as it looked." He opens the door to the apartment and steps aside to allow Miaow to precede him. As he closes the door, Rose comes out of the bedroom, already in shorts and a T-shirt.

"You should get out of that monkey outfit," she says.

"Miaow was just telling me that Pan's little show was on TV."

"It was," Miaow says, heading for her room.

"That was fast." Rose stops at the kitchen counter. "I'm going to make some Nescafé," she says. "Want some?"

"Have I ever wanted any?"

"Not that I remember."

"But I might want it at this hour?"

"You'll never truly become Thai until you learn to enjoy Nescafé."

"Then I guess I'm locked out of paradise."

"I don't know about you," Rose says, crossing the kitchen, "but I had enough of paradise tonight. The kids were pretty, though, weren't they?"

"Enthusiastic, too."

"I could never do that," Rose says with one hand on the handle of the cabinet. "Work naked like that. I was offered more money to move to the upstairs bar and do shows—you know, *shows*—but the idea made my stomach—" She pulls the door open, and there is a white blur of motion, and Rose takes an enormous, instinctive leap backward as something explodes off the shelf toward her. Packages tumble to the counter, pushed aside by whatever it is. Rose's scream is so high that Rafferty squints against the sound, and he stands as though he has been nailed in place, staring at the thing that has landed on the floor only a few inches short of Rose, who is backing away, both hands out to fend it off.

It raises itself to a vertical position, perhaps three feet off the floor, its hood spread wide, its tongue tasting the air.

Rafferty later has no memory of having grabbed Rose. All he can remember is the two of them in the living room, his fingers digging into her upper arms, as Miaow charges down the hall toward them. He stops her with a single barked syllable. The cobra remains upright, swaying from side to side.

"*Miaow.* Stay there. Rose, go over there, near the front door, with Miaow." He grabs the white leather hassock from beside the coffee table with both hands and pushes it across the room to the edge of the kitchen counter. It blocks the entrance to the kitchen.

The cobra drops flat, out of sight beneath the edge of the hassock.

"It can get over that," Rose says.

"Yell if it does," Rafferty says, already on the run. "Then go into the hallway and close the door."

He shoulders open the bedroom door and leaps onto the bed, belly-first. He pulls over his head the chain he wears around his neck and slides aside a panel in the headboard to reveal a locked metal door.

"I can't see it," Rose calls.

"Don't try!" Rafferty shouts. "Don't go near the kitchen." He fumbles with the key dangling from the chain, trying to get it into the lock. It keeps skittering away from the slot. "Yell if it starts to come over the hassock." He finally gets the key into the slot, cranks it to the right, and yanks the door open. His hand hits the heavy cloth bundle, and he pulls it out and unwraps it.

The Glock is cold and oily to the touch. It takes him three attempts to ram the magazine home, and when he tries to rack a shell into the chamber, his hands slide uselessly over the slick metal. He has to dry them on the bedspread before he can snap the barrel back.

Rose screams his name.

He rolls off the bed and charges into the living room to see the cobra slithering over the hassock as though it were a molehill. Rose and Miaow are backing toward the door to the hall. Its attention attracted by all the movement, the cobra rises up again, and Rafferty sights down the barrel.

"Don't!" Miaow shouts. "*Look*. It hasn't got any fangs. It's been—"

Her voice disappears in the roar of the gun, three fast shots, and a bullet hurls the snake backward as though it's been yanked by an invisible wire, over the hassock and back into the kitchen. Rafferty runs to the edge of the hassock and looks down to see it writhing on the floor. He fires two more times, the first bullet digging a useless hole in the linoleum. The second goes straight through the cobra's flat head, and the writhing slows.

"It was defanged," Miaow says from behind him. She sounds accusing.

"I don't care if it subscribed to the *Ladies' Home Journal*," Rafferty says. His legs are shaking violently. He puts a hand on the counter to steady himself. "Any cobra that comes into this apartment is snake meat."

"It obviously didn't *come in* here," Rose says.

Rafferty's cell phone rings.

He and Rose hold each other's eyes until Miaow says, her voice high and unsteady, "Aren't you going to answer it?"

"They already left their message," Rafferty says, but he takes the phone out of his pocket, flips it open, and says, "Yes?"

"There won't be any story in the newspaper," says the man who sat next to him in the Lincoln. "You won't try anything cute again. I assume you got our present by now. If not, you might want to skip tomorrow's breakfast cereal. The next one will be in your daughter's bed, and it'll have fangs."

"Got it," Rafferty says, but his eyes are searching the apartment. He sidesteps Rose and Miaow and looks under the coffee table. Nothing.

"And we're not happy that you're spending time with Pan."

"Oh, use your fucking head," Rafferty says. "He can make a lot of trouble if he thinks I'm not writing the book he wants. This is going to be hard enough without that." There is nothing under the counter either.

"Just a minute," the man on the other end says. Rafferty can hear a palm cover the mouthpiece and a muffled conversation, both voices male. "Okay," the man says. "You can stay in touch with Pan. But don't get fancy again, because you're all out of warnings."

"One more thing," Rafferty says, "and then you can hang up and high-five each other on scaring a little girl half to death. That skinny old guy, Porthip. The one who sells the steel. He won't talk to me until someone calls to tell him he should. I thought you assholes were on top of details."

"He'll get a call tomorrow."

"*Now* would be the time to hang up on me," Rafferty says, "but I'm hanging up on you instead."

He closes the phone and looks at Rose and Miaow. More bad news to deliver. He puts his finger to his lips, then uses the same finger to make a circle that indicates the room in general, and then he touches his ear. He says, "I'll clean this up. Miaow, go to bed." He gestures her not toward her bedroom but toward the room he shares with Rose.

She says, "I'm frightened."

Rafferty is checking the underside of his desk, but he turns and goes to Miaow. Kneeling, he wraps his arms around her. She fidgets, but then she puts an arm around his neck and presses her forehead against his chest.

Rafferty says, "So am I."

PART II

THE EDGE

24

Luck Will Have Nothing to Do with It

At 12:42 A.M., Captain Teeth says, "They've got cops."

"I'd imagine so," says the man who had sat next to Rafferty in the car. "He fired that thing four or five times." He gets up from the soft black leather couch, turning back to center his drink, straw-colored liquid over ice, on a thick coaster. In this house, rings on the tables are strongly discouraged. When he is satisfied with the placement of the glass, the man noiselessly pads across the carpet to the console, where he grabs the second set of headphones. The console, just a cheap black table with the receiver on it, has been shoved up against a wall, displacing an ornate teak-and-suede sofa that is now jammed haphazardly into a corner, where it disrupts the meticulous feng shui of the room.

The room is a home office, all dark-wood-and-leather furniture and the half-hidden glint of gold on the spines of unread books. The walls are the color of strong coffee, a deeply grained mahogany that's been varnished to a reflective luster. Three flat-screen televisions are hung on one wall in a perfect vertical, and two computer screens flicker on the console behind the desk. The desk is empty but for a small thicket of expensively framed photographs, each one showing a handsome, richly dressed man standing with other richly dressed men, mostly less handsome, who face the camera with the air of having been interrupted in the middle of something important. There is one photograph of a thickset woman in her forties, her wrinkles retouched but her disappointment intact. She is flanked by two younger women and a teenage girl, forcing the requisite smiles, who are clearly her daughters.

The room is completely silent. The entire house has been sound-proofed because its mistress does not sleep well. The men at the console press their headphones to their ears, one standing and one sitting, for several moments. The man who had spoken to Rafferty in the car drops his phones onto the console for a moment and returns to the couch, moving in and out of bright areas beneath the recessed pin spots in the ceiling. He grabs the drink and totes it over to the console, sits in the wheeled black leather office chair beside Captain Teeth, and slaps the phones back on.

"Pretty dumb story, even if they're telling it to cops," he says, listening. "Wonder where they put the snake."

"Probably the refrigerator," says Captain Teeth. A new bandage, pristine white, is neatly wrapped around his left thumb.

"She'd never let him do that. Listen to her. She's not going to have any cobras in her refrigerator."

"She's extremely fine," Captain Teeth says. "You didn't see her."

"If you're a good boy," the other man says, "you can have her when this is over."

Captain Teeth shakes a cigarette out of a pack, holds it beneath his nose, and inhales the fragrance. He knows better than to light it. Only one person is allowed to smoke in this house. "I'll never be that lucky. But I'll tell you, if she'd be nice to me, I'd spend my life keeping snakes out of her refrigerator."

"I can fix it. Give you a few hours with her before we put her away."

"Better-looking than Eve. You didn't get to see Eve either."

"I saw her on TV."

"Yeah?" Captain Teeth squints against a burst of static, puts down the unlit cigarette, and fiddles with the volume knob. "You see me? I was right up front. Till I had to leave, anyway."

"The wife's better than Eve. And she's yours if you want her." The man from the car slips one of the earphones off and tucks it behind his ear. "Okay, you got the story? The kid was playing with the gun, no damage done except the holes in the cabinet and the floor. The cops went through the place, probably looking in closets and under beds to make sure nobody was dead, and everybody said good night, and they left. I leave anything important out?"

"No."

"I mean, if himself decides to listen to the tape. Have I left anything out?"

"No. That's all of it."

"When they go to bed, you rewind the tape and go through it again. Just to make sure."

The two of them listen for a few minutes. The man from the car drains his drink. Then he asks, "Why'd you have to leave the party early?"

"Just business," Captain Teeth says. "Listen. They're going to bed." He reaches over to the other man's glass and loops a finger through the hole in the center of one of the ice cubes. He pulls the cube out and drops it into his mouth. Around the cube he says, "You really think I can have her?"

A voice behind them says, "It'll be a waste if you don't." They turn to see the man in the photographs on the desk, wearing a dark blue silk robe. "Because no one else ever will."

The men at the console leap to their feet. The man in the robe goes to the desk, opens the top drawer, and pulls out a pack of cigarettes and shakes one loose. "Kai," he says to Captain Teeth. He picks up a gold lighter and flicks it. "Have you told Ren here what you did earlier this evening, after you deserted the party?" He regards the two of them over the flame.

"No," Kai says.

"Didn't tell him how you hurt your thumb?" The man in the robe is in the darker half of the office, away from the desk lamps on the console, and the flame of the lighter brings his face out of the gloom and plants bright pinpricks in the center of his eyes. "Nothing?"

"No, sir."

"How sensitive of you not to embarrass him," the man in the robe says. "Then I'll tell him. What Kai did tonight," he says, his eyes on Ren, "was pick up the shit you dropped."

Ren licks his lips and says, "Excuse me?"

"The elevator," says the man in the robe. He lets the lighter go out, throwing his face back into darkness. His voice is soft, but the edges are rough enough to remove skin. "You made three mistakes, didn't you?"

"Three?" Ren asks. He puts a steadying hand on the console.

"One of them was just stupid. Taking the *farang* up in that elevator. Stupid, but understandable. You could have used the service elevator, but that one was right there, wasn't it? Right there in the garage."

"Yes, sir," Ren says, around a swallow.

"So you saved a few steps. You used it. And it told the *farang* what floor we were on. And then you made a more serious mistake." He flicks the lighter again, puts the cigarette in his mouth, touches the flame to its tip, and takes a drag that brings the coal to life. Then he exhales a stream of smoke and flips the cigarette straight at Ren. It strikes Ren in the center of the chest, and he drops to his knees as though he's been shot, although what he's doing is trying frantically to retrieve the cigarette before it scorches the carpet. He scrambles after it and grasps it between thumb and forefinger. When he knows he won't drop it, he starts to rise, but the man in the blue robe says, "Stay there."

Ren freezes in a crouch. His legs are bent at acute angles, and he is balanced on the balls of his feet.

"Is that position comfortable?" the man in the blue robe asks.

"Uh, no, sir."

"Well, let's see how comfortable it is in, say, two hours." He comes out from behind the desk and stands over Ren. Then he draws back his right hand and slaps the crouching man hard enough to snap his head around and make him put his free hand down to keep from toppling over.

"I didn't say you could use your hands," says the man in the blue robe.

"Sorry, sir," Ren says. The left side of his face is flaming. His legs have begun to tremble from the strain.

"Put your hands on your knees." Ren does as he's told. The cigarette in his left sends up a lazy filigree of smoke. The man in the blue robe slaps him again and then again, and when Ren puts a hand down, the man in the robe plants a slippered foot on it and grinds it into the carpet with the edge of the heel. "What was your second mistake?"

"I told him . . . I told him not to tell you."

"You didn't want me to be angry at you," says the man in the blue robe. "You didn't want me to—what? Speak harshly to you? Raise my voice? Shake my finger at you? So, since you didn't want to endure that, since you were afraid of being *shouted at,* I didn't know the truth, that Rafferty had information that could bring him back to us. And then you made your third mistake. The one that's almost impossible to forgive."

"Sir?" Ren's face is running with sweat, partially from the strain of maintaining the position, but mostly from fear.

"You lost him. And while you didn't have him in your sights, he met with that reporter. And he told her what he knew. Do you know what that did to us?"

"No, sir."

"It took this entire operation out of bounds. This was supposed to be quick and easy. Threaten the man, set him loose, see what happens, what he finds out, and then take whatever action turned out to be necessary. Maybe nothing, maybe just give him his money and forget about him. Instead, because of you, Kai had to take definitive action tonight. He had to kill that reporter."

"I—" Ren says, and runs out of steam.

"And he hurt his thumb. Didn't you, Kai?"

"It's okay," Kai says.

"No, it's not okay. None of it's okay. It's not *okay* that Ms. Weecherat is dead. Quite apart from the fact that she had children, and no child should lose a parent like that, it means we might have to manage the police, and *that* means that more people will be on the edge of our little circle. Not to mention those who have already been added. The night editor at her paper, for example."

"He can't—" Ren says. "He can't know who it was who—"

"No, he can't. And it wouldn't affect me personally if he did. I'm not the one who's at risk here. You are. Kai is. A couple of people just above you in the company. Lifters and door openers. But I'm supposed to protect my people, aren't I? So your tiny, contemptible act of cowardice puts me in the position of having to behave like a common gangster. It means that Rafferty will almost certainly have to die, since he knows perfectly well that we killed the reporter. This was *not* the way this was supposed to work out." His eyes go to the cigarette in Ren's hand. "Are you planning to smoke that?"

"No, sir. I wouldn't. It's, um . . . it's yours."

"Well, if you're not going to smoke it, what should you do with it?"

Ren says, "Put it out?"

The man in the robe sighs in irritation. "Of course put it out."

"Then . . ." Ren says, "then I can get up?"

"No."

Ren's eyes dart around the room, looking for anything close at hand. "Then where should I—"

"Put it out," the man in the blue robe says, "on your tongue."

MIAOW CLUTCHES THE pen vertically in her fist, even though she has been trained at school to hold it at a slant between her fingers. Looking at the pen, upright as a flag, looking at the dimples in the brown knuckles as her fist moves across the paper, Rafferty sees hours of practice, wiped away by fear. It makes him so angry his mouth tastes of metal.

Miaow's eyes flick back and forth between the note Rafferty wrote and the translation she is making. In English it says, *They can hear everything we say.* She does a final check of her looping Thai script and passes it to Rose, who scans it and shuts her eyes in an expression that looks more like irritation than fear. She opens them and points at the corners of the bedroom, jabs her finger toward the door leading to the living room and Miaow's room, then lifts her palms in a question.

Rafferty shrugs and shakes his head: *Don't know.* He mimes zipping his mouth closed and then takes the pen from Miaow and writes, *We can only say things we want them to hear.*

Miaow says, "Well, duh," and then blanches and covers her mouth.

Rafferty gives her the pen, and she translates, with Rose looking over her shoulder. Even before she has finished, Rose is nodding impatiently, a gesture that means, *Yeah, yeah, yeah.* She takes the pen and begins to write in Thai. Rafferty hates including Miaow in this conversation, but his written Thai is rudimentary at best, and Rose can't read English beyond "Hello" and "I love you," the phrases every bar girl learns to write during her first week on the job, so Miaow is irreplaceably in the middle. Her shoulders brushing against both Rose's and Rafferty's, Miaow follows Rose's moving hand much as Rafferty followed hers.

The three of them huddle on the new blue bedspread Rose just bought, in a semicircle of light thrown by the lamp that stands on the bedside table. All the other lights in the apartment have been turned off. Rafferty has draped a blanket over the air conditioner in the bedroom's only window to prevent light leaks that might be visible from the street.

He is certain that someone is down in the street.

Miaow takes the pen and paper and translates quickly: *How long?*

Rafferty writes, *I'll call Arthit in the morning from the hallway. He'll send someone to find the microphones.* Miaow translates, and Rose nods and writes something. Miaow, reading over her moving hand, nods in agreement and takes the pad almost before Rose finishes. When she is done, Miaow turns it to Rafferty. It says, *Can we get out of here?*

Rafferty shrugs again and takes the pad. He writes, *They're watching.* Miaow reads it and shortcuts the process by jerking a thumb toward the glass door to the balcony and the window with the air conditioner in it and miming binoculars.

Rose surprises Rafferty by scrawling, in very large letters, a word he didn't know she could write. The word is *SHIT.*

Rafferty takes the pen and turns the page over. On the clean side, he writes, *I'll move us soon.* Without even showing it to Rose, Miaow grabs the paper and scribbles *How?* hard enough to rip the paper.

Rafferty writes, *I don't know.*

25

Like He Ate a Grenade

Snarls of dust, smeared windows, grit on the linoleum, the tiny brown cylinders of mouse droppings. In the middle of the floor, a three-inch cockroach, dead and belly-up, its legs folded as precisely as scissors. The smell of damp.

Rafferty says, "It's fine."

"It needs cleaning," says Rafferty's landlady, Mrs. Song. She looks even more worried than usual.

"I'll clean it."

"No, no, no." Mrs. Song pats the air in Rafferty's direction to repel the remark. "I'll have a crew come in."

"Today?"

"*Well*," Mrs. Song says, giving the word tragic weight. The morning light seeps through the dirty windows like sour milk. "Maybe not today," she says.

"That's what I thought. I'll take care of it."

"But you're not *moving*," Mrs. Song says. Change petrifies her. She'd probably be happiest if the building were empty and sealed. She clamps her purse firmly against her side with her upper arm as though she expects it to try to escape.

"No. I want this one and the one upstairs. Both of them."

"But why?"

Rafferty says, "Because people can't see through walls."

AS THE ELEVATOR doors slide closed behind him, Arthit says, "Have you seen this?" A copy of the *Sun* is folded under his arm. He is in street clothes, since Rafferty didn't want the people who are watching the place to see anyone in uniform. Mrs. Song, trailing anxiety like a perfume, has gone down to the utility closet in the underground garage for mops, pails, and cleaning supplies.

"I haven't gone out yet today." Rafferty is holding a roll of paper towels. "But there's no story. The guy who called last night said that there would be no story."

"Oh, there's a story," Arthit says. His mouth is pulled into an inverted U so pronounced that it makes him look like a grouper. He hands the *Sun* to Rafferty, who tucks the roll of towels under his arm to take the paper. It is folded tightly around a front-page piece beneath the headline *SUN* REPORTER KILLED.

Dark spots swarm in front of Rafferty's eyes, and he is suddenly light-headed. He hands the paper back and says, "I can't read it."

"It's who you think it is," Arthit says. "Hit-and-run. Driver fled the scene."

Rafferty pivots away from Arthit, crosses the hall, and kicks the elevator hard enough to dent the door and send a telegram of pain all the way up to his quadriceps. "She had a daughter," he says. His voice feels like it has had knots tied in it. "Seven years old."

"A son, too," Arthit says. "It was a hit-and-run in the most literal sense. The guy who hit her couldn't get the car going, so he climbed out and ran. Which is how we know the car that hit her was a taxi, and that it was stolen."

"So it wasn't an accident. What a surprise. I don't suppose there was a witness."

"It's not in the story, but there was. The driver was short and very wide in the shoulders."

Rafferty looks up quickly. "And?"

"And?" Arthit screws up his face a moment. "Oh, yeah, *and*. He closed the car door on his finger, and he apparently snarled or something, because the witness saw his teeth."

"They were crooked," Rafferty says.

"I'd ask how you know that," Arthit says, "but I don't want to hear the answer."

"Give me the paper."

Arthit hands it to him, and Rafferty drops the roll of towels to the floor and scans the story about Weecherat, then flips through the pages until he comes to the third section. Pan's fund-raiser owns the front page, above the fold. Rafferty tilts toward Arthit the two-column color photo, which shows Adam and Eve from behind, stark naked from that angle, ambling toward a conspicuously horrified crowd of well-dressed millionaires. "Right *here*," he says, putting his fingertip above Captain Teeth's head. "And this is the fucker he works for. I don't know his full name, but his nickname—"

"—is Ton," Arthit interrupts. "How do you know this is the guy?"

"He's got teeth like he ate a grenade. They go all over the place. And it makes sense, because Ton wouldn't talk to me last night."

Arthit takes the paper and refolds it carefully, as though the task were important, as though it were the national flag. He avoids Rafferty's eyes. "That's your evidence? Ton wouldn't talk to you? He'd refuse to talk to the prime minister if he felt like it. And get away with it."

"He didn't talk to me because he knew I'd recognize his voice. He's the guy who ordered me to write the book."

Arthit is still looking at the newspaper. "And you can prove that, of course."

"Check his office. He's on the thirty-sixth floor of whatever building it is. I'll bet you anything you want."

"There's nothing I want," Arthit says. "Which is a good thing, because I'm not making that inquiry."

"Here's what happened: Weecherat files her story. It goes into a computer. The computer has been programmed to flag anything with Pan's name in it. The flag kicks the story to someone at the paper, who calls someone higher up at the paper, who calls Ton. Ton sticks his little warning in my kitchen cabinet, and then he thinks it would be tidier if Elora wasn't floating around with the number of the floor he's on. So he sends Captain Teeth to take care of her."

"Ton is untouchable," Arthit says.

"Oh, *fuck* that."

"Listen to me, Poke." Arthit has crumpled the paper in his fist without even knowing it. "Ton could run over an entire nursery school, on purpose, right in front of me, and back up to get the ones he missed the first time, and I'd probably offer to pay for his car wash. I'm telling you, these people are not accountable. Remember that miserable kid of General Aparit's? Shot two cops and killed one of them in a drug bust at a rave club? He's assistant to a cabinet secretary now. Aparit is a panhandler compared to Ton. It would be worth my job to look cross-eyed at him. And right now, with Noi the way she is, I can't even entertain the fantasy."

Rafferty turns away and looks through the open door of the unoccupied apartment. He hears himself say, "Right." He bends down and picks up the roll of paper towels and pitches it underhand at the floor. The towels unroll clear across the empty room, making the only clean path on the floor. "Here's something else you won't want to do anything about. Weecherat had a tape recorder. My interview was on it. What do you want to bet it's missing?" He hears the elevator doors open and glances over his shoulder, expecting to see Mrs. Song struggling mournfully with an armful of cleaning stuff. Instead it's Lieutenant Kosit, whom he hasn't seen since he dealt the card game that got Rafferty into this mess.

"Pretty impressive stuff," Kosit says, "and expensive, too. Cost maybe eight hundred, nine hundred U.S. apiece. Three of them." He's wearing olive drab shorts and a camouflage T-shirt in green and brown.

"Where?" Rafferty says.

"Center of the ceiling. They bored a little hole for each microphone. Theory is that nobody ever looks up. The holes are only about half an inch in diameter, and just to make sure they wouldn't catch your eye, they glued some kind of white cloth over the openings. The mikes are omnidirectional, sensitive across three hundred sixty degrees."

"Which rooms?"

"Living room, kitchen, bedroom. Nothing in the bathroom or Miaow's room. They feed to a transmitter inside your couch. They unstitched the liner on the bottom, put the thing inside, and tacked the cloth back."

"What's the range?" This is Arthit, and it's purely an instinctive re-action. The moment the question is out, he squeezes his eyes shut and shakes his head.

Kosit throws Arthit an inquisitive glance and then squints down the hallway for the answer. He has a seamed, leathery smoker's face, and the squint creates a fan of deep creases radiating out from the corner of each eye. "Mile? Maybe a little more. So forget finding the listening post. It's somewhere in a two-mile circle of Bangkok. And even if the sun shone straight down through the clouds to show you exactly where it was, you'd probably just find another transmitter to boost the signal and pass it along."

Rafferty has no intention of looking for it. "Nothing in the hallway outside?"

Kosit shakes his head. "No."

"Cameras?"

"No, and it's a good thing. I was quiet, but not invisible." Kosit grins. "You should have heard your wife and daughter, arguing about school and her hair color as though there was nobody else in the place."

Rafferty says, "Her *hair* color?"

"Poke," Arthit says. "What are you going to do about this?"

Rafferty turns back to the filthy, empty apartment. "What do you think I'm going to do? I'm going to take advantage of it."

WHEN DA AND Peep are pushed into the van that morning, there is only one other woman inside. She balances a very dark-skinned, black-eyed child, perhaps two years old, in her lap. The woman with the skeletal child is not there. Da assumes they will wait for her, but the man in the awful blue shirt—what was his name? Kep?—slides the door closed behind her with a bang. It is too angry a sound for so early in the morning.

"Where are they?" Da asks quickly, before Kep can get around the van and climb behind the wheel.

"Who knows? One of the tough men from the business came and got them very early." The child in the other woman's lap tilts its head to one side and trains its enormous eyes on Peep. Peep has been whimpering, fretful at being jostled as he and Da were hurried downstairs, but when he feels the other child's gaze, he goes quiet, and the two of them regard each other like members of some rare species unexpectedly come face-to-face.

"Will she be all right?" Da asks, but before the other woman can answer, Kep pops open the driver's door and slides his bulk onto the seat. An unlit cigarette hangs from his lips. Before he starts the car, he twists back to speak to Da, although he doesn't bother to turn his head far enough to meet her eyes.

"No giving money back today, got it?"

He seems to expect a reply. "I heard you the first time."

"And get off your ass. Don't just sit there."

Anger flares in the center of Da's chest. "I made money yesterday."

Kep throws an arm back and swipes halfheartedly at her, but she easily ducks out of reach. "Listen to me, you snotty little bitch. You make as much as I tell people you make. If you don't want to wind up in some dirt-road whorehouse, you'll be nice to me."

"I'll never work in a whorehouse."

"You remember that when I bring a bunch of my friends by to break you in."

"You have friends?"

The other woman puts a cautioning hand on Da's arm. This time Kep turns all the way around to glare at her. He closes his fist and slowly brings it up into the center of her field of vision. "Women with bruises on their face make money," he says. "If you don't shut your mouth, you'll find out." For a moment Da is too furious to care whether he hits her or not, but the woman squeezes her arm, and Peep chooses that instant to begin to cry. Da lowers her gaze, and after a brief eternity, stretched out by Peep's squalling, Kep turns away and starts the van.

He guns the engine, throwing the two women back against the seats, and then the van hits a pothole. Kep lets go of the wheel with one hand long enough to light his cigarette and say, "There must be a better way to earn a living."

A CARPET TO muffle the echoes, maybe tack a blanket to a wall, hang something over the windows to cover them when the lights are on at night. Some soft, absorbent surfaces. The place sounds like an empty swimming pool, and that won't do. Grab a few chairs, a table. Something to sit on, and around, while they do what they have to do.

Bare minimum.

Once the floors are clean, just fold some more blankets on them. Haul the spare pillows downstairs. If they have to sleep there, which he doesn't think they will, it'll only be for one night. With what he has in mind, they won't have much time for sleep anyway.

Mrs. Song had helped for a while, running water and sloshing around in the bathroom before making her retreat, scattering excuses and tracking water behind her. As soon as the elevator doors had closed, Rafferty had gone into the bathroom for a look, but he couldn't see that she'd accomplished much, other than getting it amazingly wet. So he'd balled up a bunch of the paper towels and scrubbed at the floor, walls, and toilet until he was certain the room wouldn't horrify Rose. He found that the tight coil of anxiety that was wrapped around his heart seemed to ease when he was cleaning.

At least he was *doing* something.

Now, back in the living room, he uses the widest of the brooms to push a quickly growing ridge of dirt across the floor. He can still feel the scrape of it beneath his shoes, but the floor looks better. The air is razor-sharp with ammonia, and the windows are cleaner. A couple of hours more and the place will be almost presentable. Ugly, empty, and not home, but presentable. There's no balcony for some reason, just a window where the sliding glass door is in their own apartment. It could be worse, he thinks, and anyway it's just for a couple of days.

He won't be able to stretch it any longer than that.

He feels eyes on him and turns to see Rose standing in the doorway, her shoulders high and her hands pushed deep in the pockets of her jeans. He says, "No problems?"

"Someone followed us to the school. A dark blue Lexus. Two men in the front seat. They didn't try to stay out of sight."

"They want us to know they're watching."

Rose takes in the room and nods at the clean window. "You've got talent."

"Don't get any ideas."

She steps back, into the hallway. "I've been in the building three or four minutes," she says. "We'd better go upstairs and make some noise."

IT'S SUCH A relief for Rafferty to be back in his apartment, away from that forlorn, filthy space, that he can almost forget about the microphones.

But only almost.

"I'm worried about Miaow," Rose says. She doesn't look particularly worried. She looks like someone deeply focused on filing her nails, which is what she is doing.

His fingers halt above the keyboard, but just for a moment. "You mean the thing with the snake?"

"No. I think that's past. But she's not as happy as she usually is."

"I've noticed. But whatever it is, she'll get over it," Rafferty says for the microphones, without taking his eyes off his laptop. He is making a list, and he pauses to come up with something fatherly. "She's just at an awkward age." This is his third pass at the list, and it gets longer every time. Only Item One remains the same from draft to draft: *Get Rose and Miaow out of the way.*

"She doesn't want to be called Miaow anymore," Rose says, and something in her voice makes Rafferty look up. "She wants to be Mia."

Rafferty frowns a question at her, and Rose lifts her eyebrows and nods. *No bullshit,* in other words. Then she says, "And she's ashamed of being so dark."

Rafferty gives up on his list. "Oh, boy."

"She asked me about whitening creams. She'd like to dye her hair reddish brown, too."

"Yeah, well, I'd like to be Johnny Depp," Rafferty says, "but that's not going to happen either."

Rose says, "Johnny Depp's got a girl. A French girl."

"Not that part," Rafferty says. "I'd like to be Johnny Depp selectively."

"It's easy to make fun of it," Rose says, "but it's important to Miaow. You probably remember, maybe not very clearly, what it was like to be young."

"I'm not that much older than you are."

"Actually," Rose says, "compared to me, you're a big, sheltered baby."

She extends her arms and gives her nails a critical survey. "But we're going to have to figure out what to say to Miaow. She's already worried about being short, and she doesn't think she's pretty. And now she feels like a dark little peasant girl with the wrong name."

"I don't know," Rafferty says. "This seems like mother territory to me."

"No problem. I'm just being polite, sharing the situation with you. I've already decided how to deal with it."

"Yeah? How?"

"I'm going to dye her hair and buy her some whitening cream."

"The hell you are."

"As you said, it's mother territory."

"Well," he says. Nothing authoritative comes to him. Then he says, "What are you going to call her?"

"Whatever she wants."

"Not Harold," Rafferty says. "I draw the line at Harold."

Rose says, "Children need a strong father."

He reviews his list, which now has two items on it, and he's not sure about the second one. "So I've done my part?"

"You're everyone's dream father."

"Okay." He looks at his watch. "It's late enough to start to bother people about this book." He picks up the phone, glances involuntarily at the patch of cloth covering the microphone in the ceiling, and dials a number high up on the yellow list. "Mr. Porthip, please," he says. He covers the mouthpiece with one hand and says to Rose, "The way this guy looks, I think I should talk to him first, or he won't be around."

26

There's Another One Gone

Porthip seems even more frail than he had at Pan's fund-raiser. The enormous office, jammed with Chinese antiques, has an unpleasantly sour smell, like damp, dirty cloth that has been allowed to mildew. The black lacquered desk is bare except for a glass and a matching pitcher of water with slices of lemon floating in it. Ringing the pitcher in a semicircle are seven vials of prescription drugs. Porthip follows Rafferty's gaze and points a knotted, quivering finger at each vial in turn. The skin on his hand is hairless and yellow, the veins like blue highways.

"Pain, pain, nausea, pain, diuretic, antidepressant—if you can imagine that, an antidepressant for death—and these big ones that don't do anything." His voice is taut, making Rafferty think of wire being drawn through a hole too small for it. He is speaking English.

"But you take them," Rafferty says.

"Because I'm supposed to. That's what they're for. They're nothing, but they make me feel better because I take them. They give me the illusion I'm doing something, not just lying down to die."

"You never know."

"If that comforts you, go ahead and believe it," Porthip says. "But

I'll tell you: Every cell in your body knows. You know with every breath you take. You know every time the second hand on your watch goes all the way around, and you think, 'There's another one gone.'"

Rafferty takes a longer look at the man. The face is taut and shrunken, but the tightly cut Chinese eyes are bright with fury, the eyes of an animal in a trap. "What does it make you want to do?"

"Be twenty," Porthip says. "Twenty with a hard dick."

Rafferty says, "I wouldn't mind that myself."

What happens to Porthip's face could be a smile or it could be pain. When it passes, he says, "This isn't what we were going to talk about."

"No. Pan."

Porthip puts both hands flat on the desk. They still tremble. "Are you going to ask me questions, or am I supposed to make a speech?"

"He's a complicated character," Rafferty says, feeling sententious. "I want both the good and the bad in the book. Let's start with—"

"He's as complicated as a cow patty," Porthip says, waving off Rafferty's assertion. "You've got the basics, right? I mean, someone gave you the background: Isaan, poor kid, farmer's son, couldn't read, probably never saw a roll of toilet paper until he was sixteen or seventeen. Came to Bangkok and made his fortune, a little shady at first, maybe, what with the poking parlors, but that was the only route open, since we evil rich control all the access to capital. But he ran circles around us with his native Isaan wit. That's the hero version, how he used all that peasant cunning to make half the baht in Thailand and now he sprinkles them around like lustral water, anointing whole areas of the country, and he's become the Bodhi tree people sit under to find enlightenment."

"Yeah, I've heard all that."

Porthip shakes his head in what could be disgust. "And you've met him."

"Three times."

"What did you think?"

"I don't know. Good and bad, I guess."

"'Good and bad,'" Porthip repeats scornfully. He pours himself a glass of water, the edge of the pitcher rattling against the glass in his unsteady hand. A slice of lemon falls into the glass, and water splashes on the desk. Rafferty wants to help but knows the effort won't be appreciated. "First thing I'm going to tell you . . ." Porthip says, and he raises the glass to his lips and drinks. He holds up a finger. Rafferty waits until the man has swallowed, and Porthip picks up the sentence. " . . . is, don't believe anything he tells you. Not *anything*. If he says it's sunny, buy an umbrella. If he tells you he's giving you something, put your hand over your wallet. He lies every time he exhales."

"Poor people have a different impression. He funds hospitals, he—"

"Bullshit. He never gives away a nickel. He'd steal from a corpse if he could find anybody dumb enough to lend him a shovel."

"So where do these stories come from?"

Porthip allows his eyes to roam over Rafferty's face, long enough for the scrutiny to be rude. He does not look impressed by what he sees. "He's not complicated, but he's smart. Do you understand the difference?"

"I like to think I'm capable of making basic distinctions, yes."

"The whole thing—the outrageous spending, the gold Rolls-Royce, the rough edges, the awful clothes, the beautiful women, the fuck-you attitude—it's all for effect. It's all lies. The philanthropy, which isn't even his money. He never uses a dime of his own. He's got half a dozen backers, guys who are tired of being on the edges, and they bankroll all this crap. He wants to build some little health clinic and pay some quack doctors who couldn't get work at a real hospital if the plague hit, and these guys pony up. If he wants to create a Potemkin village, some feminist paradise where all the women are *empowered* at their looms while the men sit around and drink all day, those guys not only pay for the looms, they buy the goddamn fabric. He's got warehouses full of the fucking stuff. Mice chew on it. It never seems to occur to anyone that the world isn't clamoring for an infinite supply of amateur weaving. It's good for potholders, junk to sell the tourists, but come on, they're making miles of the stuff. You could cover the road from here to Chiang Mai with it. And it would be uglier than the asphalt."

"Why would these people give him money? What's the payback?"

Porthip puts the glass on the desk, hard enough to crack it, and glares at Rafferty. "You know the answer to that, and if you don't, get out of here. You're not worth talking to."

"Power," Rafferty says. "Money."

A wide expanse of yellow teeth, either a smile or a grimace. "Of course. Pan's aiming high. These guys, the ones who are backing him, want to be in the middle of everything. They want access to the well. Because, of course, it's not just *money*. It's a torrent of money, a tsunami of money. They're rich now, but nothing compared to how rich they could be if Pan makes it."

"Makes it to what?"

"Some high national office," Porthip says. "I'm not saying prime minister, but I wouldn't be surprised if that wasn't the ultimate target. Cabinet level anyway."

"He hasn't said anything about that. Not to me, and not publicly."

"He will," Porthip says. "He'll lie about it first, but he will." Porthip dips his index finger into the glass of water and touches it to his tongue, as though to cool it. "Look at the political landscape. Look at what that idiot Thaksin did, paying all those farmers for their votes. The people who raise pigs want to rule the country."

Rafferty says, "Maybe they should have a say in things."

The lower lid of Porthip's left eye begins to twitch rhythmically. "Maybe they should," he says, "but if they ever get it, they'd probably deserve a chance to vote for someone who's *really* what Pan claims to be."

"Which is?"

"Someone who gives a shit."

"So," Rafferty says, "at one point he's a pimp with some massage parlors, and now he owns the rights to trademarks, he's got factories, he's a possible political force. He's somebody that people like you have to put up with. How did he make the jump? What's missing?"

Porthip passes a hand over his brow and closes his eyes. He keeps them closed so long that Rafferty is on the verge of asking whether the man is all right. When the eyes open, they are pointed at the ceiling and the muscles surrounding them are tightly bunched, the left eye still twitching. The man breathes raggedly, catches the breath in his throat, and then lets it out in a rush. He breathes deeply two or three times, and only then does he look back down at Rafferty.

"He owned . . . somebody's soul," Porthip says. The four words require two breaths. He blots perspiration from his upper lip. "He knew something about somebody big. Maybe he did something to put that person hopelessly in debt. Whoever it was, he paid it back by putting up millions and millions. He opened doors. And he kept quiet about it. Makes you think there were only two possible options: give Pan everything he wanted or kill him, and for some reason Pan couldn't be killed. So the little whorehouse owner disappears, and six months later we've got the tycoon on our hands."

"And even someone like you doesn't know who it is."

Porthip swivels his chair ninety degrees so he is looking out the window at the brightness of the new day, and at the sight the muscles of his face soften. Something about the reaction strikes Rafferty as almost infinitely sad. For a moment he thinks Porthip will drop the shield that's been in place throughout the conversation, but what Porthip says is, "Nobody knows. Nobody's talked." He turns back to face Rafferty, the mask of pain tightly in place. "And don't forget, we're talking about years ago. Whoever it was, he could be dead by now."

RAFFERTY DOESN'T EVEN have to look at the yellow sheet to punch in the number. It rings once, and then it is picked up, but the person at the other end doesn't say anything.

"This is stupid," Rafferty says. "If you don't talk, how am I supposed to know I've got the right number? You want me to blab about all this when I don't even know who's on the line?"

"Jutht a minute," says the man on the other end, a voice Rafferty recognizes from the car that sped him away from Miaow's school. But the man sounds like he has a mouthful of potatoes.

A moment later a new voice says, "What is it?"

"What's wrong with the other guy?"

"He ate something hot. Why are you bothering us?"

"I want to tell you that I just wasted an hour talking to Porthip. I'm supposed to be filing some sort of report in a couple of days, and if they're all as uninformative as he is, it's going to be pretty thin."

"That's not our problem."

Rafferty is almost certain the voice belongs to Captain Teeth, Ton's enforcer, next to him in the photo from the Garden of Eden. "I'm supposed to be writing a book here. These are my sources, remember? The ones you gave me. The information value of the conversation I just had was zero. Porthip doesn't like Pan. That sound like a chapter to you?"

"Like I said, not our problem. Make something out of it."

"I'm beginning to wonder about your competence."

"You're beginning—" The other man starts to laugh. "Our *compe-tence*. I'll tell you what. We're competent to make a hole where you and your family used to be. Just do your fucking job. Himself doesn't like excuses." The man hangs up.

Rafferty stands there, weak with anger. What he wants to do is phone Arthit and ask his friend to find out whatever he can about Porthip and Ton, but he knows that's not possible. For the first time since he met Arthit, they might as well be strangers.

Noi, he thinks, with a jolt of despair. He can't even ask about Noi without feeling like he's imposing. And he still hasn't told Rose that Arthit's afraid Noi is planning to kill herself. It's almost enough to make Rafferty's own troubles seem trivial.

Except for Rose and Miaow.

He considers calling Kosit, but the people Arthit fears could obviously erase Kosit from the equation even more easily than they could Arthit, since Kosit is a much more obscure cop than Arthit. The second obvious source of information, newspapers, is also closed to him. He figures it's not just the *Sun* where the computers are programmed to let out a squawk every time someone enters Pan's name. It's easy to see himself sitting in the empty morgue of some paper, suddenly being joined by Captain Teeth and a couple of lifters who specialize in joint dislocation and eardrum ruptures.

He could say it's research, of course. He resolves to hold that option for later.

So.

So, he guesses, that makes it time to eat.

He turns idly in the direction that most of the foot traffic is moving in, looking for someplace where he can get a salad or something light. In this heat he'd rather eat a bowling ball than a chunk of meat. He figures he'll grab a table big enough to write on, clear a space, and go back to work on his list. Maybe start playing with scenarios. He's long known that he thinks more clearly when he writes, that the act of waiting for his hand to finish forming the words slows his thought processes in a way that opens them up, allows him to see three or four possible alternative paths rather than just the most obvious one.

One problem is that there's been no time to reflect. This is Thursday, just minutes into P.M. The card game had been Tuesday night, the phone calls and the abduction in front of Miaow's school had happened on Wednesday morning. Looking back, Wednesday seems a week long: the threats, the abduction, the office suite, leveling with Pan—which he still thinks might have been a mistake, especially in light of what Porthip had to say about him—the meeting with Weecherat and then with Arthit, the encounter at the party with Captain Teeth, the event in Pan's sparkling garden.

Ton. The snake in the cabinet. Miaow's terror. The microphones in the apartment.

And today: Learning about Weecherat's murder. Arthit's remoteness. The fourth-floor apartment, and then Porthip, the dying man, smelling of mold and bitterness behind his desk.

And almost willfully uncommunicative. Why had he been on the list?

The thought stops Rafferty midstep, and someone passes him, brushing him lightly, as though he or she had sidestepped at the last moment in order to avoid bumping into his back. Rafferty glances up as the person passes, but the question about Porthip claims his attention and leads to another question: What if they're all like that? And then to a third: *Does anyone actually want this book written?*

And, if not, what the hell is going on?

But before he can begin to consider that, his consciousness is flooded by a detailed, high-definition visual memory of the person who had brushed past him. The shape of the shoulders, the way he carried himself, the color of his clothes.

The hair.

Rafferty breaks into a run, dodging between people, pushing his way through the crowd and the heat, not seeing anything ahead of him, no one that could be who he thinks it was. An alleyway opens to his right, and he stops.

Alleyways.

If it's who he thinks it was, *if* he went into an alley, *if* he doesn't want to be found, well . . .

He won't be found.

Still, it could have been someone else. It probably was. In Bangkok there must be a thousand people who look like that.

And it doesn't do Rafferty any good to wonder about it. He needs to get to a table, he needs to start writing. He needs to stop reacting and begin to plan. He needs to solve the problem of Rose and Miaow.

TODAY IT'S FLIES.

They land on Da's wrists and hands and ears. They swarm Peep's face and crawl toward the moisture in the corners of his eyes. He swings his fat little fists back and forth, but seconds after the flies take off, they land again. She hears their buzz even over the noise of the crowd, and that thought straightens her spine.

She's grown accustomed to the sound of the crowd.

Was it *yesterday* that it was so deafening?

Was it yesterday that she met that woman across the street, with her skeletal, shining-eyed child? Remembering that the woman and the boy hadn't been in the van that morning, Da scans the sidewalk across the street and sees her. But the boy's not with her.

There's no question that it's the same woman who's sitting there: same color blanket, same long, loose hair, same faded denim blouse. But she's not upright, not up on her knees with her bowl out. She sits hunched over, like someone who's been kicked in the stomach. And in place of the skeletal child, she holds a bundle, tightly wrapped in a blanket.

A passing schoolchild tosses a sidelong glance at Peep. Da has almost stopped noticing how people avoid her eyes; they look at the baby, they look at the bowl, but they don't look at her. She is becoming *used* to this.

Da shakes her head, and Peep stares up at her. She *will not* become used to this.

A schoolchild, she thinks. Kep may be eating. This is the time he disappears to eat; the woman said so.

After three or four minutes of searching the sidewalk for the awful blue shirt, she gets up. The traffic hurtles by, all gleam and glass and chrome and steel. She has not actually crossed a Bangkok street yet, except when many others were crossing, too, but now she is alone. A big *something* goes by, and there is enough open air behind it that she grasps Peep so hard he squeals, and then she steps out onto the pavement. Two motorcycles beep at her and split up, one going behind her and the other in front of her, and when the one that went in front of her is gone, there is room enough between cars for her to run into the second lane. She stops as a truck barrels past and a boy sitting on top of it shouts something down, and then she's in the middle of the street, dripping sweat, watching the traffic come from the other direction. But this time she gets a break, because a bus makes a turn at the corner, stopping all the cars, and she has enough time to crawl across on her hands and knees if she wanted to.

The woman does not look up, not even when Da says, "Hello."

This close, she can see that the bundle in the woman's lap is a baby, not much older than Peep. The woman holds it carelessly, as though it were a newspaper or something else that can't be damaged by letting it roll onto the pavement. The child's eyes are wide and startled, like the eyes of someone who has just learned that people sometimes hurt each other on purpose.

"Are you all right?" Da asks. She sits back on her heels, village style.

The woman says, "Go away."

"Kep's probably eating."

"Who cares? Go away." She has not turned her head, not given Da so much as a glance.

"Where's . . . um, where's . . ." She doesn't know the name of the missing child.

"Gone. I don't want to talk about it." She reaches up and scrubs the palm of her hand fiercely across her cheeks. "Little idiot. He never even learned to button his shirt right."

"Gone where?" People are pushing past them now as the afternoon rush intensifies, but neither of them pays any attention. Their bowls are on the pavement, forgotten.

"I had to button it every morning. Can you believe that? Seven years old and he couldn't—" She stops talking abruptly.

"He's seven? He looks so much younger."

"They let him starve," the woman says. "When he was three, his mother knew he was wrong. He didn't look at things. He didn't learn. So she fed her other kids, and after a while she pushed him out of the house. He didn't get enough to eat, so he stayed small."

"But then how . . . why did you have him?"

"I took him. Nobody wanted him. He just sat and cried because he was hungry. His mother had three healthy kids and no money; she couldn't take care of an idiot. I didn't . . . I didn't have any. Children, I mean. When I ran to Bangkok, I brought him with me."

"I thought they gave him to you."

"No. I was different." She passes her sleeve over her face and sniffles. "I told them that people would give more because he was an idiot. I mean, he wasn't really an idiot, he was . . . he was just a little . . . a little, aaahhh, slow. And he was—" She loses her voice for a second and clears her throat. "He was sweet."

"I don't understand," Da says. "He was yours. You mothered him, so he was yours. Where is he? And why do you have *this* baby?"

"*I told you,*" the woman says in a tone of pure rage. "I told you not to name yours. They'll take him. They take *all of them.* I thought I was safe, because nobody would want him, but I was wrong. I wasn't making enough money. They said he was too stupid, he was a freak, people didn't want to see him on the sidewalk. So they took him away from me."

"Where is he? Why do they take the babies? Where do the babies come from? Can't you get him back?" The questions are tumbling out, and Da has to pause, get a breath. "Where have they taken him?"

The other woman says, "I don't know. I'll never know. Because he's not . . . not normal. When they take yours, and they will, they'll sell him."

Da feels like she has been punched. "*Sell* him."

"Of course, you idiot. What do you think they do with them? Send them to school? Buy them toys on their birthdays? They sell them. They sell them to anyone who wants them, anyone who can afford them. But Tatti—I mean . . . I mean, the boy—I don't know what they'll do with him. No one will see how sweet he is. No one will see that he needs to be loved. They'll just see an idiot who can't button his shirt. He's not worth anything." She bends forward and begins to weep in earnest, the child on her lap wide-eyed and frightened.

"What can I do to help you?" Da asks, and a heavy hand lands on her shoulder. She looks up to see Kep glowering down at her. His red face proclaims several beers, or possibly whiskey, with his lunch.

"What are you doing here?"

"I . . . ah, she seemed upset, so—"

"It's none of your fucking business. You get your ass across that street before I count to ten, or I'll kick you all the way across it." He reaches down and grabs Peep, snatching him from her lap and hauling him up by one arm, and Peep starts to scream. Da is up immediately, reaching for Peep, and when Kep is slow to release the boy's arm, she sinks her nails into the man's wrist.

He yanks his hand back as she struggles against Peep's sudden weight. Kep looks in disbelief at the red welts on his skin. "That's it, you bitch," he says. "You have no idea what you're in for. Now get over there."

With Peep in her arms, she negotiates the traffic, her heart pounding in her throat. She is so shaken she can't follow what's happening around her: It's a series of quick, still, semitransparent pictures as though the world were reflected in a bubble that pops after a moment, and then there's another bubble inside that, and then that pops, and inside that one . . .

Then, somehow, she is on the other side of the road. She spreads her blanket and sinks trembling onto it, absently bouncing Peep against her breast to quiet him. To quiet herself. Across the way, the woman holds her bowl up, her arm raised at the awkward angle of someone imploring mercy, her head sharply down. Kep is nowhere in sight.

When she can keep her hands steady, Da takes her bowl and puts it in front of her on the pavement. Upside down.

27

This Place Was His Forest

First, get Rose and Miaow out of the line of fire. Somehow. Second, separate Ton temporarily from his muscle, even if it's only for personal satisfaction. The muscle is vulnerable, even if Ton isn't. The muscle can be made to bleed. Third, disappear.

Fourth, work out what they really want.

It can't actually be a book. The timing doesn't make sense. If they're worried about Pan suddenly announcing that he's running for office, what good is a book going to do? It'll take months to print and distribute, assuming that Rafferty lives long enough to write it.

Whatever it is, they'll need it faster than that.

He studies the list of names on the yellow sheets, looking for what they have in common beyond their animus toward Pan. All but two, one of whom was Weecherat, are male. All but three are in business, according to the addresses, which are either in care of a company or are suite numbers in business buildings. He tries to pair the names with the faces he saw at Pan's party and realizes they are all approximately the same age, in their late fifties or early sixties. Once again Weecherat was an exception. They probably chose her because she'd written unflatteringly about Pan, and, of course, when they'd put her name on the list, Rafferty hadn't yet heard the number of the floor Ton's office was on. They had no way of knowing he'd try to use that information for insurance.

The yellow scarf comes into his mind's eye, her preoccupation with the drape of the scarf. The way her face had softened when she mentioned her daughter.

He fights down the anger and the guilt and makes notes, just to process the information with both his mind and his hand, to see what links might open up. Doesn't see a meaning behind the patterns, although there's an elusive little flicker there somewhere.

His mind keeps wandering into scenarios, based on assumptions about what it is that Ton and his accomplices might really want. He follows one line of plausibility to its end—a bad end—and backs up and starts over. This time, with slightly different variables, the process takes him to a different end, different but still bad. Start again, factor in a new initiative on his part, and this time the ending is, to view it charitably, ambiguous. Maybe ambiguous is the best he can hope for. Maybe ambiguous should sound good to him.

The tuna salad in front of him has warmed to room temperature as the restaurant has filled and then emptied around him. Now the waitresses straighten the room, squaring the chairs and dusting the seats, laying down new linen, folding napkins and wiping their fingerprints off clean glasses, joking and talking quietly, and glancing over at him from time to time. They notice that he seems to be completely unaware of them, just staring through the window and sometimes making a note in the little notebook in front of him.

And he's cute, one of them says. Is he part Thai? *Hasip-hasip,* fifty-fifty? After a whispered conversation at the far end of the room, the boldest of them takes the matter in hand.

"Have problem?" she says.

Rafferty almost jumps out of his seat. He had no idea anyone was near, much less standing at his elbow. He looks up to see a girl of seventeen or eighteen, cute in a baby-puffy way, wearing the kind of accessories that girls her age in the United States would either scorn as cluelessly uncool or embrace as post-retro irony: Hello Kitty earrings, little butterfly hair clips, a long curved comb at the back of her head, decorated with a row of hearts, to pull the long black hair out of the way.

"Just thinking," Rafferty says, ripping himself, with a certain amount of relief, out of the latest lethal scenario. "Sometimes thinking is the only thing I know how to do."

"Food not okay?"

He's forgotten about the food. He has to look down at it. "It's fine."

"How you know?"

"Excuse me?"

"You no eat." Just a ghost of a smile to acknowledge that she won the exchange, and then it evaporates.

"I thought I was hungry, but I wasn't."

She opens a graceful hand, palm up, slightly curled fingertips a few inches from the plate. "You want I take?"

"Sure. Thanks. Sorry to waste it."

"Not waste," she says. "Can give to kid. You know? Some kid not have eat." She raises the fingertips to her mouth, looking uncertain. "Boss not know."

"Don't worry. I won't tell him." This girl, and others like her, had helped Miaow survive, sometimes with their boss's knowledge and sometimes without, when she was on the street.

When she was being protected by—

The vision of the boy who pushed past him on the sidewalk is suddenly in his mind again. And it brings with it a jumbled confusion of impressions and emotions: kindness and violence, hope and disappointment, failure. Mostly, and most deeply, failure. A failure he has hoped a thousand times to be able to rectify. He has prayed for a chance to rectify it.

But he looks at everything he's facing at the moment, at the danger and the isolation, and his only thought is, *Please, not now.*

THE BOY DOESN'T come.

Da sits there, the inverted red bowl as conspicuous to her as a fire on the sidewalk, terrified that Kep will suddenly materialize, swearing at her, threatening her. Maybe snatching Peep away from her.

She constantly scans the crowd for the blue shirt. Twice she glimpses blue and grabs the bowl and holds it upright, but it's someone else both times. Someone who doesn't look anything like Kep.

She thinks, *I could get up and walk away myself.*

And go where? says a voice in her head. *And do what? You couldn't take care of yourself before, when you were alone. And now look at you, you're stuck with a baby. And you're waiting for this boy? You don't even know anything about him.*

"I do too," Da says aloud, without realizing it. "I saw him disappear." One minute he had been there, and an instant later he wasn't. She had recognized it then. This place was his forest, just as the land around her village had been her forest. She'd grown up there, gotten into danger there, escaped it there. She'd known where to go, how to live there, what was safe and what wasn't. If someone had been lost there, Da would have been the person to trust.

Trust, the voice says. *Why do you think you can trust him?*

Da thinks, Because his face was clean. Because his clothes were dirty but his face was scrubbed. There was something about him that said he was more than he seemed to be. And because she believes that she can sometimes see things in people that are invisible to others.

Blue down the sidewalk. She grabs her bowl and turns it upright. As she watches Kep stride down the sidewalk, she pulls the coins from her pocket and drops them inside. Looking away, as though she doesn't know he's coming to get her, she raises the bowl.

RAFFERTY CLAPS HIS hands twice. With the floor covered by the cheap, worn rug, taken from a dusty room full of stuff that tenants have abandoned over the years, and with blankets tacked to two walls to create a soft corner, the sound of the clap dies immediately. The sheets hung over the windows soak up the echoes, too. When he'd started putting the pieces together, two hours ago, the sound had reverberated with a *spang* like a gunshot in a tunnel. The acoustic revisions were made between trips to the eighth floor every seven or eight minutes to make some noise for the microphones until Rose and Miaow came home, but for the past ninety minutes he's been able to stay on the fourth floor. He's finished making the place functional with a chipped and splintered coffee table flanked by two rattan chairs adopted from the leave-behind room, one of which sags drunkenly to the right, and a wooden stool, painted apple green, with a crack running down the center of the seat that widens when it's sat on and snaps back closed again quickly enough to pinch the sitter's bottom.

Pinch or not, this is better. This will work.

His watch says 4:50. Miaow had been sulky when she peeked into the fourth-floor apartment on her way up, practically rolling her eyes at Rafferty's efforts. For all Rafferty knows, she and Rose are planning her new life, her life as Mia, right now. Father of the year, he thinks, not even realizing that his newly introverted daughter is going through a crisis. When he finds his way out of this mess, he's going to rethink this whole fatherhood thing. He's obviously not doing it right. He knows *nothing* about little girls. And his own father, who abandoned the family when Rafferty was seventeen, didn't provide much in the way of a paternal role model. But he'll do better.

It's comforting to look forward to a time when he can focus on being a better father. When Miaow's problems will be as important to him as they are to her.

"Looks great," someone says. "You've got a real eye for decoration."

Rafferty turns to see Lieutenant Kosit leaning against the edge of the doorway. He is in street clothes, and looped over his thick fingers is the handle of a fancy plastic shopping bag from an electronics shop on Silom.

"I think the blankets provide a kind of unexpected élan," Rafferty says. "Who would ever have believed those colors would go together?"

Kosit says, "No one." He holds out the bag. "You owe me seven thousand baht."

"Jesus. I'm not using it for opera."

"You needed some way to jack it into your speakers, right? Well, that's where they get you. Connectors. That's where they got *you*, anyway." He fishes out a receipt and flaps it in Rafferty's direction. "See? Connectors, twenty-three hundred baht."

"How about we forget the money and I come over and redecorate your apartment?"

Kosit looks around the room with great interest. "Sure. I have a cute little French maid's outfit, all black and white with ruffles. I haven't been able to talk anyone into wearing it."

Rafferty says, "Will you take a check?"

IN THE ELEVATOR Rafferty says, "Seen much of Arthit?"

"Nobody has. He's like the Ghost of the Station. You see him around corners once in a while, but by the time you get there, he's disappeared."

Rafferty sags against the wall. "Hell."

"What's wrong?" Kosit asks. "You two are close. I tried to ask him what was going on, and he practically bit my nose off."

"Problems of some kind. He won't talk to me either."

"Must be bad, then. You guys are like a pair of gloves."

"It's bad. Listen, do whatever you can, okay? Even if he acts like you're imposing and he'd be happy if you fell off the edge of the earth, just sort of take his temperature every so often. He may need help any time, and you know him. He'd rather die than ask for it."

"I know. I mean, *I'm* a guy, but he takes it to ridiculous lengths."

The elevator stops. Before the doors open, Rafferty says, "Remember, don't say anything inside."

Kosit nods and claps a hand to his mouth, and Rafferty crosses the hall and opens the door.

Rose and Miaow are in the living room. A heavy, unmistakably toxic chemical odor punches him in the nose. Miaow is sitting on the hassock with a towel over her shoulders and something slick and gleaming—vegetable oil or petroleum jelly, maybe—spread over her forehead and cheeks. She's as shiny as a potato bug. Rose, who has a mouth full of Q-tips, is wearing rubber gloves and combing something viscous through Miaow's thick hair, which has been parted even more ruler-straight than usual. His daughter doesn't meet his eyes, but she registers Kosit behind him and slams her lids shut as though that could make both men disappear.

Rose says around the Q-tips, "Don't distract me. Whatever you want in the kitchen, you know how to find it."

"Yes, I love you, too. I think it's time for a beer." He gives Kosit raised eyebrows and gets a nod, so Rafferty goes into the kitchen, the bullet holes in the linoleum and the cabinet looking as big as lunar craters, and pops the refrigerator door. "Which do I want?" he asks aloud. "Singha," he says, holding up one finger, "or Tiger?" He holds up another.

Kosit gives him two fingers back, so Rafferty pulls a Singha for himself and a Tiger for Kosit. "And does my brusque little honey want anything?"

"Half an hour without being asked what I want."

"This is wonderful," Rafferty says, uncapping the beers. "We've reached the point in our relationship where we no longer have to be careful of each other's feelings. We're finally finished with all that tiptoeing around the real issues, all those secret resentments." He hands Kosit his bottle and takes a haul off his own. "Our long national nightmare is over at last."

Rose pulls a couple of Q-tips from her mouth and uses them to wipe carefully at Miaow's hairline and then, with the other end, the curl of her ear. "Go away. Go in the other room. This is girl business."

"If you want me—"

"I won't," Rose says.

"—you know where to find me. Just hovering aimlessly at the end of an invisible thread, putting my entire life on hold while I wait to see how I can be of service."

Miaow says, *"Poke,"* in a tone that practically takes the paint off the walls.

"I guess it's unanimous. Okay," he says to Kosit, "the bedroom it is."

The two of them sit on the bed and drink. Rafferty slides open the headboard and grabs a wad of baht. He counts out seven one-thousand-baht notes and hands them to Kosit. Kosit pulls out the receipt again and puts it on the bed, smoothing it with the side of his hand, to show that it's actually for sixty-eight hundred. Then he fishes around in his pockets until he comes out with a sweat-damp clump of smaller bills, which he pries apart with blunt, tobacco-yellow fingers. He hands Rafferty a salad of twenties and fifties and a couple of coins. While Rafferty drops the money uncounted into the compartment in the headboard, Kosit probes his shirt pocket and pulls out a crumpled pack of Marlboros, undoubtedly Korean street fakes, and wiggles his eyebrows in interrogative mode. Rafferty reaches down to the floor on Rose's side of the bed and comes up with the swimming-pool-size ashtray she uses at night. Kosit looks at it so gratefully that Rafferty thinks he might take a bite out of it, but instead he shakes a bent cigarette free and lights up. His face assumes an expression of such relief that Rafferty toys with the idea of lighting one himself, but he muscles it aside. The two men sit in companionable silence in the middle of a miasma of smoke, sipping their beers, while feminine mysteries unfold unwitnessed in the living room.

Finally Kosit stubs out the filter and puts the ashtray back on the floor. He dips a hand into the bag and begins to pull out the items he has bought: two four-packs of long-life AA batteries, a handful of microcassettes, the overpriced connectors, and a glossy box decorated with a photo of a small recorder that Rafferty recognizes, with a pang, as identical to the one Elora Weecherat had used. He takes the box from Kosit, opens it, and shakes the contents free onto the bed. Yes, it's exactly the same. He picks it up, expecting it somehow to be much heavier than it is, and slides open the compartment at the back, where the batteries go. Kosit picks up a thin black cord with a little square power brick at the outlet end and shows Rafferty where the male end of the jack slips into the recorder. He uses his index finger to flick a package of batteries and leans to whisper in Rafferty's ear. "Insurance," he says. It's not much louder than a breath. "In case there's a power outage."

Rafferty nods, but he can't take his eyes off the tape recorder. Weecherat's daughter was seven, she had said. *It's a magical age.*

Whatever it takes, whatever he has to do, he's going to make Captain Teeth pay.

ON THE TRIP to the abandoned apartment house, Da and Peep share the van with the woman and baby they had ridden with in the morning. There is no sign of the third woman. Before Kep gets into the front seat, the woman with the dark baby says, "They're taking her somewhere else. They always move a woman when they change her baby."

"Why?"

"They don't want people talking too much."

Kep climbs in, slams the door, and starts the van without so much as a glance at Da. But three or four times during the long ride, she feels his eyes on her in the rearview mirror. When she looks up to meet his gaze, he holds hers until it becomes necessary for him to pay attention to some kind of static on the road. And then, a few minutes later, his eyes are on her again, weighing her, appraising her. He has never looked at her like this before, and it brings a warm, faintly dirty-feeling prickle to her neck and cheeks, as though she has not washed in several days.

She stops checking the mirror.

When he pulls to a stop in the dirt yard, the first day's routine is repeated. As the women get out of the van, Kep holds out a heavy envelope to each of them. Each of the women empties into the envelope with her name on it all the money she has taken in, and Kep adds the bills he has seized during the day.

He adds no bills to Da's envelope.

"Wait," she says as he licks the flap.

Kep says, "Shut up."

"You took eighteen hundred—"

Kep gives her a flat gaze. He looks sleepy. "I don't remember that. Anybody see you give it to me?" He runs his thumbs over the moistened flap, sealing the envelope. Then he pulls the envelope back and brings his hand around, slapping her across the face with it.

It's not a particularly forceful slap, but all the coins in the envelope have slid to the end that is moving fastest, and the hard weight of the jumble of coins strikes her cheekbone with enough force to jar her and bring tears to her eyes. Blinking to clear her vision, she takes an inadvertent step back, almost a stumble, and comes up against the hot, unyielding surface of the van. Kep follows her, his nose practically pressed to hers, and the sleepy look has been replaced by something dark and tightly focused, and Da recognizes it, with a sharp, sinking feeling, as joy.

"I *told* you," he says. "You make as much as I say you make." She can smell the alcohol on his breath, and out of the corner of her eye she sees the other woman backing away with a hand placed protectively over the eyes of the child at her chest. Da curves her spine, pulling her waist and pelvis away from him as far as she can, not because she fears him sexually but to make space for Peep, who is beginning to squall in alarm. "You've made almost nothing in your first two days," Kep says. "Barely enough to feed yourself. And you haven't been nice to me."

"I don't—" Da begins.

"We could get along much better," Kep says, and he brings up a hand and brushes the backs of his fingers over her cheek. "Up to you. You can be nice to me, or maybe we should take the kid and give him to somebody else."

She knows he sees her eyes widen in alarm, but she tries immediately to wipe it out. The only way to handle a bully, she has learned, is with a quick kick. She spits into her free hand and scrubs the cheek where he touched her. Then she snaps, "Fine," and holds the baby up. "Take him now. He's wet and he stinks, and I'm sick of him. Here."

Kep has backed up as she thrusts Peep at him, and he takes another step back with her pursuing him, holding Peep at about the level of his face. "Take him," she says. "Do me a favor and take him. I'm sick of him, I'm sick of the whole thing. Take him. You can eat him for all I care." She keeps pushing Peep at him, hearing the child squeal and seeing the spark of panic in Kep's blunt, dark face, and she knows that he's frightened. He can get into trouble over this, she realizes, losing a new beggar, having to take back the child. It's a problem, and the man in the office won't appreciate a problem. Kep has put two feet between them now, and she uses it. "Here," she says, holding Peep out and turning halfway away, as though to walk to the road. "I'm leaving. Is that what you want? You want me to leave?"

There is no response, and she turns to Kep and sees him looking not at her but up at the windows on the second story of the building. There are faces there, looking down, watching everything that's happened. Some are laughing. Others stare openmouthed, waiting for the resolution.

And Da knows, sure as a fist in the stomach, that she has failed.

Kep can't lose this kind of face in front of the others. She no sooner realizes this than she feels his fingers dig into the muscles at the sides of her neck. "Don't be in such a hurry," he says. He squeezes hard enough for her knees to go weak. "We've just begun our talk. And you're not going anywhere, you little bitch. I've got someplace special for you tonight."

He knots her blouse in his hand and half drags her around the van and toward the front door. Da struggles, but she can only do so much without dropping Peep. Finally she grasps the child with one arm and reaches out and twists her fingers through Kep's thick hair. She yanks hard enough to pull some of it out.

And he rounds on her, his face flaming, and hits her in the face with his closed fist. The blow snaps her head to the left, and her ankles tangle as she tries to step back to keep her balance, and she goes down, falling sideways to the left. It takes everything she has to land on her back, with Peep on top of her. The child is screaming. There is blood in Da's mouth, salty and warm.

"You like to pull hair, huh?" Kep says. He is so furious that his eyes have practically disappeared. He knots his fingers into Da's hair and hauls her to her feet. Then he drags her through the door and into the corridor and pushes her up against the wall on the left while he fishes in his pants pocket for something. When his hand comes out, it holds a jingling ring of keys. He chooses one and slips it into the lock on one of the doors that were closed the night Da first came into the building. He pulls the door wide, puts a hard, heavy hand on the back of Da's neck, and shoves her through the door into the dim room. Then the door slams closed, and she stands there, swallowing blood and aching, the baby crying with all its being, in total darkness.

She hears the click of the lock.

28

The Queen of Patpong

This is silly," Miaow says. She has been even crankier since Kosit saw her getting her hair dyed. The newly reddish hair, still slightly damp from the post-coloring shampoo, looks to Rafferty like a wig. He has to make a continuous effort not to stare at it.

He fights a surge of irritation. "I don't care. Just do it. And don't try to win an Oscar, okay? All you're doing is talking to your mother."

Miaow says what she's supposed to say: "I've got a lot of homework." Her tone is so flat she sounds like she's reading.

Rafferty gets up from the green stool, which pinches him good-bye. He has to move around for a second or he'll explode. When he has his breathing under control and all the little black spots have stopped swarming in front of his eyes, he says, "But not winning an Oscar doesn't mean we're going to act like we're dead either. It just means we sound normal. We're going to do this until I'm happy with it, if it takes until the sun comes up." He looks at his watch. "It's twenty past eleven, and even if we get all of it right the first time, it's going to take us until one or two. It's up to you, Miaow. Either you can help with this and get it over with, or you can sit here all night long."

"Poke," Rose says.

Rafferty holds up both hands. "We're *doing it*, Rose. And that means Miaow's doing it. As far as I'm concerned, we can all sleep on the floor down here, but we're getting this done."

"You don't have to be a jerk about it," Miaow says.

Miaow is on the wobbly chair in front of the pink blanket, and Rose is on the solid one. The tape recorder is on the battered coffee table. More than an hour ago, they all said good night to one another upstairs, and then Rafferty led them to the elevator and down to the fourth floor. Until the anger picked him up and towed him around the room, Rafferty was balanced on the stool. Now he goes to the table and sits on the threadbare carpet, in the least confrontational stance he can adopt.

"We're in some trouble," he says to her. "I don't want to go into detail, but it's about that book, okay? Just take my word that what we're doing is important, that I wouldn't be asking you to do it unless it was important. Do I often ask you to do things that aren't important?"

"All the time," Miaow says. "And I do them."

"Then put yourself out there one more time and do this one for me, too. And then, someday, you can ask me to do something stupid, and when I don't want to do it, you can remind me that I owe you one."

Miaow says, "Promise?" This is her kind of currency.

"Absolutely. Here, in front of Rose and everything." Without taking his eyes from hers, he pushes the "record" button, counts silently to three, and says, "I like the hair."

"Really?" She puts both hands against it, palms down, and smooths it. "You're not just trying to make me feel better? You don't think it looks dumb? And fake?"

Rose says in Thai, "It's not supposed to look real, Miaow, not any more than lipstick is. It's *stylish*. And it catches the light well. Lots of highlights."

"Honest? I mean, you really think so? Do you think the kids at school will, um . . . ?"

"If they don't like it," Rafferty says, "it'll just be because they're envious."

"Oh, come on," Miaow says, but she looks happier than she has all night long.

Rose says, "It makes you look older."

Miaow grabs the thought with both hands. "How much older?"

"Ten," Rose says, and Miaow's face falls. "Maybe eleven."

"Eleven." Miaow's expression is deadly serious, and Rafferty suddenly realizes there are several conversations going on at the same time.

"Why is that important, Miaow?" he asks. "What's so magical about eleven?"

"I, um . . ." She looks down at her lap. "I didn't want to tell you this until I was pretty sure, you know? I didn't want to be the kid who yelled . . . who yelled, uhhh . . ."

"Wolf?"

"Yeah. Wolf." She still hasn't looked up. "What's a wolf?"

"It's like a tiger, but not. Go ahead with the story."

"Well, Mrs. Paris, that's my teacher?" Her head comes up halfway, and her eyes go back and forth between Rafferty and Rose.

"We know Mrs. Paris," Rose says.

Miaow finds a thread loose on the elastic waistband of her pajamas and picks at it, giving it all her attention. With her head down, she says, "Well, I've . . . um, I've been having some trouble in class."

"Really." Rose's voice is cool. "What kind of trouble?"

"Just, you know." Miaow wraps the thread around her index finger and tugs at it. "Uh, talking, writing notes to other kids, drawing a lot, making jokes when I shouldn't. Going . . . um, going to sleep."

Rafferty says, "Going to *sleep*?"

"Only twice." Miaow lets go of the thread and holds up two fingers.

"But your grades," Rose says. "Your grades are better than ever. They're practically perfect."

"That's what Mrs. Paris says. She says—" Miaow grabs a breath. "She says I'm not paying attention in class because I'm ahead of the level. Because it's too easy for me. Even though it's fourth grade and I've only been in school three years." She is wearing her bunny pajamas, looking all of five to Rafferty, although apparently this is not the time to point that out. "Anyway, about a week ago, she—Mrs. Paris—said she thought maybe I should skip up to fifth grade."

Without thinking, Rafferty says, "You're shitting me." Rose's glance hits the side of his face like a slap, and he amends it to, "I mean, that's amazing."

"But she wanted to talk about it first with the Dragon—sorry, Mrs. Satharap, the principal. And she did, and the Dragon said it was okay and that she was going to talk to you about it. That was yesterday? So she'll probably call tomorrow. And, I mean, I'm really happy about it, but . . . but . . ."

"But what?" Rafferty says. "You *should* be happy about it. I never got asked to skip a grade."

"But I'm so *short,*" Miaow says. "I'm a *baby.* And everybody's practically *eleven,* and I barely look nine. I'm a pygmy. And I can't get any taller, and I'm going to be in the class with all those really big kids. So I thought . . ."

"Oh, my gosh," Rafferty says, having rejected half a dozen less acceptable expressions of delight. "I'm so *proud* of you. Fifth grade. My God, you'll be in junior high before I have to shave again."

Rose says, "Do the girls in fifth grade wear makeup?"

"*Rose,*" Rafferty says.

Miaow looks at Rose as though she's just turned into a Christmas tree. Her eyes are shining. "A little."

Rafferty says, "*How* little?"

"Like, you know"—Miaow passes the tip of her index finger over her upper lips—"a little lipstick, kind of pale, and maybe some—what do you call it?—some stuff on their eyelashes."

"It better be very pale," Rafferty says.

"Poke," Rose says, "it's not going to surprise anybody that Miaow has lips."

"That's not the point."

Rose says, "What *is* the point?"

"The point," Rafferty says, knowing he has no chance whatsoever of prevailing in this discussion, "is that I'm proud of Miaow, but I'm not having her going to school looking like the Queen of Patpong."

Rose bursts out laughing. "The Queen of—" And she's laughing again, and then Miaow starts to laugh.

"Okay, okay," Rafferty says. "Not the Queen of Patpong. But, you know, too much makeup on a young girl looks . . . um, tarty." And at the word "tarty," Miaow laughs even harder, her arms crossed low over her stomach.

"Trust me, Poke," Rose says. "Mia will be beautiful." The name "Mia" ends Miaow's laughter as though a door has been shut on it. "Your own mother would like the way she's going to look."

"That's not actually much of a recommendation," Rafferty says. Then he says, "Mia?"

"You mean," Miaow says to Rose, with a quick detour glance at Rafferty, "you mean I can buy some makeup?"

"Tomorrow," Rose says. "I'll go with you tomorrow." She slides her eyes to Rafferty, daring him to say anything. "Does that sound okay, Mia?"

An hour and a half later, Rafferty turns off the tape recorder, and they take the elevator upstairs and go to bed for the second time, more happily than they had the first time.

"SOMEONE'S UP," CAPTAIN Teeth—Kai—says. He's had the phones on so long that he's stopped feeling them against his ears. "I hear moving around."

"So someone's going to the bathroom." Ren is stretched out on the couch, facing the cushions on the back, with a throw blanket over him. The air-conditioning in the big house is more than he can take. "Give up for the night. You trying to earn points or what?"

"Fuck you," Kai says, without much heat behind it.

"Anybody flushed yet?" Ren speaks carefully, but his tongue feels as if a nail's been driven through it, and to Kai it sounds like he's got rocks in his mouth.

"No mikes in the bathroom, remember?" Kai says. "She can be a little bitchy, huh?"

"Who? What do you mean?"

"This afternoon. When she told him to go in the other room and leave her alone. Kind of bitchy."

"It'll add spice." Ren plumps up the throw pillow beneath his head. "When she's tied to the bed. Beauty's fine, but spice is better. You want it a little hot."

Kai shakes his head. "Never happen."

"Stop listening to that crap. Nothing's going on. Just let it record. I'll fast-forward through it tomorrow. Get some sleep."

Kai takes off the phones. "You going to stay here?"

"I think so. They get up early. The little girl's up before seven. And that way, when Four-Step comes down from upstairs, he sees me sitting here being vigilant."

"Up to you," Kai says, rising. He stretches.

Ren pulls the blanket higher so it covers his shoulders. Unfortunately, that exposes his feet. He says, "Do you really think we're going to have to kill them?"

"After what happened to the reporter?" Kai says. "Sure."

29

So He Likes Sad Music

She has no idea what time it is when Kep comes for her. The room has no windows, and she has nothing to help her gauge the passage of time. It could be midnight, it could be three in the morning when she hears the singing.

The first sound to get her attention is an engine. It can't be the van; it's too loud. Probably a motorbike. She hears it approaching, out on the street, and she thinks of the moto driver who brought her here, only two nights ago, kindly waiting to make sure she was in the right place. But the bike doesn't go past and fade in the distance. It gets louder, and then it drops to an idle, and over it she can hear him singing. He is obviously drunk.

An Isaan song. It surprises her. She would have figured him for Bangkok pop, some stupid jangly song about love and pretty girls. Instead it's an Isaan song about losing a child to the city, a daughter who has gone away.

So he likes sad music. So . . . tough.

She's spent her time in the room getting to know it by touch, and she is familiar with every square inch of it. It had been used for storage by the builders. Probably all three downstairs rooms were; probably that's why they have doors with locks on them.

What was stored in this room was lumber, mostly scraps. Her heart had leapt when she found the wood, and she had passed her fingers over every surface in the room, hoping for a hammer, a screwdriver. A knife. But there was only wood. Not even any with nails in it.

The first thing she has to do when she hears the singing is to get Peep out of the way. He had fallen asleep in her lap, so she gets up slowly and edges four or five steps to the right, where there is a large wooden box, which she turned upside down to create a flat, raised surface. After turning it over, she had pushed it against the wall to make it more secure. She has already folded her blanket and put it there, and now she lays Peep in the center of the blanket and feels for the big pieces of wood.

Outside, Kep cuts the engine and sings louder. His voice is true, the notes solid. The child who went to the city does not send letters. Da's mother sang this song sometimes.

The wood is right where she put it, leaning against one end of the box. Each piece is about a meter long and as thick as a man's arm. She takes the four pieces she already selected and builds a square perimeter of wood around Peep. There's no way to anchor them to the top of the box, but she thinks the wood will at least prevent him from rolling over the edge.

She hears boots on the steps that lead up to the building's door.

The hinges of the door to the room are on her right and the door opens in, so it will swing to the right. There is no light in the hall, and the moon, as far as Da can remember, is just a sliver. It will be dark, unless he has brought a light with him.

No way to know about that. No advantage to worrying about it.

The piece of two-by-four, about a meter long, is propped against the wall to the left of the door. It's heavier and rougher than she remembers, and her fingers are too short to wrap around it securely, but she's invented a grip that works by interlocking her little fingers.

Scuffing in the hallway, like sand between teeth. In the last line of the song, the child comes home so changed that her own mother doesn't recognize her. Kep slows it down and packs it with heartache. He sings very well.

Da steps to the left, stopping near the wall, her eyes on the bottom of the door, looking for a spill of light, anything to tell her whether he's carrying a flashlight. If he is, he'll see her. But he'll also have only one hand free. She brings the two-by-four up over her right shoulder and waits.

Key in the lock.

Nothing.

Then the door opens *fast,* banging against the wall, and Da swings the piece of wood with an effort that begins at her ankles. But it sails through space, hitting nothing, until it cracks against the frame of the door, having passed straight through the place where Kep's head should have been, and the force of the impact flips the piece of wood out of her hands, and then the flashlight comes on and blinds her.

"Awwwww," Kep says. "You waited up for me." He kicks the piece of wood aside. "Don't pick it up," he says, "or I'll take it away and beat your teeth in with it." He pans the room with the light, fast sweeps to right and left, and then brings it back to her face. "Where's the little monster?" He leans to his right until his shoulder hits the doorframe, almost missing it. He's drunker, Da thinks, than he knows.

"Asleep," she says, backing away. There is a pile of wood behind her.

"Good. No interruptions." He points the light at the concrete floor for a moment. "Not too comfy, huh? Where's your blanket?"

"Under Peep." The heel of her shoe has touched the edge of the woodpile.

"Well, up to you. He can have it or you can. You're going to be on the bottom. You want to get your back dirty?"

"I'm not getting my back dirty."

"Yeah? You wash the floor or something?"

"If you touch me," she says, "I'll mark you for life."

"I don't think so. Look here." He shines the light down at himself. His left hand flashes silver, and the flash turns into a long, curved knife.

Da reaches behind her, her fingertips brushing pieces of wood, just odd pieces, nothing with any weight to it. She says, "Are you ready to kill me?"

"Oh, don't be silly. I won't have to kill you." He brings the knife up and wiggles it from side to side. "You know that web between your thumb and your first finger? You got any idea how *much* it hurts when that gets cut? I mean cut deep? You're going to be very surprised. And then you'll do anything I say not to get the other one cut."

There's nothing behind her that she can use. She brings both hands forward, arched into claws. Then she registers surprise, looks past him, over his shoulder.

Kep laughs. "Oh, yeah," he says. "Right. And I turn around and look behind me, like I haven't seen ten million stupid movies. Like I haven't—"

Da sees a blur of dark motion and hears something that sounds like a coconut hitting the ground from a high tree, and Kep's knees turn to water and he pitches forward flat on his face, the flashlight spinning on the floor, lighting the room, the boy from the street, the room, the boy from the street.

30

You Couldn't Comb It with a Tractor

I have a stomachache," Miaow says.

It is 6:45 A.M., and she is fully dressed: jeans with an acute crease, which she irons in herself because she's never satisfied with the way the laundry does it, and a bright red T-shirt featuring the Japanese teenage girl samurai Azumi. Her bunny slippers are on her feet, but her shoes are lined up beside the front door like well-trained pets. Rafferty sits at the kitchen counter, grimly waiting for the coffee to drip, and if someone challenged him to describe his own clothes without looking down, he'd fail completely.

"Sorry to hear it." His pre-coffee voice is, as always, a croak. "Do you feel well enough to go to school?"

"I don't think so. I really hurt." She goes to the counter and takes the can of Coke he's pulled out for her and pops the tab.

Rafferty says, "Alka-Seltzer? Good idea," and watches her down about half of it and then lower the can. She burps discreetly. Breakfast.

The door to the bedroom opens, and Rose, who is rarely at her best before noon, feels her way into the living room. She regards the two of them without conspicuous goodwill and squints defensively at the red of Miaow's T-shirt. She is leaning against the wall, so loose-limbed she looks as though she plans to go back to sleep standing there, but she is dressed to leave the apartment, in a pair of white shorts and one of Rafferty's freshly laundered shirts. Her hair has been slicked back with damp hands, but it's still a gloriously anarchic tangle.

"Miaow's not feeling good," Rafferty says, getting up. At the sink he runs hot water into a cup that already holds two heaping tablespoons of Nescafé and stirs it quietly, trying not to make a clinking noise with the spoon.

"Me neither," Rose says furrily. "My stomach hurts." She watches Rafferty cross the living room with the cup in his hand. When he gives it to her, she does something with the corners of her mouth that she probably thinks is a smile.

"I'm feeling okay," Rafferty says on his way back to the kitchen. He pours just-dripped coffee into his cup. "Did you two eat anything last night that I didn't?"

"The spring rolls," Miaow says.

The bottom half of Rose's face is hidden by her cup, but she lowers it long enough to say, "Right."

Rafferty swallows the day's first coffee. An invisible film between him and the rest of the world begins to dissolve. "That's probably it. You both look a little punk." He knocks back half of the cup and picks up the pot with his other hand. Miaow goes to the door, kicking off the bunny slippers, drops to her knees, and pulls on her sneakers. Rafferty continues, "They probably sat too long, maybe under heat lamps. Maybe you guys should both go to bed for a while, see how you feel in a few hours."

"All right," Miaow says, opening the front door.

"Don't make a lot of noise, okay?" Rose says. She sounds sleepy and irritable, and it's not an act. "I want to sleep."

"I'll work on my notes for the book. That'll be quiet." He drinks again and heads for the front door, which Miaow is holding wide. "You two go to bed. Get some rest. You won't even know I'm here. I promise."

Rose precedes him through the door, cup in hand, and Miaow closes it quietly behind him as he punches the button for the elevator. Two minutes later, down on the fourth floor, Rafferty inserts a new cassette and pushes "record" again.

DA WAKES ON a village farmer's schedule, maybe six in the morning, and finds herself on her back, looking up at a rough wooden ceiling. After a moment shaped like a vague question, she rolls over to see where she is.

The room is dim, with interruptions of brilliance. Sunlight shoulders its way through the cracks between the planks that make up the walls. When she withdraws her focus from the vertical strips of glare, the gloom resolves itself into backs, seven or eight of them, between her and the nearest wall. Peep is asleep beside her, nestled up against a child Da has never seen before.

She smells children, none too clean, but not filthy either. Just the slightly salty pungency of child's sweat. She could be back in the village.

Suppressing a grunt of effort, she sits up and looks around. The room is full of sleeping children, literally wall to wall. The floor beneath Da's hand is packed earth. It takes her a few seconds to assemble the pieces in her memory. The sad song, the light in Kep's hand, the silvery fire of the knife, the blur of motion behind him, the sound of the stone hitting his head. The stone that turned out to be in the toe of a sock. And the boy standing in the doorway when Kep went down.

She had quickly picked up the flashlight and snapped it off. She was certain that the sound of the motorcycle and Kep's singing had awakened the others in the building, and the light seemed dangerous. The boy had nodded acknowledgment and then made a cradling motion with his arms: the baby. By the time Da had Peep hugged to her chest and the blanket folded over one shoulder, the boy had pulled the ring of keys from Kep's pocket. He rolled the man farther into the room so the door could swing shut without hitting him. Then he motioned Da into the hallway, closed the door, and locked it. She had followed him outside into the night. Without even looking back at her, he climbed onto a motorcycle that had to be Kep's and started it with one of the keys on the ring. He waited until she climbed on. As he pulled the bike away from the building with her hanging on behind, she looked back to see the pale shapes of faces at the windows.

Then there had been miles of Bangkok unrolling on either side of her and sliding by, bright lights and tall buildings, all of it looking alike to Da. The noise of the bike, the wind filling her eyes with tears. The boy, whiplash-lean in front of her, Peep cradled to her chest. Now and then a last-minute zigzag between cars, making her gasp as the boy laughed. Then the streets had gotten narrower and darker, and they began to slope slightly downhill, and soon there was the river, broad and black and spangled with reflected light.

He had parked the bike and climbed off, then brought his arm way, way back to sling the keys in a long, high arc that ended with a splash in the water twenty or thirty yards distant. The two of them had walked from there, a kilometer or more, along the edge of a road that paralleled the river, both of them looking down the mud-slick bank, seeing the occasional rough wooden structure in the spaces between the build-ings that are increasingly fencing in the River of Kings. Above one of the shacks, the boy had turned to her and taken Peep from her arms and tucked him into one elbow with a practiced gesture, then grabbed her hand with his own and led her down the path. A rusted latch, the creak of a wooden door, and then twenty, maybe twenty-five sleeping children. Here and there, half-open eyes shone at them, and she heard the soft sound of breathing.

He had not spoken a word to her the entire time. He led her, stepping over the sleeping forms, to a corner far from the door. He indicated the open space and whispered, "Sleep. We'll talk tomorrow."

She had whispered, "They can't find—"

"No," he had said. "Nobody knows we're here."

She had dropped off almost before she was finished making certain that Peep was comfortable.

THE DOOR TO the shed opens, just a few inches, and the room brightens. He looks in, his eyes going straight to her. When he sees her sitting up, he puts a silencing finger to his lips and motions her to come out. Being careful not to jostle the children on either side of her and Peep, she gathers the baby to her and stands, stiff from a night on the ground, and threads her way between the sprawled children to the door. Here and there, kids roll over and mutter, but they quickly lapse back into sleep. Peep throws out an arm but doesn't open his eyes.

"They stay up late," the boy says after he closes the door. "They need to sleep when they can. If you have to go to the bathroom, there's a hut around the side. I'll wait for you."

"Thank you," she says. She has taken eight or nine steps when she turns back to him. "My name is Da," she says. "What's yours?"

The boy says, "I'm Boo." He looks even slighter in the bright morning light. He can't have an ounce of fat on his body, and once again she is struck by the concentration of life in the tight-cornered eyes. "When you come back, we'll get something to eat."

The hut is the most primitive kind of toilet, just a hole in the earth with four walls built around it and a length of cloth hanging in the open doorframe. There is no roof, but even without one the reek is overwhelming. Da looks down in the hole, as village children learn to do, not eager to squat over a snake or a poisonous spider, and is surprised to see water only a foot or so beneath the edge of the hole. Then she thinks, *The river,* and takes care of her needs. She unwraps Peep and takes off his soiled diaper, suddenly realizing that she'd left the shopping bag with the clean diapers, with the towel, with the milk and whiskey, at the beggars' apartment house.

Well, there's no way she can put the old one back on him. She folds it and drops it into the hole, then cleans him up with paper from the roll beside the hole and totes him back outside with his bottom bare to the breeze. When she comes around the corner, Boo sees Peep and grins. It is the first time she has seen him smile. She feels herself smile back at him, and her heart lifts. Just for a moment, she isn't worried about anything.

"Cute butt," Boo says.

"It works, too. I have to get some diapers and a couple of towels and some of those little packets of wet tissues, and—"

"Relax," he says. "There's a Foodland a few blocks that way."

"Open this early?"

"Foodland is like Bangkok," Boo says. "It never closes." They are climbing the path, Boo first and Da following. The day opens around them as they get higher, the river flowing below and buildings rising ahead. The mud has a fetid smell, but as they approach the top of the bank, it gives way to the stench of exhaust. Da prefers the smell of the mud. Boo looks back over his shoulder at her. "How old are you?"

"Seventeen. What about you?"

"Fourteen. Or maybe fifteen. There was kind of a disagreement about when I was born."

"Who disagreed?"

He glances across the road and raises his eyebrows to indicate a lane that runs off it, away from the river. "My sister and my brother."

They cross the road and enter the lane, lined on both sides with old-style Bangkok buildings, shopfronts at street level with one or two stories rising above them. "Where are they now? Where are your parents?"

Boo says, "Gone," in a tone that does not encourage further discussion. "Up here about half a block," he says. "The woman makes good noodles."

"How do the kids eat?"

He stops and waits until she is beside him, and the two walk on together. "We work with some cops," he says. "I go to the places where the guys go who are looking for children, and I talk to them, I tell them I have what they want. Then I take them to look at the kids—the ones you saw asleep in there—and they pick out the ones they want. We get a room at a sex hotel and deliver the kids. Two minutes later the cops bang on the door."

Da can hardly believe it. "And the men go to jail?"

"No. The cops are crooked. They take all the guy's money and drag him to an ATM to get more, and then they tell him if he doesn't leave Thailand the next day, they'll lock him up forever. They pay me, maybe thirty, forty dollars, depending on how much the man had. Sometimes more. They keep most of it."

"The man doesn't get arrested?"

"No, but he's out of Thailand. And the kids can eat."

They walk as Da considers it. There's not much traffic yet, and the lane is almost peaceful. "Who thought of it?"

"I did."

"How did you find the cops?"

He gives her a quick glance. "You mean crooked ones?"

"Yes."

He laughs. "What's hard is to find straight ones."

Small bright plastic chairs, red and blue, are drawn up on the sidewalk, flanking a sloping table covered in a burnt-orange oilcloth. A frilly, smooth-trunked tree provides shade. Over a charcoal fire burning in a black metal drum at the curb, a wok smokes and sputters, and four people are already slurping out of faded plastic bowls. The smell of the food makes Da realize she's starving, and that Peep must be, too. "I've got to get something for Peep," she says.

"After you eat. One thing you learn on the street is to take care of yourself first. You're no good to anyone unless you're strong." He waves at the woman beside the fire, broad and brown and sturdy, who gives him a bright good-morning smile and starts throwing things into the wok without asking what he wants.

"Your girlfriend?" she shouts, stirring in some chopped garlic and a handful of cilantro.

Da is surprised to see Boo blush.

"Look how shy," the woman says, laughing. She pours liquid down the sides of the wok, and fragrant steam billows up as the others at the table, three men and a woman, laugh, too. "Such a handsome boy, if he'd only get his hair cut. Honey," she says to Da, "cut it while he's asleep if you have to."

"I just need to comb it," Boo says. His face is scarlet.

"You couldn't comb it with a tractor," the woman says. This time Da laughs with everyone else, and after a moment Boo smiles, too.

"I have very fresh chicken this morning," the woman says. "An hour ago it was a customer."

"Two of everything," Boo says. "Except jokes."

"You should always start the day laughing." The woman is throwing things into the wok with both hands. "If you don't, you'll end it crying, my mama used to say." She looks at Da again and says, "Isn't *she* pretty?"

There's unanimous agreement among the customers, and it's Da's turn to blush.

Da sits there, in the shade, smelling the food, watching the woman's sure, quick hands and listening to the flow of chatter and laughter, and suddenly the entire scene blurs and ripples, and she is surprised to realize that she has to wipe her eyes.

"Don't cry, honey," the woman calls out. "He's not *that* ugly."

"I'm sorry," Da says, drying her cheeks on her T-shirt. "I just felt like I was back home."

WITH ANOTHER NINETY minutes on tape in the apartment downstairs, and with Rose back in bed and Miaow reading in her room, Rafferty has time on his hands. When he came home the previous evening, he'd been able to spot two of the people watching the apartment. He'd guess that there's one more, one assigned to each of them. The third one had undoubtedly been behind Rafferty, following him, and probably peeled off when he saw Rafferty was going home, probably called the others for confirmation that Rafferty had actually arrived and entered the building. There's not that much traffic on Rafferty's *soi*. No point in the follower drawing attention to himself.

Probably two shifts, possibly even three, since apparently money is no object. Not much use trying to memorize all the faces when they'll change in a few hours. He figures that they've chosen their surveillance spots and that by and large they'll stick to them, so he'll keep an eye on those places. He needs to find spot number three.

And soon. His best guess is that he can continue for another day, two or three at most, to do a convincing imitation of someone who thinks he has a book to write. If they're unconvinced, there's nothing to say they won't grab either Rose or Miaow as a way of holding his feet to the fire.

To get whatever it is they really want.

How would Ton be working the surveillance? The watchers are in the street. The microphones are in the ceiling. Presumably someone is listening in real time, and the two groups, the watchers and the listeners, are communicating. When the information from inside the apartment indicates that the family won't be going anywhere, all but one of the watchers are probably encouraged to leave their positions. No sense drawing attention to themselves needlessly. They'd be somewhere nearby, most likely someplace crowded out on Silom, with cell phones. When the listeners hear that someone is going to leave the building, all of them would get a call and move into their spots.

Maybe the best thing to do is to separate them. The three of them go out and head in a different direction, put some distance between them, and then . . .

And then . . . what? If one member of the family disappears, Ton's guys will probably kill the other two. Rafferty has to take Weecherat's murder as a message. Rose and Miaow need to vanish at the same time, and then Rafferty needs to become invisible, too.

Information overload, he thinks. There's a lot of information going to Ton's men, between the sounds coming in over the microphones and what the watchers are seeing. They'll be comfortable, maybe a little lax. All those eyes, all those ears. He needs to exploit that. Create a disconnect of some kind, a contradiction between what they hear and what they see, and use the confusion to make two people vanish in plain sight. Up until now he's been focused on figuring out how to make them think that Rose and Miaow are still in the apartment for a day or so after they've left it. He's been trusting himself to come up with the way to *get* them out, postponing dealing with the big illusion while he putters around preparing this beginner's parlor trick, which will be useless until they've gone.

Putting second things first.

He looks at his watch: 9:25. Time to imitate a writer. He puts the yellow list on the table and starts to dial numbers. He starts with the cop and then moves to the gangster.

THEIR BELLIES ARE full. Peep is clean and freshly diapered, engrossed in a bottle of formula from Foodland. Da and Boo sit on the riverbank in the shade, watching the river slide by.

"I don't know what I can do for you," Da says. "I'm probably too old to help you with those cops. Peep's too young. We're just two more mouths for you to feed. And you did all that—I mean, Kep and all of it—for me."

Boo watches a gleaming white cruiser speed upstream. The reddish brown water parts before it, sluicing up over the sides, all the way up to the big red letters that say RIVER QUEEN.

"Rich people," he says. "That's from the Queen Hotel. Rich *farang* being taken up to look at the ruins at Ayutthaya. Do you know how much it costs to sleep there for one night?"

Da says, "In Ayutthaya?"

"No, Da," Boo says with exaggerated patience, "not in Ayutthaya. At the Queen Hotel."

"How would I know? I've never even been in a hotel."

"Three hundred, four hundred dollars," he says. "Some of the rooms cost more than a thousand dollars."

Da looks over at him. It sounds like a lot of money. "How many baht?"

"More than thirty thousand."

"*Thirty thousand?* My whole village didn't have thirty thousand baht."

"The people on that boat could buy your village with what's in their pockets. They wouldn't even have to go to an ATM. But they wouldn't want your village." The boat is well upstream by now, and Da can make out some of the men and women gathered at the back of it. Most of them wear white clothes, and many of them look fat. "But you know what some of them *would* want?"

"What?"

"Peep."

Da says, "Oh," and she sees it all. Poor mothers, rich people, and the currency a baby. She holds Peep a little more snugly.

"I didn't get you away from them because I need your help," Boo says. "What I want you to do is talk to somebody. About you and Peep."

"Who? Who would want to know about us?"

Boo shakes his head. "I have no idea whether he'll want to know. I don't even know if he'll let me in. But if he'll talk to us, he can do something about it."

"What? What can he do?"

Boo takes her hand in his. Hers is cold, but his is warm and dry. It feels natural to her. He says, "If he wants to, he can tell the world."

PART III

ALL THE WAY DOWN

31

A Man Who Has Just Been Hit by a Train

As always lately, the first thing Arthit sees when he comes into the room is Noi's face in the photograph.

What he really sees is the back of the photograph, since it's turned toward his swivel chair on the far side of his dented, olive drab steel desk. What he's actually looking at is a cardboard stiffener with a fold-out triangle to make the frame stand upright. But what he *sees* is the two of them, ridiculously young and fate-temptingly happy, the immaculate white linen thread of marriage tied loosely around their foreheads. He'd had a couple of drinks for courage before the wedding, and his face is a bright red that's part alcohol, part blush. Noi's is alive with mischief. Below the edge of the photo, she had just made a trial grab at the part of him that now belonged exclusively to her. Although of course all of him actually belonged exclusively to her.

As he drags himself in, he doesn't see the window he fought to get, or the dull, industrial, alley-bisected view it looks out onto, or the rattan cricket on the table, or the couch pillows covered in yellow silk that

Noi picked out, or the photographs of himself on the wall, standing next to men-of-the-moment, mostly forgotten now but worth pointing a camera at, back whenever. He doesn't see the rug he hauled in a year ago, grunting under its weight, because he hated the brown linoleum.

Just the photograph. Just his wife's face.

Of course he *knows* that he's not seeing the other things. He's stopped seeing them in self-defense, amazed to learn how much sadness inanimate objects can give off, an emotional vapor that says, *When I bought that / was given that / put that there, I didn't know.* I thought the world's natural state was to be whole, I thought it would remain whole.

I thought if anything ever happened to one of us, it would happen to me.

Beside the framed photograph, a stack of work waits for him. Papers he needs to review pointlessly, reports he needs to initial pointlessly, a calendar of pointless meetings he'll drag himself to, just a little late, so he can sit on the periphery, against the wall instead of at the table, and try to look attentive. Try not to look like a man who has just been hit by a train.

He trudges across the room and sits down with a sigh he doesn't hear. The chair makes its invariable squeak of complaint, something he has meant to take care of for weeks—a squirt of WD-40, what could be easier? It would just take a second. The can is on top of the filing cabinet, put there at his request by one of the secretaries a million years ago. Picking it up would take more strength than he possesses. He thinks briefly about getting up and throwing the chair through the window. That's something he can visualize doing. Breaking things. For that he could find strength.

He reads the first sentence on the top page of the stack and then reads it again. Halfway through he goes back to see what the memo's subject is. It's got something to do with a new copying loop, a list of people who are to be copied automatically on several sorts of documents, very few of which ever cross his desk. He takes the page, rips it lengthwise down the center, and sits there, holding half of the sheet in each hand, looking right through the photograph.

In the three days since he found the pills buried in the flour, Noi has paled and lightened. She seems to walk more weightlessly, to absorb more light, to carry her pain more easily, as though it were a cloak she can lift from her shoulders when the weight becomes too much for her. Today, as she stood at the stove heating the water for his coffee, he had the sense that if he squinted hard enough, he could see the stove through her. That she was some sort of colored projection in the air.

That she was already beginning to fade.

Of course, the impulse, the instinct, is to hold on, to wrap his arms around her and anchor her. To do whatever it takes to keep her beside him. But to do that would be to keep her in her pain, the smoldering in her nervous system that will simply get worse until she bursts into flame like a paper doll. Fire no one can put out. Won't it be better if she simply goes to sleep?

Of course it would. Of course it wouldn't.

That morning, as he drank his coffee, trying to act the way he acted every morning—as though this were just the beginning of another day in an infinite progression of days—Noi pulled her chair around from the side of the table where she usually sits and put it beside his. She wound her arms around his neck and leaned against him. He sat there cup in hand, inhaling the smell of her shampoo, feeling the heat from her skin, listening to the flow of her breath and watching the room ripple through the tears in his eyes, while his heart slammed against his ribs like a fist. They sat there until the coffee was cold. Neither of them spoke a word.

His phone rings.

He looks at it as he might look at a scorpion on his desk. It continues to ring. Finally he drops the scrap of paper in his left hand and reaches for the receiver, seeing the glint of his wedding ring. Picks up the receiver and says his name.

"This is Thanom," says the voice on the other end, a voice with some snap to it. "We need to talk. Now. Come up here."

Arthit hangs up the phone, thinking, *Poke.*

"I'VE JUST HAD an interesting chat," Thanom says as Arthit comes through the door. Today Thanom is in his usual uniform, not the ceremonial outfit Poke had described him wearing at Pan's fund-raiser. He has a short, flattened nose and an upper lip that's longer than the nose above it. Those features, plus round black eyes as expressive as bullet holes, have always made him look to Arthit like a monkey. But he's not a monkey one should underestimate. Thanom has a perpetually wet index finger raised to detect the slightest shift in the political winds.

"Really," Arthit says. "A chat with whom?" He has not been invited to sit.

Thanom gives a tug at the left point of his collar. "A friend of yours. The *farang* who's writing Pan's biography. What's his name?"

"Rafferty," Arthit says. "More an acquaintance than a friend."

"Is that so," Thanom says, not making it a question. "I'd heard otherwise."

"Obviously I have no way of knowing what you've heard."

Arthit's tone sharpens the interest in Thanom's face, but he puts it aside for the moment to pursue his topic. "I'm apparently on some sort of list of people he's supposed to talk to about Pan, although I can't imagine why."

Arthit says, "Who gave him the list?"

Thanom leans back in his chair and regards Arthit speculatively. "That's an excellent question. I should have asked it."

"You've been behind a desk for a while," Arthit says, pleased to see the spots of red appear on Thanom's cheeks. "Focused on more important things than nuts and bolts. First-year-patrolman stuff."

"No, no," Thanom says between lips that are stretched tight enough to snap. "A really good policeman never forgets the basics."

Arthit says, "I couldn't agree with you more."

Arthit can practically see Thanom make an imaginary mark: *One to get even for.* "Did he tell *you* who gave him the list?"

"I don't know him as well as you think I do."

"It's been a while since we talked, hasn't it?" Thanom says. "It's a shame my responsibilities don't give me more time with my men. One thing about your friend interested me. He kept asking to see the files on Pan. When I said it wasn't possible, he asked whether they were even accessible. As though we might have misplaced them somehow."

"That *is* interesting."

Thanom lifts his tie and glances at it, as though he expects to find a stain. "Any idea where he might have gotten the idea?"

"None. Is it true?"

Thanom's eyes come up. "Of course not. We don't misplace files."

"That's a relief," Arthit says. "Since we're the institutional memory of law and order in Bangkok and all that."

"You don't know where he could have picked up such a notion? Your friend, I mean."

"Acquaintance. No, of course not. But if he's got whole lists of people to talk to, maybe one of them suggested something of the sort."

"Yes, yes," Thanom says, holding up a hand. "And you personally," he says. He squeezes some feeling into his voice, as persuasive as food coloring. "How are you bearing up?"

Arthit has no idea how Thanom knows anything is wrong with Noi. "Beating against the tide," he says, "as we all do."

"Do we?" Thanom says, standing to signal the end of the conversation. "I don't think so. I think some of us learn to ride it."

FOR PURPOSES OF his work, Rafferty's favorite kind of people are the ones who are dumber than they think they are. The policeman, Thanom, had practically redefined the category. Yes, of course he'd be happy to help Rafferty, especially in light of the call he'd received. Rafferty certainly had prominent friends, didn't he? Heh, heh. And the time was long overdue for a book about this disgusting man, this scab on the Bangkok social scene. Practically a common criminal, for all the flash and the . . . um, amazing girls. Here Thanom had actually stopped talking long enough to press the side of his index finger against his upper lip, blotting sweat Rafferty couldn't see.

But of course Rafferty knew a few things about beauty himself, didn't he? Thanom said when his finger was out of the way, considering the rare orchid Rafferty had been parading at the event at Pan's house. And then Thanom brandished the official elbow: Amazing how resilient women are, isn't it? he asked. Take them out of the mud and six months later they look like they've never been dirty a moment in their lives. Not that Thanom thinks of Patpong as mud, of course. It's just regrettable that there aren't better career choices for these flowers of the northeast. And how fortunate she was, Rose, to find a good man to rescue her, one who wouldn't object to . . . well, to all that. But change was coming. Surely Rafferty could feel it in the air, after—here Thanom glanced down at a single piece of paper sitting in regal splendor on his desk—after three years and nine months in the kingdom. Why, he said with an admiring shake of the head, you must feel half Thai yourself.

And no, he didn't know how Pan had gotten his start, how he had climbed from thugdom to the top of the industrial heap, or even—for sure—that there *was* any thugdom back there in the first place. "Common criminal" had just been a figure of speech based on, you know, how he dresses and behaves in public. There were rumors, of course. There were always rumors wherever there were envious people, but nothing official. And of course he'd be delighted to let Rafferty look at the official records, especially considering who had called him to suggest that he find time for this meeting, nothing would make him happier, but he would have to exceed his authority to do so. No matter how high you rise, there's always someone higher, isn't there? Although Rafferty, as a freelance writer with two—no, three—books to his credit and another one in the pipeline (isn't that the term you use, "pipeline"?), yes, Rafferty probably lives a much freer and less constrained life than a simple civil servant. How I envy you that freedom as I sit chained to this desk all day, working for the people's good.

And now you've got this fascinating project about one of Bangkok's most . . . uh, visible citizens.

And I'd like nothing better than to show you the files, but it's impossible. Just procedure, rules and regulations, you know. But of *course* all of Pan's records are accessible. The police didn't *lose* records. There were backups of backups of backups. To purge anything, even something inconsequential, would be a vast enterprise, requiring hundreds of man-hours. But nothing of that kind had happened in Pan's case. The records are there, but unavailable, I'm sorry to say.

By now Thanom had taken the paper clip off the sheets and was flicking one end of it with an index finger to make it spin. The activity had the unfortunate effect of making him look even more like a monkey, one who is on the verge of inventing a tool but probably won't. When Rafferty asks him about Pan's political aspirations, the paper clip sails off the desk and lands in Rafferty's lap.

On the street, having wasted much of his morning and with yet another interview in front of him, Rafferty asks himself again: What do they actually want?

SEVERAL HOURS LATER Arthit has made a third improvement to his new paper-plane design when someone knocks on his door. Elaborately folded official reports, symmetrically streamlined and sharply pointed, most of them with a downturned nose borrowed from the Concorde, litter the carpet. The nose *looks* good, but it seems to impair the lift a good paper plane needs, so Arthit has just counterweighted the tail with a staple and launched it across the room.

He doesn't bother to tell whoever it is to come in.

Arthit doesn't have anything as grand as a secretary, but he has access to a pool of women with widely varying skill levels. The one who comes through the door is his favorite: in her sixties, dressed and made up like a nineteen-year-old, she calls herself Brigitte, after Brigitte Bardot. Except for Arthit she is probably the only person in the station who remembers Bardot in all her pouting, carnal glory.

"For you," she says. She has an envelope in her hand.

"So I assumed," Arthit says. "Since this is the office you brought it to. What is it?"

"I don't know," Brigitte says, although her eyes say she does. "It's sealed."

"Unseal it, then. Unseal it and read it to me."

Brigitte shifts from foot to foot, obviously wishing she were elsewhere. "I'm not sure I should."

"Whoever sent it to me probably wants me to know what it says, right?"

"Well . . . I suppose."

"Then open it and read it to me. I can promise you that if you don't, it will probably be weeks before I get around to opening it myself. I have far too much on my hands." He rips out another page of another report and folds it lengthwise, already visualizing a triangular tuck in the tail section that might make the staple redundant. Staples seem like cheating.

"Well." Brigitte chews the inside of her cheek. Then she opens the envelope, which is not in fact sealed; the flap has merely been slipped inside. "It's . . . um, it's a Form 74."

"Really. And a Form 74 is?"

"Leave. It's the form granting compassionate leave."

"Ah," Arthit says. He creases the page with his thumbnail to sharpen the fold. "Does it say when the leave begins?"

"It starts today," Brigitte says. She blinks rapidly, and for a moment Arthit is afraid she will burst into tears. "In fact, it starts now."

Arthit says, "Mmm-hmm." He launches the plane, which sails across the room rewardingly. "And is there anything about how long this compassion will last?"

"Until further notice," Brigitte says.

"That's a very generous serving of compassion," Arthit says. "Definitely something to remember."

32

Innocent as a Dusting of Snow

I hope you know what a big favor this is," grumbles the man behind the desk. Through the floor-to-ceiling window with the desk positioned in its center, Rafferty sees the silvered windows of the office tower across the street.

"And I hope you know how much I appreciate it," Rafferty says to Wichat with the smallest smile he can manage. "The people who want this book written feel you might have a special perspective on Pan."

"I was around," Wichat says. His shoulders are hunched and high, and it looks protective. "I was just a foot soldier then, but I was around."

"That's not what I hear. I hear you were already on the way up."

Wichat shakes his head. "The big guy then was Chai. He was generous with his men. He took care of me. I did what he needed done, and he took care of me." Wichat tilts the chair back, dangerously close to the plate glass behind him.

"Doesn't that scare you? It's, what, twenty-eight stories down?"

Wichat says, "Nothing scares me."

"Well, lucky you. Did anything scare Pan?"

"If it did, he didn't show it. He could have been pissing his pants, but he looked like something carved into that wall of his. Nothing showed except what he wanted to show. Had a way of bringing down the corners of his mouth so hard they almost touched. Scared the shit out of people."

"You knew him when he made the move, right? The move to the massage parlors."

"The Mound of Venus," Wichat says lightly, as though he's been asked an unexpectedly easy question. "Sure."

"Where'd he get the money?"

Wichat picks up a battered pack of cigarettes and tweezes one out between his first and second fingers. He puts it in his mouth and picks up a gold lighter. "Trying to quit," he says.

"Yeah, well, lighting one is a surefire method."

"I don't light as many as I used to," Wichat says, blowing a plume of smoke across the desk. "Don't smoke them so far down either."

"Where'd he get the money?"

"He didn't need money. How do I know my name isn't going to be all over your book?"

"If it is, you can kill me."

"Funny," Wichat says dourly. "No names, got it?"

"Got it."

"I wouldn't tell you shit if you didn't have so much fucking weight behind you."

"As I said, I appreciate it. Where'd he get—"

"I told you," Wichat snaps. "He already had some. And he didn't need as much as you'd probably think. He got the first Mound pretty much free, just the old gun-to-the-head negotiation. The guy who owned it had made the wrong decisions about who to be friends with. It would have been a small funeral. So he signed it over to Pan for maybe enough baht to buy a week's worth of chewing gum, and Pan fixed the place up."

"And then?"

"And then he made a bunch of money from the first Mound and opened the others. Business, right? Make profit and reinvest it. Selling pad thai, selling pussy. Same-same, you know?"

"What else?"

Wichat reaches up and passes a palm over the surface of his oily hair. Then he makes a palm print on the desk's smooth surface and looks down at it as though evaluating its worth as evidence. "What else, what else." He drags on the cigarette again and examines it, obviously thinking about what he's going to say next. "Two things," he says. "You didn't hear this from me, but there were two things." He glares at the half-smoked cigarette, stubs it out, and drops it in the ashtray. "Hard not to pick these things up and light them later, you know? Especially when you were poor once."

"Get a jar of water," Rafferty says. "Drop them into it."

Wichat's eyes widen slightly. His complexion is rough and pitted. He must have had terrible acne as a kid. Acne plus poverty; if Rafferty didn't know the man was a killer and perhaps worse, he might even feel sorry for him.

"Hang on," Wichat says. He picks up his phone and punches a single number. "Get me a jar of water and bring it in here. No, not a glass. If I wanted a glass, I would have asked for a glass. A jar, and a coaster to go under it. A little more than half full. No lid." He hangs up. To Rafferty he says, "Good idea."

"You were about to tell me two things."

"Bunch of half-smoked cigarettes floating around, that's going to stink."

"Yeah. And?"

"Good idea." His eyes drop to the surface of the desk, scanning it as though he's looking for an objection to what he's about to do. "Two things," he says. "First, the Mounds of Venus weren't the whole story, okay? He also owned a bunch of handcuff houses, you know handcuff houses?"

"Pretend I don't."

"Houses where the girls aren't . . . eager, you know? Where they're handcuffed to the bed. Some guys *like* that. They like to punch the girls a little, too, a few of them. So Pan had, I don't know, maybe four or five of those places. Only Burmese girls, trucked in. He wouldn't use Thai girls, they had to be Burmese."

"Are you sure of this?"

"You've got to be kidding me. This is dangerous stuff I'm telling you. I don't want to know it myself. You think I'd make it up?"

"Pan acts like prostitutes are his fallen sisters."

"Pan's one of the world's great liars." Wichat brings both hands up, scrubbing the air to erase the remark. "But the Thai girls, the ones who worked in the Mounds? He took good care of them. They got paid good, and they got time off and everything. I even heard he takes care of some girls who got sick. But that's just Thais, you understand? Just Isaan. The Burmese, he treated them like shit."

"And the second thing?"

"You seen his hands?"

"You mean the scars?"

"Yeah. You've never seen him in a short-sleeved shirt because those burns, they go all the way up to his shoulders and even the front of his chest. It looks like he dived headfirst into a fire to pull something out. He disappeared for a couple of months, and when he came back, he had those scars. He wouldn't talk about them, but it was only about six months later he got his first factory and started closing down the whorehouses."

"A fire," Rafferty says.

"Yeah. He came through some sort of fire, and then he was a different guy."

"What year?"

"Oh, shit, who knows? He was still closing down the knock shops, so—"

The office door opens, and an exquisite young woman comes in carrying a jar of water. The jar has a label that says "Jif" on it.

"Oh, come on," Wichat says angrily. "It's bad enough to have a fucking jar on my desk without the whole world knowing what kind of peanut butter I eat. Peel that thing off."

"Yes, sir," the girl says. She wears a pale salmon-colored business-formal office suit, all in silk. Wichat watches her rear end as she goes back out.

"More butt than brains," Wichat says admiringly.

Rafferty says, "The year."

A heavy blink. "Yeah. Like I said, he still had one of the Mounds, or maybe two. Must have been—this is a guess—1993? Maybe '94. In there somewhere."

"Do you have anything to do with him now?" Rafferty asks. "With Pan?"

Wichat picks up the pack of cigarettes again. "I don't care who called me about you," he says. "Just pretend you didn't ask that question."

THE SIDEWALK IS at full bake, heat ripples so pronounced that pedestrians look like he's seeing them underwater. Rafferty ducks into an air-conditioned drugstore, one in a British chain that's established itself in Bangkok's high-rent commercial districts. He pulls out the cell phone and dials the number from memory.

"I need to access the morgue at the *Bangkok Sun*," he says without returning the greeting from the other end. "Somebody has to call and set it up."

"You can't get in yourself?" It is the first man, the man from the car again. His speech is still mush-thick, but at least it's understandable.

"Sure I can get in myself. I'll make a request, and then the request will get processed, and then they'll let me in, and it'll be the middle of next week. You guys want to sit around playing blackjack or whatever you do while I go through all that, or you want to move things along?"

"How'd you do with the cop?"

"I did better with the crook. It'll be in my report."

"Give me a preview."

"I think I'll wait," Rafferty says, "until I'm talking to someone who matters."

"You're just making it easier," the man says.

"If it wasn't easy, you wouldn't be able to do it."

A pause, although Rafferty can hear the breathing on the other end of the line. Then the man says, "How long will it take you to get there?"

"Twenty, thirty minutes."

"It'll be set up." The man disconnects.

Thirty-five minutes later, Rafferty discovers he's in luck. Both 1993 and 1994 have been computerized and cross-indexed. It takes him less than an hour to find fires.

Five show promise. Two of them are the most melancholy of all crimes, the burning of a slum that had the misfortune to occupy land earmarked for more profitable purposes. People died in one of these fires. Both had been euphemistically designated as accidental. Then there are two house fires that destroyed or damaged the homes of the powerful. Nobody

died, so the fires were probably just attention-getters. The fifth is a factory conflagration, a virtual explosion of highly flammable materials in
a facility that turned out stuffed animals for an American toy maker.
The fire had happened around 3:00 A.M. during a "ghost shift," a shift
the American company knew nothing about. After the workers on the
night shift left, the ghost-shift workers were brought in to use inferior
materials to bootleg identical animals for direct sale at the bazaars of
Asia. One of the differences between the superior and the inferior materials was that the inferior materials weren't fireproofed.

The fire killed one hundred twenty-one people. The factory's windows were barred, and the iron doors had been locked from the outside.
People had been stacked in front of the doors in smoldering piles, like
kindling. Some had died with their arms protruding between the bars
on the windows, reaching frantically for the world. The company that
had rented the factory to the Americans had proved to be a shell corporation owned by another shell corporation. No one who supervised the
ghost shift had been found. No one had ever been charged.

Rafferty prints out all five stories. Each of the pieces ultimately dith-
ers off into the vague language the Thai police use to describe their
lack of progress in an investigation that's aimed directly at somewhere
they're not going to be allowed to go. And there's no doubt there are
heavyweights behind at least some of the fires. The slums were burned
to make way for buildings, the houses probably burned as warnings,
and the toy factory burned through inhuman stupidity, coupled with
greed for yet more profit.

The odds were good that Pan had been involved in one of them. And
Rafferty would guess it was one of the ones that involved death, given
the magnitude of the favors he had been granted.

Rafferty had misquoted Balzac: *Behind every great fortune is a great
crime.* Pan's fortune might have begun in fire.

THE TIME CRAWLS past.

Arthit refuses to go home early. He doesn't want to explain to Noi
that he has effectively been suspended from the force. She'll take the
blame, knowing that his work is the only thing he has now. She doesn't
need the guilt.

So he does something he's never been good at: He wastes time. He's been busy his entire adult life. He doesn't take vacations—something he regrets now; he should have taken Noi to Hawaii, to Los Angeles, to Tahiti—*somewhere* that would have made her happy. He should have done a million things, but he didn't. He was who he was, and she had loved him—she still loves him—anyway.

He spends half an hour trying out pens in a stationery store, writing the names of everyone he knows, including Noi's doctors. He browses shelves of books he wouldn't read if they materialized one morning under his pillow. He walks through unfamiliar neighborhoods, seeing some of Bangkok's remaining small villages, seeing how the people stiffen and grow quiet at the sight of his uniform. Tasting the bitterness in the back of his throat that it should be so.

He thumbs through stacks of bootleg DVDs, eyed nervously by sidewalk vendors who yanked the albums of pornography out of sight at his approach. To his immense surprise, he finds a film by Buster Keaton, *Sherlock Jr.,* that he's never seen. There it is, sandwiched in between more usual titles like *Terminator 48* and *Revolving Door of the Dead.* Noi loves Keaton and his modern disciple, Jackie Chan. When he tries to pay for the movie, the vendor waves his money off, but Arthit takes a thousand-baht note, puts it on the table, and slams a DVD case on top of it, harder than he had intended to. With the Keaton in a plastic bag, he trudges off, ashamed to be dressed as a policeman.

He thinks about calling Rafferty, but what would he say? He doesn't know how to ask for help, and even if he did, he can't imagine what help Rafferty could offer. Rafferty has more than enough to deal with now. Struck by the thought, he stops and dials Kosit.

"How's Poke doing?" he asks.

"You mean other than being outmatched and outweighed and not having any idea what to do about it?"

Arthit says, "Right."

"This is stupid," Kosit says. "You're worried about Poke, and Poke's worried about you. Why don't you talk to each other?"

"Because I can't help him."

"And vice versa. So let me make a suggestion."

"Go ahead."

"Get drunk together. Get drunk and sloppy and say a bunch of stuff you'll regret tomorrow. You'll both feel better."

"Go catch a crook," Arthit says, and hangs up.

But the talk has lifted his spirits slightly. He dials Rafferty's cell and gets no answer. He checks his watch—4:45. Close enough, and he's got the Buster Keaton to distract her from the fact that he's half an hour early.

When he goes into the house, he automatically enters it his new way. The house is essentially a rectangle. The front door opens directly into the living room, which stretches the full width of the house. To the right is the hallway that leads to the two bedrooms and the bathrooms that adjoin them. The hallway ends in the kitchen. To the left is the dining room, which opens into a small breakfast nook that in turn opens into the kitchen. For the past few months, since Noi's pain took its quantum leap, he's gone to the left, through the dining room, so he won't wake her if she's asleep.

He kicks off his shoes just inside the front door and pads through the silent living room, smelling the lemon scent of the spray wax Noi uses anywhere there's a square foot of exposed wood. Without slowing down, he drops the Keaton DVD, still in its plastic bag, next to the cascade of unopened mail on the dining-room table, and goes through the nook and into the kitchen. As he comes into the warm, yellow room, as he unbuckles his gun belt and puts it on the table, his stockinged foot hits something slippery, and he looks down at the floor to see a spill of flour.

His heart literally stops.

Then it kicks itself back into life with tremendous force, and he stands there with it thumping in his ears, staring down at a sifting of flour across the tile, as clean and innocent as a dusting of snow.

Feeling like a man walking against a stiff wind, Arthit forces himself across the kitchen and into the hallway, where he stops, two steps in, and looks at the envelope taped to the closed bedroom door.

33

If He's a Friend, He'll Wait

The tail is wearing a yellow shirt.

He's been back there for blocks now. Rafferty has glimpsed him three times as he did experimental zigzags between boulevards and *sois*. He thinks it might be time to get a look at his shadow's face, for future reference.

The office building is unremarkable, neither new nor old, certainly not architecturally distinctive, and there's not a soul in it Rafferty knows. He enters the lobby anyway, walking with the brisk purpose of someone who actually has a destination. Without looking around, he pushes the call button for the elevator and waits. When it comes, he turns to face front as he punches the button for the sixth floor. He doesn't see the yellow shirt as the doors close.

He gets off on the sixth floor, trots down a couple of flights on the fire stairs, and hits the button for the elevator again. He rides it down to the underground parking garage, which opens not onto Silom but onto a small cross street. Up the slope of the exit ramp and then a quick right, away from Silom. A short jog brings him to an alley, which he takes to the next little *soi*, one that will lead him back down to Silom.

He crosses it and takes it to Silom, then crosses that and waits on the sidewalk, watching the building he just went into.

Looking for someone else who's watching it.

And almost misses him, because he's looking for yellow, and what he finally sees is navy blue, a dark T-shirt that says BAJA CALIFORNIA on it. The man in blue is short but broad-shouldered, with medium-length hair that's been parted in the middle and then gooped with mousse to make it fall in spiky curls over his forehead. A small soul patch clings to his lower lip with all the uncertainty of a misplaced comma.

No yellow shirt. Is he being double-teamed?

Rafferty watches for a few more minutes, just to make certain that Yellow Shirt isn't around, then turns and follows the flow on the sidewalk until he gets to a recessed doorway, leading into a shop that sells fantasy underwear. Rose laughed out loud at the display window once, although Rafferty still sneaks a look at it now and then.

He punches a number into his cell, waits a moment, and then says, "Floyd. It's Poke. I need a favor."

"Why am I not surprised?" says Floyd Preece.

"It's not a conventional favor, Floyd. There's money in it." He looks down the street and doesn't see either the blue shirt or the yellow one. Blue Shirt worries him a little, because he'd gone unnoticed the whole time Rafferty was isolating Mr. Yellow. The last thing he needs right now is to be followed by someone with real skills.

"How much?" Floyd Preece is a freelance journalist hanging on in Bangkok by his badly chewed fingernails. He's a first-class investigative reporter, but his talent is significantly outweighed by an avid enthusiasm for controlled substances and a total lack of interpersonal skills. Preece has never crossed a bridge he didn't burn behind him, and he's now living in a thin-towel, short-time hotel and maybe six months away from having to teach English, which is the wrong end of the rainbow altogether. Nobody in Bangkok will work with him, but he's got the gifts Rafferty needs right now.

"If you get me what I want, five hundred U.S. If you don't, two-fifty for trying."

"Sounds low."

"You don't even know what it is yet."

"Still sounds low." There is a pause and the scraping of one of the wooden matches Preece favors, and Rafferty listens to the man suck a cigar into life. "You landed the whale, didn't you? Mr. Pick His Nose in Public himself. Got to be a big fat advance there. How much did you get?"

"I don't know. I haven't checked. Okay, a thousand if you get it, five hundred if you don't, and if that's not enough, I've got other numbers in my speed dial."

"I'll need the five up front." Another big, wet inhale, followed by a muted cough.

"You'll get half of it, later tonight or tomorrow morning. I'll call and tell you where we can meet. Have you got a pencil?"

"Sure. But I need—"

"I don't care what you need, what you're getting is two-fifty up front. Now, take this down and get it right, okay? I haven't got time to repeat it." Up the street, maybe two-thirds of a block away, he catches a glimpse of the yellow shirt. He backs farther into the doorway and gives Preece the dates and details of the fires. "I'm most interested in the slum fire where there were fatalities and in the factory."

"This for the book?"

"That doesn't concern you—"

"—'cause if it is, you're really pitching me low."

"Yes or no, Floyd? Before I count to three. One . . . two . . ."

"Okay, okay. Jeez. I thought we were friends."

Rafferty says, "You did? Well, good, then this will clarify things. What I want is everything you can get, but especially this: Who built the new buildings on the sites of the slums that burned, and who owned the factory? Both before and after the fire, if there was enough of it left to sell." The yellow shirt is gone again.

"I remember it," Preece said. "Went out there, tried to get some pix to sell. Brought along a stuffed bunny, put it on the dirt in the foreground, and shot past it. Used a wide-angle for depth of field. Like irony, you know? Building was solid concrete. Not much damage, except to the stuff inside. And the people, of course."

"Right, the people."

"If it turns out the fire has anything to do with your guy, you should look at these pix. I'd let you have a couple for the right price. Great story angle, you know? Up from the flames and all that."

"Listen, I also want to know if anyone died in either of those fires who shouldn't have been there. Somebody with some rank, somebody who didn't belong."

"Got it."

"Tell you what," Rafferty says, feeling a prickle of guilt. Preece is almost at the stage where he'll have to start reusing toothpicks. "We'll make this a sliding scale. I'll pay you the thousand if you get me the basics. Anything past that, I'll pay you more, up to a total of twenty-five hundred."

"Why?" Preece's voice is sharpened by suspicion.

"Because we're friends. And because I'm in a hurry. I need this like day after tomorrow at the latest, but call me anytime you get anything good. And, Floyd. Be a little careful, okay?"

"Oh, come on." Another draw on the cigar. "Bangkok is my beat."

"Fine. But keep your eyes open." Rafferty disconnects.

At the edge of the doorway, he looks back up the street. No followers he can identify. He turns to continue in the direction he'd been going in, and there's Mr. Yellow, flanked by two others. Both of the others are wearing suit jackets, and their hands are thrust into their jacket pockets.

"You haven't been good," says the man in yellow.

"Do we know each other?" Rafferty asks.

"Good question," the man in yellow says. "You know how a scientist looks at a bug? He gets to know the bug pretty well, but does the bug know him?"

"Shoot me," Rafferty says, "but spare me the metaphors."

"Come on. We've got to talk. You walk next to me, okay? And Mr. Left and Mr. Right will follow us so they can shoot you and disappear quickly if they have to." He puts a hand on Rafferty's arm, which Rafferty shrugs off, but to no effect—the man grabs him again.

Rafferty says, "I am so fucking sick of this."

"You've been making me look bad," the man says. He's average height for a Thai, maybe five foot nine, a little meaty, with a receding hairline that gives him a thinker's forehead. A pair of round, black, resolutely opaque sunglasses straddles a shapeless, fleshy nose. A few hairs straggle despairingly across his upper lip as though they've slowed to wait for the others to catch up.

"Hard to believe anyone could make you look bad," Rafferty says. "Where are we going?"

"Right here." The man opens the door to a large black SUV that Rafferty recognizes, his stomach clenching like a fist, as the one that had been idling in front of Pan's Mesopotamian wall. "Get in," Yellow Shirt says, holding wide the rear door.

"I'd rather not."

"Okay, then, we'll kill you."

"And if I get in?"

The man in the yellow shirt smiles. "Wait and see."

Rafferty climbs up onto the step that will take him into the SUV's backseat, and his cell phone vibrates in his pocket. "Hold it," he says, pulling it out.

The man's hand is immediately on Rafferty's wrist. "Put that back. Now."

The readout says ARTHIT.

"Whoever it is," the man in the yellow shirt says, "you can talk to him later." And he plucks the phone out of Rafferty's hand. It's a very fast, very precise move.

Rafferty says, "Hey," but someone pushes him hard, between the shoulder blades, and he lurches face-first through the door, cracking his shins on the second step. He lands on the leather backseat and is pushing himself up when the man in the yellow shirt, who is now in the front seat, points a small silvery automatic at him over the seat back.

"Just sit up," he says. Rafferty sees his own face reflected in the dark glasses. He looks frightened. "In the middle. Don't do anything stupid."

Rafferty does as he's told, and seconds later Mr. Left and Mr. Right climb into the car on either side of him. For a moment they sit there in silence, and Rafferty listens to the engine ticking as it cools. The tinted windows make them invisible from the sidewalk, but he doesn't think they'd have shut down the engine if the plan called for them to shove a dead man out of the car and peel off into traffic.

"You're not taking us seriously," says Yellow Shirt. He looks at the phone. "Who's Arthit?"

"A friend."

"If he's a friend, he'll wait. I'm running out of patience with you. We called to tell you not to write the book. We did that little show outside Pan's place. But here you are, running around and talking to people. As I said, it makes me look bad. So here we are again." He waits.

Rafferty feels like the slowest person in the car. It hadn't occurred to him that he was dealing with the other side. He'd half figured that the ones who warned him away from the book had been Pan's guys, despite Pan's denial, and that they'd be put on hold after he and Pan had their little talk. "What do you want me to say?" he asks.

"Nothing. And I want you to *do* nothing, and I mean nothing. No more meetings, no more conversations, no more research. This is the third time we've had to interact. The fourth time you'll die. Understand?"

"Yes."

"Are you right-handed or left?"

There is no way to know how to answer this question. Rafferty makes a blind choice. "Left."

"See how you are?" Yellow Shirt says sadly. "I've been *watching* you, remember? Look at this gun." He lifts it from the seat back and moves it slowly to Rafferty's right. Rafferty is tracking it with his eyes, watching the light through the front windshield glint off the barrel, when Mr. Left shifts his weight, and then something cracks down onto the muscle between Rafferty's neck and his left shoulder. His arm goes numb, and as his head jerks toward Mr. Left and he registers the blackjack in the man's hand, the same thing happens to his right shoulder.

He makes a sound that's all *U*'s and *H*'s, a sound someone might make as a bull plows into his midsection, and he realizes he can barely lift his arms. Through the roaring in his ears, he hears Yellow Shirt.

"You're right-handed, and you should have realized I'd know it. But to show you that we can get along if you'll drop the project, we'll leave your right hand alone."

As though from a spot four or five feet above his own head, Rafferty watches his limp, numb left hand as Mr. Left picks it up and puts it on the back of the front seat. He holds it there as Mr. Right brings his blackjack up and then *down* onto the intricate latticework of bones in the back of the hand, and Rafferty's scream tears his throat ragged.

"You should see a doctor," Yellow Shirt says. "Probably a couple of fractures, and hands need to be looked at fast." He waves the gun back and forth again. "This will take hours to treat. You'll be out of circulation for the rest of the day, and then you're going to stop, right? I'm going to tell my principal that you're quitting, and you're not going to make me look bad again."

"No," Rafferty says, through a windpipe that feels narrower than a pencil. "I mean, yes. I'm quitting."

Yellow Shirt nods. "Good, good. You can get out now. Wasn't this better than getting shot?" He leans over the seat and drops the cell phone into Rafferty's shirt pocket. "You can call your friend back," he says. "Although it may be a while before you can dial."

34

You'll Probably Be Sterile

"This is for *teeth*," Dr. Pumchang says. From the speaker in the corner of the room, the Carpenters are singing "Rainy Days and Mondays," a song Rafferty had hoped never to hear again.

"It'll do," Rafferty says, between jaws tight enough to have been wired together. "I just need to know whether it's broken."

He sits with his left hand throbbing in a steel bowl of ice water while his dentist, with doubt animating every muscle in her face, lines up small pieces of dental X-ray film to create a rectangular area a little bigger than Rafferty's hand. Out in the waiting room are the pumpkin-colored chairs where he and Elora Weecherat had talked.

"The machine can only photograph a small area at a time," Dr. Pumchang says. "I'm going to have to take a dozen pictures. Why can't you be like everyone else and go see a real doctor?"

"It's not like I play the piano," Rafferty says, and then grabs a breath and holds it as the nerves in his arm stand up and do the wave to pass a burst of pain along to the part of his brain that keeps track of such things. When he can talk, he says, "I use this hand mainly to comb my hair."

"How did this happen?" Dr. Pumchang puts the last piece of film in place and studies the quiltlike rectangle she has created. With a long, meticulously lacquered fingernail, she pushes one edge piece half a millimeter toward the center. The picture painted on the nail is Hokusai's famous ocean wave.

"I closed a car door on it."

Dr. Pumchang makes a noise Rafferty's mother would have called a raspberry. "Single point of impact," she says. "Not a straight line of force, like a car door. No abrasions, no broken skin. If you're not going to tell me the truth, don't tell me anything."

"Fine," Rafferty says. "Don't ask me questions."

"What it *looks* like," she says, "is that someone slammed it with something small and heavy."

"That's what it looks like, huh?"

"Dry your hand," she says. Her lips are drawn so tight that they've practically disappeared.

He takes the towel and very gently pats the hand dry.

"Flap it around. Let the air get to it. Get it dry."

"The film gets wet in my mouth. How come it can't get wet now?"

"Just listen to the nice music and do what I say. Or go see a hand doctor."

"Nobody listens to the Carpenters anymore."

"I do."

"Probably cheaper than anesthetic."

Dr. Pumchang pulls the X-ray unit toward him. "Put the hand down carefully, fingers as close together as you can get them, palm flat, if you can do it, and *don't mess up my film*. If you move the pieces around, I'll have to do the whole thing over again, and I'll probably think better of it."

"So much for bedside manner," Rafferty says, lowering his palm carefully onto the pieces of film and hoping she doesn't notice how they spread out beneath his hand.

"Just be quiet and hold still." She positions the lens over the center of his wrist, leaves the room, and Rafferty hears a short buzz. Then she comes back in and moves the lens a couple of inches. "I really don't know why I'm doing this."

"Because you're a good Buddhist."

"Don't push it." She leaves again, and Rafferty hears the buzz again. "By the time we finish this," she says, coming back into the room, "you'll probably be sterile."

"OKAY," DR. PUMCHANG says, "what you've got is two fractures. Second and third metacarpals." She is peering at the pieces of film, which she's joined together with transparent tape and clipped onto a light box. "They're pressure breaks, like you'd get if you bit down too hard on a chicken bone. Can you visualize that?"

This was exactly what Rafferty hadn't wanted to hear. "All too vividly."

"The good news is that almost all the pieces are in place. In other words, the splinters are right where they should be. More or less. Properly cared for, the bones should knit without any real lasting damage."

"And what constitutes 'properly cared for'?"

"A splint, then a cast, a month or so of not using it." She looks over at him. "Say something so I know you're listening to me."

"Okay. I'm listening to you. Here's what I want you to do: I want you to take the case this awful Carpenters CD came in, and I'll put my palm on it with my fingers jammed together, and you just tape the hell out of it. That way I'll be back on the street in about ten minutes."

"This is your *hand*," Dr. Pumchang says. "You've only got two of them. You're risking severely impaired function. How would you like not to be able to bend your fingers?"

"For how long?"

"For the rest of your life."

"Oh."

"In the best prognosis, you might be able to use it as a Ping-Pong paddle."

"Well, then," Rafferty says, "you'd better tape it really well."

DOWN ON THE street, it takes him three one-handed tries to bring up "recent calls" on his cell phone and press the "connect" button to dial Arthit. He puts the phone to his ear, looking down at the white adhesive-taped rectangle of his left hand, and waits.

"Hello," says someone who is not Arthit.

The hair on the back of Rafferty's neck stands on end. The tone is recognizable the world around. "Is Arthit there?"

Not-Arthit says, "Who is this?"

"I'll call him back." Rafferty folds the phone one-handed and puts it into his shirt pocket. There's no question in his mind that Arthit's phone has just been answered by a police officer. Immediately his phone starts to ring. He doesn't even have to look at the readout to know it's the cops, calling him back.

35

Off the Board

The envelope says, DON'T COME IN. CALL A FRIEND. It sits, meticulously centered, on the coffee table in front of the couch in Arthit's living room. It is the only thing on the table. The characters are written in thick black felt-tip. Noi's usual handwriting was slapdash, the lines of text slanting up to the right in a way that Arthit always saw as optimistic. But these words are ruler-straight and meticulously formed. The kind of care she would take with the last thing she would ever do.

Where did she sit to write it? he asks himself, and immediately knows the answer: the kitchen table. There had been a half-drunk cup of tea on the table. He'd seen it before his foot slipped.

"Can I get you anything?" Kosit asks.

Sitting in the center of the couch, Arthit shakes his head. He says, "She didn't finish her tea."

Kosit blinks and says, "I hadn't noticed that."

"She was in a hurry," Arthit says. "She wanted to make sure."

"Sure?"

"That I didn't come home too early. That the . . . that the pills had time to work." He can't find the voice to continue, so he clears his throat and looks back down at the envelope. He hasn't opened it yet. He's not sure he'll ever be able to open it.

The front door stands wide open, and an ambulance's red lights blink on-off-on through the window. A few people have gathered curiously on the sidewalk. Arthit can hear the medical technicians talking in the bedroom. When they wheel Noi out, it will be the last time she ever leaves the house. Their house.

Of course he *had* gone in.

After all, he'd come home early. She might still have been . . .

"A glass of water," he says. His voice is husky.

"Sure," Kosit says. He gets up but stops as two uniformed patrolmen come in. "What?" he asks. "Why are you here?"

"We got called. Fatality, right?" The senior patrolman is in his early fifties, nut brown. He's got a nose as bulbous as a head of garlic, the skin covering it a miniature map of broken veins. Beneath a flop of dirty hair are tiny eyes, the whites a disconcertingly sweet pink. His younger partner looks embarrassed, his eyes fixed on the carpet.

"Suicide," Kosit says. "The survivor is a cop. You're not needed."

"We got a call," says the senior patrolman. "From headquarters."

"It's a mistake," Kosit says. "Go away."

"From whom?" Arthit asks.

"Excuse me?" The senior patrolman scratches the back of his neck, revealing a dark, damp circle under his right arm.

Arthit says, "I asked who put out the call."

"You're the husband, right?" says the senior patrolman. He waits for an answer, letting the silence yawn between them.

"I am," Arthit says at last.

"Yeah, well, then, I don't see that you need to know who put out the call." His partner shifts his gaze from the carpet to the tops of his own shoes.

"You're being offensive," Kosit says. "This man is a lieutenant colonel on the force. We have a note, in the handwriting of the deceased."

"Where?" asks the senior patrolman. He takes two more steps into the room, claiming it as his own.

"It's—" Kosit says, glancing down. The coffee table is bare. "It's in the . . . um, kitchen," he says.

"We'll need it to take it," says the senior patrolman. "And, sir," he says to Arthit, "we'll need your weapon."

Arthit says, "What's your name?"

"And where's your name plate?" Kosit demands.

"In the car." The senior patrolman rests his hand on the butt of his automatic. "I want the weapon, sir. Now."

"*Why* is your name plate in the car? And him"—he lifts his chin at the embarrassed partner—"did he forget his, too?"

"For the third time," the patrolman says, "I want your weapon."

"I'll have to get it," Arthit says, standing up. He goes toward the dining room, then stops and says over his shoulder, "Surely you're not going to let me go alone. How do you know I'm not going to come back shooting?"

"Go with him," the senior patrolman says to his partner, who swallows convulsively at the prospect.

"I'll go," Kosit says. "This man's rank deserves that kind of respect."

The wheels of the gurney squeal from the hallway. Arthit forces himself not to turn to look, but the senior patrolman's eyes flick toward the noise, and he watches with some curiosity. "Go," he says.

Arthit leads Kosit through the dining room, listening to Noi's progress down the hall on the other side of the house. "This is about taking me off the board," he says very softly to Kosit when they're crossing the breakfast nook. "It's about the thing Poke's involved in, the thing with Pan."

"Who put out the call?" Kosit says.

"Thanom. He's probably the guy who scrubbed Pan's records."

"That tapeworm. What can I do?"

"Give me your money."

Kosit pats his pockets, locates a wad of bills folded so tightly they look like they've been ironed, and passes them to Arthit. Arthit pulls out his own money, puts the two stashes together, and slips them back in his pocket.

By now they are in the kitchen. Moving quickly, Arthit goes to the kitchen table, the table where he and Noi ate breakfast only that morning, where she rested her head on his shoulder, the table where they'd eaten all their meals since it became more difficult for her to carry the food even as far as the breakfast nook. The table where she probably wrote the note.

Next to the half-empty teacup, on which he now sees a pale lipstick print that stabs him through the center of his heart, are the gun belt and holster. Arthit pulls the automatic free and lets the belt and holster fall to the floor. He stares down at the gun in his hand long enough to make Kosit put a hand on his arm.

Arthit looks up. "Count to thirty," he says. "Then knock over the table and call for help."

"Got it."

Arthit opens the back door. "I'll call you after I buy a new phone. They'll be looking out for calls from this one." He takes his phone out of his pocket and hands it to Kosit. The two men regard each other for a long, silent moment.

"I'm counting," Kosit says. "One . . ."

Arthit takes one last look at Noi's kitchen. Then he says, "Thanks. I won't forget this." A moment later he's out the door and into the dark, wet warmth of the night, the gun cold and reassuringly solid in his hand.

36

Head-On

H e should have accepted the painkillers Dr. Pumchang offered.

If he bends his elbow sharply and holds the taped hand
against his chest at about heart level, the throbbing subsides to a point
at which it's just a hairsbreadth on the wrong side of unbearable. He
cradles the left wrist in his right hand, with the result that he has no
hands free. It's getting dark, but the sidewalks are still crowded, and
he negotiates his way through the oncoming crowd, hands clasped to
the center of his chest like someone who is about to open them to sing,
his elbows pointed out in front of him to keep anyone from blundering
into the rigid, swollen, white-wrapped rectangle that used to be his left
hand.

His cell phone rings, and he lets go of the bad hand long enough to
bring the phone's display into his field of vision. Arthit's number again.
He'll have to answer sooner or later, but right now he hasn't got the
courage to find out what's happened. Not that a cop will tell him. But
why doesn't Arthit have his phone? He'll face it when he gets home.

Rafferty is a city boy by choice, and this is normally the hour he likes
best, when the day shrugs its shoulders and allows the night to slip back

in, when Bangkok goes through four or five kinds of light in an hour. The show begins with the gradual softening of dusk, the buildings' windows growing brighter and their edges sharper against the darkening sky as the first bats flap raggedly across it, and finishes with the sidewalks chalky with the spill of light from stores and restaurants and bars, and the bluish electric snap from the buzzing streetlights high overhead. He's often thought that Tolouse-Lautrec would have loved it.

But tonight it seems hellish and sulfurous, as though the world were lighted by Lautrec's gas-lamp footlights, turning faces into irregular expressionistic assemblages of light and shadow, concealing eyes and washing the color out of clothes. Making it harder to spot Yellow Shirt or any other extra, unwanted wheels he might be hauling along. Rafferty is keenly aware that he's the next thing to helpless—he'd do anything to prevent a blow to his hand—and the anxiety makes him scan the faces around him with an added degree of intensity.

Which is how he spots the girl.

As he nears the turn that will take him to his apartment, he becomes aware that the makeup of the crowd on the sidewalk has changed. There are more children than he is used to seeing, street children by the look of them, feral and filthy-faced and wearing dirty, ill-matched clothing. They weave in and out among the larger figures, sometimes passing him in the direction in which he is going, sometimes coming at him head-on. He notices one girl, perhaps twelve or thirteen, who has a tangle of wild hair above a scar that slashes diagonally down her forehead through her left eyebrow, mercifully skips the eye, and begins again as a furrow plowed into her smooth cheek. He watches her in profile as she overtakes him and disappears into the throng. Four or five minutes later, he sees her coming toward him.

Okay. Not random.

The girl doesn't glance at him, doesn't even seem to feel his eyes on her, but he knows she has registered his gaze, sees it in the almost undetectable increase in the speed at which she walks, in the sharper downward tilt of her head. Clutching the injured hand against his chest, he works his way over to a shop window and backs up until his shoulders touch the glass. Whatever is coming, it will at least have to come head-on.

And then, of course, he knows what it is that's coming.

He is already looking for the boy by the time the familiar face appears down the street, moving along at precisely the pace of the crowd, angling slowly toward the window where Rafferty waits, feeling his heart thrum in the vein at his throat and wondering how in the world he can factor *this* into his life right now. And then he realizes that whatever the boy wants, it would not be good for whoever is tailing him to see the connection between them, so he pulls the bandaged hand away from his chest and uses his right to hike the sleeve above the adhesive tape so he can check his watch. He does his best to register impatience and scan the crowd like someone who's being stood up, and then he turns and moves with the flow, but more slowly, keeping the buildings at his left shoulder.

The boy moves beside him without a glance. He has a hand on the arm of a young woman—a girl, really—who holds a baby. Neither of them seems to notice Rafferty, but the boy, without turning his head, says, "You're being followed."

Lowering his gaze to look at his watch again, Rafferty says, "How many, and what color shirt?"

"One. Blue. Can I get rid of him?"

"Don't hurt him. I'm in enough trouble already. Nobody in yellow?"

"Not for the last three blocks anyway."

"Let's lose him."

The boy shrugs assent and moves on. The girl beside him risks one short look at Rafferty, then snaps her head forward again, but not before her eyes slide down to the white-wrapped hand. She tosses a quick, puzzled smile and hurries on beside the boy, putting her free hand on his arm in a way that makes Rafferty think, *Hmmmm,* even under these circumstances.

A broad incline of steps opens up to Rafferty's left, rising to a complex of shops and restaurants that's anchored by an enormous and brilliantly lit McDonald's, in front of which Ronald offers the passing crowd a permanent plastic *wai,* hands palm to palm against his chest in greeting. Halfway up the steps, Rafferty turns idly and surveys the crowd, still trying to look like the man whose date hasn't shown.

His phone rings again, and again it's Arthit's number.

The sidewalk teems with people: those who left work late, those who are starting the evening early, those who are squeezing in some last-minute shopping, those who just want to move around now that the day's heat is lifting, those whose fingers are happiest in other people's pockets, those who are always on the street. Rafferty's attention is drawn by a shout and a sudden knot of people on the sidewalk, a little eddy like a whirlpool twelve or fifteen feet away. Another shout, a curse this time, and the knot dissolves, and three children streak for the curb. One of them holds a wallet straight up in the air like the Olympic torch. The children pause in the parking lane, tossing the wallet back and forth, and then there's an eruption of people, shoved forward from behind, and the children take off, heading back down Silom, away from Rafferty, with Blue Shirt in pursuit, screaming after them and stretching his arms in front of him as he runs, as though they were as elastic as chewing gum and he could suddenly extend them and snag the nearest kid.

"Now," the boy says, suddenly beside him. "Down, into the crowd, and around the corner. We'll be there." He descends a step and then turns back and says, "If you'll talk to me, I mean." Then he hops lightly down the stairs and melts into the crowd, and Rafferty, feeling old and fragile by contrast, pulls out his cell phone and, with some difficulty, opens it, then presses and holds the 1 key to speed-dial Rose. By the time she answers, he is already at the foot of the steps, pressing the bad hand to his chest.

"Rose," he says. "Get Miaow and leave the apartment." He finds an entry point in the crowd and steers himself into the stream of people. "No, nothing's wrong. I just need you to get your two watchers out of the way. I want to get into the building without being seen. Tell Miaow you'll buy her an ice cream or something. Call me when you know you're being followed." He folds the phone against his chin and drops it into his shirt pocket, then grabs his left wrist again as the hand seems to balloon with pain.

Five minutes later, standing on the side street with the boy and the young woman looking at him expectantly, he answers the phone, and Rose says, "The apartment's clear. They're behind us."

"THERE ARE TWENTY-FOUR right now," Boo says. He reaches up to the wall behind him and rubs the hanging blanket between his thumb and forefinger as though he's thinking about buying it. "Sometimes there are more, sometimes not so many."

"Twenty-six," says the girl, who has been introduced as Da. "If you count us."

"Twenty-five and a half," Boo says, and Da grins, and Rafferty has to tighten his jaw to keep it from dropping. The kid made a *joke*? In the old days, a little less than two years ago when the boy—then known by his street name, Superman—first barged into their lives—he'd rarely smiled at anything lighter than a five-act tragedy.

"Excuse me," Da says politely. "Why is your hand like that?"

"I don't want to forget my Carpenters CD," Rafferty says. "This way I never do."

"But—" Da says, looking puzzled.

The boy says, "Don't joke with her. She believes everything."

And Rafferty watches in amazement as the girl takes one hand off the baby and swats Superman—*Boo*—across the head.

"But you can't *play* it," Da says, glaring at the boy, who's cringing in mock terror, "if it's all taped up like that."

"This is my contribution to the evening, wherever I go," Rafferty says. "Making sure that there's at least one Carpenters CD that nobody can play."

"Who stomped on your hand?" Boo asks.

"Someone you'll never have to meet."

The boy shrugs without much interest and looks around. Despite Rafferty's efforts, the apartment on the fourth floor is dingy and cheerless. Through a six-inch gap between the sheets and pillowcases he hung over the windows, he can see wet-looking streaks of whatever the hell is left on glass after it's been badly washed.

"Why are we here?" Boo asks. "Where's Miaow?"

"We're here because we can't go upstairs for a bunch of reasons," Rafferty says, "and Miaow is out right now with Rose."

"What reasons?" the boy asks.

The girl asks, "Who's Miaow?"

"My daughter," Rafferty says, and suddenly an idea breaks over him like a wave. It's enough to make him sit forward and forget about the hand for a moment. "Twenty-four kids? You've got twenty-four kids?"

"Give or take," Boo says.

Da says, "How old is Miaow?"

"Then you can help me," Rafferty says, closing his eyes. He's been in another poker game for the past few days, he realizes, playing against pros this time, and he's suddenly been dealt a hand full of wild cards. He's already seeing it in his mind, setting up the bluff, figuring out what he'll need.

"Good," Boo says, settling into his uncomfortable chair, "because we need you to help us, too."

Da says again, "How old is—" but the boy cuts her off with a glance.

"WHERE ARE YOU?" demands Captain Teeth.

"Outside the apartment," says the man who had been watching Rafferty. "I only lost him for five or ten minutes this time."

Captain Teeth rests his forehead in his hand. "What do you mean, *this* time?"

"He went into a building an hour or so ago. He must have come out the back way or something, because I was out front the whole time. I picked him up about half an hour later, and he'd hurt his hand somehow. He went into another building and got it bandaged, and then . . . well, then—"

"Kid stole your wallet." Captain Teeth turns up the volume on the console. He has one earpiece of his headphone still in place, and the cell phone pressed to his other ear. Rafferty's apartment is silent.

"Three of the little bastards. But I got it back."

"I don't give a shit about your wallet. You shouldn't have chased them."

"It was my *wallet.*"

"Oh, golly," Captain Teeth says, listening to the silence in Rafferty's living room. "A few baht, some fake ID, maybe a condom. No wonder they tossed it."

"They got eight hundred baht."

"You'd already lost him once, you idiot. You should have stayed with him."

"Okay." When Captain Teeth doesn't say anything, the man adds, "Sorry."

"Any chance it was a setup?"

"You mean, do I think he's running a ring of homeless kids? No. The sidewalk was full of them. Must have been twenty."

Captain Teeth says, "Is that normal?"

"No," the man says grudgingly, "but come on. They move around. If they didn't, everybody'd be on the lookout all the time."

"What about the hand?"

"I don't know. Maybe cut, maybe broken. All wrapped up in bandages."

"Any lights on in the apartment right now?"

The man on the street counts balconies and corner windows until he gets to Rafferty's floor. "The one in the living room."

"Well, I can't hear him."

"Are the woman and the girl in there? I don't see the guys who follow them."

"No," Captain Teeth says. "They went out ten, fifteen minutes ago. The guys are behind them."

"So," the man on the street says, "what's the problem? There's no one for him to talk to."

"The woman got a phone call just before they went out," Captain Teeth says. "And what it all adds up to is that we don't really know where Rafferty is, and the building went for ten minutes or so with nobody watching it." He sits back in his chair and takes the nail of his uninjured thumb between his straggling incisors.

The man on the other end of the phone says, "Kai?"

Captain Teeth—Kai—says, "I'm thinking." The door to the office opens, and Ren comes in, looking sleepy. He's breathing through his mouth to cool the burned spot on his tongue. He looks at Kai, with the phone to one ear, and raises his eyebrows questioningly.

"Go inside," Kai says into the phone.

"And do what? Knock on his door?"

"Yes."

"He's *in* there, I'm telling you."

"Based on what?" Kai hears something in his other ear. "Hold on," he says. To Ren he says, "Grab the headphones."

Ren pulls out his chair, sits, and clamps the phones to his ears. Together the two of them listen to a ringing telephone in Rafferty's apartment.

Ren looks over at Kai and says, "So?"

"So some kids picked Dit's pocket, and Dit chased them and lost Rafferty, and the other two followed the woman and the girl out of the apartment, and now it's Dit's best guess that Rafferty's at home."

"Sure he is," Dit says on the phone.

"Then *why isn't he answering his phone?*" Kai demands. "The fucking thing has been ringing for twenty or thirty seconds."

Dit says, "Oh."

"Get your ass up there. Knock on the door. If he doesn't answer, pick the lock and take a look. If he *does* answer, just turn around and go down the stairs. Don't answer any questions, just get out of there."

"Wait," Ren says. "Let me try something." He takes out his own cell phone and dials Rafferty's cell number. Listens as it begins to ring.

Fails to hear it in his earphones.

"Go in," Kai says to Dit. "Go in now."

"I TOOK CARE of Miaow for a while," Boo is telling Da. "Way before she met Poke. She was only four or five then, but she was already on the street. Four or five, right?" he asks Rafferty.

"That's what she says. She also says you saved her life."

"She could take care of herself, even then." But Boo's cheeks have gone pink. "And I didn't take very good care of her when I started using *yaa baa,* did I?"

Da says, "You did *what?*"

"All day and all night."

Rafferty's cell phone rings.

"Why would you do that?" Da asks.

"I was crazy," Boo says. To Rafferty he says, "Aren't you going to answer that?"

"Not yet," Rafferty says. It rings again.

"Then when?" Boo asks. "What are you waiting for? A sign of some kind?"

"Oh, for Christ's sake," Rafferty says. "Everybody except me knows what I should do." He pulls out the phone and looks at it. His forehead creases for a moment as he looks at the number, and then he's up and running toward the door.

"Stay here," he says. "Don't go anywhere, don't open this door."

He takes the stairs three at a time, catching his foot once and landing on his outstretched palms, and he screams at the pain, but even while he's screaming, he's pushing himself to his feet again and running upstairs for all he's worth. If someone *was* watching the building, he has to be in the apartment. On the seventh floor, it suddenly occurs to him that the door to the eighth might be locked, and although he thinks it's impossible for his heart to beat any faster, it accelerates in his chest anyway and doesn't slow until the eighth-floor doorknob turns in his hand. He hurries down the corridor, fishing out his keys, and mutes the phone before slipping the key into the door.

Behind him the elevator moans and shudders into motion, bringing someone up.

He pushes the apartment door open slowly, breathing through his mouth to silence his panting. He pulls out the phone again, but it's no longer ringing. Tucking the reinjured hand beneath one arm and forcing himself to breathe regularly, he closes the door slowly, tiptoes to the bathroom, and flushes the toilet. Then he closes the door sharply. Still in the hallway outside the bathroom, he mops his forehead and pushes the button to return the most recent call.

RAFFERTY'S VOICE IN his earphones brings Ren bolt upright. Rafferty says, "Yeah?"

Kai has his cell phone to his ear. "Where were you?" He's pulled the earphones off and is looking at them as though they'd suddenly started transmitting classical music.

"What do you care? And aren't you supposed to *know* where I am? Something wrong with your terrific surveillance system?"

"You . . . ahhh, you didn't answer." Kai puts one of the phones back over his free ear.

"I was washing my hands, if you actually need to know. Something I usually do after I go to the bathroom."

Kai turns to Ren and gestures frantically at his own telephone. Ren looks at him, bewildered, and Kai puts a hand over the mouthpiece of his cell phone and rasps, *"Dit."*

"Oh," Ren says, dialing. He waits as the phone on the other end rings.

"Huh," Rafferty says. "Sounds like someone's in the hall."

"Oh, yeah?" Kai says. "You're . . . um, you're home, then?"

"Where else would I be? Hold on, somebody's just standing out there while his cell phone rings."

Ren says into his phone, *"Dit. Get out of there."*

"It's probably nothing," Kai says. "How did the interviews go?"

"Are we *chatting*?" Rafferty says. "And don't tell me it's nothing when it's at the door of my own apartment." There's a pause. "Well," he says. "Nobody there. Didn't even leave a copy of the *Watchtower*." Kai hears the door close. "So was there a reason you called?"

"Just reminding you there's a deadline coming up."

"That's very thoughtful of you." He disconnects, and a moment later Ren and Kai hear him in their earphones, saying to the empty room, "What a bunch of idiots."

37

I Might as Well Be Fluorescent

His first stop, maybe a quarter of a mile from the house, is an ATM. He withdraws the limit on his bank card, then inserts a credit card and does it again. Standing with his back to the sidewalk and his head down, panting from the run and feeling his shirt plaster itself to his spine, he watches the crisp new thousand-baht notes slide through the slot.

Put it together with what he already has and what Kosit gave him, and he's got twenty-three thousand baht. Not enough, not when he has no idea how long he'll be on the run.

On the run. Considering who he's running from, tonight may be the last time he'll be able to do this without sending skyrockets through the computer system. By tomorrow he probably won't even get his card back.

He wants to try the credit card again, but someone is waiting behind him, and he doesn't want anyone looking at him for long. He's pulled his shirt free of his trousers to hide the gun and opened his collar, but he's still unmistakably in uniform.

A police car speeds by, lights blinking, going in the direction of his house. Time to move.

At the curb he flags a motorcycle taxi, and the driver fishtails to a stop with an alacrity that makes it obvious he's registered that Arthit's a cop, loose shirttails or no loose shirttails. This does not make Arthit any happier than he is already.

"Pratunam," he says, and wraps his hands around the coward's grab bar on the rear of the rider's seat as the bike leaps forward.

And finds himself looking at the denim landscape of the driver's back and seeing his wife's eyes. *Noi,* he thinks.

In self-defense he conjures up Thanom's monkey face and waits for the surge of good, cold, cleansing fury. But instead something hollow and dark spins in a widening whirlpool beneath his heart, and he thinks again, *Noi.*

"THEY DUG A new river," Da is saying in the fourth-floor apartment, "and then they built a dam just below where they dug, so all the water went into the new riverbed and our river dried up." She tilts a plastic baby bottle, bought at Foodland that morning, into Peep's mouth. "They were smart," she says. "They did it toward the end of the summer, when the river always got low anyway. When the water stopped, we all thought it would start again by the time the rains came. But it didn't."

"Where did it go?" Rafferty says.

She is studying the baby's face. "To a golf course. When we went and looked, everybody was Japanese. All the golfers, I mean. The people who chased us away were Thai."

"You went and looked?"

"Well, sure," she says, meeting his eyes. "We wondered where our river had gone, so we followed the new one."

Boo is watching her as she talks. She glances over at him, and he holds his arms out to take the baby. She hands Peep to him without a moment's hesitation. When the child is comfortable in Boo's lap, he slips the nipple of the bottle between Peep's lips. Da watches long enough to make sure Peep is drinking before she returns her gaze to Rafferty. For a moment she seems to have forgotten where she is in her story, and Rafferty wonders for the third or fourth time about the relationship between them.

"They chased you away," he prompts.

"They didn't want us there. The place was so green and pretty and full of important people, and we were all dusty and had holes in our clothes. About a week later, they brought the big machines and knocked our houses down."

"Where did everyone go?"

She shakes her head. "Wherever they could. My mom and dad took my sisters and went to live with my mother's parents. But my grandfather doesn't have any money, so I came here." She flicks her eyes toward Boo. "To beg."

"Was there any kind of piece of paper? Did anyone ever show you anything that said they had the right to take the river? Or knock down the houses?"

She slips her index finger into the hole above the knee of her jeans and tugs at its edge. "The policemen who came with the machines had something, some piece of paper a lot of the people in the village had signed."

"What, a deed? Did someone pay you all something?"

"My father said it was something they were told to sign so they could vote. All the people who signed it were old enough to vote."

"Did it *say* anything about voting? Did it say anything about—I don't know—a bill of sale or anything?" He stops because she is looking down, working the finger in the hole in her jeans, and her face is darkening.

After a moment she says, "I don't know."

Rafferty says, "I see." He should have known she couldn't read.

"But that's not why we're here anyway," Boo says into the silence. "It's about the baby. It's about Peep."

HE BLOWS OUT in relief as the machine yields five thousand baht more. That's twenty-eight thousand, roughly eight hundred American dollars. The credit card worked again, but he's hit the limit for twenty-four hours, and by then the cards will be dead anyway. Thanom has the clout for that, and the people who are screwing with Rafferty have enough power, and probably enough foot soldiers, to put a man on every ATM in Bangkok.

His shirt is soaked through, the sweat turning the chocolate brown material almost black. It's still hot out, but this is the sweat of fury. When he thinks of Thanom, his hands involuntarily clench at his sides. The man has deprived Arthit of his time to mourn.

What would Noi want Arthit to do now? The answer comes as clearly as if she were standing beside him, whispering in his ear. He should take care of himself.

He briefly asks himself whether the best way to take care of himself would be to turn himself in, then dismisses it. The two cops who came to his door had removed their name plates. If only one of them hadn't been wearing his name, Arthit might have chalked it up to sloppiness or a memory lapse. But both of them? Something very wrong there. Kosit was the one who had called in the death, so whoever took the call knew there was another cop in Arthit's house. The two who came to the door didn't want Kosit to know their names.

He doesn't think Thanom would have him killed. But *something* was going on, something outside the normal course of official detention and questioning. Maybe it was just a stall for time; maybe he was going to be lost in the system for a while, stuck in some cell somewhere with no way out until he could be "discovered" and apologized to, maybe even given some sort of token, a raise or something. But that could be weeks from now, after whatever it is Thanom thinks Arthit knows will no longer have value.

And that something has to be connected with Pan. This all began with Pan.

He catches a whiff of his own sweat and glances down at his shirt.

Right, clothes. The booths that crowd the sidewalks of Pratunam are beginning to shut—there's a dark spot here and there where the spotlights have already been doused—but the sellers who are active are eager to accommodate a policeman. Within twenty minutes he has bags containing three anonymous plaid shirts, a couple of generic T-shirts, and two pairs of preshrunk, precreased, totally indestructible and wholly synthetic pants that will probably be the last man-made objects on earth. His shoes are a dead giveaway, cop from soles to laces, but they fit well, and if anyone gets close enough to look at them, he's finished anyway. He makes a final stop at a booth that sells toiletry articles and buys a razor, some shaving foam, a comb, and a toothbrush. The woman studies him as she puts them into the bag, wondering why a cop needs to buy the stuff for a night out and concluding that he's got some action lined up somewhere. She practically winks at him as she hands him his purchases.

She'll remember him, too.

So far, he thinks, tucking the bag under his arm with the others, *I might as well be fluorescent, leaving glowing footprints everywhere I go.* How the hell did crooks manage?

Still, with the change of clothes in a bag and the night stretching out around him in all directions, he can feel a sort of *click* inside, a hardening of purpose and sharpening of focus he has come to regard as his cop mode. When he feels like this, he occasionally visualizes himself as a human flashlight, pointed forward, sharp-eyed, able to ignore the irrelevant and cut through the fog of confusion. This is when he does his best work.

But the lift in his spirits doesn't last long. He's looking for someplace he can change clothes when he sees the blinking lights. Regular, steady, red flashes, coming from the intersection half a block in front of him. He turns around to put some distance between himself and the police van, then halts. There are red lights in the street behind him, too, at the other end of the block. And he stands there, clutching the bags as the illusion of competence recedes, asking himself why on earth he took the time to go shopping on the same street where he used an ATM.

"THEY TOOK THE kid away from her," Da says. "Like it was a lamp or something, not a . . . a child. And next time I saw her, she had a new one. They gave her a baby. The same way they gave Peep to me."

"Wichat did," Rafferty says, just trying to keep track.

Da says, "I guess so."

"He's been sending beggars out with babies for at least a year," Boo says. "Everybody on the street knows it. But nobody says anything. He's not a friendly guy."

"Where does he get them? Any idea what he's doing?"

Boo says, "What I think he's doing is selling them. I think he's buying them someplace, maybe from people who steal them, and then keeping them until he can find a buyer. And giving them to beggars, so that . . . well, that way he doesn't have to draw attention by storing a whole bunch of babies somewhere."

"And beggars with babies make more money," Da says. "At least that's what he told me."

"You say babies," Rafferty says. "How old is a baby?"

"A year," Superman says with a shrug. "Maybe a year, eighteen months. Like Peep."

"So they can't talk," Rafferty says.

Da says, "No. I didn't see any that were old enough to talk, except some who were injured and the boy they took away, and he was simple or something. He never said a word."

"Why does that matter?" Superman says. He squints, working it out. "Because . . . what? Because babies can't tell the people who buy them that they were stolen?"

"Sure," Rafferty says. "And maybe because if they *could* talk, they wouldn't speak Thai."

Da looks down at Peep as though he could answer her question. "Not speak Thai?"

"Three or four years ago," Rafferty says, "there was a big baby racket in Cambodia. People went there from America and Europe, thousands of them, to adopt children who were supposed to be orphans. But they weren't orphans. They'd been bought from poor families for fifty or a hundred dollars. Sometimes they were just stolen. The new parents paid anywhere from thirty to fifty thousand dollars for a baby. The money was supposed to pay some sort of official fees."

Boo says, "Thirty to fifty thousand per *kid*?"

"Per kid."

"There were four or five babies at the place I was staying," Da says. The numbers are unimaginable. "And I think they may have more places."

"They have three more," Boo says. "My guess is that they've got fifteen or twenty babies at any time."

Rafferty says, "A while back I heard something about babies being brought here, carried across the border by women who pretended to be their mothers. Makes sense, I suppose, just thugs shaking hands across the border. The racket was too profitable to let it go. But I'm not sure what you want me to do. Do you want to find a way to get— What's the baby's name?"

"Peep," Da says.

"Do you want to get Peep back to his mother or something?"

"Oh," Da says, looking like someone who has just been surprised by a loud noise. "I don't . . . I mean, I don't—"

Rafferty's phone rings. He pulls it out of his pocket and checks the display, which says KOSIT.

THERE IS NOWHERE to go. Another van has pulled up at each end of the block, straight across all the lanes to cut off the traffic, and Arthit sees six or eight uniformed policemen climb out of each. They obviously intend to work toward one another in the hope that Arthit is somewhere between them. He sees them split up, some moving slowly, trolling the sidewalk, while others stop and talk to the vendors.

The uniforms have fanned out onto both sides of the street, which is now empty of traffic and too wide and well lit to cross comfortably. Arthit knows he'd never make it to the other side. He's closer to the vans in front of him, so he turns around and moves with the crowd, which is gradually slowing to a stop. The cops at either end are funneling people down to single file, peering at faces.

He stops walking. *Faces?* How would they know what he looks like? It's surprising enough that Thanom could scramble a force so quickly; there's no way he's had the time to print out and distribute a stack of Arthit's file photos. He moves a bit farther along until he's in front of a booth that's gone dark, and he steps back into the gloom and squints at the group of cops that's working its way toward him from his left.

He *knows* some of them. He sees three men and one woman he has worked with, nobody he could call a friend but people who can identify him on sight. Even a change of clothing isn't going to allow him to slip away.

The nearest pair of cops reaches the booth where he bought his shirts. The vendor keeps his face down, not wanting to challenge the cops in any way, but then he looks up and nods an answer. He talks for a moment, waving his hand along the sidewalk in Arthit's direction. Then he comes out from behind his counter and indicates the booth where Arthit bought the razor.

The dark spot where Arthit is standing suddenly feels quite a bit brighter than it did a moment ago. Without looking left or right, he crosses the uneven sidewalk to its far edge and begins to move slowly along, his left shoulder almost brushing the walls of the buildings that face the booths. Unlike some areas of Pratunam, where booths hem the sidewalks on both sides, here they're only on the traffic side. Opposite them are older, somewhat run-down buildings, mostly four- and five-story structures with shops at street level and apartments or offices above them. The street windows are mostly dark now, the shops locked, but he's hoping that one of the doors leading upstairs will be open.

Keeping his movement small, using nothing but his left arm, he pushes on doors as he goes past them, twisting the occasional handle. He's getting too close to a group of three cops who are stopping people on the sidewalk. If they look up and survey the crowd, they'll see his face. Arthit is on the verge of taking a desperate chance and crossing the wide, empty street when the door he's pushing on swings away from him.

He'd actually given up, and the open door takes him by surprise. He has to back up a step to go through it. It's a glass door, framed in weathered, pockmarked aluminum. When it shuts behind him, he checks to see whether it can be locked from inside, but no—it needs to be keyed.

He finds himself in a small, murky space with just enough room for the door to clear the bottom step. The only light other than the splash from the street comes from a fluorescent tube at the top of the stairway. Without a backward glance, he turns away from the street and starts to climb the stairs, trying not to hurry. Hurry draws attention.

The night opens to the *whoop-whoop-whoop* of another police vehicle forcing its way through traffic. They must have called for additional support after they talked to the vendors in the booths. Thanom is serious, or whoever is pulling Thanom's strings is serious.

At the top of the stairs, he finds a door and a switchback leading to another flight of stairs. He reaches up and pops the fluorescent tube loose and stands for a moment in the welcome darkness. Then he climbs the next flight of stairs.

There are three floors above the shop, then a short flight of stairs that leads to the roof. Each stair landing has a light, and after a moment's thought he leaves the others on. If the cops come up the stairs and discover that the first fluorescent has been detached from its connection, additional tampering on the higher floors will just give them a trail to follow. He might as well put up a sign that says LOOK HERE. At the very top of the stairs, he checks out the door to the roof and finds it padlocked on the inside. He goes back down to the door on the first landing and gives it a shove. It opens onto a hallway, only ten or fifteen meters long, with two doors on each side. Four apartments in all.

He knows that finding an empty apartment is too much to hope for, but he quietly tries the doorknobs anyway. All locked. At the third one, he hears a questioning voice from inside: Someone must be waiting for a visitor. He barely makes it back to the stairwell before he hears the apartment door open. A moment later it closes again. He leans against the wall on the dark stair landing, fighting to get his breath under control.

Then, forcing his legs to move again, he turns and hauls himself up the stairs to the next floor. The apartment doors here are also locked, but at the end of the hall is a fifth door, which he pulls open. He finds himself looking at mops and brooms. A big, rust-stained, industrial-size basin hangs from one wall. A sagging shelf above the sink holds floor wax, powdered cleanser, paper towels. Nothing he can use. He thinks about taking the powdered cleanser, maybe throwing it into someone's eyes, then rejects it. There will certainly be a gun pointed at him, and he'll be dead before his target even sneezes.

He's climbing up to the third floor when he hears the door to the street open.

"Wait here," says a male voice. It's a voice that sounds comfortable with command. "We'll go up. You guys keep your eyes on the side-walk. And nobody gets out through this door."

RAFFERTY IS IN the dirty, empty master bedroom of the fourth-floor apartment with no memory of how he got there. "He can't come here," Rafferty says. "This place is being watched twenty-four hours, and it's the first place they'll look. If he calls you, tell him not to come here."

"I don't know whether he'll call me," Kosit says. "And there's no way for me to reach him."

Rafferty's bandaged hand fires off a telegram of pain. He's accidentally put it against the wall to steady himself. He tucks it safely under his right arm and considers whether to ask the next question. "Did you see her?"

A pause. Then, "Yes."

"Did he?"

"The envelope on the door said not to go in, but you know him. He figured she might still be alive."

Rafferty's eyes are closed so tightly he sees red fireworks. "How bad was it?"

"She was an angel," Kosit says. Rafferty can hear him swallow even on the phone. "She put on a really nice dress and even some makeup. She got all pretty, lay on her back, spread her hair out on the pillow, and went to sleep."

"God bless her," Rafferty says around the stone in his throat. "Hold on." He tucks the phone under his left arm, wipes the cheeks he hadn't known were wet, and dries his hand on his shirt. Then he puts the phone back to his ear. "Do you have any idea where he might have gone?"

"Nope. I'm at the station now, and there was kind of a flurry a little while ago. Thanom sent a bunch of guys out to Pratunam, but even if it was Arthit, I'm sure he's not there anymore."

Rafferty sniffles and says, "He'd want to buy clothes. Pratunam would be good."

"Yeah. But you know he's not going to hang around anywhere. He's probably in some hotel by now."

"I hope so. What did her note say?"

"He didn't open it."

"No, I suppose not. He'd want to be alone when he did that."

"Right. God forbid he should get emotional in front of somebody."

"If he does call you, tell him I'll be out of here by the end of the day tomorrow. All three of us will. Tell him I'll have my cell phone."

"If they can put a flag on his phone, they can do the same to yours."

"I'll buy a stolen one as soon as I'm off everybody's radar and call to give you the number. Tell him I can meet him any time after about three tomorrow. We should all be free and clear by then."

"Just call me," Kosit says. "That fucker Thanom."

"Thanom could monitor your phone, too."

"I'm not important enough."

"You were at the card game. You're Arthit's friend. You should get another cell phone. When you've got it, call my landline at the apartment to leave the number. Make something up—you're calling about the carpeting or something. I can retrieve it from voice mail even if I'm not there."

"Will do."

"I've got to call you back in a few minutes, after I finish something here. I need you to buy some stuff for me tomorrow morning." Rafferty disconnects and wipes at his cheeks again. Then, blinking fast, he goes back into the living room. Boo and Da look up when he comes in.

"You okay?" Boo asks.

"It's a rough time." Rafferty sits on the stool with the cracked seat. "Listen, I can either write this story or put you together with someone who can do it better than I could. But I want to do something else, too. I want you to meet a guy named Pan."

Boo's eyes widen. "The rich guy? The gold car?"

"That's the one."

Da says, "Why?"

"I don't know what I think about him," Rafferty says, "and a lot depends on who he really is. What he does after he meets you might answer some questions. But I have to tell you that it could be dangerous. I don't think it will be, but I can't be certain. And at least we'll walk in with our eyes open. So it's up to you."

Da says, "Everything I've done for weeks has been dangerous."

"You're a brave kid," Rafferty says. He turns to Boo. "Let's talk about what I need you to do tomorrow morning."

"How many do you want?" Boo asks.

"Fourteen or fifteen, boys and girls. Is that a problem?"

Boo says, "You're the one with the problems."

TWO PAIRS OF feet, coming up. They've already checked the first floor. For a moment, Arthit had thought he might be able to get past them while they were checking out the apartments, slip down the stairs, and deal somehow with whomever they left at the door. But they were smarter than that. At the first-floor landing, there was a short silence, and then the fluorescent light came back on.

"Well, look at that," said the authoritative voice. "Is the light out on the next floor?"

Arthit heard one pair of shoes go up three or four steps. "No," said the younger voice. "It's on."

"Okay. You wait here. And take your damn gun out. You think you're in line for dinner or something?"

"No, sir."

"Don't move, got it? If you hear something, you just stay here. Yell if you have to, but wait for me."

"Fine."

"And remember. He's dangerous and he's armed. Nobody's going to get crazy if you shoot him."

"But he's— Do you really think—"

"Doesn't matter what I think. It's what I've been told."

"Yes, sir."

The door had closed, and Arthit had waited motionlessly for five or six minutes on the steps just above the third-floor landing until the older cop came back into the stairwell on the second floor and the two men began to climb. Shoes in hand, Arthit moved on flat feet, letting the noise below him drown out the sound of his own movement until he was at the padlocked door to the roof. He can go no farther.

It's just a matter of time.

While the other two are still moving, he puts the bags at his feet, laying them down in slow motion so the plastic won't crackle. On the second floor of apartments, the two cops go through the same routine, the younger one waiting in the stairwell while the older one goes into the hallway. As Arthit stands there, his back to the door to the roof, waiting for them to come, waiting for whatever will happen when they do, he realizes he feels nothing except an overpowering loneliness. For fourteen years Noi has been the first person he saw every morning, the person he held as he slept. The sound of her laughter was the world's most beautiful music.

They were going to get old together.

She had put on lipstick for him. Before she sipped at the tea that she used to wash down the pills, she had put on the light pink lipstick he loved best. That morning, when she moved to his side of the breakfast table and rested her head on his shoulder, she had known it would be the last time.

Arthit finds he doesn't care whether he lives or dies.

He waits, his body feeling as heavy and inert as stone, as they finish on the second floor and climb to the third. He can probably measure the rest of his life in minutes. The gun at his waist is sharp and hard against his stomach. He takes it out and looks at it for a second, then very slowly lays it down beside the bags. There's no way he's going to shoot a policeman.

The two cops climb the final steps to the third floor. Nothing remains between them and Arthit but a corner and a short flight of stairs. The door to the apartment hallway closes, and Arthit waits, his arms hanging down and slightly apart from his sides, his hands open and empty, with the palms facing outward.

Shoes scuff concrete. The younger cop comes around to the bottom of the stairs, his gun extended, and looks up.

Arthit stands there, waiting. He knows the young cop's face, although he can't put a name to it. They worked together on something, sometime.

For five or six very long seconds, the young patrolman stands perfectly still, staring up at Arthit. His eyes drop to the automatic on the floor and come up again to meet Arthit's. Then, slowly, he transfers his gun from his left hand to his right. He works the free right hand into his trouser pocket, and Arthit follows the movement, expecting a throwdown gun or maybe a taser, but when the young cop's hand comes out, it holds a fold of currency. He puts the gun barrel to his lips like a hushing finger and tosses the money underhand. The money transcribes a graceful arc and lands at Arthit's feet. The young cop holds out his free hand, palm out—*Wait there*—then climbs three steps and turns his back to Arthit, listening.

After a couple of minutes, the door to the third floor opens, and the young cop makes a point of scraping his shoes against the concrete as he goes down the stairs and disappears around the corner. "Nothing up there except the door to the roof," he says. "It's padlocked from inside."

"Okay," says the older cop. "Maybe they've already got him down below."

Arthit hears them descending. The moment he hears the street door swing shut, his legs fold beneath him and he finds himself sitting among the bags of clothes.

38

Nobody Sees Street Kids

When the door opens, Miaow pushes around Rose and stops as though she's walked into a window. Her eyes almost double in size as she sees Boo, and then—immediately—they jump to Da, and from Da to the baby in Boo's lap. She says, "Ahhh, ahhhh."

"Why are you down—" Rose starts to ask Poke, and then she sees Boo, too, and her smile fills her face. "Oh," she says. "*You're* here."

"I—" Miaow says, and stops, her eyes moving back and forth. "I mean, *you*—"

"This is Da," Boo says. "And the baby is named Peep."

"Baby," Miaow says, as though the word were in a brand-new language.

"Not mine," Boo says. "Not really Da's either."

Rose says, "We should get upstairs, Poke. They were behind us when we came back. They're going to expect to hear something."

"Fine," Rafferty says, heading for the door. "Coming, Miaow?"

Miaow gives him a look that could turn him to ash.

"Guess not," Rafferty says. "We'll pretend you're pouting. For a change. Open the door quietly when you come in." To Superman he says, "See you tomorrow." The boy nods, but he's looking at Miaow.

Rose says, "What's all that stuff on your hand?"

"Tell you in the elevator," he says. He closes the door behind them. In the hall he says, "And I have to tell you something else. About Noi."

"WHAT HAPPENED TO your hair?" Boo says.

"I fixed it," Miaow says. Her eyes go to Da again.

"I liked it better the other way."

"Who cares?" Miaow says. Her fists are brown knots at her sides. "Who cares what you like? Where did you go? Where have you *been*? And who's she?"

"I told you. She's Da."

"Who's Da?"

Boo says, "Why don't you ask Da?"

"I'm asking you."

"He's my friend," Da says. "He got me away from some bad people."

Miaow chews on the inside of her cheek for a moment. "How long have you known him?"

Da's eyebrows contract. "How long?" she asks Boo.

"Couple of days."

Da says, "It feels like a week."

"What does he mean, it's not your baby?" Miaow says. "What kind of bad people?" She abandons that line of questioning and turns her eyes to Boo. "Why did you go away?"

"I made a mistake. About Poke. I thought he was—you know, a bad guy."

Miaow says, *"Poke?"*

"I was wrong. But I didn't really go away, not at first. For a few months, I kept an eye on you. To make sure you were okay."

"Did not," Miaow says.

"I did."

She gives him hard eyes. "I never saw you."

"I was careful. And I had some other kids watch you from time to time."

"If he wants to disappear," Da says, "he just disappears."

"*I* know that," Miaow says. "I was with him for a long time. Not just two or three days, like *you*."

"Miaow," Boo says.

"He took care of me," Miaow says, and suddenly she's swiping at her cheeks with her forearm. "I was almost a baby, and he . . . he—" She breaks off, grabs air, and dives in again. "I thought . . . I thought you started again. Started the *yaa baa,* I mean. I thought you went away because you wanted that. More than you wanted anything. More than you wanted to—I don't know—to stay with me. With us."

"No," Boo says. "I don't use that now. Remember Hank Morrison?"

"Sure." She scrubs her arm over her eyes as though she's punishing them. Then she sniffles. "He helped Poke adopt me."

"He got me into a monastery up north. The monks got me through it."

She looks at him over the top of her arm. "A monastery?"

The corners of his mouth lift. "I meditated. I even ate vegetables."

"But you're back," Miaow says. "You're here. Why did you come back?"

"I belong here. Where else would I go?"

"It's his forest," Da says.

Miaow looks at Da as though she doesn't understand, but then she nods. "It is," she says. "But why are you here now? I mean *here*, in this apartment?"

"I came to ask Poke for help," Boo says. "But it turns out I'm going to help him."

"How?"

Boo lifts Peep to his shoulder and begins to pat the baby's back. "I'm going to get you out of here."

"A FIRE," TON says.

"That's what he looked for," says Ren. "They checked the search history on the computer he used in the morgue at the *Sun*. He was looking for fires. He printed out stuff on four or five of them, a factory and some houses and a couple of slums."

Ton is wearing a suit that cost more than three thousand dollars and looks every penny of it. He leans against the edge of the desk, the unbuttoned, silk-lined jacket hanging open in a way that gives Ren an almost sickening pang of envy. No matter what he does, no matter how much money he eventually makes, he will never in his life look like that, like a man who was born to wear expensive clothes.

Captain Teeth—Kai—has one earphone in place and is listening to Ton and Ren with the free ear. Now he swivels his chair around to face them and says, "So he's looking for a fire? So what? Anyone could see that Pan's been in a fire, with those hands."

"He saw Pan's hands the first time they met," Ton says. "Why go looking for fires *now*?" He runs his own hand over his jaw as though checking on his shave. "Who did he talk to today?"

"The cop, Thanom," Ren says. "And Wichat."

"Thanom knows part of it," Ton says, "but he'd never say anything, not after what he went through to erase those records." He lowers his eyes, studying an area of the carpet. "Wichat might say things he shouldn't—he's stupid enough—but I doubt he knows much of anything. Still," he says, "Wichat."

"But you . . ." Ren says. He looks like he's trying to hear something that's just out of earshot.

"Yes? I what?"

"You *gave* him Wichat."

"Of course I did. Anybody good would have found Wichat. When someone really digs into Pan—and they will if we continue—it'll be somebody good. You've got to assume that the people you go up against will be good, or you'll be caught stretching your willie when you should be wondering what's around the corner. And after he talked to Wichat, he went to the morgue at the *Sun*?"

Ren says, "He called me to set it up."

Ton straightens. "Timing," he says. "Wichat doesn't know what the fire means, any more than you two do, but he knows when it happened. He probably gave Rafferty a year, maybe two. Rafferty went looking for fires during that period. Anybody who puts it together is going to have a new set of questions." He pushes himself away from the desk and puts both hands into his trouser pockets. Ren hears change jingle. "This exercise would have been worth it," Ton says. He glances at Ren.

"If it weren't for having to kill the reporter. As it is, it may be worth it anyway."

He goes to the door and opens it, but instead of going through, he lets it swing closed again and turns back to Ren. "Anything else? I mean anything at all."

Ren swallows before answering. "His tail lost him twice today. Just for a few minutes."

Ton blinks slowly, leaving his eyes closed for a second. "How? When? Where?"

"The first time was after he finished at the *Sun*. He went back to Silom, probably just going home, but he kept looking behind him, like he knew someone was back there."

"He undoubtedly did," Ton says, putting his teeth into it. "I more or less told him he'd be followed."

"But Dit—that was who was following him—Dit figured that he shouldn't let Rafferty see his face. Rafferty went into a building, and when he got into the elevator, he turned around again, so Dit ducked back, and he couldn't see what floor Rafferty went to."

Ton waits. After a long moment, he says, "And?"

Ren licks his lips and winces as his upper lip brushes the burn on his tongue. "And there was an exit on the side of the building. Rafferty must have used that, because Dit waited in front for a long time. After he found the side exit, he started working his way up and down the block. Checked all the stores, anywhere Rafferty might have ducked inside. About twenty, twenty-five minutes later, he saw Rafferty, back on the sidewalk. He'd done something to his hand. He was holding it like he'd broken it or something. And then Rafferty went into a building that has a lot of doctors in it and took the elevator to the sixth floor. About an hour later, he came back down with bandages on his hand."

"This is wonderful," Ton says. "He goes missing for a few minutes and then shows up injured, and we don't know how. Where is he now?"

"In the apartment," Kai says, pointing at his headphones. "With his wife."

"Well, that's something," Ton says. He turns to Ren. "You said twice, we lost him twice."

"Right after he came out with the bandages. Some street kids stole Dit's wallet, and he chased them."

Ton says, "I am surrounded by idiots. Pull Dit off and put somebody better on it. In fact, pull off everyone who might know who you're working for."

"Dit's the only one. What do you want me to do with him?"

"I don't care. Give him something unpleasant to do."

"Anyway, Rafferty went right back to his apartment. We heard him. So nothing happened."

"Dit should be thankful for that," Ton says. He opens the door again. "We'll give Rafferty one more day, just to see how much closer he gets. By tomorrow night we'll be done with him. But don't lose him again. Don't lose any of them."

"After tomorrow," Ren says, "what should we do with him?"

Without looking back, Ton says, "You didn't ask me that question, and I don't ever want to hear how it was answered." The door swings closed behind him.

Ren waits a minute or two to make sure Ton isn't coming back. He gets up and goes to the door and opens it on an empty hallway. Then he closes it and says, "This makes me very uncomfortable."

"What would it take to make you comfortable?" Captain Teeth asks. "It could have taken you years to get this close to the man. You're almost living in his pocket."

"That's what makes me uncomfortable."

"You know why. He couldn't involve a bunch of people in this thing. It's too . . ." His voice trails off.

"It's too what?" Ren prompts. "Too dangerous? How about 'Get rid of everyone who knows who we're working for'?"

Captain Teeth puts the other earphone in place and swivels to face the console. With his back to Ren, he says, "I'll think about it."

BOO WATCHED ME *to make sure I was all right,* Miaow writes. Her face is glowing. *For a long time after he ran away.*

Rafferty reads the note and takes the pen. *How long?*

Miaow grabs the pen away from him and turns the page over. *I don't know. He had other kids watch me, too.*

Did you see any of them? Rafferty writes.

No. I wasn't looking. She chews on the end of the pen until Rafferty reaches out and pushes it away from her mouth. *But nobody sees street kids,* she writes. And she watches Rafferty read her sentence three or four times and then sit back and stare at the opposite wall.

Wild cards, he thinks again. *Street kids can follow anyone.*

39

Replay

Rafferty says, "I like the hair."

Miaow says, "Really? You're not just trying to make me feel better? You don't think it looks dumb? And fake?"

Rose says in Thai, "It's very stylish. It's not supposed to look real, Miaow, not any more than lipstick is. And it catches the light well. Lots of highlights."

"Honest? I mean, you really think so? Do you think the kids at school will, um . . . ?"

"If they don't like it," Rafferty says, "it'll just be because they're envious."

"Oh, come on," Miaow says.

Rose says, "It makes you look older."

The morning light pours in through the sliding door to the balcony, bouncing off the glass top of the coffee table to create a rectangle of sunlight on the ceiling. Other than the sunlight, nothing in the apartment is moving. The small tape recorder is hooked up, via its expensive connectors, to Rafferty's amplifier, and the voices come out of the bookshelf speakers on either side of the empty room.

Down on the fourth floor, Rose says, in person, "This is ridiculous. It's way too big."

She is wearing a gray uniform jacket and matching slacks. The slacks have a black stripe down each side. Under the jacket are a white shirt and a black clip-on tie. Her shoes are cheap black lace-ups with rubber soles.

"Hair down inside your shirt," Rafferty says. "All of it. Tie it back with a rubber band or something."

"So? Everything will still be too big." She pulls at the waistband of the pants. "I'm swimming in it."

"Don't worry, you won't be." Rafferty goes behind her and tries to gather her hair between his hands but gives up immediately. "Two-hand job," he says. "I'm disqualified."

"Do you actually think this will work?" She has tugged the back of the shirt away from her neck and is stuffing hair down inside it. "I look like a clown."

"It'll happen fast," he says, "and we'll set it up. Like a bluff in poker. They'll see what we want them to see. They'll hear a male voice just before they see you. They'll put it together themselves and see a man for the three or four seconds you're visible. And don't forget, there will be other stuff going on."

"But why is everything so big? Did Kosit get the wrong size?"

"No. You and Miaow each have three shirts, two pairs of pants, an extra pair of shoes, a couple of towels, and the other stuff on the list, right?"

"I put it together myself."

"And you brought the wide scarf I took out of your closet."

"It's a shawl," she says, "and yes, I have it, although I can't imagine where I'm going to wear a cashmere shawl when I'm supposed to be running for my life."

"You're going to wear it under your shirt, tied around your middle. With all those extra clothes inside it. You're going to be a guy with a gut. And the uniform will fit once you've got your belly on."

She gives the collar a tug and puts on the cap. "So?" she says. "Is it me?"

"Tilt the cap back a little bit to close the gap between it and the collar."

Rose uses both hands to reset the cap, being careful not to allow any hair to fall out of it. "Maybe I should just cut it off."

"It'll be fine. We'll bobby-pin the cap so it can't slip."

"Listen to you," she says. "I married a hairdresser."

"You wish."

"Poor Arthit," Rose says. "How will he get by? She was the only thing he loved in the world."

"I have to find him," Rafferty says.

"Let him lick his wounds. He's not someone who asks for help."

"No, but that doesn't mean I don't want to give him some. And I have to see whether there's any way I can get him out of this jam with Thanom. Especially since it's basically my fault."

His cell phone rings. "Put the shawl on the table and put the stuff on it," he says. "Try to get it even. You don't want a lumpy stomach." He opens the phone and says, "Yeah?"

"Snakeskin Industries," Floyd Preece says. "Am I good or what?"

"I don't know, Floyd. What's Snakeskin Industries?"

"A *snakeskin*. It's something that's empty when it's left behind. It's the company that owned the factory that burned down, the one that made Buffy the Bunny, remember?"

"I remember. But I also remember, from reading the newspapers, that it *was* empty—it was a holding company that was held by another holding company, and nobody could identify any of the officers."

"Yeah, well, Snakeskin didn't own it when it burned down."

"I'm not following you. You just said—"

"You're right about the cops; they couldn't find anything about the company that owned the place when the fire happened. The American corporation that made the bunnies or whatever they were leased the place, and the company they leased it from was a system of double and triple blinds. But eighteen months later the factory, the shell of it anyway, was sold, and the company it was sold to, the company that sold it a second time, was Snakeskin Industries."

"I guess that's interesting. Sort of."

"Oh, it's interesting," Preece says. "Because of who Snakeskin sold it to."

Rafferty waits for a second or two and then says, "This is an irritating pause."

"They sold it to Pan."

Rafferty watches Rose pile Miaow's and her things in even layers as he thinks. "You're right," he says, "that qualifies as interesting. It'll be even more interesting if you know who owns Snakeskin."

"I don't know who the Thai principal is, but a special permit was issued to Snakeskin Industries to operate in Thailand under partial foreign ownership."

"Foreign as in?"

"As in a guy named Tatsuya Kanazawa. And, as you might guess from the name, old Tatsuya isn't Thai."

"Japanese," Rafferty says, and a little jolt of electricity fizzes through him. "Is he—did you read anything about him being yakuza?"

"No," Preece says patiently. "But it's still morning."

"And there was nothing on the other partner, the Thai partner?"

"No again. But Tatsuya's part owner of another business in Bangkok, too."

"Let me guess," Rafferty says. "Steel."

"Awwwww," Preece says. "Tell me you didn't already know all this."

"You've done great, Floyd."

"Money," Preece says. "You were supposed to give me some last night."

"I'll call you later and let you know where to meet me."

"You'd better," Preece says. "Or I won't tell you the rest of it." He hangs up.

"I don't know about this," Rose says, looking down at the strata of stuff she's spread over the shawl.

"Don't worry about it," Rafferty says. "You're going to be a great-looking fat guy."

"IT'S HOT DOWN here," says the man who's been assigned to Rose. "Gotta be thirty-one, thirty-two degrees."

"You're breaking my heart," Captain Teeth says on the other end of the phone.

"All I'm saying, why can't we take turns? One of us goes to get cool for a few minutes, then comes back and—"

"Not the plan," Captain Teeth says. "The man wants everybody on the job."

"Well, what are they doing? Does it sound like they're coming out or what?"

"They're sitting around talking about hair color."

"Must be the little girl. She had it dyed red a day or two ago."

"Apparently it looks great," Captain Teeth says. "Stay where you are." He closes the phone and drops it onto the console.

Out on the street in front of Rafferty's apartment house, the man who's been assigned to Rose watches a few street kids float by. Five or six of them. They've been up and down the street a couple of times, just straggling along, peering through the windows of parked cars and generally looking for trouble. One of them had asked him for money, and the man had shown the kids the back of his hand and told them to beat it. But they were back.

If he had his way, the man who's been assigned to Rose thinks, they'd all be rounded up and put in jail. Little animals. They invade neighborhood after neighborhood, looking for pockets to pick, things to steal. Give *real* crooks a bad name. Lock them all in a cage, drop the key in the river, and drop the cage on top of it. Or do like they did in that Japanese movie, whatever it was called—*Battle Royale,* that was it—and strand them on an island and force them to kill one another until only one's left. And then write a new ending and kill the one who's left.

At the corner the kids turn around and drift back aimlessly, and suddenly one of the kids at the rear of the pack lets out a scream of warning, and about ten new kids round the corner at a run. The gang the man has been watching breaks into a full-out sprint with the others in pursuit. The ones in front look terrified. Two of the bigger boys in the group that's chasing them are waving something that look like ax handles. They chase the smaller group like a pack of wild dogs.

The man settles back in his doorway to enjoy the show. The kids in front make a rapid turn to their right, as tightly knit as a flock of swallows, and disappear down the ramp into the garage beneath the apartment house. The other group, the larger group, follows.

A man in the garage bellows in Thai, "Out! Get out!" and a second later the kids erupt onto the street again, the groups mixed now into a single cloud of children, and there's another deep shout, and a tall, fat guard in uniform runs out of the garage behind them, brandishing a billy club. The kids pick up the pace, and five or six seconds later they've all vanished around the corner, the guard in pursuit.

The man who's been assigned to Rose realizes he's stepped out into the sunlight to watch the spectacle, and he retreats back into the shade. For a few seconds, it occurs to him, he was so interested he hadn't given a thought to how hot it is.

IN THE GARAGE, Rafferty puts his unbandaged hand up to the spot on his cheek where Miaow kissed him just before she joined the swarm of kids and charged up to the street, her ragged clothes fluttering as she ran. The sight produced a surprising pang. When he first met her, she'd been running with kids just like these.

He goes to the elevator and pushes the button for the fourth floor. Time for Part Two.

40

It Corrupts the Corruptible

Sunlight as thin and unsatisfying as gruel, not even intense enough to throw shadows. The phone at Rafferty's ear is slick with sweat, an aftereffect of Rose and Miaow's escape. "He's not in," says Porthip's secretary.

"When will he *be* in?" The floor he spent so much time cleaning has gotten gritty again, and he drags his feet over it, enjoying the sound.

"I have no idea."

Just for the hell of it, he kicks the stool that's pinched his butt so many times and watches it topple over onto its side. He doesn't think he'll ever have to see it again, and he won't miss it. "Is that usual?" he asks. "That you'd have no idea when he'll be in?"

"No," she says. "When he gets in touch with me, would you like me to tell him what this concerns?"

"He'll know what it concerns," Rafferty says. "Can't *you* get in touch with *him*?"

The woman does not reply for a moment, and then she says, "No."

"Really. Is *that* usual?"

"Oh, well," she says. "It'll be in the paper tomorrow anyway. He's in the hospital."

"Which one?"

"I can't tell you that."

"Sure you can." He looks at his watch. About forty minutes more on the tape that's running upstairs. He'll have to go up, do his stuff in the apartment, and put in the next cassette. "Anyway, there's only one hospital he'd go to."

"Really," she says neutrally.

"Sure. Bumrungrad."

There's a short pause, and she says, "Well, that'll be in the paper, too. But before you get smug, Bumrungrad's a very big hospital."

"Right," Rafferty says. "I'll never manage to find him."

He hangs up and calls Kosit.

"OUT OF THE question," Dr. Ravi says. He'd answered the phone at Pan's office. "You can't just stop by and see him any time."

"It's not any time," Rafferty says. "It's half an hour from now."

"This is a very bad day. Extremely busy."

Rafferty has no trouble visualizing the little man, probably wearing another ambitiously pleated pair of slacks, seated behind the desk in the small office outside Pan's big one. "Sorry it's a bad day, but I'm coming anyway."

"He won't see you."

"He'll see me. Just say one word to him. Say 'Snakeskin.'"

The pause is so long that Rafferty thinks Dr. Ravi has hung up. When he does speak, all he says is, "Half an hour?"

"Yes. But two other people are going to get there first, two kids. Let them in and have them wait. It's important that they're not out on the street when I arrive."

"Any other orders?" Dr. Ravi says.

"That'll do for now," Rafferty says.

He folds the phone and sits on the stool, which he has put upright again. The day in front of him is a maze, an urban labyrinth with several ways in and probably only one safe way out. Within an hour Rose should call to tell him they're with Boo's kids down at the river. They'll be fine down there, at least until dark, when he'll move them. Assuming that he's alive to do it.

The taped hand goes into spasms, sending a long, dark line of pain up his arm. When he stands up, the stool pinches him, and this time his kick sends it all the way to the opposite wall, where it breaks into pieces.

There are at least three places he needs to go. At some point he'll have to dump the final tails, so no one from either side is riding his slipstream. He's pretty sure he knows how to do it, but he's been wrong a lot recently, so he turns his mind to it, and while he worries about that, he also worries about time. This is Saturday, and his bank will close early. He focuses on the schedule, trying to factor in imponderables, such as bad traffic or a sudden bullet in the back of the head.

Instead he finds himself worrying about Arthit. His best friend, alone for the first time in his adult life, is floating somewhere on the tide of the city, adrift over depths of abandonment and grief. Running from his loss, running from whatever it is that Rafferty has let out of the bottle. And as hard as it is for Rafferty to imagine Arthit needing help, he probably does. He probably needs several kinds of help.

HE CAN GIVE himself ten minutes, no more. The seconds tick off in his mind as he moves through the apartment silently while he and his wife and child chat with each other over the speakers.

From the headboard of the bed, he takes the Glock and the spare magazine. His closet yields up a pair of running shoes and his softest, most beat-up jeans, since he may have to wear them for some time. He chooses a big linen shirt that's loose enough to conceal the gun. After he changes, he slips his cell phone into his pocket, where it will stay until he replaces it later in the day. He goes to the sliding glass door to close it but stands for a moment looking past the balcony and out over the city. Its sheer size is a comfort. It unfolds around him in all directions, block by block like giant tiles, fading eventually into the perpetual smog and water vapor that obscure the place's real size, but he knows that it goes on and on. People have hidden in it for years, just another stone on the beach. He turns and goes over to the little tape recorder, rests his finger on the "stop" button, and waits for a natural pause.

"Hang on a minute," he says out loud. He pushes "stop." "I'm going out for a couple of hours, but I'll get back in plenty of time for dinner.

Anybody want anything?" There is no reply, since he's pulling out the cassette in the recorder and slipping another in. He rewinds the new tape all the way to the beginning of the leader, which will give him twenty seconds or so of silence before Miaow and Rose start talking. He says, "Okay, then, bye," pushes "play," and goes out the door, putting some muscle into closing it so it can be heard. He's still standing out there, waiting for the elevator, when he hears Rose's voice through the door.

The new tape is a little less than two hours long, the product of their trip down to the fourth floor on the previous morning. He has that much time until the apartment goes silent. After that they'll begin to wonder. When the curiosity gets too strong, they'll come through the door.

And then they'll probably be looking to kill people.

THE GUY BEHIND him isn't trying to be inconspicuous. He stays two or at most three cars back all the way, a cell phone pressed to one ear. When Rafferty's taxi stops at the gates to Pan's earthly paradise, the follower cruises past slowly, then pulls in to the curb halfway down the block.

When the guard opens the gate, Dr. Ravi is already standing there. He lifts his left hand to study his watch, says, "Seven minutes late," and turns to climb into the swan. "As I told you, time is very tight today." The vehicle is moving while Rafferty still has one foot on the ground.

"Are my guests here?"

Dr. Ravi purses his lips around something small and sour and says, "They are."

Rafferty says, "You were never poor."

If the comment surprises Dr. Ravi, he doesn't show it. "No. We weren't rich, but we weren't poor."

"You managed to pay for Oxford."

"Cambridge," he says, biting the syllables. "I was on a partial scholarship."

They are cresting the hill that blocks the view of the garden. "You don't like street kids."

Dr. Ravi's shoulders rise and fall. "I don't mind them in the street. In the house is a different matter."

"Is that a sentiment your employer shares?"

"I have no idea. He was more like them when he was young than I was."

"People change," Rafferty says as the apple tree gleams its way into sight.

A diplomatic head waggle of disagreement. "In some ways. At the core, though, I think they stay the same."

"Really? You don't think power corrupts?"

Dr. Ravi makes a tiny adjustment to the steering column with no discernible effect. "It corrupts the corruptible."

"Ah." Rafferty sits back and watches the garden slide past. "You knew what Snakeskin meant."

"Of course. The first thing I did when I came to work here was to go through the documents that spell out Khun Pan's past."

"Why would you do that?"

Dr. Ravi turns to face him for a moment, a glance that's meant to put Rafferty in his place, and then looks back at the road. "I'm his media adviser, remember? I need to know what's back there, what's on record, in case something gets dredged up. It probably wouldn't surprise you to know that there are people in the media who don't like him."

"So you're an expert on his past."

Dr. Ravi worries the idea for a few seconds and says, "To some extent."

"Then how'd he get burned?"

They glide past the empty little village, as deserted now as Da's is. The pigs watch them go with lazy attention, as though wondering whether the swan is edible. "That"—Dr. Ravi accelerates slightly, as though the talk has gone on too long—"you'll have to ask *him* about that."

THE FIRST THING he hears when he opens the front door is laughter, coming from the back of the house, the direction of Pan's office. Then he hears voices, Pan's surprisingly wispy one and Da's. Whatever Pan says, Da starts laughing again.

She turns to smile a greeting at Rafferty as he pushes the door open.

Pan is standing in the middle of the room with Peep in his arms. The baby's dirty blue blanket looks incongruous against the yellow silk covering Pan's chest, beneath the unsettling pink of his mouth. Boo lounges behind Pan's desk with his hands folded over his nonexistent belly, apparently completely at ease, and Da occupies the chair Rafferty had claimed four days earlier, the afternoon before the gala fundraiser.

"What a treat," Pan says to Rafferty, although his smile is measured. "You have very interesting friends."

"She's from Isaan," Rafferty says.

"Yes," Pan says, "we've had a few minutes to get that on the table. And he's a flower of the pavement, isn't he?"

"Or a weed," Boo says. He grins, but his eyes are watchful.

"Have they told you why I brought them here?"

"We just got here," Da says. "And we don't really know."

"Well, it's probably rude to bring up business so quickly, but Dr. Ravi says you're pressed for time."

Pan gives Peep a little bounce. "Dr. Ravi is an old woman. When you're as rich as I am, time is elastic."

"It's elastic when you're poor, too," Boo says.

"That's true, isn't it?" Pan says. "I hadn't thought of it, although I should have. I was poor long enough. But for everybody else, everybody who has something but not enough, time is rigid. It's a floor plan for the day, isn't it? You can only stay in each room so long."

"So," Rafferty says, "are we going to sit around and philosophize, or should we get down to it?"

Pan's smile dims a notch. "You seem to be in more of a hurry than I am."

"Cute baby, isn't it?" Rafferty says.

"Adorable." Pan raises Peep and makes a little kiss noise. Peep screws up his face, waves a fist, and starts to cry. Da rises and goes to take him, then carries him back to her chair.

"Did Da tell you where she got him?"

"Where she *got* him?" Pan's smile widens again. "I've been familiar with those mechanics since I was, let's see, about twelve."

"He was handed to her," Rafferty says. "Five days ago. By an old acquaintance of yours."

Boo sits straighter behind the desk.

Still watching Peep, Pan says, "You think I know someone who gives away babies?"

"Well, you used to know him. His name is Wichat."

Pan turns his head a few inches to the left and regards Rafferty as though he's favoring his dominant eye. "You've been busy." He leans back, resting part of his broad bottom on the edge of the desk. "If you wanted to know about all that, you could have talked to me."

"You *did* work with Wichat."

"Of course. I started out with him. Dozens of people could tell you that. *I* would have told you, if you'd asked. It's no secret. I was a crook. There weren't a lot of other employment opportunities for someone like me. And if you wanted to be a crook in those days, at least in the part of Bangkok I was being a crook in, you did business with Wichat. Actually, with Wichat's boss, Chai. Is this going to be in the book?"

"Unless you can come up with something better."

Pan seems suddenly to remember that Boo and Da are in the room. The smile returns, and he looks down at Da, who is holding Peep. The baby's cries have faded to a damp snuffle. "Girls always look most beautiful holding babies," he says.

Rafferty says, "Not a really contemporary point of view."

Pan lets his gaze linger on Da for a moment, and then he says, "I'd rather it weren't in the book, but if it is, you should be very clear on the point that I've had nothing to do with Wichat, or anyone like Wichat, for twenty years. I have no idea whether Wichat is—what?—giving out babies? Why would anyone give out babies?" He tugs at the crease in his sky-blue slacks. "And why tell me about it now?"

"I'm sorry," Rafferty says. "I haven't done this right. We're actually here to ask for your help."

Pan's eyebrows climb half an inch. "Help."

"See, this is what I think is happening. Wichat is buying babies from poor families, some of them probably Cambodian, and selling them to rich people, to *farang*. And he stashes the kids in the interim with female beggars. He hides them in plain sight and even makes a little extra money. Da says people give more to—"

"A woman with a baby," Pan says with badly masked impatience. "Obviously. But how in the world do you think I can help?"

"I'm not completely sure," Rafferty says. He leans against the wall beside the door. "Da and Peep ran away from Wichat's guys because she was going to get raped. Boo helped them escape. And of course they have something that belongs to Wichat, which is to say Peep. So they're on the run now, and I'm hiding them."

Pan lets his eyes drift back down to Da and Peep. Behind him, Boo looks past him at Rafferty, his eyebrows elevated in a question. Pan says, "Why? Why are you hiding them?"

"I owe Boo a favor. So I guess the question is whether you can do anything, considering that you used to be buddies with Wichat, to get him to let go of Da and Peep, just stop searching for them."

Pan surveys the room, not really looking at anything. "I suppose what he really wants is the baby. Why not return it to him?"

Da says immediately, "No."

"Right," Pan says. "Of course not. Well, you say he's for sale, right? If it's just about money, if Wichat just doesn't want to lose his profit, then I can probably do something, maybe compensate him. How much is he getting?"

"Thirty to fifty thousand U.S."

"You're joking."

"That's my best guess," Rafferty says.

"Still," Pan says, "even if I bought Peep for Miss . . . Miss Da here, Wichat might be more worried about what she could tell people. Especially if he's making that much money."

"I think he is," Boo says. "Both making that much money and worried about Da talking to people."

Pan's eyes flick to Boo as though he's surprised at the certainty in the boy's voice. "So, you see, it's a little awkward. If I talk to Wichat, let's say to offer to buy Peep, then he knows that I'm in touch with these kids. It opens up a raft of questions. That's awkward. He and I aren't friends anymore."

"If you say so," Rafferty says.

"Let me think about it," Pan says. "They're safe for the moment, I suppose?"

"I think so."

"Would they be safer here?"

"I don't know," Rafferty says, watching Pan's eyes. "Maybe."

"Well, where are they staying now?"

"In my apartment house. An empty unit, down on the fourth floor."

"Do you have security? Is there a doorman or anything?"

"It's not that kind of apartment house," Rafferty says.

"Maybe here, then," Pan says. "If there's one thing I have a lot of, it's guards."

Rafferty says, "What do you guys think?"

"I like it at your place," Boo says. It's what Rafferty told him to say if the question came up. "We don't get in anybody's way." He looks at Da, who nods.

"Fine," Pan says. "I'll think about Wichat. I'm sure something will come to me."

"That's all we can ask," Rafferty says. He pushes himself away from the wall. "You kids mind waiting for me outside? You can walk down to the village. I'll be out in a minute." He turns to Pan. "That okay with you?"

"Sure. Just don't get too close to the pigs. Shinawatra can be aggressive."

Da says, "I know all about pigs." Then she says, "Shinawatra? Like the prime minister?"

"I'll explain it later." Rafferty turns his back to Pan and opens the door to let them out. With his left hand, he pulls the automatic from his pants, and as Boo passes him, Rafferty glances down at it. Boo follows Rafferty's eyes and takes the gun without missing a step. When Rafferty closes the door and turns back to Pan, nothing in the big man's face suggests that he registered the transfer.

"So?" Pan says. He turns and goes behind his desk. He sits and pulls a drawer open.

"Da tell you about how they turned off her town's river?"

"Actually, the boy told me. Terrible, terrible." He takes the tube of lip balm out of the drawer and applies it. "The sort of thing that should never be allowed to happen."

"What can you do about it?"

"Me?" Pan drops the tube back into the drawer. "I have no formal power."

"And if you did?"

"Oh, well. If we're going to be hypothetical, then hypothetically, I'd prevent it."

"Would you give them their river back?"

Pan shakes his head in irritation. "It's done. It's over. What I'd do is make sure it never happens again."

"What do you mean, over? A few bulldozers, an afternoon's work, they'd have their river back. And how long could it take, how much could it cost, to rebuild a few shacks like the ones you put up in that postcard village in your front yard?"

"That's not the point. The money's been spent, the golf course has been built, probably a hotel put up. The people who did this are powerful. They're not going to let go of it. They've got clout."

"In short," Rafferty says, "it wouldn't be expedient."

"You're oversimplifying, and you know it. The point is to prevent it next time."

Rafferty gives it a minute, turns and takes a circuit of the office. When he's facing Pan again, he says, "So. How'd you burn your hands?"

"Sooner or later," Pan says. He sounds weary. "I knew you'd bump up against that sooner or later. I told you I was in protection, right?"

"Right. With Wichat's boss, Chai."

"Chai," Pan says. "*That* was a guy. Balls of steel. That was when we had real gangsters, not store dummies like Wichat."

"Wichat means business."

"Yeah? You talk to him?"

"Sure. I've talked to half a dozen people on the yellow list. A lot of them have wondered how you got burned."

"Right, the burns. One of the women I was protecting had a three-wok restaurant on the curb, and some guys who had wandered onto the wrong block tried to rob her. I was just down the street. Protection, right? If I'm extorting money for protection, the least I can do is protect them. So I . . . um, got involved, and while I was taking care of the first guy, the second guy threw a wok at me. Full of hot oil." Pan opens the top two buttons of his shirt and shows Rafferty an expanse of shiny, hairless flesh. "So naturally, like a total idiot, I reached out and tried to catch it. Not just my hands, but all the way up my arms and across my chest. Hurt like nothing else in my whole life."

"So," Rafferty says, "it happened back when you were working with Wichat. Before the Mounds of Venus."

"That's right." Rafferty holds Pan's gaze until Pan looks down at his shirtfront. He rebuttons the shirt and pulls a cigar out of his pocket.

He centers it in the moist-looking mouth and fires up the smoke.

When Rafferty feels as if the silence has been stretched far enough to snap, he says, "Uh-huh."

Pan drags on the cigar with every evidence of being completely absorbed in it, but when he finally looks up at Rafferty, he has the eyes of someone who suspects that the guy across the card table has just filled the holes in his straight. "You asked Ravi about Snakeskin," he says.

"Actually, I didn't. I just said the word to see whether it would persuade him to let me in. And it did."

"How interesting," Pan says. "You know, I'm beginning to wonder whose side you're on."

"What a coincidence," Rafferty says. "So am I."

41

Off to Brunch

"Hang on to the gun," Rafferty says. "Just in case. I'll get it later."

The three of them are walking the curving path to the front gate, since no swans were volunteered. Da carries Peep in both arms, staring openmouthed at the garden gleaming in the sun to her right. Boo has the gun wedged into the pocket of his too-large jeans, covered by the tail of his shirt.

"Why do I want a gun?" Boo says. "We're leaving."

"I'm leaving first, and you're waiting about five minutes. There's someone watching me, and I don't want him seeing you. I don't want anyone to see you."

"Why not?"

"Tell you later."

Instead of answering, Boo reaches over and slides a fingertip down the side of Da's neck. She shrugs as though there's a spider crawling on her, but the smile gives her away. "But the gun?" Boo asks.

"In case they try to keep you here."

Da turns away from the ruby light of the Tree of the Knowledge of

Good and Evil and looks across Boo at Rafferty. "Do you think they will?"

"No," Rafferty says. "But right now I can't come up with a single thing that would surprise me."

CAPTAIN TEETH SAYS, "He's at Pan's."

"That's not a problem, not now." Ton's Saturday-morning outfit is a splendid pair of beige slacks with an almost invisible herringbone weave and a navy silk blazer that sports gold buttons. From his seat at the console, Ren figures they're probably real gold. Ton checks his cuffs and tugs the left one another tenth of a millimeter out of the jacket sleeve. "Where are the females?"

"At home," Ren says, holding up the earphones. "Being boring."

"I'll be at the club," Ton says. "I've got the cell, but don't call unless it's important. I'll be back in a few hours."

A cell phone rings, and Captain Teeth fishes his from his pocket and listens for a moment. "He's coming out of Pan's. Flagging a cab."

"Who's following him?" Ton asks.

"Nobody you know."

"Good," Ton says. He pushes the door open. "I'm off."

When it has swung completely closed, Ren says, "Off to *brunch*."

"It's Saturday," Captain Teeth says. "Tell me you wouldn't rather be at brunch."

"Me?" Ren drops the headset onto the console, leans forward, and rests his head on his crossed arms. "Would I rather be at brunch? I'd rather be anywhere. I'd rather be in a Burmese prison."

"FLOYD," RAFFERTY SAYS, the phone squeezed between ear and shoulder. "Got another question for you."

"You got some money that belongs to me, too," Floyd Preece says. "Shoulda paid me by now."

"Coming right up. Listen, this is a very important question, and you don't give me the answer until I hand you the money, okay?"

Preece pauses, probably looking for the catch. "Let's hear it," he says at last.

"What's being done with the factory right now?"

"That's it? I mean, that's the big question?"

"You want something harder?"

"No, no. Happy to get paid for nothing. I could answer you right now. I won't, not till I'm a little richer, but I could."

"Yeah, well, save it until I give you the money."

"And when will that be?"

Rafferty looks up and down the street to make sure he's still unaccompanied. "Well, next stop is the bank."

"ALL OF IT," he says.

The teller takes the withdrawal slip. The amount to be withdrawn is blank, since Rafferty has no idea how big the "advance" was. The teller says, "You're closing the account?"

"If emptying will close it, I guess so." It's nearly 1:00 P.M., closing time on Saturday, and he's one of the last customers in the bank. He'd like the place to be much more thickly populated, absolutely jammed with potential witnesses. This is the stop that worries him most.

Punching keys with bright orange nails, the teller says, "Has our service been unsatisfactory in some way?"

"Excuse me?" Rafferty had been looking back, through the picture window that shows him a long, hot-looking rectangle of Silom. The sun is in full beam now, showing off to a world that was already hot enough. Lots of people, a normal crowd for the weekend, sweat their way past the window, going in both directions. "No, no. You've all been great. Seriously. I'd live here, if I could."

"Live here?" The teller has the beginning of a smile on her lips.

"Right in the lobby," Rafferty says, checking the sidewalk again. "Nice and quiet, good class of people. Put an easy chair over there, get a key to the restroom, have meals sent in."

"All by yourself?" the teller asks, glancing sideways at him. She's in her early thirties, tailored, with every hair in place, but something in the way she looks at him makes it easy for Rafferty to imagine her barefoot in some green field, a little perspiration gleaming on her face.

"Oh, no," Rafferty says, banishing the image. "With my money."

The teller leans forward and peers at the screen.

"Problem?" Rafferty says.

She comes up at him with a bright bad-news smile. "I'm sorry," she says, "but I have to talk to my supervisor."

"Something wrong?"

"Oh, no. Just . . . um, big withdrawal. It has to be authorized." She gets up.

"Fine." Rafferty feels the lightness where the Glock used to be and wishes he owned a spare. He turns back to the window, puts his hand into his pants pocket, and finds the 3 on the touch pad of his phone, which he's assigned to Kosit. He presses it down and counts to five to activate the speed-dial function. After ten seconds or so, long enough for one ring, he hopes, on Kosit's phone, he disconnects and goes back to scanning the sidewalk. He doesn't recognize anyone on the street.

Yet.

The teller is in a rear office, visible through a window, talking to a fat man at a desk. The fat man scrabbles at the keyboard of his computer, studies the screen, and then picks up a telephone. The teller stands there for a moment, waiting for another instruction, then turns and comes back through the door.

"It won't be much longer," she says. She sits down, takes a strand of hair, wraps it around her finger, and checks the ends. "Sorry to make you wait."

Rafferty is now the only customer in the bank. The other tellers are counting out, snapping rubber bands around stacks of currency, and slipping dust covers over their terminals. He'd known that the withdrawal would attract attention eventually, but he hadn't figured it would happen in real time.

"I'm going to be late," he says. "Either let's wrap this up in a minute or two or let's forget it and I'll come back on Monday."

"I'm so sorry. Let me go talk to him." And she's up again, on her way back to the fat man's office.

The guys at the apartment, Rafferty thinks. They're three minutes away. They've got phones. But Rose and Miaow are talking in the apartment, and he doesn't think Ton's controllers would move the watchers while they're hearing—

It feels as if his stomach plummets two feet.

Did he plug in the tape recorder?

42

Open Season

Rose's voice has dropped several tones, abandoning its normal alto in favor of something that's beginning to sound like a drug-wobbled baritone. She finishes her sentence, and there is a long pause. When Miaow answers, her voice is almost as low as Rose's, and her words have a kind of ripple, like something seen underwater.

"Hey," Captain Teeth says to Ren. "Listen to this."

Ren puts on his own headset, squints at the sound for a second, turns up the volume, closes his eyes, opens them again, yanks his headset off, throws it onto the console, and says, with considerable vehemence, "Shit." He meets Captain Teeth's gaze. "Brunch or no brunch," he says, "he's gotta know about this." He reaches for his phone, and it rings. He grabs it.

"Yes?" he says.

"I just got a call," Ton says. "Rafferty's withdrawing all the money. It's the Thai Fisherman's Bank on Silom, around the corner from the apartment. I think he's going to run. Get the other two guys over there right now."

"The conversation in the apartment," Ren says. "It's a tape."

Ton says nothing for long enough that Ren asks, "Are you there?"

"I'm here. That means the woman and the girl are gone. He's the only one we've got. I'll have them stall him in the bank. I want those men there *right now*. They should try to take him."

Ren says carefully, "Take him."

"*Take* him," Ton says, as though he's talking to an idiot. "Get him under control. Take him somewhere. Are we speaking different languages?"

"And if they can't? I mean, if he resists? Or if he goes nuts? What happens when they get him where they're—"

"Just make me happy," Ton says, and disconnects.

"He wants us to make him happy," Ren says, tossing his phone onto the console. "Who's making us happy?" He gets up and goes behind Ton's desk and sits in the big chair. "If Rafferty's dead, the man doesn't need us. We could be hanging in the breeze."

"You worry too much," Captain Teeth says. He gets up. "Where is he? I'll go over there myself."

"Thai Fisherman's Bank, Silom."

Captain Teeth checks the holster in the middle of his back. When he's satisfied, he slips into a sport coat and heads for the door. As he goes through it, he says, without looking over his shoulder, "If he catches you in that chair, you'll need a new ass next time you sit down."

THE SWEAT POPS on Rafferty's upper lip in less than a heartbeat. He'd been timing himself in the apartment, staying within his ten-minute limit, hurrying to get to Pan's early enough to let him come here so he could walk into a trap. And he hadn't done the most important thing. He'd left the tape recorder running on batteries. He hadn't plugged it in.

He turns to face the sidewalk. Still busy, still full of people he doesn't recognize.

And then he sees one he *does* recognize, the man who was driving the car behind him all the way to Pan's. He's leaning against a parked truck, doing nothing. Looking everywhere except at the window.

"Umm," says the teller, and Rafferty turns to her.

"You've been banking here a long time, right?" Her face is full of uncertainty.

"Years."

"I see you in here sometimes," she says. "With a little girl?"

"My daughter."

"That's what I thought." She picks up a pad of old photocopies that have been turned blank side up and stapled together to create a scratch pad. She begins to draw a girl's face, all big eyes and long curling hair. She inks a heart above the girl's head, then several more, a little cloud of hearts floating in midair. Without looking up, she says, "It's a police hold."

"Police."

"That's who he's talking to. It was on the computer. A police number to call for any withdrawal from your account for more than two thousand U.S."

"It's a mistake of some kind," Rafferty says. He needs to mop his forehead, but he doesn't want to draw the attention of the man in the office. "Was there a name?"

"No," she says. "But I'm sure you're right. It's a mistake."

"Of course it is." The teller's station is behind a plate of glass, and by taking a step to his left, Rafferty can see a reflection of the window that opens onto the street, but not clearly enough to identify any individuals. He looks instead for quick movement. "You draw well," he says, his eyes on the reflection.

"I draw like every other girl in Thailand," the teller says. "We all imitate Japanese anime."

"I like the heart." Someone hurries past the window, head down.

"Which heart? There are five of them."

Rafferty focuses through the glass at the drawing. "The first one," he says. "The big one. I like big hearts." He has nothing he can use as a weapon.

"We all do," the teller says. "But try to find one. Ah, here he comes."

And the fat man has come out of his office, wearing a smile that looks like it was crimped into his face with a vise. Circles of sweat turn his white shirt translucent beneath the arms.

"Sorry, sorry," he says. "Just a bit of delay." He looks down at the scratch pad, at the girl's face with the hearts around it, and winces. "Do you have enough in your drawer?"

The teller says, "No," in a tone that makes it clear that the answer was obvious.

"I'll get the rest from the vault," the fat man says. "Get started. Give the man his money."

"Yes, sir." She slides the cash drawer open, pulls out a three-inch stack of thousand-baht bills, and drops it into the counting machine. The bills flip by as the total on the readout increases. "That's five hundred twenty thousand baht," she says. "We need another seven hundred thousand. How are you going to carry all this?"

"Carefully," Rafferty says. It's more money than he'd expected— about forty thousand dollars.

"You'll never get it into your pockets," she says. "I'll lend you a bag, okay?" She lifts an inexpensive nylon bag above the counter. "It's my shopping bag. I'm going to buy groceries after I punch out here."

Reflected in the glass partition, two men peer through the window behind him. "I'll buy it from you."

She gives him a smile. "Just bring it back." The fat man returns, a banded stack of bills in each hand.

"If it's humanly possible," Rafferty says. He turns around, and the men at the window separate quickly. One of them turns away to show the back of his head, and the other slides out of sight to the right. The first one he saw, the one who had been following him, is still leaning against the car, so there are at least three of them—the one who was behind him, and the two who were supposed to be watching Rose and Miaow, which certainly means that the tape recorder ran out of juice and wound down.

Which, in turn, means that it's open season.

And there might be more out there. He hears the bills snapping through the machine behind him.

"Here we are," the teller says. She holds up the nylon bag, which has what look like coffee stains on it. "I'll go around to the door and give it to you," she says. "It's too thick to slip under the partition."

"Thanks," he says. He follows her, and she buzzes the door open and hands him the bag, which is heavy enough to tug his uninjured hand downward.

She says, "Take care."

"I'll try," Rafferty says. "It's murder out there."

"I think the door's locked," she says. She precedes him, rattles the door once, and slips a key into the lock. Pulling it open, she steps aside and gives him a little back-and-forth wave.

Rafferty smiles, fills his lungs with air, and goes through the door.

The day is even brighter than it had seemed through the tinted windows of the bank. It takes him a second to adjust to the glare and scan the sidewalk. The man leaning against the car turns away as Rafferty's eyes find him. Rafferty looks left and sees one of the men who had been waiting outside the apartment building coming toward him, one hand in his pocket. This one doesn't look away. His eyes drift beyond Rafferty, who turns to see a third man coming from the other direction. The third man doesn't have a hand hidden in a pocket, so Rafferty heads toward him, moving briskly, and then something catches his eye from the left, and he sees Captain Teeth getting out of a cab.

Captain Teeth is shorter than Rafferty remembers him, and wider. He's got the chest and shoulders of someone who bench-presses Chevrolets. All that overdeveloped muscle tissue has been wrapped in a sport coat, and in this heat he might just as well be wearing a sandwich board that says HEAVILY ARMED. He throws some bills at the cabdriver and makes for the curb.

Rafferty carefully slips the bag over the bandaged hand, slides it up his arm, and crooks his elbow so the money dangles from his forearm. He puts his good hand under his shirt and leaves it there, at waistband level, and strides forward purposefully. The man who is coming toward him falters, his eyes on the concealed hand. The question is clear in his face: keep moving toward Rafferty and maybe get shot now or back off and maybe get shot later by his friends? Getting shot later wins, and the man veers off to his right, toward the parked cars.

That leaves the other two and Captain Teeth, and Rafferty doesn't think Captain Teeth is going to be so easy to bluff.

When in doubt, take the offensive.

Rafferty moves left, on a course to intercept the man who chose being shot later. The man works farther to his right, his eyes flicking side to side, until he's almost brushing a parked car, and then Rafferty cuts behind him and steps up against him, circling the man's neck with the arm that has the bag hanging from it and pushing the index finger of his good hand hard into the man's back. The man throws his hands into the air spasmodically, striking a glancing blow off Rafferty's bandaged left, and Rafferty emits a hiss of pain that loosens the other man's knees. Rafferty has to hold him up until the man can get his feet under him again. Captain Teeth is closing fast, reaching back beneath his sport coat, undoubtedly for a gun.

"Stop there," Rafferty says.

Captain Teeth comes to a halt about five feet away. He keeps his hand hidden. "You think I care if he dies? Shoot him. When he falls, I'll have a target."

"Move that hand," Rafferty says, "and I'll shoot you instead."

Captain Teeth bares his awful incisors in a grin and says, "Watch the hand move," and then his eyes lift and widen, focused behind Rafferty, the teeth disappear, and his hand comes out empty and open. He takes a few steps back. Something cold noses the nape of Rafferty's neck.

"Drop the gun." The tone is businesslike.

"Love to," Rafferty says. "But I haven't got one."

"Hands behind you." The gun is pushed half an inch forward. "*Now*."

"Okay, okay." He lets go of the man he's been holding, who stumbles away and then turns to face him. Whatever he sees over Rafferty's shoulder, it freezes him.

"Don't move," says the man behind Rafferty. The bag is lifted from his arm, and something circles his wrists, and he hears a sharp *click*. The cuff is tight around the bandages on his left wrist. "You two," the man says, "go." Captain Teeth and the man Rafferty has been holding pivot in unison and retreat down the sidewalk without a backward glance.

"You're going to turn around, and I'm going to stay behind you," the man says. "Don't do anything stupid. Don't do anything I might *think* is stupid."

A sharp tug yanks Rafferty's cuffed hands to one side, and he turns, the other man pivoting with him so the gun never loses contact with the back of Rafferty's neck. A circle of people has gathered around them, a safe five or six paces away, their eyes wide. "Walk now. Toward the van."

Rafferty heads for a vehicle that's double-parked in the first traffic lane. It's a police van, its windows covered in a silvery reflective coating. The rear door has been slid open. Another man in a police uniform comes around the front end of the van. It takes Rafferty a moment to recognize him as Kosit.

"Hey," Rafferty says, and the gun probes the back of his neck as though it's looking for a path between the vertebrae.

"*That's* stupid," the man says.

The face Kosit turns to Rafferty as he approaches the van is all cop. Without a glimmer of recognition, he yanks hold of Rafferty's shirt and pulls him toward the open door, and Rafferty sees another man in the van, hunched down on the floor behind the driver's seat. He tries to stop, but the man behind him adds a shove to Kosit's pull, and with his wrists cuffed, all Rafferty can manage is a stagger-step to keep from falling forward. Kosit grabs his shoulders, puts an expert hand on top of his head, and pushes him down onto the seat of the van, and as the door slams shut, the man crouched behind the driver's seat brings his head up and regards Rafferty.

It's Arthit.

43

She Has a Different Life Now

From the corner where she had folded the cashmere shawl to give her something to sit on—Rafferty was right, it *had* come in handy—Rose watches the kids. The younger ones are manic, adrenaline-jacked from the adventure of the escape. They've replayed the chase, argued over their speed and their acting skills, and they've had occasional words about the value of their individual contributions. A couple of these ended in minor tussles, broken up by the older kids, who are maintaining a disdainful cool that's either assumed or, in the case of a few of the more frayed and weathered of them, hard-earned.

Miaow had tried to join in the roughhousing for a while, but the kids kept their distance from her. None of them had been with Boo when she was, and they're all strangers to her. It's obvious that they don't see her as one of them. They skirmished with one another, but they treated her as though she were made of glass and already chipped. Watching them, watching her daughter try to enter the field of play, Rose is struck by how much Miaow has changed. The filthy, tattered clothes can't conceal the differences between her and the others. It's not just the weight she has gained, although she probably weighs 20 percent more than any other kid her height in the room. It's not just the newly colored and carefully cut hair, or her obvious cleanliness. She moves differently than they do. Her reactions aren't as fast, and she seems to have a narrower awareness. Boo's kids appear to be able to track simultaneously everything that's happening in the big room, while Miaow focuses only on what's in front of her. Rose sees the kids behind her and on either side exchange glances, and it's obvious that the unspoken topic is Miaow.

Now Miaow is sitting beside Rose, her head lowered, plucking at the shawl. Her lower lip protrudes, and there are little dimples in her chin. Her end of the conversation, when Rose attempts to start one, is limited to monosyllables, some of them not even words. Looking down at the top of her adopted daughter's head, at the part in her hair, straighter— as Rafferty once said—than the path of a subatomic particle, Rose feels her heart swell. She feels as if her heart has a color, a kind of sad, bruised purple. She slides a hand over Miaow's, but Miaow pulls away and puts her hand in her lap. It looks lonely there.

Rose gives up and rests her back against the wall. The kids are settling down now, and the temperature in the room, which was fearsome when they arrived, is dropping slightly as the light outside dims. Rose looks at her watch—four o'clock.

Where is Poke?

She pulls out her phone to dial him and then thinks better of it. He was going to buy a stolen phone and use that to call her, in case they— whoever "they" are—are triangulating on his old number. Maybe he just hasn't bought the new phone yet. She's trying to visualize "triangulating" when the door to the shack opens and Boo and Da come in, Boo carrying Peep in the crook of one arm as if he's had a baby in his arms his entire life. The other hand is full of white plastic bags, as are both of Da's. Even across the room, Rose can see Da follow Boo with her eyes, watching him as though he changes into something more interesting every moment he's in sight. Exactly, Rose thinks, what Miaow doesn't need.

Miaow sits bolt upright as the door opens. She leans forward, trying to shorten the distance between them without getting up.

But Boo doesn't even look in their direction. He has stopped and bought supplies: brooms, toilet paper, bags of food, bottled water, and he begins immediately to parcel them out and give orders, delegating three kids to clean out the toilet room, handing money to another and assigning five to go with her and bring back hot food. The smallest kids are handed the new reed brooms and told to sweep the dirt floor.

Not until the the random energy in the room has been harnessed and the kids are all engaged in their tasks does Boo lift his eyes to them and wave them over. Rose gets up and then leans down to pick up the shawl, and by the time she straightens up again, Miaow is already all the way across the room, standing next to Boo.

"Let's go outside," he says. "It gets dusty in here when they sweep." He turns, Da following in almost perfect synchronization, and Rose and Miaow trail along behind.

"How long have you all lived here?" Miaow asks as she passes through the door.

Rose can't hear the beginning of the boy's reply, but when she comes out into the late-afternoon sunshine, he is saying " . . . maybe three or four more days, and then we'll move."

Miaow says, "Where?"

Boo laughs. "You *have* forgotten," he says. "When did I ever know where we'd go next? What did I used to say?"

" 'Whatever opens up,' " Miaow says.

"Well, that's where we're going."

"Why do you have to move?" Da says.

"Too many kids in one place. People see us. Sooner or later somebody says something to the cops or the weepies who help us poor kids so they can make enough money to buy SUVs and live in villas. Then they show up in the middle of the night and we all have to run, and sometimes one or two of us get caught."

"The small ones," Miaow says.

"Listen to that," Boo says. "You haven't completely turned into a schoolgirl. There's still a little bit left."

"I haven't—" Miaow begins.

"Even *with* that hair."

Miaow's hand goes to her hair. "There's nothing wrong with my—" Suddenly she's blushing.

"What's next, skin-whitening cream? Now you're an American?"

He is keeping his voice light, but Rose can see the tension in the cords of his neck.

"Wait," Miaow says. "I'm not trying—"

"You're not?" he demands. "Okay, you're not on the streets now. But why pretend to be something you aren't?"

"I don't know what—"

"Have you told anybody at your *school* about it?" He squeezes the word "school" as though he's trying to juice it. "Does anyone know you were on the street? If I showed up, would you introduce me to your friends?"

"But . . ." Miaow says, "but they're . . . those kids, they're—"

"Leave her alone," Da says.

"*No,*" Miaow snaps, just barely not stamping her foot. "Don't you tell him not to . . . uhh, not to talk to me the way he . . . um, the way he wants to, to talk to . . ." And then she's crying, and she turns to Rose and wraps her arms around her mother and buries her head against Rose's blouse.

"Well," Rose says, looking at Boo. Miaow's shoulders are shaking, but she's absolutely silent.

Da says, "That was *mean.*"

"She has a different life now," Rose says to Boo.

Boo says, "Obviously," but he doesn't meet her eyes.

Rose's phone rings.

She looks at the number on the display but doesn't recognize it. She thinks, *Poke's new phone,* and answers, putting her free hand on the back of Miaow's neck, which feels damp and hot. When she says, "Hello," there is no reply. The line is open, but the person at the other end doesn't speak. "Hello?" She waits a minute, listening to the hiss of distance, and then closes the phone and puts both arms on Miaow's shoulders. Boo looks out over the river, as though he wishes he were somewhere else.

Da rubs her arms as though she's cold and says, "Someone is watching us."

CAPTAIN TEETH SAYS, "She answered. She's there."

Ren doesn't even look at him. "Where?"

"Wherever the phone is."

"That's helpful," Ren says. He is back behind the big desk, even though he knows that Ton could walk in at any moment.

"It's something," Captain Teeth says. "She probably thinks the phone is safe unless she uses it. She doesn't know it's searching for a tower all the time. I wanted to make sure she hadn't just left it somewhere to lead us in the wrong direction."

"Goody," Ren says acidly. "You may get your chance with her yet."

"Fine," Captain Teeth snaps. "You worry about what's going to happen to us if the man gets everything he wants. I'll worry about what happens to us if he doesn't. Maybe we can't find Rafferty, but we know how to find the woman, once the man calls whoever it is at the cell-phone company. Which probably means we know where to find the kid, too."

Ren says, "We know too much."

Captain Teeth says, "So figure out how to live through it."

THE ROOM SMELLS of carpet that was at some point wet for a very long time. The carpet is wall-to-wall and well worn, obviously installed during an optimistic interlude in the past when someone thought the hotel would be a success. Shag of a long-unfashionable length, dyed a color that has no counterpart in nature, it curls slightly at the corners as though something were trying to claw its way out.

If this is the last act of my life, Rafferty thinks, *I'd rather it didn't begin on a carpet like this one.*

Kosit sits, legs dangling, on top of the cheap, chipped, four-drawer bureau in front of the mirror, and Arthit is up on one elbow on the bed nearer the door. The bag of money is at the foot of Arthit's bed, tipped on one side to spill bundles of currency across the bedspread. Rafferty is standing inside the bathroom door, just to get off the carpet. The toilet is running behind him. It has been running since they got there.

Kosit's patrolman accomplice, the man who stuck the gun in the back of Rafferty's neck, has gone back to the station to dig out some pictures.

"I'm not a cop now," Arthit says.

Arthit's face is puffy and bloated, especially beneath the eyes. For the first time since Rafferty met him, his friend is unshaven, despite the new and unwrapped razor on the bureau where Kosit sits, and the stubble on his jaw is dusted with white. The hair on one side of his head sweeps forward, probably from having been slept on.

"Of course you are," Kosit says. "We can straighten this out."

Arthit waves the thought away. "If I want to."

"Oh, that's good," Kosit says. "Let Thanom win. Give him what he wants. That'll show him."

"Of course you want to be a cop," Rafferty says.

Arthit puts out a hand, palm down, and slowly pats the air. The meaning is clear: *Back off.* "Poke," he says, "I know you're trying to keep me focused on *stuff.*" He reaches out a white-stockinged foot and kicks the bag of money a few inches toward the end of the bed. "Make lists, *do* things, get even, clear everything up. Keep me busy, keep me from thinking too much. And I appreciate it. But you know what? Everybody, and especially you, is just going to have to leave me alone. I don't need a tow boat. I'm going to work through this the way I have to, and I don't need anyone dragging me along. For the first time in years, I'm not a cop. I can do it my way, not their way. I don't have to—" He stops and looks down at the bed for a moment, then lifts his chin as though his neck were stiff. "I don't have to worry about Noi now. And I'll tell you something. I am *going* to be at Noi's cremation in two days." He holds up his first and second fingers, V style. "Two days. Monday afternoon. That means I need to get this straightened out by then, because if I don't, I'm going to get arrested before I'm even inside the temple. And while I don't particularly care whether I get arrested, I won't allow it to happen at Noi's cremation. Noi's cremation is going to be the kind of ceremony she deserves." He waits, holding Rafferty's gaze.

Rafferty says, "All right."

Arthit reaches into the pocket of his trousers and withdraws an envelope, crumpled from his movements. "Do you know what this is?"

"Noi's letter?" Rafferty asks.

"Has it been opened?"

"Not that I can see."

"And it won't be," Arthit says, "until her spirit has been sent on its way with the peace and dignity it deserves. I won't know what my wife's last words to me were, Poke, until we get through this. So forget about motivating me, or helping me work through issues, or finding closure, or whatever it is you think you can do for me. I'll do what I have to do. I'll do anything that's necessary to let me read this letter."

"Okay," Rafferty says.

"And that means we're partners," Arthit says. "Your jam is my jam." He folds the envelope once and puts it back into his pocket. "I'm not a cop for now, and I want revenge. I can bring you my skills, and Kosit's, and you can bring us everything you've figured out. Between us we're going to get you out from under, and we're going to put Thanom away, since he's involved in your situation. I've had to leave Noi's family to handle the ceremonies. You think I'll forgive that? I'm going to boil his balls, dip them in hot sauce, and feed them to him."

"How?" Kosit asks.

"It's obvious. We learn what's up and we fix it. Just come all the way in here, Poke. Stop lurking in the fucking bathroom, sit on this awful bed, and tell us what you know."

Rafferty comes out of the bathroom, pulling the door closed behind him so he doesn't have to listen to the toilet running. He glances at the bedspread, which is shiny with dirt, before he takes a seat, inches from Arthit's feet.

"At the beginning it was simple," Rafferty says. "We started with two sides. One of them is Ton, and I don't know for sure who the other one is yet, although I've got a theory."

"Let's hear it." Arthit reaches over to the other bed and grabs the pillow. He puts it on top of the pillow he already has, and then he sits up with them behind his back.

"No. I'm not sure, and I don't want to plant anything in your minds, yours and Kosit's, yet. I could be wrong. Let's see how things shape up as we start to screw with them." He rubs his face with his good hand, realizing how tired he is. But at the same time, there's a kernel of excitement deep in his chest: He's part of a team now. "So we had two sides, both threatening my family, one side if I wrote a book and the other side if I didn't. And then it gets more complicated. Ton's side is connected to Thanom. And Pan is connected—was connected, might still be connected—with this crook Wichat, who's selling the babies."

"Was connected or is?" Arthit asks.

"I think we'll know in a few hours. I put some bait in a box. If Wichat goes for it, we'll know they're still an item."

"Okay," Arthit says. "Tell me about that ridiculous bandage on your hand."

"This is courtesy of what I think of as the *other* side, meaning not Ton's guys. I thought it was Ton's side at first, but it wasn't. Is this complicated enough?"

"I have extensive training," Arthit says. "Cosmic string theory is complicated. Imaginary numbers are complicated. This is just two bunches of thugs tussling over a blanket, and you're unlucky enough to be the blanket. Does the hand hurt?"

"Yes."

"Well, don't let it slow you down."

"That's what I needed. Sympathy."

"Tell me about the money," Arthit says, touching the bag with his foot.

"It's Ton's. I thought I'd enjoy spending it to stick his finger in a socket. And I'm hoping we're at a point where we might be able to do that."

" 'Hoping,' " Kosit says. He reaches down and pulls out one of the drawers in the dresser and puts one foot up on it. " 'Might be' at a point. This is all very reassuring."

"Why?" Arthit says. "Why are they any more vulnerable now than they were before?"

"Because they know that things aren't working. They thought they had me under control, but now they know they don't. They thought Thanom could put you on ice, but he couldn't. Wichat, who's probably involved in this, is worried about some kid wandering around who could bust his baby racket open. Nobody knows where we are or what direction we might come from. This is the kind of situation that makes people improvise, makes them do stupid things to get the world under control again."

"But what was the point in the first place?" Kosit asks. "I mean, what were they all after?"

"Arthit called it," Rafferty says. "It's politics. Ton's side, which is the elite who would hate to see Pan elected, aimed me at people who don't like him. The kind of people who might spill the dirt if there were dirt to be spilled. We know—lots of people know—that there's dirt back there, but I think there's one thing, one horrific thing, people *don't* know about, except as a rumor of some kind, and they wanted to see whether I could find it, so they could use it against him if he decides to run for office. The other side, call it the pro-Pan side, tried to scare me off because they were *afraid* I'd find the dirt, and they don't want anything to surface that could keep him from getting elected. Whatever it is, Pan has managed to keep it a secret till now, and that's why none of those biographies got written: He bought people off, or threatened them, or burned down a printing press."

Arthit says, "Any idea what it is?"

"I'm pretty sure it's exactly what we talked about the very first night, after the card game. It's the missing step from ambitious thug to budding billionaire. At some point Pan acquired a guardian angel, and he did it by doing something unforgivable, something indelible. Something that could destroy Pan, and probably the guardian angel, too, if it came out. And I think it had to do with a fire. He was burned a few months before he made the leap. I located half a dozen fires in that time frame, but I think the one we want is a toy factory."

"I remember that," Kosit says. "It was awful."

Arthit says, "Have you not listened to the radio today?"

"Actually, Arthit," Poke says, "that was high up on my to-do list, but I haven't gotten around—"

"Then you *don't* know," Arthit says. "This is no longer a hypothetical discussion." He sits up and leans forward, grunting as he stretches his lower back. "I sat here, in this awful room, with nothing to do, and in self-defense I turned on the radio. Big story. Pan's office announced today that he's going to hold a press conference on Monday. The spokesman wouldn't say what it was about, but all the radio commentators seem to think he's going to announce that he's running for office."

"Monday," Rafferty says.

"Day after tomorrow." Arthit draws a deep, slow breath and blows it out. "The day of Noi's cremation."

"Well, then," Rafferty says. "We'd better get going."

"Finally," Arthit says. "Where?"

"First," Rafferty says, "we're going to a camera store to spend some of Ton's money. Then we'll go down to the Indian district and spend some more of it to buy stolen goods. Third, we'll go see some street kids, and after that we'll pay a compassionate visit to someone in the hospital."

"Compassion," Arthit says. "One of my favorite words."

44

The Old Skyrocket

They haven't been out of the taxi more than a minute when Rafferty sees the first one, but only because he's looking. The kid is about nine years old, dirty enough to have spent most of his life underground, and he's lurking on the other side of a line of parked cars, watching them through the windows.

Rafferty says, "See him?"

Kosit, who is toting a big shopping bag, says, "See who?"

"Exactly," Rafferty says. "Nobody sees them." He turns to the kid and waves him over, but the boy squints at Kosit's uniform and takes off at a run, and then two others appear, both girls, visible but just out of reach, dangle themselves in sight for a second, and sprint in different directions. It's the same maneuver they did when they stole the wallet from the man who'd been following Rafferty.

"The old skyrocket," Arthit says approvingly. "Everybody goes in different directions, and the fastest kid runs last." One of the girls, thin as a piece of paper, with an explosion of fine hair framing a nervous, high-boned face, has slowed and is watching them over her shoulder. "That one," Arthit says. "Nobody's going to catch her." He takes a couple of steps in her direction, and she accelerates like a startled hare, threading her way between the cars on the road and disappearing around a corner. "Olympic caliber," Arthit says, coming back.

"It's down there somewhere," Rafferty says, thumbing over his shoulder at the Chao Phraya. All three kids had put the river behind them when they ran.

"Sure it is," Arthit says. "If they run east, home is west."

"Boo says it's a shack, nothing but weeds and mud on either side of it. Just old wood with a tin roof. Right along here somewhere."

They walk the cracked, weedy sidewalk that runs along the top of the riverbank. Across the river the city's lights are beginning to flicker on, casting long yellow threads over the surface of the water. The sky is deep blue-black above them, reddening to an eggplant purple at the horizon. The river exudes a dark, sweet brackish smell.

Two more kids approach them from the front, and Rafferty turns to see the other three coming up from behind. They all look wary. "Put your hands on your wallets," he says. "They're artists with wallets." To the speedy girl, who has come closest, he calls, "Where's Boo?"

"Don't know Boo," the girl says, slowing. Her eyes are on Kosit, and she's ready to run again.

"Oh, sure you do. Look at me. I was the guy in the garage this morning when you helped my wife and kid get away. On Soi—"

"Soi Pipat," she says, and she gives him a big grin. "We were good, huh?"

"Amazing."

Arthit says, "You can really run."

The girl says, "Sometimes I need to." She looks back at Rafferty, then over at Kosit, with a passing glance at Arthit. "You didn't have cops with you this morning."

"They're okay," Rafferty says. "Boo knows this one." He angles a thumb at Arthit.

The girl grabs her lower lip between her teeth. Then she swipes her nose with an index finger and says, "They're down there. Near the water. You want to see them?"

"Sure. But I need to talk to Boo, too."

"Then we have to hurry," the girl says. She gives Kosit another critical glance. "You're sure about the cops?"

"Look at the bag, the one in uniform's carrying," Rafferty says. "He's Santa Claus. Why do we have to hurry?"

She turns toward the path and says over her shoulder, "Because we're going to work soon."

"Actually," Rafferty says, "you're not."

IT'S TWENTY THOUSAND baht," Rafferty says, passing the fold of currency to Boo. "It's to keep the kids from going to work, pay for food and stuff, and buy a little of their time."

"For twenty thousand you can have them for a week," Boo says, fanning the bills. The only light in the room is a yellowish glow from four kerosene lanterns, one placed in each corner, a cautious distance from the wooden walls. The flames throw golden highlights on sweaty foreheads and noses. "What do you want them to do?"

"Hang around on the street. Be invisible. Stay out of reach." Rafferty has one arm around Miaow, who is not only sitting closer to him than usual but actually leaning against him. Her knees are raised, and she has both arms wrapped around them, folding herself into the smallest space possible. She hasn't said a word. Rose sits several feet away, watching them both. Da is clear across the room, as far from them as possible, with Peep out cold in her lap.

"Out of whose reach?" Boo asks.

"Everybody's. Send them in threes, so they can do the . . . the . . ."

"Skyrocket," Arthit says.

"I remember you from before," Boo says to Arthit. "You were at Poke's. Aren't you a cop anymore?"

"I'm on leave."

"Cops are always cops."

"Speaking of cops," Rafferty says, "this is Kosit. Kosit has some toys."

"I'm Officer Santa Claus," Kosit says. "Is there something I can put on the ground? I don't want this stuff to get dirt in it."

"Here," Rose says. "Real cashmere." She takes the shawl, folded in half, off her lap and spreads it on the dirt floor. Rafferty starts to protest, but it doesn't seem worth it.

"Get two of those lanterns," Boo says to the room at large, and immediately two of the smaller kids jump up and thread their way through the seated children, lanterns in hand. Boo takes them and sets them on either side of the cashmere shawl.

"Here goes," Kosit says, clearly enjoying himself. He reaches into the bag and brings out several black objects, then dips back in and gets more. When he's finished, there are eight of them, sleek and compact, made of gleaming plastic and shaped like cylinders, small enough to fit easily into a child's hand. "Look," Kosit says. He picks one up, unfolds a small screen on one side, holds the cylinder up, and moves the barrel slowly across the room. Then he turns it around and pushes a button, and suddenly kids are scrambling over one another to get closer, to see their own lantern-lighted faces on the tiny video screen. "You're all in the movies," Kosit says.

"You think everybody can use these?" Rafferty asks.

"Are you serious?" Boo says. "They're *kids*. Kids can figure this stuff out while they're sleeping. You're the guys who read the directions."

"They need to keep them out of sight," Rafferty says. "Under their shirts or something, until they absolutely have to pull them out. And the people they're photographing can't see them." He picks one up. "Watch. The screen swivels up, so you can look down at it. Hold the camera at chest or even belt level, just don't bring it up to the eye. Anything held up to the eye is a dead bust."

"Anything else?" Boo says. "I mean, anything we can't work out ourselves?"

"Yes. I'm deadly serious about them staying out of reach. If anyone even looks at you, beat it. Walk away. If they come after you, run. But these things have a zoom lens, so don't get close. Is that understood? Because if it isn't, we can forget it right now."

"Relax," Boo says. "This isn't as dangerous as what they do every night. Sooner or later one of the pedos is going to grab a kid and hold him hostage while he tries to talk his way through the cops."

At the word "pedos," Arthit and Kosit both look up at Boo. Before they can ask a question, though, Rafferty says, "But I'm not responsible for that. They're not doing that for me. They're doing *this* for me, and they'll be careful, all right?"

" 'Pedos'?" Kosit demands, his eyes narrow.

"I'll tell you later," Rafferty says.

Boo says, "Who are we watching?"

"A bunch of guys," Rafferty says. "You've met Pan and Dr. Ravi, so you should be on the team at Pan's place, but stay out of sight. Officer Kosit has pictures of most of the others."

"They just brought me along to carry stuff," Kosit says. He reaches back into the bag and takes out a manila envelope. From the envelope he withdraws several black-and-white photographs, pulled from police files by the patrolman who helped him arrest Rafferty. He puts the first one on the shawl.

"Wichat," Boo says sourly, looking down. "Some of us already know him by sight."

"I do," says the girl with the exploding hair.

"Okay," Boo says, "you and two others will be on Sathorn." To Kosit he says, "Who else?"

"A cop," Kosit says, putting a photo of Thanom on the shawl. "This is someone to be very careful of."

"Looks like a monkey," Boo says.

"He *is* a monkey," Arthit says. "He's the world's only man-eating monkey."

"And there's also a rich guy," Rafferty says. Ton looks up, startled by the camera, in one of the photos taken at the malaria event. Captain Teeth glowers over Ton's shoulder "The guy just behind him is not anyone to get close to."

Rafferty spreads the pictures out. "There's one more," he says. "But we haven't got a photo. He'll probably be with these two, or with the one with the bad teeth, there, in the picture. You'll pick them all up at the house where the rich guy, whose name is Ton, lives, or maybe at his office."

"You have addresses?" Boo is examining the photos one at a time.

"Sure," Rafferty says.

"And what you want . . ." Boo says.

"I want everything they do, wherever they go. And I'll say it one more time: I want the kids to stay as far away as possible. I'd rather have bad pictures, or no pictures, than to have a kid get caught. Teams of no fewer than three, so they divide up if they get chased."

"Phones," Kosit prompts.

"Right. Here's how you talk to me, and to each other, if anything happens."

Kosit upends the bag, and a dozen cell phones, all makes and several colors, cascade out. "Stolen and resold," Kosit says. "Although as a cop I'd never say that. The SIM cards are all new, bought for cash. Prepaid up to five thousand baht each. No records, nothing that can be traced."

"And one each for you and Rose," Rafferty says to Miaow, picking up two of them. "Get out your old ones."

Not speaking, Miaow shifts her weight so she can reach into her pocket. She comes up with her phone, holding it without looking at anyone. She seems to be staring through the nearest wall and all the way across the river. When Miaow moves, Da's eyes go to her. Rafferty takes the phone and hands it to Rose, who's holding her own.

"Throw them in the river," he says.

Rose nods, but for the moment she puts them on the dirt floor.

"Are we clear on all this?" Rafferty asks Boo.

Boo puts down the photos and picks up one of the phones. "Starting when?"

"Right now. I'll give everybody money for moto-taxis. Just wave the bills at them. And listen, if anybody gets something out of the ordinary—for example, if any of these people meet each other—I want a phone call the moment you've got your video and you're out of sight." He gets up, dusting his jeans, and Arthit and Kosit follow suit. "I'm going to say it again, and I'm talking to every single one of you. If you're in any kind of danger, forget the video. Just run."

"We already know about running," says the girl with the exploding hair.

"Good," Rafferty says. "Let's get started."

"SHE NEEDS TO work it out for herself," Rose says.

"She and Arthit," Rafferty says. "Nobody needs my help." They have their arms comfortably dangling from each other's waists, and they stand only a few feet from the edge of the water, now just a black, flat, featureless plain with an upside-down city glittering near the opposite shore.

"Don't be silly," Rose says. She turns and lightly kisses the side of his neck. "You help just by being there."

He leans toward her, forcing her to prolong the kiss. "That's not enough."

"She can't confide in you," Rose says. "She doesn't know what's wrong. All she knows is that she doesn't fit anywhere. Not at school, not with the kind of kids who used to be her friends. She's somewhere between here and there, and no one in either place really accepts her."

"We accept her."

"Come on. We're wallpaper. In a kid's life, the only people who really exist are other kids. Parents are like large, troublesome stuffed animals."

"So what you're telling me, in your tactful Thai way," Rafferty says, turning to face her and cupping her chin in one hand, "is that I should keep my mouth shut."

"Until she asks you," Rose says. "Which she probably won't." She looks up at him for a moment, and then she says, "I never tell you how handsome you are."

"And I know why."

"Don't even try that," she says. "You know perfectly well how women look at you."

"They sense solidity," Rafferty says. "They know I'll keep a fire burning in the mouth of the cave and that there will always be a haunch to gnaw on. Even if I put them in danger all the time. Rose, I'm so sorry about—"

"What they *know*," Rose interrupts, "is that you'd give them a great time if you decided to pile on."

Rafferty says, "Pile on?"

Rose leans forward and brushes his lips with hers. "Go away," she says. "Do what you and Arthit have to do. Be careful. Watch out for Arthit. I don't know how much he wants to stay alive. And don't worry about Miaow. She's tougher than you are."

Rafferty says, "Pretty much everyone is." He starts to climb up the bank but turns back and says, "Get rid of those phones."

45

You're Not Hopeless After All

T hey don't know where he is," Captain Teeth says, putting down the phone and following Ton with his eyes. "He's out with the wife somewhere."

Ton is agitated in a way that unnerves Ren. The man paces the room, running his fingertips over the surfaces of the furniture as though expecting dust. He straightens everything he touches: photos, pens, ashtrays, knickknacks, but he never looks down at the result. He continually tugs at the sleeves of his jacket, as though they're riding up on him. He buttons and unbuttons his sport coat. He hasn't sat down in the twenty minutes since he burst into the room, swearing about Pan.

"Call back whoever you talked to," Ton says. "Tell him if he can't find his boss and put me in touch with him in half an hour, it'll be years before he gets another job. I need the woman's phone located, and that man's boss is the only one who can authorize it."

"Fine," Captain Teeth says, dialing. He turns his back to Ton and, looking at Ren, rolls his eyes.

"Pan's going to make an announcement," Ton says. "He's going . . . to make . . . an announcement. After everything we've learned from this . . . this fishing expedition with Rafferty, he's going to make an *announcement*? You," he says to Ren, "get on the phone and—" He is still for the first time since he came through the door. "No," he says. "Forget it. I'll be back in a minute."

Ton goes through the door and into a long, dim hallway, paneled in reflective mahogany. The only lights gleam above paintings: a darkly polished Vuillard, two gauzy Renoirs, a pallid, drooping Madonna by the Dutch Vermeer forger of the 1930s, Han van Meegeren. Three doors down, he pushes his way into a room that's empty except for some bare bookshelves, a grand piano, and a cello, leaning carelessly against a chair. On one of the bookshelves near the door is a telephone.

Ton picks it up, dials a number from memory, and says, "General? I'm sorry to bother you, but I think we should talk." He listens for a second. "No, sir, I don't think it's anything fatal. But if you could give me a few minutes— Fine. I'll wait for your call." He hangs up and blots the bead of perspiration that's gliding down toward his jawline.

THE NURSE'S CREPE-SOLED shoes squeak on the linoleum as she hurries after them. "Please, *please*," she says. It's an urgent whisper. "You can't go in there. He's not allowed to have visitors right now."

Kosit speaks in his normal tone of voice, without looking back. "Did you see my uniform when we passed you?"

"Of course," she hisses. "But still, the doctor says—"

"Tell the doctor to say it to me," Kosit says. He pushes open the door to the patient's room. "Now go away. We're not going to interfere with your curing him."

The nurse says, "There's no curing him."

"Then what are you worried about?" Kosit stands aside and lets Rafferty and Arthit precede him. Then he follows and closes the door in the nurse's face. He turns his back to it and leans against it, his arms crossed.

The room is as dim and airless as a sealed cave. The flame on a candle, Rafferty thinks, would burn straight up, without a flicker. Porthip has been assigned to a high floor, with a view of Bangkok in all its sloppy, energetic life, a decision that seems to Rafferty to be tactless. Through the gauze-curtained window, arteries of light mark the prog- ress of traffic down Sukhumvit, and neon smears the darkness with the vibrant colors of the city's nightlife. By contrast, the single light hanging above the bed is a chalky bluish white, turning the face above the tugged-up covers into a pallid waxwork.

Porthip is flat on his back. His eyes are closed. The fat around his eyes has been burned away, and the eyeballs beneath the lids seem unusually large, as spherical as marbles. Suspended halfway down the intravenous drip that snakes under the covers to attach to the man's wrist is a morphine-delivery unit with a plunger the patient can use when the pain is too much to bear. Beside the bed, green screens monitor the struggles of the heart that gave out yesterday, abandoning the depleted body to the cancer that is devouring it. As he approaches the bed, Rafferty studies the face. Stripped of the energy that had animated it, it seems a frail mask, bones hollowed out to create a thin shell over emptiness. Rafferty feels a cold prickling between his shoulder blades, seeing his own face in forty or fifty years.

Porthip's eyelids flicker.

Rafferty says, "You're awake."

The eyes open, focused somewhere beyond Rafferty. With evident effort, Porthip brings them to Rafferty's face. His forehead creases for a second and then clears. "You," he says. "I wondered."

"Wondered what?"

"How long," Porthip says. "Before you . . ." He lifts his chin, indicating the morphine drip. "Push that thing, would you?"

"Sure." Rafferty depresses the plunger, and a moment later Porthip's eyes slowly close and then reopen.

"Nothing," he says. His voice is a husk, just a rough surface wrapped around breath. "I've pushed it too often. The limiter's kicked in. But when it works, it's great stuff. I've . . . seen things. On the walls. On the insides of my eyelids." His back arches as a spasm runs through him. His eyes close. "Death," he says.

Rafferty says, "So what?"

"Ah," Porthip says, opening his eyes. "You're angry."

"You lied to me."

Porthip says, "Why should you be different?"

"You're dying. Why waste the effort now? What possible difference could it make to you at this point?"

"Habits," Porthip says. "Hard to break."

"Snakeskin," Rafferty says. "It owned the factory that burned down. And you owned Snakeskin. With Tatsuya."

"Tatsuya," Porthip says, and this time he does smile. "The partner every businessman dreams of. Dead for years and years. Tatsuya is a signature machine back in Tokyo."

"I don't care about Tatsuya. You owned that factory."

"Not according to the records," Porthip says.

"No, of course not. But if you didn't own it when it burned, then you did something that doesn't make any business sense at all. You, as Snakeskin, bought a destroyed factory, paid good money for it, and then just let it sit there. You didn't clean it up, you didn't put it to use. It could be making money again. So why buy it if you weren't going to do any of that?"

"Interesting question," Porthip says.

"I don't think you *did* buy it. I think you already owned it. You just quietly sold it to yourself, passed it from one company to another. You couldn't sell it to someone else because it might have attracted media attention. The papers would have been interested. A lot of people died there."

"One hundred," Porthip says, and takes a breath. "And twenty-one."

"And around the time of the fire, Pan disappears, and when he comes back, he's got burns all over him and there's suddenly some serious weight behind him. He's doing big-boy business, the kind of business that requires someone to open doors. Someone like you."

"You know," Porthip says, "you can push the plunger on that thing up there until your thumb falls off, but it only delivers so much. They let you control your pain, but only up to a point. There's a limiter that won't let you go all the way to where I want to go. For that you need a doctor who's so high up nobody would ever question him."

"You owned that factory," Rafferty says. "Pan got burned there, somehow, and you wound up owing him. And you're high enough up that no one would, as you say, question you."

Porthip's body goes rigid, and his mouth tightens into a line as straight as a slice. Then his lips part and he lets out a long sound that's just his breath traveling over his vocal cords, wind through a pipe organ.

"Pan put the locks on," Porthip says when he can talk. His voice is frayed and ragged, and he's taking more frequent breaths. "He put the bars on the windows. We had a . . . a problem with the ghost shift. Day jobs, some of them had day jobs. They were tired. People kept going outside, going into the sheds where the stuffing was stored. Big . . . soft piles of stuffing. For the bunnies, for the kittens. The ghost shift . . . they took naps there." He struggles under the covers until he has an arm free, and then he lifts a twig-thin hand to the plunger and pushes it home. "Nothing." He is panting with the effort. "But I can pretend I feel better."

"They took naps," Rafferty prompts.

"I hired Pan from Chai, who was the top crook then. I needed four or five heavyweights to keep the workers on the ball. Except for Chai, Pan was the only one who knew who I was, the only one—" His body arches again, his eyes slam shut, and a stream of air hisses between his lips. "He was the only one who knew anything. The others were just . . . muscle."

"What happened?"

"There was . . . a rule," Porthip says. "There had to be two guards outside. One of them had to have the key. One of them always . . . always had to have the key." His eyes close again, and the lids flutter as though the eyeballs behind them are rolling up. Rafferty puts a hand on the arm Porthip extricated from the covers. The man's eyes open. "Key," he repeats.

He turns his head to the right, as though it eases the pain. "So Pan stops by the place in the middle of the night. He used to do that, just to . . . to keep everybody awake. And there's smoke coming out of the windows, and people inside are screaming. He runs around the building, looking for the men who were supposed to . . . to be there . . . but they've gone . . . to . . . to eat. They've got the key. Pan went crazy. He tried to knock down the doors. They were iron, hot iron, and he was trying to push them open. He tried to pull the bars off the windows, even though flames were already coming out of them. He reached between the bars, into the fire. He tried to pull people through. He actually pulled one set of bars out and yanked three people through the window, but they were dead. They were on fire, but he pulled them over the windowsill and fell backward. They landed on top of him, burning. He rolled out from under them and tried to go in through the window, but he couldn't. It was an inferno." Porthip licks his lips. "Can I have some water?"

Rafferty picks up the glass with the straw in it and positions it under Porthip's mouth, then waits as the man drinks.

"He was burned. Badly. His clothes were synthetics. They melted into his skin. He was in terrible pain. But when the guards came back, he killed them. Then he loaded them in the trunk of his car and dumped them in the river. At five A.M. he came to my house. He could barely stand up."

"And you took care of him."

"He almost died there. He tried to save those people. Never, not once, did he do anything that would have . . . exposed me. He was the kind of man you wanted to do something for."

Arthit says, "But you're exposing him now, aren't you?"

Porthip looks past Rafferty and lets his eyes settle on Arthit. "He's not the same man. Before, he had . . . he had honor."

"What does that mean?" Rafferty asks.

"You're doing so well," Porthip says. "I'd hate . . . hate to deprive you of the satisfaction."

"You backed him. You put him into businesses he never could have gotten into on his own."

"At first," Porthip says. "For a while."

"And then you sold the factory to him."

"No," Porthip says. "You're missing it."

"Missing what?"

"Snakeskin. *Snakeskin* sold the factory to Pan."

Rafferty says, "I just said that."

Porthip shakes his head. "You said *I* sold it to him."

From behind Rafferty, Arthit says, "It's a corporation, Poke. It's not an individual. It remains Snakeskin no matter who owns it."

"Oh, Jesus," Rafferty says. "You sold the company."

Kosit closes his eyes and nods.

"To whom?"

Porthip's lids open, and he looks at Rafferty out of the corners of his eyes. He lifts his hand toward the morphine-delivery unit and caresses the plunger with his fingertips, then lets the hand drop. "You don't know?" he asks. "You haven't figured it out?"

Rafferty tilts his head back and closes his eyes and lets the realization wash over him. When he opens them again, he finds Porthip looking at him with some of the old energy.

"Ton," Rafferty says. "You sold it to Ton. And *Ton* gave the factory to Pan."

"See?" Porthip says. "You're not hopeless after all."

46

It's Hard to Put a Positive Spin on Mass Murder

They haven't even gotten into the hospital's parking lot when Rafferty's phone rings.

"Wichat came out of his office," says a child's voice. "With three big guys."

"Who is this?"

"Nit," says the child. "I'm the girl who runs fast."

"Good work, Nit. Stay away from him. Be careful."

"I'm always careful."

"Has he met anybody?"

"No, but he went to your apartment building, where we were this morning. He's in there now."

Rafferty's heart sinks. He'd been pretty sure it would happen, but he hadn't wanted to believe it. He puts out a hand to stop Arthit and Kosit. "Where are you?"

"In front of the building. Across the street."

"You know the garage door, where you went in before?"

"Sure."

"Okay. Stay across the street but move left, so the garage door is to your right. Keep moving until you're looking at the left edge of the building. You should be able to see the balconies that stick out on that side."

"Hang on. Yeah, sure. I can see them."

"Okay. Count up eight stories. Tell me whether you see any lights in the windows next to that balcony."

" . . . six . . . seven . . . No. It's dark."

"Okay, now count down four floors. Wait. Is someone keeping an eye on the entrance, in case they come out?"

"Sure." The tone is edged with impatience.

"There's no balcony on the fourth floor, but there are windows in the same—"

"Got it. Yeah, there are lights on."

"Son of a *bitch*," Rafferty says in English. "Okay, thanks," he says in Thai to the girl. "Get out of sight. The people Wichat wants aren't there, and he'll be out any minute. Wait around the corner on—"

"On Silom," Nit says, and this time the impatience isn't just at the edges.

"Right." He snaps the phone closed and pops a sweat that's pure anger.

"Well," he says to Arthit, "we've got the answer to one question. Pan and Wichat still keep the chat line open."

"On what evidence?"

"Pan just tried to sell Boo and Da to Wichat. I told Pan they were staying on the fourth floor of my apartment house. I didn't tell anybody except Pan. And Wichat's up there right now with some goons, probably punching holes in the walls."

"What does that prove?" Arthit asks. "In the larger picture, I mean."

"Well, I think we can assume that Pan is no longer the self-appointed guardian of the poor of Isaan. If he ever was. Da's about as poor and as Isaan as it's possible to be, and he tried to hand her to a Bangkok crook who probably wants her dead." He kicks a tire on the nearest car, hard enough to set off a whooping alarm. "This is going to kill Rose. She thinks he's a great man."

Arthit says, "And then there's Ton." He grabs Rafferty's arm and hauls him away from the squalling car.

"Yes," Rafferty says. He can't get a breath that's deep enough to unlock his chest. "There's Ton."

"What do you think that's about?" Kosit asks.

Rafferty says, "The word that comes to mind is 'sellout.' "

"EVERYBODY ELSE IS staying put," Rafferty says, putting the phone away. "The kids say nobody's moving." The three of them are sitting on plastic chairs at an outdoor noodle stall off Sukhumvit. Kosit is slurping rice noodles loudly enough to be heard over the traffic, while Arthit pushes his spoon through the broth as though he expects to discover something of value at the bottom of the bowl. Occasionally he stops shoving the utensil around and passes his hand over the bristle on his chin. All the while his eyes burn a hole in the center of the bowl.

Rafferty watches Arthit brood, thinks of three or four modestly helpful things to say, and rejects all of them. Instead he takes a mouthful of noodles and boils his tongue. He forces the scalding liquid down and grabs a glass of water, holding the coolness in his mouth on the theory that it will keep his tongue rare, as opposed to well done. He lets the silence stretch and then swallows the water and says, "It's the only thing that makes any sense."

Without looking up, Arthit says, "What is?"

"A deal. A terrifically secret deal. Between Ton—Mr. Establishment—and Pan. Ton must have taken a look at him and seen a guy who had peasant roots and lots of charisma, was terrifically popular, and was an obvious candidate sooner or later. The worst-case scenario would have been that Pan runs and gets elected, and Ton's guys have got to get him out somehow. The best-case scenario would have been that he runs and gets elected—"

"And they own him," Arthit says. He drops the spoon into the bowl. "Ton's group aren't against Pan running for office. They're *for* it. Because they made a deal with him. They think they're going to control the first Isaan prime minister."

"Why would he go for it?" Kosit asks with his mouth full. "He could get elected without them."

"I'll make a few guesses," Arthit says. "They tell him he won't get assassinated during the campaign, for one thing. They say he won't have to worry about a coup if he gets elected and that they can make everything a lot easier for him once he's in office. Cooperation from the legislature. No pesky investigation every time he slips a million baht into his pocket."

Rafferty says, "And I was, to use a business term, due diligence. They set me up to see whether the man could really get elected."

"Meaning what?" Kosit says.

Rafferty takes another mouthful of water. "Ton wanted to know whether I could discover the monstrosity in Pan's past, the thing that would make it impossible for him to get elected. I think they saw the same blank space Arthit talked about at the very beginning, the link missing in Pan's story, the link between Pan the pimp and Pan the great industrialist. They wanted to see whether I could find out what it was. If Pan runs for national office, how likely is it that the fire at the factory will come out? If it did, it'd be fatal. People will put up with a lot from a candidate, as American politics prove over and over again, but it's hard to put a positive spin on mass murder. Ton figures only a very small number of people know about it, and they're all on his side. So he set me loose to see whether I'd find it. He gave me clues, put me in touch with some of the right people, because after Pan goes public as a candidate, he'll be investigated by the best, and they won't miss anything obvious. I was his way of knowing whether the campaign could survive the attention of the press."

"And he doesn't know you've figured it out," Kosit says. "That's why the announcement on Monday."

"I don't actually understand that," Rafferty says.

Arthit pushes his chair back and says, "Neither do I."

Kosit picks up his bowl in both hands and drains the broth without apparent injury. "Why not?"

"Because I'm on the loose," Rafferty says. "Because Arthit's on the loose. Because there's no way he can know what we've learned or what we're up to, so why not just wait until we're under control? What's so special about Monday? They could announce any time in the next few weeks, but no, it's Monday, and here *we* are rattling around all over Bangkok, and Ton has no idea what we do or don't know. It's not . . .

characteristic. He's careful, and here he is allowing Pan to go public while these wild cards are all over the table."

Arthit says, "Maybe Ton's not in charge."

Rafferty is about to fill his mouth with water again, but he puts the glass back down. "Right. What's happening right now? Porthip's dying. Porthip might be the only person who actually knows firsthand what happened at the factory. Everybody else just has hearsay." A thought strikes him. "Except maybe Wichat. Wichat was working for the same crook Pan was, back when it happened. Maybe that's why Pan tried to hand him the kids, because he can't piss Wichat off."

"Could be," Arthit says, nodding. "Keep going."

"So with Porthip about to vanish from the scene, Pan wants to redefine the relationship. He tells Ton he's going to announce–"

"And Ton says no," Arthit says. "And Pan doesn't like to be told no. So let's say he decides to announce anyway. The announcement is a demonstration that he's going to be more independent now, that it's going to be a collaboration or nothing."

Rafferty says, "Works for me."

"One thing I can tell you," Arthit says. "This is bigger than Ton. He's rich and nice-looking and he married well, but he's not in charge of anything this big. There's someone else, someone up in the nosebleed echelons of society. Military or conservative for a dozen generations. And what that means . . ." He looks at Kosit, who's been shifting eagerly on his chair, practically raising his hand to speak. "What does that mean?"

"That Ton's on the spot," Kosit says. "He's sitting on a burner."

For the first time, Arthit looks like himself. He leans over and swats Kosit lightly on the head. "That's exactly right."

Rafferty says, "Hold on," and opens his phone. "What?"

"Pan and the little guy," Boo says on the other end of the line. "Dr. something, the one with the big nose and the slacks with all those pleats?"

"Another player on the move," Rafferty says to Arthit. To Boo he says, "What are they doing?"

"They pulled out of Pan's right after I talked to you, about ten minutes ago. Big black car, not the gold one. They're heading away from town, on some nowhere road."

"What direction? Where are you?"

"North, sort of. Out toward Chatuchak. Bunch of factories."

Rafferty says, "Factories."

"The guy with the nose is driving," Boo says. "Pan's in the back."

"How far behind are you?"

"A few blocks. We're on three motos, no lights. You're going to have to pay these guys extra for that."

"Who's 'we'?" Rafferty realizes he's standing, and a sudden stab of pain tells him that he's tried to reach into his trouser pocket with the bandaged hand, looking for small bills to pay for their meal. Kosit gets up and drops a few fifty-baht notes on the table.

"Just kids," Boo says.

"Which kids?"

"Nobody you know."

Something in his tone rings wrong, but Rafferty dismisses it, since there's nothing he can do about it anyway. "Stay far back. I'm pretty sure we know where he's going. We're way the hell on the other side of town, but we'll be there as soon as we can. And listen to me. When they stop, you call to tell us where it is. And that's *it*. You do not go in until we get there. Not you, not any of your kids. You wait outside and out of sight until we arrive."

"You worry too much," Boo says. He disconnects.

"I worry too much," Rafferty says to no one.

"We'll be where?" Arthit asks. Kosit is already out on the street, hailing a cab.

"The famous factory. Dr. Ravi's taking Pan out there as we speak." A taxi flashes its headlights and cuts through traffic at an acute angle to reach them. "And I think the time has come to get their attention." Rafferty climbs into the back, beside Arthit, as Kosit slips into the front seat and pushes his badge at the startled driver.

"Right now," Kosit says, "it is impossible for you to drive too fast."

47

Kinder That Way

Boo waves the motorcycle taxis past the gate that Dr. Ravi's car pulled through. The gate is high and rusted, twisted as though someone drove straight through it, and it sags disconsolately to the right, like it's hoping for something to lean on. There are no lights visible on the other side, just tall, spiky weeds and the looming hulk of a building.

Not until the bikes are almost a quarter of a mile down the road, with the gate behind them, does Boo wave the convoy to a stop. The road is just heavily oiled dirt, spotted with patches of asphalt to fill in holes. On either side, vertical screens of foliage climb chain-link fences to mask the squat industrial buildings they surround. Razor wire spirals its silver teeth along the tops of some of the fences. Except for a weak wash of moonlight diffused through ragged, gauzy clouds and a single spotlight shining uselessly on an empty parking lot across the street, the area is dark. Two feral-looking older boys climb off the bike behind Boo's, but when the person on the third bike begins to dismount, Boo waves her to stay put.

"You're going back to the shack," he says.

"No, I'm not," Da says. "I'm going where you go." She has made a sling of Rose's cashmere shawl, and Peep peers over the edge of it, curious now that the movement of the motorbike has stopped.

"This isn't the same as watching a house," Boo says. "We don't even know what's in there."

"You should have said that before we all got on the bikes," Da says. "And there are four of us, and Khun Poke is bringing all his police, right?"

"You're not coming."

"You don't understand, do you?" She looks at him as though he's slow and she's grown impatient with waiting for the idea to drop. "I'm going where you're going." She steps toward him, and he backs up. "What's your problem? I'm a *girl*?"

Boo licks his lips, looks away, and then his eyes come back to her and he says, "The baby." The boys are watching, and to Boo's irritation they look amused.

"Peep?" Da says, her eyes wide and innocent. She puts a hand, open-fingered, against her heart. "Peep, in *danger*? Peep's been in danger ever since he got stolen. He's used to it. If he wasn't in danger, he'd probably start to cry. His karma has kept him safe until now, and either it'll keep him safe tonight or it won't. Just like yours. He'll be fine or not. Just like you."

One of the boys laughs, and Boo rounds on him, fists clenched.

"See?" Da says. "Even your friends aren't afraid of you. I'm not letting you go in there without me."

The night's silence breaks open as something mechanical sputters, coughs, and gradually works its way up to an irregular chug. A motor of some kind. The half-moon emerges from behind a scrap of cloud to reveal an area that looks post-human. The world is a narrow oiled road, fences, weeds, and empty black buildings like giant boxes dropped to earth at random.

"Generator," says one of the boys. "Must be back there."

Boo has wheeled around to face the sound. While his back is turned, Da hops off the bike and taps the driver on the shoulder. He glances at her, takes the money in her hand, and pops the clutch. By the time Boo's head snaps around, the bike is ten meters away, accelerating into the night.

Boo glares at Da. Da reaches into the shawl, brings up Peep's hand,

and waves it from side to side at Boo. The other boys start to laugh, then cover their mouths to muffle the sound. Da is grinning, too, but Boo's lips are a tight line. He stands perfectly still, waiting for silence.

"We're doing this my way, and anybody who thinks I don't mean that can find a new bunch of friends and a new way to buy food tomorrow." His voice is a sharp-edged whisper. "Everybody understand that?" He looks at Da. "*Everybody?*"

Nods all around. The boys study their feet. Da busies herself with Peep, but she makes a syllable of assent.

"I'm going through the gate first. You all"—he focuses on Da again—"*all* of you, you wait until I wave you in. Once we're all in, you do what I say unless I'm dead, and then it's up to you. Anything there you don't understand?"

"Yes," Da says, for all of them. "You're not supposed to go in. Rafferty said we were just supposed to watch."

"And that's what I'm going to do. I'm going to watch. And if I see anything I don't like, I'll come back out and we'll wait."

"You will not," Da says. "You'll show off, do something brave. And stupid."

"You know," Boo says, "I was doing just fine until you came along." He turns and faces the road, a dark ribbon in the moonlight. "We've got some brush on this side of the road. Stay close to it, and duck in if you hear a car." Without waiting for a response, he starts toward the factory.

"IT'S THE CELL network guy," Ren says, holding out the cordless phone to Ton.

"Give me the phone number for Rafferty's woman," Ton says. Into the phone he says, "Hi, Poy. Thanks for calling. I'm sorry to interrupt your evening, but this'll just take a minute. Listen, I've had a theft from one of my businesses. . . . No, nothing serious, but you can't let these things go. Got to make an example, or other people start to get ambitious, you know what I mean?" He laughs, extending a hand for the slip of paper on which Ren has written Rose's phone number. He opens and closes the hand quickly several times to hurry Ren. "She's got her cell phone on," he says into the telephone, "and I need a location." He takes the slip of paper from Ren, glances at it, listens for a moment, and says, "Wait." To Ren he says, "How long since you checked to see whether she's still got the phone?"

"Kai called a few hours back."

"Call again, now."

"But we already—"

"Do it. I'm not going through all this and then sending out a bunch of people to find a phone that's in a trash can somewhere."

"Fine." With a glance at the paper from which he copied the number, Ren dials. He closes his eyes as he waits and then opens them, listens, and disconnects. "The little girl answered," he says.

"Fine. They'll be together." Into the phone Ton says, "Here's the number. How close can you get?" He goes to the big desk, sits down, and powers up a computer. "No," he says. "I doubt she's got a GPS phone. Probably just some junk she bought used. Does it matter?" He clicks a mouse to bring up Google Earth and positions the cursor over Bangkok. "Really," he says. "Within fifty meters? That's amazing. Listen, give it to me in coordinates if you can. I want to try to locate it on the computer."

Kai comes into the room and looks first at Ton and then at Ren.

"It's the guy at the phone company," Ren says quietly. "Tracking down the woman and the girl."

"I'm ready," Ton says, with a pencil in his free hand. "Just read it to me." He writes some numbers on the pad and says, "As close as fifty meters, huh? Well, I owe you. And I'm sorry about the bother. Go back to your party." He drops the phone on the desk and starts to punch numbers into the computer. "Where are you?" he asks out loud. "Let's just zoom in a little bit—" The sentence ends in a surprised puff of air. He sits perfectly still, staring at the screen. Both Kai and Ren are looking at him.

Finally Ton tears his eyes from the computer. "Get me four guys right now," he says. "Guys who don't much care what they have to do and don't have any idea who you work for. You won't believe where you're going to take them."

"WHOEVER IT WAS," Da says, looking at the phone, "they hung up."

"Where did you get that?" Boo says, taking the phone out of her hand.

"It was on the floor at the shack."

"And you picked it up."

She reaches for it, but he puts it behind his back. "Nobody wanted it," she protests. "Everybody else had one."

"And you left it on."

"Well," she says, "what good is it if it's off? Oh, come on, I never had one before."

"And you haven't got one now," Boo says. He powers the phone off, brings his arm back, and throws it over the nearest fence.

"Hey," Da says.

He steps toward her, showing her a face that's all muscle. "Suppose it had rung while we were inside? Suppose we're watching something we're not supposed to see, and your damn phone rings. Has anybody else got one that's on?"

One of the boys holds one up. "It's on silent."

"Turn it off."

"Okay, okay."

"Anything else stupid?" Boo asks. "Any alarm clocks? Talking dolls? Anybody got squeakies in their tennis shoes?"

Nobody answers him.

"When we get to the gate, you two"—he points at Da and one of the boys—"you wait across the street. Get behind some bushes. You," he says to the other boy, the smaller of the two. "You come just inside the gate and to one side of it. Keep your eyes on me as long as you can. Relay any signal I give you. If I want you, I'll just wave you in. Two fingers means call some more kids. But if there's trouble"—he holds up his right hand, fingers splayed—"five fingers means run for your lives, got it? In different directions. When you know you're clear, get back to where we got off the bikes and find a place to hide there. We'll meet up there and figure out what's next."

Nobody says anything. Boo holds up his hand again, two fingers extended. "Means what?"

"Phone kids," says the smaller boy.

"And?" He displays all five fingers.

"Run," Da says.

Boo looks directly into her eyes. "And you'd better."

AFTER REN AND Kai leave to pick up their muscle, Ton remains at his desk. It seems like a long time since he's been alone in this room. He interlaces his fingers and rests his chin on them, and then he closes his eyes to eliminate distraction while he works his way through a conversation he does not want to have.

The position he's in now is the one he dreamed of when he was a young man, the outcome he'd hoped for when he married into a ranking family by taking the scandal daughter, the one no one could manage, the woman who has become the wife he never sees. It's taken him years of patient labor to build the trust of those above him, but he's in his element now: behind the scenes, working in partnership with the kingdom's most powerful men to maintain the order of things. To keep the kingdom secure, to keep the proper class—the educated class, the traditional leaders—in charge. To keep the nation moving forward. Thailand is already the wealthiest state in Southeast Asia, and Ton has become an important part of the group that has worked in an unbroken line, generation after generation, to accomplish that.

And, of course, he's gotten very rich doing it.

But there are things about it he hates. There are times in the past week when he's felt like a thug. Having to associate with Ren and Kai—having them in his *house*—has been almost physically painful at times. But there was no alternative. There was no possibility of allowing the usual four or five levels of management to know about the arrangement with Pan. It would have been in the papers within weeks of their agreement. He'll have to do something about Ren and Kai, but he can worry about that later.

Now is the problem. Things are going outside the lines and have been ever since the reporter had to be killed, and he's moments from a conversation that actually frightens him. He can't remember the last time he was frightened.

He is working on his third possible opening, trying to find a way to position the discussion without its leading to something disastrous being said, when he becomes aware of a regular fluctuation of light, visible even through his closed eyelids. With a sigh of resignation, he opens his eyes and looks at the halogen lamp on his desk, which is blinking on and off. He pushes his chair back a foot or two and reaches down to the lowest drawer, which he pulls open. The files stacked inside are bulky and hard to handle, and he needs both hands to remove them and put them on the desk. The desk lamp continues to flicker as he leans back down to the drawer. On the bottom edge, his fingers find the small metal tab and pull it forward. A little snicking sound signals the rise, no more than half an inch, of the drawer's false bottom. Ton lifts the bottom panel to a vertical position and pulls out the flat telephone that's stored beneath it.

Only one person has this number.

Ton breathes twice, swallows, picks up the receiver, and says, "Yes, sir."

"My boy," says the man on the other end. "How are you?"

"I'm somewhat preoccupied. I'm sorry to have bothered you, but there's a problem."

"No bother, no bother. Before we get to the problems, I want to apologize."

This line had not arisen in any of his visualizations of the conversation. "For what, General?"

"I didn't like your idea, the *farang* snooping around in Pan's past. Too fancy, I thought. Well, I was wrong. It was obvious almost immediately that Pan wouldn't get to election day without all that bothersome material coming to light. Got me thinking in other directions."

"It did?"

"Yes, and I have exactly what we need. But first, tell me about this bullshit announcement he's threatening to make."

"It's Porthip. With Porthip dying—"

"Your *farang* went to the hospital tonight," the general says, as though Ton weren't speaking. "With a cop and another man. The other man could have been a cop, too."

The back of Ton's shirt is suddenly damp. "He did?"

"He did. And Porthip told him."

"He *told* him? You mean, about Snakeskin?"

"About Snakeskin, about you. You personally. You want to hear the tape?"

"No. That . . . um, that won't be necessary."

"You didn't know your *farang* was there, did you?"

This is the topic he knows he can't control. All he can do is step up to it. "No. He shook his tail. I can't use my best people, because they know who I am, and of course I'm connected to you. So I have to use contract guys, and they're not—"

"I understand," the general says.

Ton tugs his shirt away from his skin and manages not to sigh in relief. "Thank you. But if Porthip's talking—"

"Don't worry. We've had the limiter removed from his morphine drip, and the nurse has traded his pain pills for junk. An antifungal medicine, I think. Without the pills he'll medicate himself out of existence by morning. Kinder that way, really."

"If there's an autopsy—"

"Not your business," the general says, and his tone has stiffened. "You already have more, apparently, on your plate than you can handle. But even if there *is* an autopsy, even if some zealot decides to check the cause of death for a man who was, after all, a terminal-cancer patient, they'll be expecting to find morphine in his system, won't they? Worst comes to worst, it's a compassionate death, maybe a slap on the hand for the supervising doctor."

"Yes, sir."

"The announcement."

"I told Pan early this morning that we'd discuss things further in a couple of weeks. He said I wasn't in charge."

"Excuse me?"

"With Porthip dying, he said, there wasn't anybody who could hold the factory over his head anymore. At least nobody who had actually been part of it. So he said we were no longer running his campaign. He'll still work with us, he says—he'll need help when he's elected—but he thinks he'll win in a landslide now that the fire can't come back to haunt him. In fact, he said he was going to use it."

"How the hell does he propose to do that?"

"Without Porthip, he says, he's the hero of the fire. What he's going to do is to get the press together—and you know how they'll show up, especially after the malaria party—and he's going to announce his plan to turn the factory into a monument to the people who died there. He'll talk about how he saw the smoke from the road, about how he tried to save them, show his scars. He's going to say that's why he bought the place, so he could consecrate it. He'll clean it out some and make it safe for the public to visit, and he's going to carve into the walls the names of the people who died there and turn the big workroom in the front into a gallery, with melted machines and photos of the place after the fire. He's finding pictures of the people who worked there—while they were still alive, I mean—and he's going to put those with the other pictures. And then he'll announce a grant of five million baht to fund a commission to look into the working conditions of people who do bottom-wage piecework, especially people who come to Bangkok from the northeast. And after all *that,* he'll close things out by announcing that he's running for the National Assembly, where he can really do something about these issues."

"That's it," the general says. "*That's* why he insisted on getting hold of the factory. And it's brilliant. He'll have every vote in the northeast. Too bad we can't work with him."

"He's going to make the announcement at the . . ." Ton trails off, looking at a spot in the air in front of him. His face is suddenly warm.

"At the factory?" the general says.

"Yes, sir." Ton picks up his cell phone but drops it again. He rapidly flexes the fingers of his free hand, looking down at the phone.

"It would be extremely effective," the general says. "You wouldn't be able to count all the votes it would bring. It would probably put me back on the sleeping pills. But thanks to you, thanks to your *farang,* I've found an alternative. Have you been following this kid—oh, well, at my age everybody's a kid—this young man who started out with the sidewalk popcorn machines?"

"I know something about him."

"Branching out. A couple of guesthouses, some gift shops in the lobbies of hotels and small airports. Got the rights to an American restaurant franchise called Greens. Heard of it?"

"No, sir."

"Just the usual burgers and junk, but they have some sort of handbook full of policies to make the business greener, you know? More environmentally responsible."

"Like what?"

"Who cares? Maybe they use the methane from cattle farts to power the stoves. How do I know? Thing is, green is good. Thing is, the kid's Isaan. Thing is, the kid will listen to reason."

"But, I mean, with Pan on the ticket—if he's running against Pan—no matter how good he is, Pan will wallop him, won't he?"

The general says nothing. In the silence that follows, Ton picks up his cell phone and scrolls down toward Captain Teeth's number. Then he stops scrolling and says, "Oh." He puts the cell phone back on the desk. "I see."

"And think how the votes would pour in," the general says, "if he were stepping into the shoes of a martyr."

Ton says, "Yes."

"Then we're finished?"

"Yes, sir."

"Good work," the general says. "Without your *farang* I never would have looked around." The general clears his throat. "You *can* get your hands on him, right? Not that he could prove anything, but just for neatness' sake."

"Yes, sir. I know where his wife is."

"Good, good. You're a valuable asset, Ton."

"Thank you, sir."

The general hangs up.

Ton puts the phone back into the the drawer and replaces the false bottom. He closes the drawer and realizes he forgot to put the files back, so he swears between his teeth, opens the drawer again, and drops the files into it. He is conscious of a prickling of sweat at his hairline.

He wishes he could talk to his wife.

When he's finished straightening the files, he sits looking down at the open drawer for a full minute. Then he picks up his phone, scrolls the rest of the way down, and presses "call." He waits, drumming the fingers of his left hand on the desk. Then he says, "Listen. I need one of them, either the woman or the girl, to be able to talk. It may be the only way to bring Rafferty in. But here's the important thing: I can't figure why they're at the factory unless Pan's there."

"Okay," Captain Teeth says.

"If he's there, take him out."

"You mean—"

"You know what I mean. Take him out, and take out anybody who sees anything. Just leave me one of those females in a condition to talk on the phone."

Captain Teeth says, "You're the boss."

"And one more thing. If Pan goes down tonight, we have to talk about what happens to the guys who are with you."

"Well," Captain Teeth says, "I'm not related to any of them."

48

Waiting Patiently for Blood

The generator sounds like it has a respiratory disease.

It sputters, coughs, hiccups. Then it makes a phlegmy, ratcheting, throat-clearing sound for ten seconds or so, and the whole pathology starts over.

It's so loud, Boo thinks, that he could ride in on horseback and no one would hear him.

The big black Mercedes sits empty at the end of the cracked drive, a car-shaped hole in the darkness, its motor ticking as it cools. Boo keeps himself to the darkest areas, moving from the shadow of one bush to another to avoid the thin, chilly-looking moonlight. The ground underfoot is littered with chunks of concrete, jagged-edged, irregular, heavy enough to pitch him facedown if he trips on one. Spiderwebs lace the spaces between the weeds, fat spiders straddling the centers, waiting patiently for blood. Boo isn't particularly afraid of spiders, but he doesn't like walking face-first into one.

And the place smells as if the hair of a million women was burned inside.

Boo can stroll the darkest, narrowest alley in Bangkok on a moonless night without so much as a bump in his pulse rate, but this weedy field with its blackened, abandoned factory makes the hair on his arms stand up. The generator goes into a paroxysm of coughing, and suddenly there is light on the bottom floor of the building.

Or is there? The interior is so black that there's nothing for the light to bounce off; it's like looking into an infinite space. If it weren't for the long rectangles of illumination spilling onto the weeds through the doors and windows and shining on the newly visible profile of the Mercedes, Boo's not sure he'd even register the light. But he knows one thing: Light or no light, the place doesn't feel any friendlier.

With the noise of the generator clattering in his ears, he doesn't hear the person behind him, and when the hand lands on his arm, he goes straight up into the air and comes down facing the opposite way, one hand clutching a five-inch knife that's normally sheathed inside his right front pocket. When he sees who it is, he gasps in relief several times and then knots her T-shirt in his hand to drag her down into a crouch, out of sight from the building.

Da says, "We have to leave."

"Be quiet. Rafferty's coming with the cops. We'll argue then."

"Now," she says. "We have to leave now."

Boo looks back at the building, sees nothing inside the big black room, just the sharp-edged rectangles of light falling through the door and windows. He registers that the windows are barred with thick rods of what looks like iron. "Why?" he whispers. "Why do we have to leave?"

"This place is full of ghosts," Da says. "They're everywhere."

"Don't be silly," Boo says, feeling the goose bumps pop out on his arms.

Da says, and her voice is shaking, "They're *on fire*."

"Well, yeah," Boo says, keeping his own voice steady. "Look at the place. Got burned to shit."

"Please. These are not ghosts you can talk to. They want blood. They've been waiting for blood."

"Go across the street," Boo says. "They'll stay here. Ghosts don't just wander around. I need to see what's happening in there."

"You have to come with me," Da says. "I can't have Peep here. If we stay, there will be blood. There *will* be."

"Then go, *go*. Get out of here. Get Peep across the street."

Da starts to reply, but her voice splinters into "Ohhhhhhh" as a figure inside walks past the door.

"Shut *up*," Boo hisses. "It's just the fat guy, Pan. The little one's got to be around somewhere. He was driving. He's not in the car, so he's somewhere else. Look, he's only a guy." Then he puts a hand on her shoulder and says, barely louder than a thought, "Don't move."

Dr. Ravi comes through the door of the factory and picks his way down the driveway to the Mercedes. He opens the trunk and leans in, and when he straightens up, he has something coiled over one shoulder and bulky objects dangling from each hand. Inside the factory door, he puts down the things in his hands and pulls the coil off his shoulder and drops it to the floor.

"Lights," Boo says. "And cord. Electrical cord."

But Dr. Ravi is already on his way back to the car. This time he removes long pieces of something that looks like pipe. Once inside again, he takes two of the lengths of pipe and begins to screw them together. Then Pan appears at the door and picks up the long coil of electrical cord. He unloops it, backing away until he is out of sight.

"What are they doing?" Boo whispers. "Are they going to light the place? And why are they doing this themselves? Pan's rich. There must be a hundred people who could do this for him." He squeezes Da's shoulder. "Go now. Tell the kid at the gate—his name is Tee—to come up here. I want him to use that video camera."

Da puts both hands on his arm. "I'm telling you. You should go, too."

"Ghosts leave me alone," Boo says. "I've come too close to dying, too often. They look at me and know it's just a matter of time."

"You don't know anything," Da says furiously. He hears the brush rustling for a couple of seconds, and then the generator drowns out the sounds of her movement.

A moment later Pan appears, pushing something black and shapeless across the floor, right to left. Things—pieces of it—fall off as he shoves, and he kicks the fragments out of the way. And then he reappears, moving in the opposite direction, picking up things as he goes, and ten or twelve heartbeats later he carries an armload of shapeless objects past the door. Whatever he's arranging, it's being set up on the side of the room that's to the left of the door.

Boo looks over his shoulder just in time to see Da slip through the gate, heading across the street. Other than the gate, there seems to be no way out; as far as Boo can see, the fence, at least three meters tall, surrounds the overgrown plot of ground on which the burned factory is centered. He's thinking, *Keep the path to the gate clear,* when he hears the boy who'd been stationed at the gate, Tee, coming up behind him. Without looking back, Boo says, "You stay here. I'm going to check the window to the left over there."

Tee says, "I don't like it here."

"Well," Boo says, "you've got a lot of company. Try to keep me in sight, but don't let them see you."

"Yeah, but . . ."

"But what?"

"But I don't want to be here alone."

"That damn Da," Boo says. "Ghosts everywhere." He straightens partway and looks down at Tee. "You going to be okay?" It's more a threat than a question.

Tee averts his eyes. "I guess."

"Won't be long."

As Boo starts to move to his left, he sees Dr. Ravi, who's still standing in the doorway, unfold three legs at the bottom of one of the pipelike objects to create a tall tripod. He bends down and picks up one of the lights and starts to screw it onto the top of the tripod. He has to stand on tiptoe to tighten the light. He handles the objects clumsily. They're obviously unfamiliar to him, and assembling them fully engages his attention.

At the edge of the driveway, Boo pauses and steadies his breathing. The driveway is about fifteen feet wide, and with the Mercedes behind him there's no cover at all. He waits until Dr. Ravi turns his back to the door, picks up the light, now securely atop the pole, and carries it left, out of sight. Then Boo crouches low, takes one last look at the door and the window, and sprints, bent almost double, over the cracked asphalt. He has made it most of the distance across when his toe catches on the edge of a fractured, uptilted piece of paving. He windmills his arms, he tries desperately to find a point of balance, but he was moving too fast, and there's no question. He's going down.

At the last possible second, he realizes he's going to land on his elbows, and he pulls them back to avoid breaking them, and he hits flat on his stomach. The grunt that the impact forces out of him can be heard even over the generator. He remains absolutely still, holding his breath, his eyes glued to the doorway, wishing fiercely for invisibility, and he hears someone inside say, "Somebody's out there."

And then something cold and wet touches his arm.

"WHY DR. RAVI?" Arthit asks.

The taxi is absolutely rocketing now that the densest parts of the city are behind them, the driver using flashing headlights, a nasal horn, and a well-oiled accelerator pedal to muscle the rest of the world out of the way.

"Process of elimination," Rafferty says as the landscape flashes past. "What it comes down to is that nobody else knows as much about what's happening in Pan's life, no one else is in daily contact with him. Let's say Dr. Ravi applied for the job because he thought, like a lot of people, that Pan was a great man."

"He probably could have been," Arthit says.

"Pan?" the driver asks. "You mean the one with all the money? What a guy."

Arthit says, "I rest my case."

"And maybe one reason Dr. Ravi wanted the job was that it hadn't escaped his attention that Pan could have a significant political future," Rafferty says. "And let's say that Dr. Ravi has unexpectedly democratic sentiments and he thinks that Pan might be the person who could finally give the poor a say in how the country is run."

"I'd vote for him," the driver says.

"Just drive," Kosit says.

"I'd like to be next in line for his girls, too," the driver says.

"Here's the thing," Arthit says to the driver. "Shut up and drive, or when we get there, I'll shoot you."

Rafferty looks over at him, and Arthit shrugs.

"Cops," the driver grumbles.

"And get us there in ten minutes," Arthit says, "and you'll make an extra five thousand baht."

The driver says, "Driving."

"So he gets the job, Dr. Ravi does," Rafferty says, "and the first thing he does is go through everything in the files, probably including some stuff he shouldn't have seen at all. As he told me, he's the media director. He needs to know whether there are any skeletons in the closet. He's expecting one or two—nobody gets as rich as Pan without a few skeletons folded away here and there—but he's not prepared for a hundred and twenty-one of them."

Arthit thinks about it for a moment. "How do you know he found out about that?"

Rafferty also thinks for a second, then shakes his head. "Actually, I don't. But he knew what Snakeskin was."

Arthit says, "Mmmmm."

"So let's say he *didn't* know about what happened at the factory. But the deal with Ton, with Snakeskin, is happening in real time, in the office Pan shares with Dr. Ravi, and Dr. Ravi found out about it."

He breaks off as Arthit touches his knee and lifts his eyebrows at the driver, whose eyes keep going to the rearview mirror.

"And that information . . . um, confounded Dr. Ravi's expectations, and all of a sudden his political allegiances shifted. I mean, drastically. Whether he knew about the fire or not, he suddenly realizes that the archangel is in bed with the archfiend. So Dr. Ravi decides to use his privileged position to work *against* you-know-who's ever getting elected to anything, and here comes the last thing on earth he wants to see: some hack writer, and a *farang* to boot, all set to crank out a biography of the no-longer-great man."

"Why would he think the book would be sympathetic?"

"My fault. I kicked him out of the office before I told Pan about the threats from the other side, before we came to our understanding. When the door opens, half an hour later, Pan and I are getting along great, so great that I've been invited to the malaria thing, and then Pan's lending my wife diamonds worth millions, and I'm apparently allowed to drop by whenever I want. So sure, Dr. Ravi figures the book will be a whitewash, a fan letter. I'm going to turn Pan into Gandhi."

Arthit scratches his head. "So it was Dr. Ravi who warned you not to write the book."

"Yeah. I don't think he was actually going to carry out the threats. He thought I'd scare off easily, and I would have if it hadn't been for

Ton. But he got some people who are *really* serious about their politics to keep an eye on me, and when he told them to discourage me for a second or third time, they went a little overboard."

Arthit glances at the bandaged hand. "I'd say so."

"I'd like to keep listening," the driver says, "but we're almost there. It's the next right."

49

At the Bottom of the Ocean

Boo rolls over four or five times, as fast as he can—sky, driveway, sky, driveway—heading for the weeds, putting distance between himself and the . . . the whatever it was. He reaches the edge of the drive and worms his way into the weeds, pulling himself along on his elbows, just as a brilliant light pours out of the window on the left. The light is pointed directly at Boo. He knows he's been spotted, and he's on the verge of getting to his knees so he can run, but the light slowly slides past him. He's just realizing that they didn't see him after all when the light picks out an old gray dog, sitting in the center of the driveway, scratching its ear.

"A dog," somebody inside says.

The light, Boo can see now, is the one Dr. Ravi was assembling. He's standing in the window, holding the pipe so he can turn the light right and left without burning his hands on the fixture. The dog gets up slowly, obviously stiff in the joints, gives its ribs a halfhearted scratch with a back paw, looks at Boo, and wags its tail. Then it starts to amble toward him.

"Where's it going?" a different voice—Pan—asks.

Boo is frantically trying to wave the dog off. A little creakily, the dog goes down on its front legs, paws wide, ready to play.

"Maybe there's somebody there," Dr. Ravi says.

"Gun," Pan says. He is still out of sight.

"It's probably some kid. Who's going to show up with a dog?"

"*Gun,*" Pan snaps.

Dr. Ravi lets go of the light, and it ends up pointing at the spot where Boo left Tee. Boo peers through the weeds, trying to see something, anything—the pale oval of a face, the gleam of eyes. But there's nothing. So the good news is that they don't see Tee. The bad news is that the dog is headed straight for Boo.

Pan's silhouette looms in the doorway, throwing a shadow twenty feet long. He holds the gun in both hands, barrel up, a stance that looks professional. Boo pulls himself farther into the weeds, and the dog trots happily along behind him. Bringing the gun down in front of him, Pan starts in the dog's direction.

"Khun Pan," Dr. Ravi calls as headlights sweep across the sagging gate. "Somebody's coming."

IN THE YELLOW cones of light, Rafferty sees kids scattering into the dark. "Well," he says to Arthit, "at least they're doing what they're supposed to do."

Arthit says, "Pull past the gate, maybe ten, fifteen meters. Stop in the middle of the road. I don't want to climb out into all that fucking plant life."

"The big man's afraid of bugs," the driver says, but he does as he's told. "Here?"

"Fine." Rafferty opens his door. "That's thirty-three hundred on the meter, plus another five thousand for speed. What the hell, call it ten thousand." He drops the money over the back of the seat.

The driver grabs the bills as though he's afraid Rafferty will regain his sanity. "Want me to wait?"

"No. Just go." To Kosit, Rafferty says, "Close the door softly. There's one chance in a thousand they didn't see or hear us."

"Amateur night," Arthit grumps, climbing out. He eases his door closed and taps the window, signaling the driver to go, but Rafferty pulls his door open again.

"Listen," he says to the driver. "Pull a little farther past and then turn around and drive out, slowly, like you're looking for something. Got it?"

"For ten thousand? I'll drive out sideways."

"Just do it like I said. Like you made a wrong turn and you're heading out again."

"Fine."

Rafferty closes the door again, and the three of them watch the driver make a three-point turn and creep back the way he came. They stand silently for a long moment, and finally Kosit says, "Think that'll fool anybody?"

"Oh, who knows? Better than nothing."

"Hurry," Arthit whispers, grabbing Rafferty's arm. He pulls them into the hedge that lines the factory wall. A moment later they see Pan come through the gate. He's carrying a gun.

All three of them hold their breath.

Pan comes into the middle of the road, looking up and down, and turns to follow the taxi's taillights as it makes the left at the end of the block. Then, gun still extended, he goes back through the gate.

"Remember," Rafferty whispers. "He's not just a fat rich guy with a gun. He did a lot of enforcement work."

"In the file that got vaporized," Arthit says, "he was figured for three killings."

THE DOG HAS given up on Boo and returned to the driveway, which is still warm from the sun. It sits down as though it owns the place and watches Pan approach.

Halfway to the dog, Pan stops as suddenly as though he's been frozen in place. He remains there, motionless, while Boo, watching, counts silently past fifty. Pan is waiting to hear something, waiting for someone to shift or fidget, waiting for anything that seems wrong. Without moving anything but his head, he slowly surveys the front of the factory and then, very deliberately, turns in a complete circle. Then he waits again, holding the gun two-handed, pointing at the sky.

Dr. Ravi appears in the door of the factory, and Boo sees Pan's shoulders relax, and the man starts to walk toward the door. He makes a detour to scratch the dog's head and ears, and when he's done, the dog stands and follows him into the factory.

"Let's get this finished," Pan says.

Boo rises, taking advantage of the fact that they both have their backs turned. He works his way farther left, his eyes fixed on the barred window. Five or six weedy meters from it, he lines up a clear view and settles in to watch.

Inside, bright light sweeps blackened walls. Dr. Ravi carries one of the tripod assemblies to the far wall and points it at the end of the room to the left, which is out of Boo's line of sight. Shortly afterward Pan shuffles past again, pushing another black object, sagging and half melted. Boo can almost identify the shape it used to have, but not quite. Still, he knows that he recognizes it.

"Give me a hand with these," Pan says, and Dr. Ravi moves across the window, heading right. With no one at either window or the door, Boo stoops, brings up a handful of dirt, and rubs it over his face and arms. Then, putting his feet down very slowly, he moves a couple of meters closer and a little to his right. If Pan and Ravi look straight out at him, they'll see him, but they'd have to be looking for him.

He hopes.

A scraping sound that sets his teeth on edge precedes the sight of both Pan and Dr. Ravi, each shoving another blackened object across the floor, the dog following happily along. This time Boo sees the things for what they are.

They're sewing machines.

For a frozen, gelid moment that puckers his flesh, Boo can almost see the women who sat at them, and he smells again, overpoweringly this time, the stench of burned hair. Suddenly Boo agrees with Da. This is no place for the living.

For another fifteen or twenty minutes, the two men inside work, pushing the machines across the floor and collecting more of the smaller, blackened things. Everything is taken left, to the area of the room they are . . . what? Decorating? Arranging? Boo can't figure it out, even when they talk to each other.

"To the right," Pan says. "Five or six on each side."

"We could get this done a lot faster with some help."

"I'm the only one who knows what it should look like. Who knows what it *did* look like."

Dr. Ravi says, "It's just theater. Just a press conference."

"It's everything," Pan says.

Boo has been so glued to the window that he's caught completely by surprise by the shape at the door, the man who is suddenly standing just outside it, and it takes him a moment to recognize the voice that says, "No. It's not quite everything."

Pan turns, and his hand goes to his belt, but Rafferty says, "Don't." He's got a gun in his hand, the gun Boo gave back to him, pointed at Pan's substantial gut, and he pushes through the door, and the two cops follow him into the room, both holding guns in a way that looks loose and expert.

Boo moves right, signaling to Tee. When the boy stands up, Boo holds an imaginary camera to his eye and points Tee to the window he's been watching through. Tee nods and wades through the weeds, and the last man to go through the door, the cop in uniform, glances back at the sound, registers the boy, and then turns around to face the room again.

"What's this about?" Pan demands.

"Oh," Rafferty says, "it's a long list. Let's start with you pulling the gun from under your shirt with two fingers and holding it out. Thumb and little finger, on the handle only. Barrel down."

Pan says, "There's no need for this," but he does as he's told, and Arthit comes forward and takes the gun. He puts it beneath his own shirt and then backs away again, his gun still aimed at Pan.

"So that's one thing," Rafferty says. "And then there's this." He turns to the window and waves Boo in.

Pan waits as calmly as though he's just enduring a pause in the conversation. He pays no attention to the guns that are trained on him. But when Boo comes through the door, he takes a sudden breath, and then his eyes close briefly. When they open, they are fixed on the floor.

Rafferty says, "Surprised to see him?"

"I'm surprised to see any of you," Pan says, but his voice is mostly air, and he still has not looked up. Color is climbing his face.

"You *sold* him," Rafferty says. He is speaking Thai. "You. The hope of the poor and downtrodden. You sold him and a little girl who doesn't have anything in the world except a baby that isn't even hers. You sold them to a gangster who was going to kill all of them, except the baby. All he'd do to the baby is sell it."

Pan keeps his eyes on the floor, but Dr. Ravi is staring at Rafferty as though he's suddenly begun speaking in tongues.

"And you didn't even have to," Rafferty says. His voice feels like it's being squeezed through a very small opening. "You could have bought Peep out of petty cash."

Pan's pink mouth contracts and loosens, then contracts again, and he says to the floor, "I tried." The dog, which has been standing next to Dr. Ravi, eyeing the newcomers, hears something in Pan's voice and goes and sits at his feet, looking up, concerned. Automatically, Pan reaches down and scratches the dog's ears.

Rafferty says, "Oh, well, you tried. That makes everything all right."

"He wouldn't do it," Pan says. "He wanted—he wanted—to deal with it his way." He straightens up. The dog paws at his pants leg, wanting more, but Pan ignores it. "He was afraid she'd talk, the girl would, to someone. He was afraid you'd *arrange* for her to talk to someone."

"And that made sense to you. So you said, 'Okay, here's where she is. Go kill them.'"

Pan says, "It wasn't like that."

"No? What was it like?"

"Wichat . . . knows things, from when we worked together."

"Right," Rafferty says. "He knows what happened here. That makes him dangerous, since you've decided it's worth selling who you are in exchange for power."

Dr. Ravi says to Rafferty, "Wait a minute. What side are you on?"

"Forget it," Rafferty says. "So you were wrong. Get over it." He comes another few feet into the room and looks at the arrangement at the far end. The lights are focused to create a sort of stage on which eleven blackened and sagging sewing machines have been arranged in a loose semicircle with a space in the middle. Two enormous photos of the burning factory have been put up on the smoke-black walls. Set in the space between the sewing machines is the platform Pan stood on when he gave his speech at the Garden of Eden. On the floor in front of the platform, ringed by the ghostly machines, is a heap of burned shoes, curled and shriveled fragments of leather and charred cloth, half-melted rubber.

"Are those really from this fire?" Rafferty says, pointing at the shoes. He can barely speak.

"Yes," Pan says.

"And you're using them," Rafferty says, "for a photo op." He spits on the floor.

"What happened here—" Pan begins.

"I *know* what happened here," Rafferty says. "I know everything. I know you tried to save people. I also know you're the one who locked them in. And I know how you used their deaths to make yourself rich, to get backing from people who normally wouldn't have pissed on you. Porthip because he felt you earned his support and Ton because he decided that he'd better own you if you were going to run for office. And you sold yourself to him."

"No, he just thought I did," Pan begins. "But, really, I—"

"And when you sold yourself, you also sold the people who died here. Is there anything left? Is there *anything* you haven't sold? And who did you sell it to? Everything you were supposed to stand for. You sold it to a man who hates the people you grew up with, squeezes blood out of them at every opportunity. You know, the kind of people you *used* to be, the kind of people who died here. And now you're going to . . . to what? Cash in on their deaths, right? You're going to use these people's deaths as currency to buy votes."

Pan says, "You don't understand. Porthip, Ton—people like Ton— *own* this country. They've owned it forever, and they'll never let go of it until there are people like me in office. People who are the real Thailand, not the Chinese Thai who have had everything for centuries. People like that will never share power with—"

"People like that?" Rafferty says. "People like that? I know about people like that. The woman I married was whored out by people like that. But let me ask you, Mr. Man of the Soil, how much of yourself do you think you can sell before *you* become people like that? A girl whose river was stolen, a baby snatched from its mother, a street kid. You were going to sell them. The people who died here, you're going to use them. Who the hell do you think you are now?"

Pan's eyes are everywhere. He clears his throat and says, "I—"

"Don't bother," Rafferty says. "It's all over your face. Look, even the dog's given up on you."

And in fact the dog has gotten up and is walking toward the door, looking past Boo. And then he stops and his ears go up, and he lowers his head and begins to growl.

"Poke," Arthit says, but the door is suddenly crowded with men, and in front of them, with Captain Teeth's arm around her throat and his gun at her head, is Da. Even with death touching her temple, she keeps an arm wrapped tightly around the cashmere shawl that holds Peep.

Boo takes an involuntary step toward her, but one of the men racks his automatic, and the boy freezes.

"Not one move," Captain Teeth says. "Nobody. Not one move. Anybody twitches and the girl and the kid are dead on the floor, got it?"

No one speaks. The only sound is the husky growl of the dog, its head now low as it looks up at Captain Teeth.

"I count three guns," Captain Teeth says. "I want those guns turned around slowly, so you're holding them by the barrel. Do it now."

Rafferty, Arthit, and Kosit reverse their guns so the handles are pointing toward Captain Teeth.

"Good. Now hold them up in the air, way up. Good, good. And turn around so your backs are to us. Now bring down the hands with the guns, hold them out shoulder length, arms stiff, by the barrel. I don't want to see any bent elbows. Bring the arm slowly behind you and just stay there."

Rafferty hears feet moving, and then the gun is removed from his hand. A moment later Captain Teeth says, "All of you, turn back around. Slowly. All the way around."

When Rafferty is facing the door again, he sees Captain Teeth, still clutching Da, at the center of a group of five men, three of whom hold automatics. They have come several feet into the room, with the door at their backs. Kosit, Arthit, and Rafferty are several feet apart, and eight or ten feet beyond them, near the podium on the other side of the hill of burned shoes, are Pan and Dr. Ravi. Nearest the gunmen, the dog at his side, is Boo.

Captain Teeth makes a show of looking inquisitively around the room. "Where are they?"

"Where are who?" Rafferty says. "The whole world's here."

"Your honey. And the kid. We know they're here."

"You're wrong," Rafferty says.

"Okay, fine. Be an asshole. You," he says, giving Da a shove that nearly makes her stumble. "Over there. With Fatso and the little guy." He points his gun at Boo. "You, too, hero. Over there. Take your dog with you." As Boo moves, the dog resists being led, holding its ground and growling. Boo lets go of him and joins the others. Captain Teeth turns back to Rafferty. "And you and your friends. Over there, with everybody else. Makes you easier to shoot." He waits there as people move awkwardly through the obstacle course of shoes and melted machines. "Nobody behind anybody, okay? Side by side." He looks at the setup. "What were you going to do, make a movie?"

"I want to talk to Ton," Pan says.

"I'll bet you do. But right now I'm more concerned with our missing girls. One more time," he says to Rafferty. "Where are they?"

"They're not here."

"Bullshit. It was your sweetie's phone that got us here in the first place. I'm not asking again, I'm just shooting somebody. You, Mr. Policeman." He aims at Kosit.

"Wait," Da says. "I had the phone. I took it, and when you called, I answered it."

"Sure." Captain Teeth turns to Rafferty. "You ready to see your cop friend die?"

"It was me," Da says in a strangled voice. "Someone called, and I said hello, and then they hung up."

Captain Teeth stares at her for a moment. "How many times did you say hello?"

Da swallows. "Once."

Captain Teeth says, "Show me the phone."

"I . . . I don't have it. He, I mean Boo, he took it away from me, and—"

"Fine. Right. You had it but you don't have it. You two," he says to two of the men with guns. "Go through this building, every fucking room. Look under stuff. Look up at the ceilings. There's a woman and a kid here somewhere, and I need them."

One of the men glances around and says, "I'd rather stay here."

"And I'd rather be in bed with five college girls. But I'm not. Get going, or I'll leave you here when we go back to the city."

"Okay, okay." The man who argued looks at the other man who's been chosen. "Do we have to split up?"

"You can go piggyback for all I care. But find them."

With obvious reluctance the two men leave the lit room and enter a hallway that leads to the back of the building.

Pan says, "You're making a mistake."

"Well, you've got the experience to know," Captain Teeth says. "You've fucked up so bad that nobody needs you anymore."

"Ton," Pan says. "I need to talk to Ton. He and I can work this out."

"He's finished with you. Just shut up and wait. Someone shut that dog up."

"It doesn't belong to anybody," Boo says. "It lives here." The dog is showing its teeth now, the hair along its spine bristling.

"Well, let's fix that." Captain Teeth lowers the barrel of his gun and sights over it. There's a sudden movement in the group of people between the sewing machines, and within the second it takes Captain Teeth to look up again, Pan has his arms wrapped around Da's shoulders and is crouched behind her, using her as a shield as he backs toward the door.

"I'm leaving," he says. He takes a few more steps backward, pulling Da along next to him. Da's eyes scour the room, looking for help.

"Fuckup," Captain Teeth says, and he brings the gun up and shoots Da.

The bullet lifts her off her feet and slams her back against Pan. He grabs her by instinct, but then her legs crumple beneath her and she's dropping, her mouth open in amazement, as she tries to bring the other arm up, tries to get it under Peep. Pan staggers forward, pulled off balance by her weight, and he looks down at her face, at her wide, sightless eyes. The generator, which has been coughing outside, shuts down, and slowly, in the new silence, Pan lowers Da to the floor, his eyes on hers all the way down. At the last moment, he slips a hand beneath her head as it nears the concrete. When she is flat on her back, he eases his hand out from under her and his head comes up, his mouth gaping, and a scream rips itself loose from the center of his belly, a scream that threatens to empty even a man so large, and he stands and spreads his arms, making an even bigger target, moves carefully around Da, and takes two steps toward Captain Teeth.

Captain Teeth fires again, and Pan staggers a half step back, arms still spread as though in invitation, and then moves forward again. Captain Teeth fires again and again, and as Pan shudders and falls, there are shots from Rafferty's left, and he turns to see Arthit pouring fire into Captain Teeth, using the gun he took from Pan, and as Captain Teeth goes down, Arthit turns and fires at the three men left in the room, dropping one of them, and the other two break for the door and disappear into the night.

The dog ignores the shooting and goes to the heap of clothes and blood that is Da, standing over her as Peep starts to cry. The dog begins to howl.

Kosit goes to Captain Teeth's body and grabs his gun, then charges back into the factory, after the other two men. Rafferty and Boo drop to their knees on either side of Da, and Boo picks up Peep and rocks him, tears streaming down his face. Rafferty is probing Da's wrist for a pulse when he hears the shots from the rear of the factory. And then it's quiet except for the dog's howls.

THE FACTORY IS a flickering wash of red and blue lights. "It's over," Rafferty says into the phone. He is sitting in a patrol car. "It's not the ending you wanted, but it's over."

"I don't know what you're talking about," Ton says on the other end of the phone.

"Pan's dead. So are three of the people you sent after him. You might want to be on the lookout for the other two. This place is wall-to-wall cops. There's nothing to tie any of it to you—"

"I should think not."

"Except a videotape of Pan talking about his arrangement with you. The quality's not real high, but there was plenty of light, and what he said will have quite a bit of news value."

A pause. When Ton speaks, Rafferty can hear the strain in his voice. "No one will use it."

"Maybe not. Maybe not for a couple of years, maybe not until things have changed. But things *will* change, and when they do, these tapes will just be waiting. And do you think there's a chance the new guys will want to nail you by the wrists and ankles to the pavement on the expressway and back a truck over you?"

"Hypotheticals."

"Here's something that's not hypothetical: My wife and my daughter and I are going home, and we're going to live there safely and happily, without worrying about looking over our shoulders. And as long as we stay that way, happy and safe, the copies of these tapes will be at the bottom of the ocean. So to speak. But the minute something happens to any of us, they'll bob up again. These are people you'll never in a million years be able to identify, people I don't even know, two or three removes from me, who will know exactly what to do with the tapes, who to give them to. And they will do it, if anything happens to my family and me. Is that clear?"

"As I said, I have no idea what you're talking about."

"You're going to have to do better than that."

After a moment Ton says, "I don't deal well with irritation. The tapes sound irritating."

"Well, they won't be, as long as you—"

"And what about you? You have the potential to be irritating."

"I won't be. I've got people to protect."

"Yes, you do," Ton says. "Go home." He hangs up.

Rafferty folds his phone, closes his eyes, and listens to the ambulance siren die away in the distance.

50

A Formless Nimbus of Light

The living room of Arthit's house is crowded and noisy. The seat of honor—the reclining chair Arthit bought to watch the American cop shows he and Noi used to laugh at—is occupied by Noi's mother, a tiny woman with a prodigiously concentrated energy field that keeps her daughters and grandchildren spinning in tight orbits around her. Her wispy silver hair, thinning and uncontrollable, creates a formless nimbus of light around her head that Rafferty thinks is an appropriate effect for a gathering that follows a cremation.

Arthit sits in full uniform on the couch, behind the coffee table. His eyes are red-rimmed, but he's laughing almost unwillingly at something that's just been said by the husband of one of Noi's sisters, an appointed official in a minor province, someone who would have been on Ton's side if it had come to that.

"He's going to be all right," Rose says, following Rafferty's gaze. "He's a good man, and he had years and years with a good woman. Everything but the end was a blessing. And who knows about the end? Karma is complicated. Maybe that was a fire they both had to go through."

"At least he can be a cop again," Rafferty says. "The kids' video makes him a hero. He's the one who took down the thug who killed Pan."

"That's such a *man* reaction," Rose says.

"Well, he's a man. What do you want me to do, enroll him in the Chrysanthemum-of-the-Month Club until he feels better? He told me he'd find his way back at his own speed, and having something to do will help. Men have spirits, too, Rose. We're not floor lamps. Men's spirits just heal better behind a screen of activity. As of the Sunday-night TV news, he's the most famous cop in Thailand, and there's nothing Thanom can do except try to crowd into the newspaper pictures alongside him. The people in the northeast would probably vote for him for prime minister. Not that he's crazy enough to do anything about it."

In the dining room, Boo carries Peep in one crooked arm. He's resplendent in the new clothes Rafferty bought him for the ceremony. Da shines in a pale yellow dress that Rose helped her pick out, with Miaow's sullen help. The once-spotless sling that supports the cast on Da's left arm has already been decorated by Boo's crew with a broad range of enthusiastic drawings that range from flowers and hearts and bright yellow suns to daggers and teeth dripping blood. The other kids, here at Arthit's insistence, cluster defensively in the breakfast room, wearing clothes so new they creak, and never getting farther than four or five feet from the food.

Boo and Miaow have avoided each other. Not a word has passed between them.

And Rafferty has lost his Carpenters album and gained a cast on his own left hand, courtesy of the doctor who took care of Da. When he'd gone to the hospital to pay for her care, the doctor had taken one horrified look at the bandages and said, "Who did this? A plumber?"

"A dentist," Rafferty said, and the doctor grabbed his sleeve and pulled him back into an examination room.

Rafferty's cell phone rings. It's his old phone, the one that's been off for most of the past two days.

"Sorry," he says to Rose. "I've got to go outside to hear this." He opens the phone and says, "Hang on a minute," then crosses the living room and steps through the front door into a warm, violet evening. "Hello."

"Hello." It's a man's voice. The English is unaccented. "I'd tell you who I am, but you don't know me. I've been asked to call you to make sure you've noticed that everyone you love is alive and well. I assume you're aware of that."

Rafferty says, "Resoundingly."

"Good. I've also been asked to point out that their present good health is in the nature of a favor. That, essentially, you've been done a good turn."

"That's one way to look at it. Another way is to say we had an agreement."

"Don't overvalue the strength of your deterrent. It was a favor. You're undoubtedly aware that favors are usually returned. It's called 'quid pro quo' in Latin, I believe."

"Very impressive."

"Thank you. A time may come when you'll be asked to return the favor. The gentleman who asked me to call says to tell you he expects a thoughtful response. And in the meantime look at it this way: Someone in Bangkok will be keeping an eye out for you. Not much point in being owed a favor by someone who's dead, is there?"

"Not unless you're very patient."

"And he wants you to redeposit his money. He'll work out a wire transfer to a safe account."

"Can't do it," Rafferty says. "It's gone."

"What? All of it?"

"Pretty much. Got a few hundred left."

"What did you do with it?"

"Paid some hospital bills. Gave a bunch of it to some street kids and to the children of a reporter who got killed. Oh, and I bought a baby."

"The man who asked me to call you is not easily amused."

"What can I tell you? It's all true."

"Well," the man on the other end says, "looks like you owe us a bigger favor than we thought."

"Looks like," Rafferty says. "So that'll give him an extra reason to worry about my safety." He thinks for a moment and then says, "Interesting how quickly another Isaan businessman stepped up to the plate, isn't it? Politically, I mean."

"Times are changing," the man says. "We all have to change with them. Just remember, you owe us a favor."

The man hangs up.

Rafferty puts the phone into his pocket and stands there, looking in through the window at the bright room, at the people assembled to remember someone whose life was faithful and compassionate and good. Like, he thinks, 99 percent of the Thai people. Like Boo's kids will be, if they get a chance.

Standing near the window, on her own at the edge of the crowd, her hands folded in front of her, is Miaow. Without discussing the situation with either Rose or Rafferty, she has apparently made a decision. She wears the "schoolsiest" dress she owns, and yesterday she bought a hair rinse that would emphasize her new highlights. Her hair is even redder than it was before. She does not look toward Boo or Da.

She's tough, Rafferty thinks. *But that doesn't mean she can't break your heart.*

The front door opens, and a group of people emerge, calling out words of parting. There is a general movement inside, people getting ready to go back to their lives. Soon enough, Rafferty knows, Arthit will be left alone to spend the first night in this house without Noi by his side. To begin something new.

IT'S ON THE coffee table, centered in front of him, still sealed. The side of the envelope that told him not to come into the bedroom is facedown, revealing the sealed flap. Kosit stands to one side of the sofa and Rafferty to the right. It seems wrong somehow for them to come too close to him right now.

Arthit looks up. He says, "Well."

"Well," Rafferty says. The look on his friend's face makes him want to burst into tears.

Arthit breathes deeply, leans forward, and uses both hands to pick up the envelope. As he does, Da comes into the room, stops suddenly, and then goes to Rose and whispers something to her.

"What?" Arthit says.

"Oh," Da says, blushing scarlet, "it's . . . um—"

Rose tells him, "She says there's someone sitting next to you."

Arthit's eyes go to Da. He blinks as though to clear his vision, and then he says, "Thank you."

He opens the envelope.

51

News from the *Sun*

BANGKOK MAN ARRESTED IN BABY-SELLING SCHEME

Exclusive to the Sun *by Floyd Preece*

A Bangkok businessman with alleged ties to the underworld was arrested yesterday by Bangkok police on charges of running a complex and highly profitable operation that purchased, and in some cases stole, infants in order to sell them to wealthy foreigners.

Wichat Kangsomthong, 57, was taken into custody at his offices on Sathorn Road in Bangkok's Yannawa district. Police officials acknowledged that the arrests were in part a reaction to two earlier stories in the *Sun* detailing the sale of babies at costs in excess of 1.2 million baht to foreigners, mostly European. The infants, both Thai and Cambodian, were taken from their birth parents and given temporarily to beggars who were "protected" by Mr. Wichat's syndicate.

In addition to facing charges of kidnapping and enslavement, Mr. Wichat is being investigated for violations of international human-trafficking laws because some of the children were allegedly transported across borders. Some of these charges carry the potential of life imprisonment.

Author's Note

Many of the Thai names in this novel, both surnames and nicknames, are invented. While the visitor to Thailand may be overwhelmed by the sheer length of Thai surnames (five or six syllables in some cases), the names of the oldest families are quite short. Relative newcomers to the kingdom are asked to submit several potential surnames, one of which will presumably be approved, and adding a syllable or four is the easiest way to retain something approximating a family's original name without duplicating the name of an existing family. Therefore, the odds are quite high that all people who share a surname are related. This means that a writer should be careful about using a "real" surname, especially for an unsympathetic character, since that could be construed as libel.

I also made up some of the nicknames, aiming at simplicity and memorability, since there are so many characters.

And I should probably stress that the Bangkok in this novel (and the earlier ones) is a fictional environment, inspired by a real one. Distances have been compressed here and there, and some geographical liberties taken, primarily because it would be impossible to maintain a thriller's pace while stranded in Bangkok traffic. Those of you who find it difficult to believe in the Bangkok that's depicted here should know that millions of people feel exactly the same way about the real-life city.

But the unstable political landscape presented here is not, in the main, fictional. It's a defining fact of present-day Thailand, and no one can say how it will ultimately play out. In fairness, it should be pointed out that murder and assassination play virtually no role in Thai politics. But, of course, this is a work of fiction.

Acknowledgments

First place in the gratitude parade goes to Jonathan Whipple, who told me about a card game in which one player won the right to write another's biography. This situation allowed me to cut by about thirty percent the amount of time it took me to get Poke into trouble. The game also gave me the alternating series of opening chapters that contrast the rich, uselessly throwing money away high above the pavement, with the people who scuffle for survival on the sidewalks.

Profuse thanks are due to my editor at Morrow, Peggy Hageman, who helped me to focus the book more precisely and to clarify some confusing story points, all the while acting as though the improvements were entirely my idea. My former editor, Marjorie Braman, suggested some key plot elements, among them the return of Superman, that made the book stronger. And my agent, Bob Mecoy, went over the manuscript with a critical eye and a mental X-Acto knife to tighten things up and reinforce some of the bearing beams.

The book's wet, wonderful jacket is the work of James Iacobelli. And the manuscript inside the jacket had the benefit (as have all of Poke's adventures) of an enlightened copyedit by Maureen Sugden, who knows her Hokusai from her Hiroshige and suggested literally dozens of improvements. Still don't know about some of those commas, though.

This book, like all the others, was written mostly in coffeehouses in America and Southeast Asia. I'm especially grateful to the people at Novel Cafe in Santa Monica, California, and Bee Bee Cafe in West Los Angeles, as well as to those angels of mercy who fed me and kept me caffeinated in Phnom Penh, at Corner 33, Black Canyon Coffee, and Freebird. Coffee World in Bangkok also gets some of the blame.

As always, the writing of this novel had a soundtrack, courtesy of an overstuffed iPod. Most frequently played were Bob Dylan, Rufus Wainwright, Rilo Kiley, Vienna Teng, Shawn Colvin, Conor Oberst, John Prine, Vampire Weekend, Angelique Kidjo, Emmylou Harris (always and forever), Mary Gauthier, Elvis Costello, Rihanna, Delbert McClinton, Taylor Swift, Patti Griffin, Calexico, Over the Rhine, Ryan Adams & the Cardinals, the perpetually heartbreaking Townes Van Zandt, TV on the Radio, The Hold Steady, Tegan and Sara, and Kyung-Wha Chung. And about four hundred others.

My deepest and most heartfelt thanks go to the person I'm blessed to share my life with, my wife, Munyin Choy-Hallinan. As this book's first reader, she helped me make parts of it better and strengthen (or at least plaster over) its weaknesses. Without her, it would never have been finished.

HALLINAN Hallinan, Timothy.

Breathing water.

DATE			